SPEAK TO MY Heart

Books by Rebecca Talley

NOVELS/NOVELLAS:

    Heaven Scent
    Altared Plans
    The Upside of Down
    Aura
    Imperfect Love
    Best Kind of Love: A Reunion Romance Novella
    Grounded for Love: A Reunion Romance Novella
    On Deck for Love: A Reunion Romance Novella
    Adding Christmas

CHILDREN'S:

    Grasshopper Pie
    Gabby's Secret

NON-FICTION

    Hook Me: What to Include in Your First Chapter

REBECCA TALLEY

DuBon Publishing

This is a work of fiction, and the views expressed herein are the sole responsibility of the author. Likewise, characters, places, and incidents are either the product of the author's imagination or are represented fictitiously, and any resemblance to actual persons, living or dead, or actual events or locales, is entirely coincidental.

Speak to My Heart

Book design and layout copyright © 2017 by Rebecca Talley
Cover design copyright © 2017 by Rebecca Talley

All rights reserved. No part of this book may be reproduced or transmitted in any form or by any means whatsoever without written permission from the author, except in the case of brief quotations embodied in critical articles and reviews.

Copyright © 2017 by Rebecca Talley

ISBN-13: 978-1987589016

ISBN-10: 1987589017

Printed in the United States of America
Year of first printing: 2018

For Grandpa Hyrum, who struggled with his speech after a stroke.

For Jared, who has struggled with his speech for years, but continues to improve each day. You've got this, J-Man.

For the speech therapists, who've dedicated their lives to helping others be more clearly understood.

For my family and my biggest cheerleader, Del. Thank you for all your support while I work toward my dream of bringing uplifting stories to readers.

Chapter 1

Hailey Baker sank her key into the doorknob and opened the door to her still-undecorated one-bedroom apartment. She kicked off her red wedges and rubbed the back of her heel where a blister had begun to form. *Why is it that the cutest shoes are the most uncomfortable?*

She made her way to her bedroom and slipped into her well-worn black yoga pants and oversized Denver Nuggets T-shirt. She didn't mind wearing business attire to the accounting firm, but the moment Hailey stepped inside her apartment, it was time to lose those stuffy clothes.

She plopped on the sofa and set her aching feet on the coffee table. It had been another long day at the office juggling accounts, creating spreadsheets, and balancing ledgers for her clients.

Her new Nikes, piled in the corner where she'd left them months ago, caught her eye. *One of these days I need to get back to running and going to the gym.* She blew out a long breath.

Grabbing the remote, she flicked on the TV. Friday night alone—again. What exciting thing could she do? She found her trusty companion as of late, Netflix, and started scanning through series she could binge watch. Nothing jumped out at her.

Hailey refused to feel sorry for herself or to think about what Kevin might be doing tonight. It had been almost three months since Valentine's Day—the day she'd expected a marriage proposal. Instead, her world had come crashing down around her when she witnessed the intimate embrace that left no doubt in Hailey's mind that Kevin had betrayed her. The memory still sent a piercing pain through her heart. She'd booted him out of her life, and she needed to stop letting him take up space in her head. He didn't deserve it after what he'd done. The lyrics to Carrie Underwood's song *Before He Cheats* popped into her head, and she smiled. *If only.*

She rose, went to the compact kitchen, and opened the refrigerator. Something smelled like it had crawled in and died. She rummaged through the contents and pulled out a Styrofoam container from a luncheon she'd had with her coworkers before the tax season rush last month. *This needs a trip straight to the dumpster.*

With the offensive container in hand, Hailey slid her feet into her flip-flops and walked to the trash area next to her complex.

She tossed in the rotting mess and began making her way back to her apartment.

Before she could avoid him, Jimmy Vaughn headed her way.

"Hailey, baby. What's going on? You are looking hot." Jimmy gave her his slimiest smile as he smoothed his stringy black hair.

"Hi, Jimmy." She said it in a monotone voice, hoping he'd get the hint she didn't want to talk to him.

"How about you and me—"

"Sorry, Jimmy. I have plans tonight." When it came to Jimmy, she had plans every night. For the rest of eternity.

"But you broke up with that slob you used to date—"

"Yeah, I know." The whole world seemed to know that she was single. Did she have a neon sign blinking above her head?

"So?" Jimmy licked his lips, then raised a bushy eyebrow.

She shook her head and started walking.

Jimmy sidled up next to her and walked in step. "Then how about me and you taking a ride on my bike up into the mountains tomorrow?

We could make it a long weekend and go to Aspen."

Ew, no. I'd rather walk barefoot across broken glass. Hailey clucked her tongue. "I'd love to, but I need to work tomorrow."

"It's Saturday," he said with an accusatory tone.

"We're open on Saturdays, and I have to go over some accounting with one of my clients." Hailey picked up her pace. She wished her apartment wasn't ten hundred miles away.

"Geez, Hail, you work all the time."

"I know, Jimmy." No one needed to remind her that her life revolved around accounting. At least numbers couldn't rip your heart out, then make mincemeat of it.

"Rain check?" he asked.

Opening her door, Hailey kept it close behind her as she backed inside. She shut the door without answering him. It'd be worth moving to another apartment to get away from Jimmy. His beady stare made her feel like she needed a shower. She was sure his mother must love him, but no way on this green earth would she ever agree to a date with him. Even if she had several cans of pepper spray with her.

Hailey popped a burrito into the microwave, and while waiting for it to heat through, she grasped her long hair, twisted it into a messy bun, and secured it with a hair tie, reminding herself she was due for a trim. When the microwave timer dinged, Hailey took the plate to the couch and sat.

After a couple of bites, her phone started playing Beethoven's "Für Elise." "Hi, Mom."

"Hi, sweetie. How are you?"

"Good. Has Brit had the baby yet?" Hailey couldn't wait to be an aunt again.

"No. The doctor says it may be a few more days. I'm staying at Brit's house so I don't have to drive all the way back to Denver every night, and I can help with Kyle."

"I'm sure he loves having his grandma there full-time to spoil him." Someday Hailey would have babies for her mom to spoil. At least she hoped so.

After a long pause, her mom said, "I have some bad news."

"What?" Hailey drew in a deep breath.

"Harry had a stroke."

Hailey's heart plummeted to her stomach. *Not Gramps.* "Oh, no. When?"

"They think it was during the night sometime."

"How is he?" She clenched her jaw while she waited for her mother's reply.

"He's stable, but he's lost his ability to speak."

"Forever?" She couldn't imagine her animated grandpa, who loved to tell tall tales every chance he got, unable to speak.

"I don't know. I'd like to go help, but with Brit having the baby any day, I can't." Hailey could hear the desperation in her mom's voice. "I'm not sure what to do."

"Do you have any details?"

"When June woke him, he couldn't speak. She wasn't sure what to do, so she called 911."

"Poor Gran. I bet she was terrified." Hailey wanted to magically transport herself to Florida, give her grandma a hug, and tell her everything would be okay—because it had to be.

"What's the prognosis?" Hailey steeled herself for the answer.

"He'll need some speech therapy for sure. I don't know what else."

Hailey rubbed her forehead. "Will he be able to live in his house anymore?"

"I don't know. You know how stressed Grandma June gets, and with all her eye problems she doesn't drive anymore. I don't know what they'll do. They can't afford to put him in a facility and—"

Rustling sounded, as if the phone had been dropped. "Mom? Are you there?"

"Yes, I'm here. Sorry. Oh, hang on a minute, Hailey . . . Kyle, I'm coming. Let me tell Aunt Hailey goodbye . . . I better go, honey."

"Okay, but please keep me updated on him. And on Brit. I'm

planning to drive up to Fort Collins when she has the baby."

"I will."

Hailey ended the call. She was no longer interested in eating her burrito, so she headed to her bedroom. Memories of her grandparents swirled around her head. After her father died, they had doted on her and Brit. They'd lived a few streets over until Gramps retired from the police force and he and Gran moved to Florida.

Hailey lay on her bed and turned to her side, anxiety and fear enveloping her. What would her grandparents do now? They needed help, and their only daughter, also known as her loser aunt, wouldn't be any. No one even knew where Regina was these days. *Probably in some bar hustling customers.*

If only Hailey could do something. But what? She was in Colorado Springs, almost two thousand miles away from Gran and Gramps. How could she possibly help, especially with her job? She tossed and turned through the night, alternating between warm, happy memories and the cold reality that Gramps had had a stroke.

After a fitful sleep, Hailey trudged into the bathroom. She gazed at her dark circles and dull eyes. *I look awesome.* She blew out a breath. *I need to do something to help Gramps.*

An idea sparked, but she wasn't sure if she could pull it off. Hailey hurried to her closet, pulled on some navy slacks and a pink paisley shirt, brushed her teeth, and then dragged a brush through her tangled hair.

On her way to the office, she practiced what she was going to say to her boss and made adjustments here and there. When she arrived at the parking lot, she knew exactly what she wanted to say.

"Hey, Jenna, is Mr. Michaels in?" Hailey asked the young receptionist who always wore vivid pink lipstick and had long manicured nails.

"Uh, yeah. He's in his office with a client. What's going on?"

"What do you mean?"

"You look stressed or something. Your face is all red."

Hailey wiped at her cheeks. "My mom called last night about my grandfather."

"Oh no." She wore a sympathetic expression. "Bad news?"

"He had a stroke." She hated saying those words.

"Does he live here?" Jenna asked, her brown eyes filled with compassion.

"No. He and Gran live in Daytona Beach."

"That's right." Jenna tapped her temple. "I remember you talking about them. I'm sorry to hear about his stroke. Is there anything I can do?"

"I don't think so, but I need to talk to Mr. Michaels." Hailey squared her shoulders as if that would give her the dose of courage she needed.

Jenna checked her computer screen. "Hmm. He should be free soon. He doesn't have another appointment until 10:30."

"Thanks. Can you let me know when this client leaves?" The sooner she could speak with him, the better.

"Sure." Jenna nodded.

Hailey made her way back to her office, still rehearsing what she wanted to say to convince her boss to let her take some time off. She was certain about what needed to happen. If she could go to Florida for a few weeks, or even a month, she could provide the help and support her grandparents needed while Gramps recovered.

About twenty minutes later, Jenna called to let Hailey know Mr. Michaels was free. He was a decent guy and had been a good boss for the last four years. Hailey hoped he'd be reasonable and let her take the time off.

Hailey knocked on his door and he told her to come inside.

"Hi, Mr. Michaels."

"Hailey, how are you today?" He adjusted his wire-rimmed glasses and focused on her.

"I've been better."

He looked at her with concern. "What's wrong?"

"My grandfather had a stroke night before last." Hailey tried to keep the emotion out of her voice.

"I'm so sorry to hear that," he said with sincerity.

"And, I, well, I," she stammered. *Don't be such a scaredy cat. Just say it.*

Mr. Michaels studied her. Asking for time off wasn't as easy as she'd hoped. "Is there something you want to say?" he asked.

All the careful rehearsing she'd done previously fell right out of her brain. She struggled to find the right words. "I . . . uh . . . you see . . . I'd like to . . ."

"Yes?"

"Can I take some time off?" Hailey finally blurted out.

Mr. Michaels pulled his dark eyebrows together and sat back in his brown leather chair, making it creak with his movement.

Hailey swallowed. "I need to go to Florida. My grandparents have always been so good to me, and they need help right now since my grandma doesn't drive anymore. There isn't anyone else that can do it. Tax season is over, and I haven't used much of my vacation time since I started working here. And," she added, "I can continue to work for clients while I'm there." She chewed her lip in anticipation.

"You are one of my best accountants. And one of the hardest workers." He smoothed his thick salt-and-pepper hair.

Hailey relaxed a bit, waiting for him to agree to her time off.

"But, I don't think I can spare you right now. We're going to start doing the bookkeeping for the Tundar Corporation and I need you to head that up."

Hailey's shoulders fell. She didn't want to disappoint her boss, but she couldn't think about anything but going to Florida. "Oh."

"I really need you to be here," he said as he laced his fingers together. "I'm sorry. I know you haven't taken much personal time and you are concerned about your grandfather, but the firm must come first. You understand."

"Yes, sir. I do." Except she didn't. Not at all. Work was important, but it shouldn't supersede family. Why didn't he understand that? "Thank you for considering my request." Numbly, she turned and walked out of his office, a massive weight hanging around her neck.

Maybe Gran and Gramps would be okay without her. Nurses and in-home caretakers were abundant there because Florida was the retirement capital of the world. She could hire some help for them and they'd probably be fine. Maybe Mr. Michaels was right and her first loyalty should be to the accounting firm, especially because she was only beginning her career and didn't want to risk losing her job at this prestigious firm. After all, that's why she agreed to work on Saturdays. If she wanted to get ahead, she had to sacrifice.

During her lunch break, she sat in her office and gazed out the window trying to convince herself everything would be all right. The more Hailey thought about hiring help, the less she liked it. Gran and Gramps had stepped in when she needed them—they hadn't hired someone else to do it. She let out a long breath.

A knock sounded at her door.

"Come in."

Jenna poked her head in. "When are you leaving for Florida?"

"I'm not." Tears built behind her eyes. Even though her boss was probably right, Hailey wasn't at all convinced. She wanted to help her grandparents, first and foremost, but part of her also saw this as a welcome break from all the memories of Kevin that seemed to haunt her.

"Why?" Jenna came inside the office and sat in the chair opposite Hailey's desk. "What happened?"

"We're getting a big client and Mr. Michaels doesn't feel like he can let me take any vacation time right now. At least not until we get everything organized for this Tundar Corporation." As she said it, her resentment built.

"Maybe you can go after that?" Jenna said in a hopeful tone.

"I have no idea how long it will be. And my grandparents need help now, not in a few weeks or months." She rubbed her forehead. "I could hire some help for them, but I hate the idea of strangers being with them. They need family, and there isn't anyone else who can help. I have to do something, but I don't know what."

"I'm sorry Mr. Michaels said no."

"Me too." Hailey felt like a week-old wilted flower.

"Do you want to go out and get some comfort food?" Jenna raised her professionally shaped eyebrows.

"No, thanks. I need to finish up some reports for Crandall Automotive." Maybe doing some work would keep Hailey's mind off Gramps. Or not.

"I can bring you something back." Jenna rose.

"I'll be fine." Hailey wasn't interested in food, only in figuring out how to help her grandparents. There simply had to be a way.

After Jenna left, Hailey cradled her head in her hands. Why was her boss being so unreasonable? Other accountants could handle this new corporation. Wanting to help her grandparents seemed like the right thing to do. Her stomach twisted into double and triple knots. All she could think about was Gramps and poor Gran, who was probably sick with worry and shouldering so much stress. Memories of all the times her grandparents had been there for her after her dad died played in Hailey's mind. Now it was her turn to be there for them. She had to do *something*.

Hailey stood and sucked in a deep breath of courage. She marched herself down to her boss's office again. Lifting her quaking hand, she knocked on the door, but didn't wait to be invited in.

Mr. Michaels gave her a sharp look and said, "Excuse me for a moment," into the receiver of his phone. He punched a key to mute the call. "Hailey, I'm speaking with a client right now."

"I apologize. I'll wait." She sat in the chair across from his desk, her heart rapping against her ribs.

When he finished his call, he glared at her and she resisted the urge to run screaming from his office.

"What is it?" he asked curtly.

"I really do need to take some time off to help my grandparents."

His jaw tightened. "We already discussed this."

"I realize I'm putting my job at risk, but, in this case, family has to come first. My grandparents desperately need help. They need their family, and I'm the only one who can go. Without me, they'll really struggle, and I can't live with that."

Mr. Michaels tapped the desk with his fingers while Hailey's heartbeat thrummed in her ears. She'd never been so bold before and wasn't sure what had gotten into her. She hoped it wouldn't result in her termination from the company, but if it did, she'd have to deal with it after she went to Florida.

Finally, Mr. Michaels said, "I suppose we can make arrangements. I will assign someone else to the Tundar Corporation. You understand you are passing up a valuable opportunity that may have significant repercussions to your career?"

She licked her parched lips. "Yes, I understand."

"If you will commit to working long distance and maintain your clients without any problems, you may take some time off."

"Thank you." Relief washed over her.

With a stern tone, he said, "I expect you back in this office before the beginning of next quarter."

"I will be here by the end of June." She'd have to make it all work somehow.

"If not," he peered at her over his glasses, "you *will* need to find another job."

"Thank you." Her gratitude outweighed her fear, but only by a fraction.

Hailey stood. Before she got to the door, Mr. Michaels said, "Hailey?"

She turned to look at him, bracing herself for more conditions to her leave of absence.

"I hope your grandfather recovers." He sat back in his chair and gazed at her. "You're doing a good thing."

Hailey let out a breath she didn't even know she was holding. She nodded and left, taken aback at his unexpected kindness. *Mr. Michaels has a heart after all. Who knew?*

Although she might lose out on some opportunities for her career, as long as she was back before the next quarter, she wouldn't have to sacrifice her job. She couldn't ask for more than that.

Chapter 2

Peter Stafford walked into the tan steel building that housed the karate school. He spotted his sister to his left, and she waved him over. "Thanks for coming, Pete."

He sat on one of the metal chairs at the edge of the gray mat. "Of course." Peter tried to attend as many functions as he could.

"Benji is so excited to test today," she said. Peter admired how much Laura loved her son.

A thin man with red hair and a goatee, who was dressed in a white karate uniform, called all the students to attention. He turned to the audience. "Thank you for coming to our demonstration and belt testing tonight. The students have all been working hard to show you what they've been learning here at Seaside Martial Arts School. Please be respectful as they complete their testing." The man walked over to the edge of the mat.

Two lines of kids formed on the far side.

"Is Benji nervous?" Peter gazed at the young boy.

She leaned in and whispered. "He's been practicing like crazy."

"He seems to like karate." It was obvious by the grin on his face that Benji enjoyed what he was doing.

"He loves it." She turned to him. "And he loves that you come to see him. I can't tell you how much it means to both of us." She smiled, but Peter could see the sadness in her blue eyes.

"You know how much I love him. I want to always be here for him. For both of you."

Laura sat up, her blonde hair falling across her shoulders. "Oh, look, Benji is testing." She clasped her hands together.

The barefoot man with the goatee yelled out some words and the boys and girls all responded by making formations with their arms.

"I know nothing about karate except what I've seen Benji do," Peter said. "I wish I could help coach him."

"I know even less than you do." She shrugged.

They continued to watch the exhibition and when it was over, Benji came rushing to them. He threw himself into Peter's arms. "Uncle Peter, I'm so glad you're here. Did you see me get my orange belt?"

"I sure did. Great job," Peter said. He held up his hand, and Benji slapped it.

"You were the best one out there." Laura tousled his light brown hair, then hugged him close.

"Aw, Mom, you always say stuff like that."

"Because it's true." She clapped him on the back.

"How about we go out for some pizza to celebrate?" Peter said.

"All right. That's my favorite," Benji said with enthusiasm and a wide grin that exposed crooked front teeth.

"I didn't know that." Peter's eyes grew large and he acted like he'd never heard that before.

"Yes, you did." Benji rolled his eyes.

"You're right. Pizza is your favorite meal and Cookies and Cream ice cream is your favorite dessert. Unless your mom makes her extra special brownies, then those are your favorite."

Benji laughed. "Yep."

"I still think you were the best one out there. And to be an orange belt at nine years old is pretty awesome." Laura put her arm around her son. "Let's get that pizza."

At Pizza Palace, after placing their order, they sat at a shiny wooden table near a window. A mixture of baking bread and garlic scents wafted through the air. Benji slurped his soda while they waited for their pepperoni and sausage pizza. When it finally arrived, Benji gulped it down in a few bites. "Slow down there, honey," Laura said. "You don't have to eat the entire pizza in five minutes."

"But I want to go play a video game." He shoved a bite in his mouth. "Can I?"

Peter whipped out some tokens. "I thought you might ask."

Benji grinned and took the gold-colored coins. "Thanks."

"You're so good to him," Laura said taking a piece of pizza and placing it on her plate. "I'm glad we decided to move here by you."

"Me too. It gives us more time together than when you lived in Orlando."

Laura's face saddened. "But he misses Grandma."

Peter sipped his soda. "With any luck, I'll convince her to move out here too. She doesn't need that house anymore."

"But that's her home." Laura took a bite of pizza.

"I know, but I worry about her living there alone." Peter bit into his piece. "I try to see her as much as I can, but life is busy here."

"Then I'm grateful you can squeeze in time for us." Laura elbowed him.

"Of course." Peter scanned the room and watched Benji playing a game. "I love spending time with Benji."

"And he needs that."

Peter looked at Laura. "I know I can't ever replace Sam, but I want to help as much as possible. I know it's been hard."

"Yeah. It's been pretty hard." She picked a pepperoni off her slice and ate it. "I understood the risk of being a military wife, but I didn't think about how it would affect my child. I knew Sam might not come home in an abstract sense, but I didn't think that would actually happen. You know?" She swished her soda around the glass with her straw. "I never thought I'd be widowed, especially before I was thirty."

Peter slung his arm around Laura. "I'm sorry. Sam was a great guy and he really loved you and Benji."

"Yes, he did." A wrinkle formed between her eyebrows. "And I don't want Benji to forget his dad."

"He won't." Peter wanted to reassure her.

Laura leaned her head against Peter's shoulder. "I'm glad we have you."

He smiled and said, "That's what brothers are for."

Chapter 3

When Hailey arrived home that night, she sat on her couch and called her mom. "I've made arrangements to go to Florida and help until Gramps is feeling better." Saying it to her mom convinced her even more that it was the right thing to do.

"You have? What about your job?" She could hear the alarm in her mom's voice.

"I already talked to my boss and he agreed to some time off as long as I maintain my clients." Of course, he'd given her a time limit, which was stressful, but she couldn't worry about that right now. She could only concentrate on helping her grandparents and hope the timeline her boss had given her would work.

"Are you sure?"

"And I need some time away. Ever since, you know, the breakup with Kevin, it's been hard. Really hard. Everywhere I go, I see memories." She shook her head. "Besides, I haven't seen Gran and Gramps for a long time. I'd love to spend time with them and soak up some Florida sunshine. I don't get to the beach much here in Colorado Springs." She laughed at her own joke.

"As soon as Brit has her baby—"

"No worries, Mom. You take care of Brit and her family. I got this."

After the phone call, Hailey felt lighter, as if the heavy burden of her failed relationship that she'd carried for the last couple months was released, and she was free to do something else besides wallow. Helping her grandparents would benefit her as much as it would them. She could focus on them and stop thinking about the cheater she'd wanted to marry.

She logged onto her computer and found a flight.

Within twenty-four hours, she'd be in Florida.

Hailey boarded the Delta plane at Colorado Springs Airport. The flight to Atlanta, where she had a layover, would take almost three hours, so she rested her head against her seat, trying to reassure herself that planes were perfectly safe. When the engines began to roar, she closed her eyes briefly and said a silent prayer that they'd make it without crashing. If she had her way, she'd never fly anywhere.

Thoughts of Gramps having his stroke suddenly bombarded her mind, and worry wormed its way through her stomach. How would he be when she arrived? Would he know her? Would he ever be able to speak again? What if he had another stroke?

After they'd been in the air ten minutes or so, the middle-aged woman with black hair and large gold hoop earrings that sat next to her said, "I love to fly. Don't you?"

"Uh, no. Not really." Who wanted to be in a large, metal object hurtling through the air at five hundred miles an hour, thirty thousand feet above the ground? *An object that could plunge to the earth at any given moment and burst into a fiery explosion.*

"Where are you going?" Her deep brown eyes seemed to peer into Hailey's soul.

"To Daytona Beach."

The curvaceous woman grasped Hailey's hand in hers. "My name is Salima."

Hailey resisted the urge to yank her hand out of the woman's grip. *Why is she holding my hand? She's a little creepy.*

"You are worried. Yes?"

Hailey gave a slight nod. *Definitely weird.*

"You should not be."

"Okay." Now that the strange woman had said there was no need to worry, Hailey felt so much better. Except she didn't. At all.

"You are on your way to your destiny."

Destiny? Is she for real? "Oh. I am." Hailey squelched the laugh that rose up in her throat. She didn't want to be rude, but this lady was a serious whacko.

"I can see the future." Salima said it with a little too much dramatic flair.

Hailey had met a woman like this once when she was with Gran at a circus. That lady was dressed in a brightly colored flowing skirt and wore a dozen or more gold bracelets. For a dollar, she would tell you your future. Hailey was sure this woman sitting next to her was as nutty as the fortune teller at the circus.

"Many do not believe. But I speak the truth. You go now because you seek to soothe those you love, but in the end," she pulled Hailey's hand closer to her and continued, "it will be your heart that receives what it needs."

Hailey nodded, then eased her hand out of the woman's. Her heart didn't need anything except lots of distance from memories of Kevin. "I'm going to help my grandparents. Gramps had a stroke."

Salima gave a knowing nod. "Ah, yes. The reason for your distress."

The plane dropped, then felt like it was vibrating. Hailey's stomach turned upside down. She squeezed her eyes shut because she was far more concerned at the moment that they'd all end up in a heap of twisted metal.

Salima placed her warm, chubby hand on Hailey's. "No need to worry. It is not your destiny to die in a plane crash. Nor is it mine."

This woman was peculiar for sure, but somehow her words calmed Hailey in an odd sort of way. She hoped Salima was right. This plane ride couldn't end fast enough. Hailey wanted to plant her feet back on solid ground ASAP.

Hailey took some deep, cleansing breaths, then pulled out a novel by Rachael Anderson and lost herself in the plight of the characters and the relaxing setting in Hawaii. When some turbulence hit again, she gripped the armrest and closed her eyes, counting backward from one hundred. When she finished, she gulped her soda and skimmed through the magazine in the seat pocket in front of her. This airplane ride was taking far too long. Finally, the plane came to a skittery stop in Atlanta.

"Remember, your destiny awaits you," Salima offered with confidence.

Hailey nodded. All that awaited her was taking care of her grandparents. And a welcome escape from the heartache in Colorado.

She found a row of chairs near the next gate and pulled out her phone to check her email and skim through Facebook and Instagram.

On the next flight, she didn't sit by any eccentric people who wanted to tell her fortune—only a lady and her crying baby. As they neared Daytona Beach, Hailey's nerves tingled. She wasn't sure what she'd find when she saw Gramps. Last time she'd seen him, he was as lively as ever, telling terrible jokes and making homemade ice cream. He loved to play gin rummy and was the family champ. Thinking about those memories warmed her heart, and she hoped he'd be back to the same old Gramps soon, so they could play cards again.

She refused to think about her grandparents getting older and having strokes and other health issues. As far as she was concerned, they would live forever.

Hailey deboarded the plane, grateful to be on the ground again, and walked over to the luggage carousel to collect her bulging suitcase. She wasn't sure exactly how long she'd be staying, so she'd crammed as much as possible into the bag.

Walking outside the glass doors to the airport, Hailey was hit with a wall of humidity. She wasn't in the dry air of Colorado anymore—that was for sure. Her skin reacted immediately, and little droplets of perspiration formed at her hairline.

She found a taxi.

"Where can I take you?" the man with a black mustache asked.

Hailey gave him the address to her grandparents' house.

She hadn't visited them here in almost four years. Moving to Colorado Springs and trying to get settled in the accounting firm had prevented any travel—something she now regretted.

Palm trees lined the streets, and the bright green grass reminded her she was in an area that received plenty of water. She missed the rugged Rocky Mountains that lined the horizon at home, but welcomed the chance to spend time with Gran and Gramps and maybe even go to the beach.

Before she knew it, the cab arrived at the small, beige house in her grandparents' retirement community. They'd moved here over ten years ago after Gramps had retired from the police force in Denver where he'd served almost forty years.

"Thanks for the ride." Hailey gave the driver some cash and retrieved her suitcase.

The front door flung open before Hailey even reached it, and Gran stood there in white polyester pants, a coral blouse, and her dangly earrings, with arms outstretched. Hailey melted into her, inhaling the familiar floral scent.

"Let me look at you." Gran eyed her up and down. "You need to put on some weight. And your hair is so much longer, and it seems darker, than the last time I saw you. But you still have the same beautiful blue eyes like your daddy. You sure look like him." Gran gave her another hug. "Come inside and see Grandpa Harry."

Hailey braced herself to see Gramps as she entered the house. The air conditioner whirred, and there he sat in his brown recliner, dressed in a red shirt that looked too big for him and gray pajama pants. His eyes met hers and he gave a slight smile. She rushed to him and buried her head in his neck. After hugging him, she pulled back and said, "Hi, Gramps."

He said nothing, but peered at her with his deep blue eyes as if trying to communicate his love. Hailey was relieved to see that he looked basically the same, maybe with a little less wavy gray hair and a few more wrinkles, but she desperately wanted to hear his familiar voice and silly jokes.

"You can put your suitcase in the back bedroom. I have it all ready for you. Then you can have some dinner with us. I made meatloaf," Gran said with pride. "It's my special recipe."

"Thanks." Hailey noticed that Gran's hair was whiter and her eyes looked tired, but her smile was still full of warmth and comfort like chicken noodle soup on a cold night.

Hailey took her stuff to the bedroom. The walls were lined with photos that captured her childhood. She laughed at some of the pictures, memories cascading through her mind. Life was much simpler when she was a little girl playing in that kiddie pool or making a face while sitting in a pile of snow.

After a trip to the restroom, Hailey sat at the dinner table. A slice of meatloaf with a hard-boiled egg cooked in the middle of it like an eye stared at her, daring her to eat it. She didn't have the heart to tell Gran that meatloaf reminded her of dog food. She simply shoveled it into her mouth without thinking about the way it smelled or its lumpy texture.

"Would you like another slice?" Gran asked with a silver spatula in hand.

"Maybe later," Hailey said, having no desire to eat another bite of meatloaf but also not wanting to hurt Gran's feelings.

"How about you Harry?" Gran said. "More meatloaf?"

He shook his head and stood. He leaned over, kissed Gran on the cheek and squeezed her shoulder, then slowly walked over to his recliner.

"How is your job?" Gran asked. "Your mom says you work all the time."

Hailey sipped her cold milk. "I do work a lot, but my job is good."

"I don't know how you deal with those numbers all the time. I never had a head for numbers and neither did your father. Must be something you inherited from your mom's side of the family." Gran adjusted her purple-framed glasses.

"Numbers make sense to me. I love that they are completely objective and they fit so nicely together. If I make the right computation, everything works out." She wished relationships were as simple as math calculations.

"But, taxes?" Gran took a sip of her milk. "Makes my head spin thinking about all that."

"Tax time is pretty busy and stressful, but I also handle accounting for clients all year long. I'll be keeping up with some accounts while I'm here."

Gran offered Hailey some watermelon. "How long can you stay?"

Hailey took a slice, the sweet aroma of fresh-cut watermelon tickling her nose. "As long as you need me. I'm sure Mom will come out after the baby is born."

"I was so relieved when your mother called to tell me. I wasn't sure how I'd handle all of this on my own." Gran placed her warm hand atop Hailey's. "You are such a sweetheart to come help."

"I love you and Gramps." Hailey glanced at him across the room. He was watching TV and didn't seem to notice their lingering conversation at the dinner table.

"I wish I'd known sooner that he'd had a stroke." A somber expression crossed Gran's face.

"You did the best you could," Hailey said, trying to reassure Gran.

"I hope so." Gran took another sip of her milk. "Your mom tells me that you and Kevin are kaput."

"Yep." Hailey used her fingers to sweep some crumbs on the table into a pile.

"He was sure a dashing young man. The two of you made a handsome couple."

"Yeah." Hailey didn't want to rehash the details of her breakup with the man everyone had thought she'd marry. The crater in her heart was still trying to heal. "So what's on the agenda tomorrow?"

"Harry has a speech therapy appointment. He can't speak, you know. The doctor says he might regain some of his speech but probably won't ever talk like he did before." She shook her head, fear flickering in her eyes.

"The doctor doesn't know everything. Gramps could speak totally fine again." Hailey wanted to be optimistic and bolster Gran's spirits.

"The stroke didn't seem to affect too much else. It wasn't a major one, thank goodness. No rhyme or reason with strokes, I suppose. Besides the loss of speech, it seems like his right side is weaker now, though." Gran glanced over at Gramps.

"Don't you worry. I'm here now. I'll make sure he gets to his appointments, practices his therapy, eats enough, and recovers as well as he can." Hailey was there for Gran as much as she was for Gramps.

Gran smoothed her short hair. "I feel bad about you putting your life on hold for us."

"Don't. I love you and want to help. Besides, there isn't much to my life but work these days. And the gym." She laughed, but a needle of sadness pricked her heart.

"You don't have to take care of us twenty-four hours a day, but Harry did all the driving because of my glaucoma. If you can do the driving, that'd be the biggest help." Gran drank the rest of her milk. "You can shop, go to the beach, have some fun. You can use our car whenever you want. Maybe you'll meet—"

"Gran, please. I can read your mind," Hailey said as she sat back against her chair. "I'm not here to meet any men." Gran needed to squelch her preoccupation with matchmaking, especially when it came to Hailey's life.

"You never know." Gran's eyes lit up. "Lots of my friends have eligible grandsons."

I can only imagine. "That's sweet. But I'm taking a vacation from dating—indefinitely. I'm here to focus on you and Gramps. That's all." Hailey picked up her plate and stood, hoping Gran would get the hint that her love life wasn't up for discussion.

Gran stood as well, then took the serving bowl to the sink.

"I can take care of the dishes," Hailey said. She turned on the water to begin rinsing.

Gran held up her hand. "No, no. I'll do the dishes. You go in and spend some time with your grandfather. It'll brighten him up."

Hailey smiled. "If you're sure."

"I am." Gran nodded and opened the dishwasher. "Go on."

Hailey walked into the living room and sat on the couch. "Hey, Gramps, what're you watching?"

He turned and looked at her. He tried to mouth something, but Hailey didn't catch it. Not wanting to make him feel bad, she said, "Oh, look at that photo." Hailey stood and reached for a framed picture of herself and Gramps. "I remember when we took that. I came to visit the summer before my senior year, and you took me fishing on that big boat."

Gramps nodded, a smile stretching across his face. He pointed at the photo and rolled his eyes.

Hailey laughed. "I know, I know. You caught a *huge* fish that day, but *somehow* it got away. Sounds fishy to me." She laughed at her corny joke.

Gramps sat up. He said some garbled words that made no sense, but Hailey knew what he was trying to say.

"Sure, sure. I believe you, Gramps." She stretched out her hands, holding them about four feet apart. "It was this big."

He shook his head, held his hands about two feet apart, and then gave her a look as if to chastise her for exaggerating.

"I loved fishing with you that day. We had so much fun." The memories began to pour in of times they'd spent together.

Gramps raised his eyebrows and pointed outside.

"You want to go fishing again?" She'd love to spend the day fishing with her grandpa, not worrying about anything except trying to catch fish.

He nodded with enthusiasm.

"I'd love to, but I'm not sure we'd convince Gran to let you go right now. You need to recover." Hailey didn't want to irritate Gran with talk of going fishing or anything else except Gramps getting better.

He waved his hand dismissively.

"I'm here to help you recuperate, not to go fishing." She leaned in closer to him. "But I'll make you a deal."

Gramps eyed her with eagerness.

In a whisper, she said, "As soon as you're all better, I promise to take you fishing."

He stuck out his hand. Hailey took it and they shook.

"You focus on recovering, and I'll concentrate on finding a great fishing spot for us." She grinned at the familiar rapport between them.

Gramps nodded and smiled his approval.

"What are you two coming up with in here?" Gran asked in an accusatory tone as she walked in with hands on hips.

Gramps wore an innocent expression.

Hailey said, "Nothing. Just reliving some memories, that's all." She tried to sound as innocuous as possible.

"I don't want the two of you cooking anything up." Gran wagged her finger. "You hear me, Harry? You need to use all your energy to get better. No big plans to do anything else."

Hailey suspected her grandmother had eavesdropped. To allay any fears, she said, "Above all else, Gramps and I are both committed to his recovery. Right?" She turned toward Gramps.

He nodded vigorously.

"Good," Gran said with a flick of her head.

When Gran looked away, Gramps winked at Hailey.

"Your bedding is all freshly washed and there are clean towels in the bathroom." Gran pointed down the hall.

"Thanks, Gran. I'm excited to spend some time with both of you." It had been way too long, and Hailey vowed to make visiting her grandparents again a much higher priority.

"We're both happy to have you here." Gran sat on the couch and pulled out her knitting. "I think there's a movie on that one channel, ACM or something like that. Harry, why don't you find us a nice one, and we can relax."

"Relaxing sounds nice." Actually, it sounded heavenly.

"I bet you're tired from all that traveling," Gran said while her needles clicked together.

"Exhausted." Hailey made herself comfy on the couch with Gran.

After watching an old movie about an annoying woman and her pet leopard named Babe, or something like that, Hailey said goodnight and made her way to the pink-themed guest room. It didn't take long for her to fall asleep.

Chapter 4

The next morning, a shrill sound echoed through the house and Hailey bounded out of bed, her heart beating wildly, before realizing what it was.

The smoke detector. What a way to welcome Monday.

Combined scents of coffee, bacon, and burned toast hit her nose. Yep, she was with Gran and Gramps. As sure as the sun rose, Gran burned the toast each morning. Hailey hoped her grandparents' house would never actually catch on fire, because she could bet the neighbors were so used to the detector going off each morning, they'd never think it was the real thing.

"Good morning," Hailey said as she sat at the table.

"That darn toaster. I need a new one. I keep telling Harry that it doesn't work right." Gran placed a plate in front of Hailey. "I hope you're hungry. You're looking a little thin."

"I like to work out." *At least I used to.* Her busy work schedule and nasty breakup with Kevin had left her with little motivation to exercise.

"Back in my day, girls wanted some curves." Gran shook her head as if dismayed. "I don't understand girls these days wanting to be bone thin. Makes no sense at all."

"How's Gramps?" Hailey took her fork, then slipped a bite of scrambled eggs into her mouth.

"He's resting. He needs to do a lot of that to get better." Gran adjusted her neon-green blouse.

Hailey laughed inwardly at Gran's familiar vibrant wardrobe. *I'm glad some things haven't changed.* "What time is the appointment?"

"At eleven o'clock." Gran poured Hailey some orange juice. "It's with the speech therapist at some building by the hospital. Rehab something or other."

"So I'll have time to do some work after breakfast and before we need to leave?"

Gran nodded, her large yellow earrings swaying.

"Have you met the therapist yet?" Hailey sipped the tangy juice.

"No. The doctor said we should go to the rehabilitation place and they'd give us someone." Gran let out a long breath. "I don't know."

Hailey reached over and squeezed her grandmother's hand, noticing the web of veins across it. "I'm here. No need to worry. I can help get Gramps ready."

"That'd be good. He's a little ornery for me sometimes, the ol' coot." Gran pursed her lips. "That man can be so aggravating at times. But I don't know what I'd do without him." Fear flashed in Gran's eyes.

"Let's not worry about that." Hailey wanted to reassure Gran as much as herself.

"Having you here is exactly what we need. You and your grandfather have always had something special."

Hailey smiled. She didn't ever mention it to anyone, but she knew that she and Gramps had a unique connection. It had always been that way, even when she was a little girl. "I'll do whatever I can to help."

"Gramps, hang onto my arm," Hailey said as she helped her grandfather out of their silver Chevy Impala.

"Come on, Harry, people are waiting," Gran said, glancing

around. She brushed at her yellow pants. "We're already late. You know how much I dislike being late."

"It's okay, I've got this," Hailey said, sensing her grandmother's growing agitation. "Why don't you go into the lobby and find out where we need to go?"

Gran nodded, then trotted over toward the entryway, her floral purse hanging down at her side.

Hailey helped Gramps shuffle into the facility, and they made their way down the hall to a large desk where Gran stood.

"It's in this room." Gran pointed ahead of them and started walking.

By the time Hailey and Gramps reached Gran, her eyes were wide and she was tapping her foot. "Maybe we should get him a wheelchair so it doesn't take so long," Gran said.

Gramps looked at his wife and said some unintelligible sounds, then reached out for her hand.

Gran's face softened as she placed her hand in his. "I'm sorry. I guess I'm a little on edge."

Gramps pulled her hand to his lips and kissed it, obviously trying to calm Gran.

Hailey wanted to alleviate Gran's stress, so she said, "Why don't you go to the cafeteria and get a soda or something. I can talk to the therapist and take care of this."

Gran studied her.

"Really," Hailey insisted. "You don't need to worry about this. I can handle it." Gramps didn't need Gran and her anxiety making things even more stressful.

Gran gave her a swift hug, then turned and walked down the hall.

Hailey looked at Gramps and he gave her a lopsided smile. "I got your back," she said with a wink.

They approached a small reception area, and Hailey signed in her grandfather. They sat on a long, upholstered bench and waited for several minutes before being called back to a small room with a dark wood table and four brown, padded chairs. Hailey helped seat Gramps.

After a few more minutes, *Thor* opened the door. Hailey's breath caught as she did a double take and stared at the tall, blond-haired man filling the doorway. She swallowed hard. *He can't be the therapist.* He wasn't at all what she expected. His piercing pale blue eyes made her heart somersault and her stomach twist. His gray-patterned shirt fit him perfectly in all the right places, and a quick glance at his left hand showed no wedding ring. *Is this room getting warmer?* She resisted the urge to fan herself.

"Hi. I'm Peter Stafford." He extended his hand.

As she took it, a jolt of energy surged up her arm, and she blinked. "I'm . . . uh . . . Hailey." *Real smooth. He's going to think I'm an idiot. Say something intelligent.*

"Nice to meet you, Hailey." His strong hand held hers a moment longer, and then he let go.

Ignoring the musky cologne he wore, she composed herself enough to say, "And this is my grandfather." She looked at Gramps trying to recall his name, but her mind was completely blank.

"Harry Baker?" Peter said.

Hailey let out a nervous laugh that made her sound kind of like a hyena. "Yes. Harry. That's him. But I don't call him Harry, of course. I call him Gramps." *Can I crawl under a rock somewhere until my brain reengages?*

Mr. Stafford acknowledged Hailey, then sat in the seat next to Gramps. "I understand you had a mild stroke."

Gramps gave a slight nod.

Peter looked over the file in his hand. "I'm here to help you restore your speech. If you promise to work with me, I think we'll have you talking again soon. How does that sound?" He smiled, exposing flawless, bright white teeth. Like the brightest teeth Hailey had ever seen.

Gramps made a few noises.

Peter turned his attention to Hailey. "Has he been able to say anything understandable since the stroke?"

Hailey chastised herself. *You are here to help Gramps, not drool over the very attractive therapist.* "Not really. He tries, but only sounds come out. No words." She stroked Gramps's hand.

"Aphasia, the inability to communicate, is common with strokes."

"What do we need to do?"

Mr. Stafford turned to Gramps. "First, I'll need to evaluate your skills. We can do that with some basic exercises and simple words for recognition. How does that sound?"

Gramps nodded.

"You might also have apraxia, Mr. Baker."

A sullen expression crossed Gramps's face.

The therapist reached over and patted Gramps on the arm. "No need to worry. If you have apraxia, we will address it and get you all fixed up."

"What is apraxia?" Hailey asked, noting how kind and attentive Mr. Stafford was to Gramps.

"That's when the muscles in the mouth don't quite work in the proper order," he said to Hailey, then looked directly at Gramps. "We'll need to rewire the connection between your brain and your mouth so that the sounds you make are in the right order to form words. I'll also evaluate your ability to swallow." He smiled, and Hailey's heart reacted without permission.

"Sounds attractive."

The therapist looked at her with a confused expression and Gramps chuckled.

"Wait, what?" Her face felt like it caught on fire. "Did I say *attractive?*" She did her hyena laugh again. "I didn't mean that. At all. I assure you." She cleared her throat. "I meant to say, sounds perfect. Yes, *perfect* is what I meant. About that plan. Your plan to, uh, help Gramps sounds perfect." *Wow. Hit me over the head. How could I have said attractive? And perfect isn't much better. I sound like a babbling idiot.*

Mr. Stafford focused back on Gramps, who wore a grin like that silly Cheshire Cat, and Hailey wished she could evaporate. "I'd also like to set a time to come to your home and evaluate your surroundings so I can create a therapy plan that will be most effective for you."

Hailey nodded, then swallowed. *Did he say he'd be coming to the house? Like as in where I'm staying? Therapists do that?*

He turned to Hailey. "It will be most important that he practice the exercises at home. What we do here won't be nearly as effective unless he's practicing at home." He glanced at Gramps, then inclined his head toward Hailey. "You'll need to make her practice with you."

Trying not to be overwhelmed with the daunting task ahead, she said, "Okay. I'll do my best."

Peter studied her. "Don't worry. I'll give you detailed instructions and show you exactly what you need to do. Together we'll help him regain his verbal communication skills."

Hailey drew in a quick breath. "I'm here to help with whatever he needs."

The therapist looked at her, making her nerves misfire. "He's lucky to have you."

"Thanks." She wanted to explain that she was actually an intelligent woman with a successful career, but worried she'd trip all over her words again and prove herself to be nothing more than a bumbling ditz.

After some questions and a few speech exercises, Mr. Stafford finished his evaluation. "I'll work on a treatment plan for you, Mr. Baker."

Gramps nodded and gave him a lopsided smile.

"Thank you," Hailey said, sending him mental commands to forget what she'd said.

"I'll see you soon." Mr. Stafford opened the door and left, his cologne trailing behind him.

Peter sat in his office logging notes about his last patient, Harry Baker. He paused when thoughts of Mr. Baker's granddaughter suddenly filled his mind. *Sounds attractive.* That's what she'd said. He smiled as he replayed it in his mind. Did she think he was attractive? That seemed to be the most logical explanation. Then again, maybe she was thinking about someone else or maybe it was merely a slip of the tongue, as she'd explained. He leaned back in his chair and glanced out the window.

From the moment he shook her hand, it took an unusual amount of energy to focus on the appointment and on Mr. Baker. Sure, she was beautiful with her long brown hair, trim waist, and smooth skin. But her eyes grabbed at him. What color were they? Blue. But what kind of blue? Almost like the color of the ocean when a wave is about to break and the sun hits it just right.

"Excuse me," a high-pitched voice jolted him out of his thoughts.

Peter turned. "Yes, Joyce?"

"You were pretty deep in thought. Care to share?" she said with a nauseating smirk.

"Thinking about my last patient, that's all," he said. Joyce was about ten years older and divorced—four times—and made it no secret she was interested in him. He'd used the excuse that office romances were inappropriate, but the truth was she was a little scary with her fiery red hair and matching temperament. He was more than happy to keep his distance.

"Maybe you were thinking about a moonlit cruise around the bay. With me." She gave him a come-hither look.

He ignored her attempt to flirt and asked, "What did you need?"

Joyce handed him a file. "Here's the info you requested on Mrs. Johnson. The hospital sent it over."

Peter opened the folder and glanced over the paperwork. "Thanks, Joyce. I appreciate it."

"How much?" She leaned against the wall and subtly eyed him up and down.

Peter shook his head. Joyce was nothing, if not persistent. But he still had zero interest. Ze-ro.

Joyce gave him a wink and walked away.

Peter looked down at his notes on Mr. Baker, which sent his thoughts back to the granddaughter. Hailey, she said her name was. He chuckled at the way she seemed to be so nervous. Was that because of him? And what was it about her that drew him in? On the one hand, he didn't want her to distract him from her grandfather, but on the other, he hoped he would see her again.

His phone vibrated so he pulled it out.

Don't forget about our lunch date tomorrow. I have the afternoon off and Benji is super excited.

Looking forward to it. He texted back.

As they left the therapist's office, Hailey motioned Gran over from a waiting area.

"How was the appointment?" she asked as she approached them.

"Everything went well." *Except for when I laughed like a hyena, couldn't say anything intelligent, and then blurted out the word* attractive. *Who does that?*

"It did?" Gran seemed surprised.

"Yeah. The therapist seems nice." Her cheeks were still warm. "And Gramps did great."

Gramps elbowed Hailey, but she paid no attention to him.

Gran looked at Gramps, then at Hailey. "What's going on?"

"Nothing," Hailey said, blinking a few times.

"Harry?" Gran said.

They both looked at him. He wore a wide grin.

"Gramps really liked the therapist, that's all." She threw him a glare. "How about we get some ice cream?"

Gramps nodded and Gran said, "Can you drop me off at the

grocery store? I need to get a few things."

"Sure. Gramps and I will eat ice cream while you shop." Sounded like a fair trade.

After they dropped off Gran, Hailey drove Gramps to the ice cream parlor that was in the same strip mall as the grocery store.

She helped Gramps inside the cheery shop that exuded the scent of thousands of delectable calories and sat him at a small white table.

"Hello, Harry. Your usual?" said an older woman with bleach-blonde hair and a diamond stud in her nose.

Gramps smiled at her, then winked.

"He's one of my regulars. Always a flirt that Harry." The lady gazed at Hailey. "You are?"

"His granddaughter, Hailey. I came to help because he had a stroke."

"Nice to meet you. I heard about the stroke, but I'm sure with his spunk he'll be fine." She handed Hailey a sugar cone topped with pink ice cream. "Peppermint for my best customer."

Hailey took the cone to Gramps.

"Can I get something for you?"

Hailey glanced over the menu. "I'd like a scoop of Cookies and Cream, please."

"Coming right up."

Hailey glanced around the room decorated in blue and white striped wallpaper and white lace curtains. "This reminds me of when I was a little girl."

"My parents started the shop years and years ago," the woman said. "They've both passed now. I can't imagine doing anything else. I love my customers, especially my regulars like Harry. Where's June today?"

"She's at the grocery store."

"June was born to bake. Brought me a delicious angel food cake dripping with strawberry sauce when I had surgery on my foot."

"Gran loves to share her strawberry cake." Hailey laughed.

"I'm glad they have you to help them out."

Hailey sat at the table and let the cold, creamy mixture slide across her tongue. "Nothing better than Cookies and Cream," she said.

Gramps nodded.

Hailey pointed at him. "You and me, we need to get something straight."

Gramps peered at her with raised eyebrows.

"I will admit that your therapist is handsome. Maybe even *attractive*." Gramps let out a laugh. "Yeah, yeah. I literally can't believe I said that. I'm so embarrassed. I hope he'll forget it."

Gramps gestured with his hand in a way that implied Hailey should pursue this man.

"That right there is what we need to get straight. Obviously, he's good looking. And has kind eyes and a warm smile and he smells divine. But," she straightened in her seat, "I'm not the least bit interested in anything romantic with him or anyone else."

Gramps questioned her with his eyes.

"I'll tell you why. First of all, Kevin broke my heart. I was planning to marry him while he was planning who else he could cheat on me with." The memory of seeing him with the other women felt like an ice pick in her chest. "We'd been dating for over a year. Over a year, Gramps. I thought he was going to propose, but he was only lying." She balled her fist while the anger and hurt bubbled up. "He's a cheat and a liar and I'm not interested at all in repeating that experience ever again. If I can't have what you and Gran have, I'd rather be single the rest of my life."

Extending his hand, Gramps stroked her arm.

"And secondly, I'm only here until you recover, and then I need to go back to my life in Colorado. I don't want any complications. Besides, Mr. Stafford is only interested in being your speech therapist." She placed her hand on his. "And I'm here to help you. That's all. Nothing else."

Hailey finished her ice cream and so did Gramps. "Are we ready to go?" she said.

He held up his hand.

"Not yet?"

He pointed at the counter.

Hailey looked over. "You want to get another ice cream?"

Gramps stood and made his way over to the counter. Hailey followed him.

"June's regular?" the lady said with a metal scoop in her hand.

Gramps nodded with a smile.

"Two scoops of Pistachio Almond coming right up." She grabbed a cup and began filling it.

"That's so sweet of you to get ice cream for Gran." Hailey hoped someday she'd find a man who loved her the way Gramps loved Gran, but she was pretty convinced that was impossible.

The woman handed the cup to Gramps and he gave her some bills. She rang up the sale and said, "Here's your change."

Gramps pointed at her.

"My tip?"

He gave her a wave and they walked out of the ice cream shop.

Chapter 5

After Hailey picked Gran up from the grocery store, she helped Gramps into the house and got him settled in his favorite, well-worn brown recliner, then brought in the groceries while Gran enjoyed her ice cream with Gramps. Hailey snuck glances at the two of them together while she put everything away in the kitchen.

About thirty minutes later, the doorbell rang. "I'll get it," Hailey said.

She opened the door to a pretty woman with wavy white hair, bright red lipstick, and blue eye shadow.

"Hello, you must be Hailey," the woman said as she stepped into the house, a fruity scent trailing behind her.

"Yes, I am." Hailey suspected she'd been the subject of at least a few conversations.

"I'm Lila."

"Nice to meet you." At least she thought it was nice to meet her. For some reason, it seemed like Lila was sizing her up and down.

Gran rounded the corner. "Hi, Lila, dear."

The women hugged each other.

"June hasn't stopped talking about you." Lila turned to Gran.

"You're right. She is adorable," she said with a wide smile. "Darren would love to meet her."

"Excuse me?" Hailey said. What was Gran up to?

"Oh, don't mind Lila, she's only talking to herself." Gran slipped her friend a sharp look.

Lila cleared her throat. "Oh, uh, yes, I came by to see if you're coming to bingo on Thursday."

"I don't know—"

"Yes, she is," Hailey said. "I'm here to keep Gramps company. We're planning to watch a basketball game that night so, Gran, you might as well go with your friends and play bingo." Hailey wanted Gran to keep up with her normal activities.

"You don't mind?"

"Of course not. That's why I'm here." A night with her friends would do Gran a lot of good. And it wouldn't hurt Gramps to have a little relief from Gran's worrying.

"Thursday night then?" Lila said.

Gran nodded. "Yes, yes, dear. That'll be quite fine." Gran looked at her watch. "I'm so sorry you need to get back home, but it was nice to see you."

"I . . . uh . . . oh, yes, I do need to get home."

Gran walked Lila to the door and stepped outside with her. Hailey could hear them speaking in hushed voices, but couldn't make out what they were saying.

After Lila left, Gran came back inside.

"What were you talking about out there, Gran?" Hailey asked.

"Us? Oh, nothing." She shrugged. "Nothing at all."

"Why are you acting so strange?" It seemed like Gran had a secret or something.

"I'm not." Gran sat on the couch and said, "Tell me more about the therapy session."

Realizing she wouldn't get any information out of her grandmother, Hailey said, "It was good. His therapist seems to be a nice man and committed to helping Gramps. He seems quite sincere. And certain that Gramps will speak again." An image of the appealing Mr. Stafford flashed through her mind followed by the prickly memory of her monumental failure to speak coherent sentences in front of him.

Gran stared at her.

"What?" Hailey shifted her weight.

"Why are your cheeks so flushed? Did something happen with the therapist you aren't telling me?" Gran sat up and perched on the edge of the sofa as if expecting some juicy story.

"It's the heat, I guess." *Or the fact that I totally embarrassed myself.*

Gran lifted an accusatory eyebrow.

Hailey held up her hands. "Gran, nothing happened that you need to know. Really. And remember, I am *not* interested in dating anyone. Not Lila's Darren, not Gramps's therapist. No one. So, you can put away your matchmaker's hat."

Gran placed her hand on her hip. "Why don't you want to date anyone?" She gazed at Hailey with a perplexed expression.

"Because."

"*That* explains it." Gran widened her eyes in the same way she always did when she thought someone was being ridiculous. But Hailey wasn't being ridiculous. At all.

"Gran," Hailey said, letting out a long breath. "I'm still trying to recover from a long relationship that didn't end well." That was putting it mildly.

"What happened with Kevin? You dated him for what, a year?"

Hailey slumped. "Thirteen months, two weeks, and four days." She raked her fingers through her hair.

Gran gazed at her with sympathetic eyes. "Your mom said you were going to marry him."

"I thought I was." Another piece of Hailey's heart broke off. She'd invested so much into her relationship with Kevin and now that it was over, she wasn't sure where to go from here to put the pieces back together.

Gran put her arm around Hailey's shoulder. "Do you want to tell me about it?"

Hailey chewed her lip. Maybe talking to Gran would help put things into perspective. After a minute or so of silence, she said, "He was working a lot—staying late at his office, working weekends—I was really proud of him for being such a hard worker." A tear edged out of her eye. "The night before Valentine's Day, I decided I'd take him some Chinese food. I had it all in my hands when I walked up to his office building and there he was." She paused. "With a woman." She let out a long, painful breath from lungs that squeezed tight at the memory. "He was hugging her and then he kissed her—really kissed her. Like there was no doubt it had happened before."

Gran stroked her hair. "What did you do?"

"I dropped all the food and ran back to my car. After I ugly-cried for a while, I went back to my apartment and stared at the ceiling most of the night trying to figure out what to do. I thought maybe I'd misinterpreted what I'd seen. Or maybe I'd imagined it. I couldn't believe the man who'd talked about marrying me would do something like that. We had plans for a life together, even talked about the names for our kids. I thought we'd be getting engaged on Valentine's. I made a down payment on this gorgeous satin wedding dress because that's what he led me to believe."

"What a two-timing rat." Gran narrowed her eyes.

"That's not even all." Hailey sniffed. "The next morning, I wanted to confront him. I drove over to his condo, still hoping I was somehow wrong." She wiped at her eyes. "I sat in my car trying to build up my courage when I saw his door open."

"Oh no." Gran shook her head.

A tear trickled down her cheek. "I couldn't believe it."

"That woman from the office came out?" Gran's tone was filled with indignation.

"Worse."

Gran gasped. "What?"

"He wasn't two-timing me. He was three-timing me. Maybe more." Hailey threw her hands up. "I don't even know."

"My poor girl." Gran hugged her close.

"How could I have been so stupid? So oblivious? He said I was the only one and I believed him." Hailey closed her eyes, the deep sense of betrayal still gnawing at her. "He said he wanted to marry me, and I believed him."

"You weren't stupid. You trusted him. That's what people do when they love someone."

"I really thought he was working and going on business trips. It never occurred to me that he was seeing other women." Hailey clenched her jaw. "I was such a fool."

"Not a fool." Gran rubbed her arm. "Just in love."

"I suppose there were signs, especially the last couple of months, but I was completely head over heels. I was sure he was going to propose, and the whole time he had a revolving front door. Who knows how many women he was seeing besides me." Hailey let the tears tumble down her cheeks, not holding anything back. She and Gran sat there for several minutes while Hailey cried. This was the first time she'd talked about it in such depth, and the emotional release made her feel light and free, as if she'd dropped a thousand pounds of dead weight.

"What happened after you saw those women?" Gran asked. "I would've socked him right in the nose." Hailey had to smile at the image of Gran punching Kevin.

"I packed up the stuff he'd given me, took it to his condo, and dumped it on his doorstep, which broke a glass figurine he'd bought me at a carnival. Oops." She laughed and cried at the memory. "He came over to my apartment the next day and tried to smooth things over. What a jerk. I told him to drop dead and kicked him out."

"Good for you," Gran said with enthusiasm.

"It was the hardest thing I've ever done. Sometimes I wonder—"

"Don't even say it," Gran interrupted. "You don't need a man that can't be faithful to you. You deserve much more than that. And you *will* find one."

"I don't know, Gran. I don't know that there are any good ones left." Hailey didn't hold much hope.

"Sure there are, sweetheart." Gran caressed her cheek. "He's out there. Don't you worry."

Hailey sat up and smoothed her hair. "For now, I'm not worried about finding a man. My only concern is you and Gramps."

Chapter 6

After checking on Gran and Gramps, Hailey spent the following morning inputting numbers in a spreadsheet for Crandall Automotive and running reports for Colorado Subs and Rocky Mountain Outdoors. She made some phone calls and sent several emails. She had lunch in her room so she could work without interruption. Finally, she finished and strode into the stifling living room wearing black shorts and a bright pink tank top. "Hi, Gran. Sorry it took me so long. I didn't realize how much I needed to do today."

"I'm glad you got some work done." Gran peered over her knitting. "Looks like you're ready to exercise now."

"I figured it was time for me to get myself back into working out again. Would it be okay if I went running? Well, maybe not so much *running*." Hailey fanned herself. "How do you people live here in this heat and humidity?" Hailey had forgotten what it was like to be in Florida during the late spring.

"We can turn up the AC," Gran offered.

"That's okay. I'll be fine." *Unless I keel over from heat exhaustion at this very moment.* "Will you be all right with Gramps while I'm gone?"

"Of course." Gran put down her knitting. "I told you before, I don't need you twenty-four hours a day."

Hailey nodded. She loved that Gran still felt so independent and committed to taking care of Gramps, but his stroke had taken a lot out of Gran with the initial scare and subsequent worrying, and Hailey wanted to give Gran as much emotional support as possible. "I'll be back in a while."

Hailey left the house and walked briskly down the street to warm up her muscles. It had been too long. Her breakup with Kevin had taken much too much out of her, and it was time to take her life back. Starting a regular running routine would help put her in control.

She plugged her earbuds into her phone and listened to one of her playlists from Spotify. Increasing her stride, she started to jog. It felt great to be outside. It was even better that she was in a place that didn't have a memory of Kevin tied to it everywhere she turned.

Huffing and puffing, she decided to slow it down. She spotted a park ahead and made her way over to a bench where she watched kids on the swings. Someday, she'd have kids and take them to the park to swing, but for now she'd find strength in her solitude.

The sun hung overhead in the cloudless sky, radiating heat. Hailey started walking again and found herself in a strip mall. *Too bad I didn't bring some money with me so I could buy a water bottle. I need one to take with me on my runs or I'll shrivel up from dehydration.*

Hailey began walking toward a restaurant when she stopped in her tracks. On the patio sat the speech therapist, Peter Stafford. At least she thought it was him. He had the same hair color and the same build. She moved closer, trying to get a better look. He turned his head. It was definitely him, and he was with a young boy. She watched the easy, natural interaction between the two of them. They laughed, then he reached over and tousled the kid's hair. *Must be his son.*

A woman with long blonde hair walked up to the table and sat down. *And that's his wife.*

Feeling like a stalker, Hailey backed up a few steps, then turned around and began to run. The warm, moist air weighed heavy in her lungs as she increased her stride. A twinge of disappointment ran down her spine. She should be ashamed that she was attracted to a married man. But how would she have known? It wasn't like she could say, "Hi. You look like Chris Hemsworth and I find you extremely attractive. Are you married?" She laughed at the absurdity. *Married men should always wear a wedding ring.*

At least she knew now that Mr. Stafford was off limits, even in her thoughts. It was for the best anyway. Her heart was still fragile, and she needed at least five years, maybe ten, to heal it.

When Hailey opened the door to the house, Gran was huddled together with three other ladies, looking at something.

"Hi," Hailey said. "What's going on?"

Gran's head popped up. "Oh. Uh, we're talking about . . . bingo."

"Uh, huh. Bingo," said a woman with short black hair and a rather large nose.

Another woman, with long gray hair and a flowing orange dress said, "Nothing to see here."

Gran elbowed that woman and gathered up something in her hands.

Obviously, the women were trying to hide what they were doing, but why? "Gran?" Hailey said.

"We're all done now. No more bingo talk, ladies. We can examine strategy another time," Gran said.

The third woman stood. She was tall with thick glasses and curly gray hair. "Thanks, June. I'll be in touch."

She'll be in touch? Something was definitely going on. Why was Gran covering it up? They were acting like they were part of some covert operation. Were they talking about cheating at bingo? Was it even possible to cheat?

"Thanks for coming, Darla," Gran said to the tall woman.

The other two women stood.

"I'll see you later," Gran said to both of them.

After the women left, Hailey eyed Gran with suspicion. "What's going on here?"

Gran walked into the kitchen and said over her shoulder, "Nothing. I told you, we were talking about bingo. That's all."

When Gran came back into the living room with a glass of water in her hand, Hailey said, "You aren't trying to cheat at bingo or something are you?" Hailey wanted to get to the bottom of it, because Gran was acting so sneaky.

"My lands, girl. You think I would *cheat*?" Gran widened her eyes and clutched at her chest.

"Well, no. Of course not," Hailey said, feeling guilty she'd accused her grandmother. "It's just that you were acting so weird when I came in."

"We were simply talking about our plans. That's all. Nothing for you to be concerned about." Gran handed the glass of water to Hailey. "Did you have a nice time doing your exercising?"

"Yeah. It felt good to move those muscles again." Obviously, Gran was finished talking about her meeting with the ladies. Maybe Hailey was being suspicious for nothing and reading something that didn't exist into a get together between Gran and her friends. Older women did talk about bingo, didn't they?

Gran sat on the couch. Hailey plopped down next to her. Gran pulled her knitting from her black-and-red-checkered bag and started clicking away.

Hailey examined the blue and white creation. "What are you making?"

"A baby blanket for my great-grandson."

"Brit will love it." Hailey touched the soft yarn. "It's beautiful."

"Thank you. I hope to get it finished before he's born." She laughed. "Guess I better hurry."

Gramps emerged from the hallway and glanced around the room

furtively. Hailey guessed he was checking to see if those women had left. He stepped over to his recliner and sat.

"Hey, how are you doing today?" Hailey asked him.

Gramps peered at her as if trying to communicate with his eyes.

"You interested in a game of cards?" Memories of numerous card games over the years flooded her mind. What she wouldn't give to have Gramps like that again. "We can play Crazy Eights."

He nodded with a crooked smile.

"I've been practicing, so you can't beat me." Hailey grabbed the deck lying on the shelf by the recliner. "I know you used to let me win all the time, but I'm going to win legitimately."

Hailey dealt Gramps his seven cards, noticing that it seemed to take him more effort to hold the cards as well as more time to process the cards he held.

She set the rest of the deck face down on the small end table between the couch and the recliner. "All right, are you ready?" she asked after giving him some extra time.

He looked at her and she placed the first card face up to start the discard pile.

Slowly, he set down a card. She followed with a three of hearts. He studied his cards, then set down a three of diamonds. Although the game took longer than it used to, Gramps beat her.

"You were just lucky. That's all," Hailey said. "I'm going to really shuffle the cards this time."

Again, she began the game. Gramps dropped his selected card a few times, but Hailey averted her eyes because she didn't want to make Gramps feel bad. By the end of the second game, she was no longer feeling bad for Gramps because he'd beat her again.

"Are you cheating?" she said with mock anger.

Gramps blinked his eyes, then displayed a wounded expression.

"Okay, fine. No more taking it easy on you," Hailey said. "Get ready to lose."

He reached over and patted her on the hand.

After fifteen minutes or so, Gramps won the game. Again. Hailey sat back against the sofa and threw her cards in the air. "I'm never going to beat you."

Gramps wore a satisfied grin.

Gran asked, "Are you two ready for dinner?"

"It's still early, isn't it?" Hailey checked her Fitbit for the time. It wasn't even four o'clock.

"We eat early here."

Hailey picked up the cards and shuffled them into a deck. "I need to play another game with Gramps. This time, it's gin, and I'm definitely going to win."

"Harry *is* an expert player, you know." Gran smoothed her purple-striped blouse.

Hailey eyed him. "He's gonna lose."

Hailey dealt each of them ten cards, then placed the next card face up. They continued to discard and then choose cards until Hailey looked at her hand with confidence. All her cards fit into melds. She called out, "Gin."

Gramps laid down his cards, and sure enough, she'd won.

Hailey jumped up to do a victory dance. "I won, I won, I won. Oh, yeah. I won." She wiggled her hips, then spun around.

Gran clapped her hands and started laughing. "Good for you. No one ever beats Harry."

Hailey looked over at Gramps, who gave her a nod.

"Maybe you'd like to take a shower before dinner?" Gran said, adjusting one of her large beaded earrings.

"Okay." After being outside in the sticky sauna air, then playing cards, she definitely needed one, but it seemed odd that Gran was suggesting it. Hailey wasn't a child who needed personal hygiene direction.

"I'll set the table," Gran said. "Don't be too long."

Hailey finished her shower, combed through her wet hair, and threw on a pair of jean shorts and a blue T-shirt. She wasn't used to the warm, almost suffocating, temperatures in her grandparents' house.

When she walked out into the living room, she stopped suddenly, surprised at the unfamiliar woman staring at her.

"Oh, Hailey. I'm glad you're out of the shower. I invited Dee over for dinner tonight," Gran said sweetly.

Hailey gave a slight nod at the lady with red hair and penciled-on eyebrows that weren't at all balanced—one eyebrow was much higher than the other.

"And this is her grandson, Roger."

Roger stood there in khaki shorts that weren't quite long enough for his gangly legs.

A setup. No wonder she wanted me to take a shower. Hailey shot Gran a stern look. *You are in so much trouble* she communicated with her narrowed eyes. Hadn't she been clear about this very thing earlier? She was not interested in dating. Period.

Hailey glanced over at Gramps, who wore a big grin. She glared at him and his grin widened.

"Hailey, your grandma is sure proud of you. She talks about you all the time." Dee reached out for Hailey's hand. Hailey reciprocated and Dee clapped her other wrinkly hand on top of Hailey's. "We thought you'd like to meet Roger. He graduated from college at the top of his class."

Roger might have been attractive—if he didn't have those big front teeth and a serious unibrow.

"Hailey, it's a pleasure to meet you," Roger said. He drummed his fingers on the side of his thigh and smiled weakly.

"Hi," Hailey said, hoping to be polite but not give Roger any idea she'd be interested in seeing him after this ambush dinner.

"You sit here, next to Roger." Gran pointed at Hailey, who pasted on a smile as she entertained ways she could strangle her grandmother.

At least the meal smelled heavenly. Hailey piled some pot roast and potatoes on her plate, then grabbed one of her grandma's famous wheat rolls. The bread melted in her mouth.

Gran cleared her throat loudly, so Hailey glanced at her. Gran squeezed her eyes shut and jerked her head. "We need to say grace."

Hailey quickly swallowed the bread in her mouth and closed her eyes.

After the prayer, Roger looked at Hailey, his gaze making her skin feel prickly. "I am glad to be here for dinner, Hailey."

Trying to have some polite conversation Hailey asked, "Where are you working?"

"I have applied at several companies in the area."

"Doing what?" She shoveled another bite of pot roast into her mouth, trying to lose herself in its deliciousness and pretend she wasn't in the middle of awkward central.

"I'm a computer engineer."

"Oh, yes. He's a whiz at computers. Always has been." Dee beamed.

After a long, hard swallow, Hailey replied, "That's awesome." What could she do? What if she feigned a heart attack? Would that get her out of this mess? She glanced over at Gramps, who was laughing to himself, which made her want to bop him.

"June and I thought you and Roger might like to go to a movie tonight," Dee said brightly.

"Oh, you know, I'd love to," Hailey started.

"Great. I already bought the tickets," Roger said, his toothy smile splashed across his face.

"Roger, I'm so sorry, but I can't. I have some work I need to finish tonight." It wasn't a complete lie. She probably needed to send another email or two to Mrs. Saunders at Rocky Mountain Outdoors.

"That can wait, can't it?" Gran asked.

"It's a client who is particularly hard to please. I've been her accountant for years and I promised my boss that I'd keep up with certain clients while I was here." She turned to Roger. "I'm sure you understand, right?"

Roger wore a crestfallen expression. "Yeah, sure."

Hailey might have felt guilty for stretching the truth a bit, but she was still mad that she'd been trapped in this uncomfortable setup tonight.

Roger's face lit up. "How about we go bowling tomorrow night?"

"Bowling?" She searched her mind for an excuse. "I, uh—"

Gramps made a sudden noise and all eyes turned toward him. He held up a deck of cards, then said some garbled words.

Hailey pounced. "Ah, yes. Gramps and I have a standing date with a card game."

Gramps nodded and Hailey wanted to rush over and kiss him.

"Maybe—" Gran started to say.

"I think we should finish dinner and not worry about any other dates right now," Hailey said. She didn't want to be rude, but the last thing she needed was a date with someone with whom she had nothing in common. Absolutely nothing.

They finished the rest of the dinner. Hailey said as little as possible while Roger talked about SQL, Linux, HTML, firewalls, and other computer lingo that held no interest for her. It all went over her head and she silently pleaded for them to leave before she passed out from boredom.

"I'll call you, Dee. Thanks for coming over," Gran said.

"Thank you for a lovely dinner. We'll have to do it again soon. Roger will be here indefinitely."

"Bye, Hailey. I'll give you a call." He raised his unibrow and smiled.

Hailey nodded. As soon as they were out of earshot, Hailey said, "How could you do that?"

"I was trying to help," Gran said, wiping at her white pants.

"I told you I don't want to date anyone right now."

"But I thought if you met Roger—"

"Really?" She gave Gran an are-you-kidding-me look. "You thought I'd like to date Roger? Seriously?"

"I guess he is a little . . ."

"No, he's a lot." She said to Gramps over her shoulder. "And you

52

only saved yourself because you came up with the card game idea. I saw you laughing it up over there."

"F-f-f-f-fu-nn-nny," Gramps said.

Hailey and Gran both whipped their heads in Gramps's direction and stared at him. "You said a word." Hailey pointed at him, tears welling in her eyes.

Gramps said it again. "F-f-f-f-fu-nn-nny."

"We'll have to tell the therapist tomorrow. This is big," Hailey said, feeling more optimistic than she had since she arrived. Maybe his speech would return and he'd once again entertain her with his tall tales. She yearned to hear Gramps share one of his big whoppers.

After Hailey replied to a few emails and reworked a spreadsheet for one of her clients, she joined her grandparents and watched an episode of *Lawrence Welk*, followed by an old black-and-white movie. Hailey wanted to soak in all the time she could with her grandparents.

Chapter 7

On Wednesday morning Hailey was up bright and early so she could get some more work done. After she'd completed several tasks, including filling out the monthly ledger for Colorado Subs, her cell phone began playing "Für Elise."

"Hi, Mom."

"Hi, honey. How is everything?" Her mom sounded cheery.

"Good." She closed some of the open windows on her computer.

"How is Harry?"

"He said a word yesterday." The memory made her giddy all over again.

"That's good."

"Today we have another therapy appointment." She refused to let any thoughts of Mr. Hunk—Stafford, that was his name—enter her mind.

"I'm so thankful you can be there to help."

"I love spending time with them." Hailey shut her laptop, then swung her legs up on the bed.

"How is June?" her mom asked with concern.

"Fine." She sat back against the headboard of the bed. "Except I'd like to kill her."

"Why?" Her mom sounded shocked.

"She had this guy come over for dinner and it was the worst."

Her mom laughed. "Good ol' June, always the matchmaker."

"It was the most awkward dinner ever." Visions of Roger grinning at her circled her head and she cringed. Setup dates were always, always awful. Especially if your grandmother was involved in any way.

"Have you heard from Kevin?"

The mere mention of his name made Hailey's heart ache. "No. And I don't expect to. We are done."

"Maybe—"

"No, Mom. We're done." She didn't want to discuss Kevin with her mom or anyone else. It was still too painful. Besides, her mom didn't know all the gory details, and she didn't need to.

"But—"

"Mom, I gotta go. Our appointment is soon and I need to get ready."

"Okay. Keep me posted."

They said their goodbyes, and Hailey tossed her phone on the bed. She didn't want to think about Kevin. Or the hole he'd left in her heart. She didn't want to remember the good times they'd had, because he'd ruined all of that with his lying. Hailey only wanted to move forward and get on with her life.

After finding a light, cotton-print dress and some sandals, she went to the kitchen to make some breakfast. Gran stood at the stove dressed in a bright green blouse and wearing mascara and red lipstick.

"You look nice today," Hailey said.

"Thank you," Gran said. "I'll make you some eggs. And some toast with jam. And sausage."

"No, that's okay. I'll eat some fruit." If she kept letting Gran feed her, she'd gain a hundred pounds.

"Are you sure?"

"Yeah. Is Gramps up and ready?"

"Yes. We've already had breakfast." Gran grabbed a bowl of fruit from the refrigerator. "He ate all of his eggs and sausage."

"I'm still trying to get used to the time change from Colorado. Two hours makes a big difference." Hailey filled a glass with some orange juice.

"I have a hair appointment today. Could you drop me off and then take Harry to his therapy?" Gran handed Hailey a plate with strawberries, blueberries, and other fruit on it.

"Sure." Hailey popped a couple of grapes into her mouth. "Don't you want to come to the session?"

Gran ran her fingers through her hair. "I really need to get my hair done, and I haven't had a chance since Harry had his stroke."

Hailey studied her grandmother. His stroke had taken a toll on Gran, too. Gran had always been strong and a hard worker, but for a moment, she seemed so small and weak. "No problem. You should take some time for yourself. I can handle the appointment."

During his lunch break, Peter sat at his desk and logged some notes from the previous patients. He checked his appointment schedule. Harry Baker was next. Without warning, a tremor shot through his stomach and his palms moistened.

He drew in a breath. *This is ridiculous. I am a medical professional, not a fifteen-year-old boy.*

Still, the thought of seeing Hailey again made his nerves tingle. What was it about this woman? Why was she having this effect on him? He hadn't been this affected by a woman in years, and it was unsettling.

He rubbed his eyes. Feelings were fleeting—he knew that all too well from experience. He simply had to focus on the patient and compartmentalize whatever errant feelings he might have about this woman. He was a professional first and foremost, and he not only needed to act like one, he needed to think like one.

Peter rummaged through his lunch sack and turned his attention to eating while he read an article about a technique for treating apraxia of speech.

Hailey helped Gramps get out of the car. "I bet you'll do some great things today."

He nodded.

They slowly walked into the outpatient facility and waited for the appointment.

After ten minutes, they were called back to a small room with photos of the beach adorning the walls.

When the door opened, Mr. Stafford walked in wearing navy pants and a blue shirt. Hailey tried not to notice how the shirt accentuated his eyes or how the faint musky scent of his cologne tickled her nose. "Good to see you. How are you today?" He reached out his hand.

Gramps reciprocated.

"He said a word yesterday. Totally spontaneously," Hailey said, using her hands to emphasize her enthusiasm.

The therapist eyed her and the corners of his mouth lifted. "Wonderful." He turned to Gramps and nodded. "Certain words may come back like that. Are you ready to do some work today, Mr. Baker?"

Gramps said a few unintelligible words.

Hailey interpreted what he meant and said, "He wants you to call him Harry."

"Okay, Harry. Call me Peter." He smiled and Hailey noticed how it seemed to sparkle. *What is wrong with you? Stop checking him out.*

Peter pulled out some cards. "We're going to work on some basic sounds and try to rewire the pathway between your brain and your mouth. Kind of like retraining your muscles to say the right words."

Gramps looked at him, then let out an expletive.

Hailey blinked and sat back against her chair. "Gramps!" Her cheeks warmed.

Gramps smiled. He let out another curse word.

Her excitement that Gramps was saying words was tempered by her embarrassment. Of all the words he could start saying, it had to be those. And in the clinic. In front of the therapist. "You can't say those kinds of words in here." She turned to Peter. "I'm so sorry. I don't know why he's saying these."

Peter held his hand up. "No worries." He patted Gramps on the shoulder. "I'm glad to see you have some words coming back."

After a thirty-minute session, Peter turned to Hailey. "I'll give you some things to take home and work with him, because that will make the most difference."

"Can I talk to you outside for a minute?" Hailey asked, reminding herself to keep any interactions with Peter on a professional level.

Peter nodded.

"I'll be right back, Gramps."

In the hallway, Hailey said, "Do you think he'll regain all of his speech?"

Without looking directly at her he said, "It's hard to say. Some stroke victims do, others don't."

"I'm sorry about, you know, what he said in there." Hailey still felt a bit embarrassed.

Peter glanced at her, then looked down at the papers in his hands. "Not the first time I've heard those words. Any progress we can make in word formation is good. Some words that are almost instinctive seem to come back first."

"He doesn't usually talk like that."

Peter took an almost imperceptible breath, then gazed at her. Instantly, hundreds of butterflies filled her stomach. "Don't stress out about it. I'm glad he's starting to say something."

"Thanks."

Peter took a step back. "Do you live with him?"

"No, I live in Colorado, but when he had his stroke I volunteered to come help while he recovers."

"That's very nice of you." His smile tugged at her heart.

"Thank you for working with him." She cleared her throat.

"I think we'll see some progress. I'd like to make the next appointment at his home and do the session in familiar surroundings."

Hailey swallowed hard. "That sounds good." A shiver raced down her spine.

"Stop by the front desk and let them know you need a home visit."

"I'll do that." She nodded. "We'll see you then."

"Looking forward to it." The way he said it made her wonder if he was flirting with her or simply being kind. *Stop thinking about him like that.*

Hailey watched him walk away, then she returned to Gramps in the room. "We're done for today. You did fantastic. Except for, you know, the whole cursing part." She shook her head and clucked her tongue.

Gramps shrugged and gave a slight smile.

"I don't know what I'm going to do with you." She helped him down the hall and they stopped at the desk.

"May I help you?" an older woman with fiery red hair asked.

"I think we're supposed to make an appointment for a home visit."

The woman eyed Hailey and it made Hailey almost feel like she was under some kind of scrutiny. "It looks like Dr. Stafford can make a home visit on Wednesday at three o'clock."

"I think that will work."

The woman wrote out an appointment card and handed it to Hailey. "Here you go. Remember, Dr. Stafford's time is valuable so please make sure to be home at that time and keep it to only thirty minutes."

Have I offended this woman somehow? What is her problem?

"Joyce, can you make a copy of this and put it in Mr. St. Claire's chart?" another lady with wire-frame glasses said.

"Sure," the woman with red hair answered in a sweet voice. She turned back to Hailey and gruffly said, "Any questions?"

"No. Thank you for your help." Hailey gave her a courtesy smile, but the woman didn't reciprocate. Hailey wasn't sure what was going on. She turned to Gramps and they walked out of the building.

"We need to pick up Gran at the salon."

Gramps said some garbled words. Hailey didn't understand most of them, but she could make out the word woman.

"Yeah, I don't know why she was rude. Maybe she was having a bad day." Hailey wanted to give her the benefit of the doubt.

When they got home, Gran said, "How about some tuna casserole for dinner?"

Stifling her gag reflex, Hailey said, "That sounds yummy. Can I help make a salad to go with it?" *Please say we can eat something other than tuna casserole.*

"I have some fruit in the refrigerator." Gran pointed.

"I'm on it," Hailey said, not wanting to appear too zealous.

They sat down to dinner and Gran said grace. Gramps picked up the pitcher with both hands and poured some apple juice into Gran's glass. "Thank you," she said.

He winked at her, then poured some juice for Hailey.

"Tell me more about the appointment today," Gran said.

Hailey turned to Gramps and cocked her head. "Well . . . he said some words."

"Really?" Gran looked pleased.

Hailey then repeated one of the words.

"Harry!" Gran's eyes widened. "You said that to the nice speech therapist?"

Gramps shrugged.

"I guess we should be grateful he's starting to say things again. But, my lands, man, can you keep those words to yourself?" Gran shook her head.

Hailey gave Gramps a you're-in-trouble-now look, but he simply smiled.

After dinner, Hailey and Gramps cleared the table. He walked over to his recliner. "Do you need anything?" Hailey asked him.

He said something that sounded like beer.

Hailey shook her head. "Nope. No beer today, Gramps. Can I get you some water? More juice?"

Gramps said a string of words that didn't make sense.

"No alcohol right now."

Gramps again said some words. Though Hailey didn't understand each word, she knew the gist. "I know you aren't happy about this, but you need to give your body time to heal from the stroke. You want to get your speech back, right?"

He nodded.

"Water or juice?" she asked again.

Gramps rolled his eyes.

Hailey brought him a glass of ice water. "Drink plenty of this so you can be hydrated. Dehydration won't help you recover."

Gramps waved his hand. He didn't need words to communicate his disdain for Hailey's advice.

Hailey turned on the TV for him and surfed the channels until he motioned for her to stop on some war movie.

Hailey went to the back bedroom and found Gran.

"Come sit down." Gran motioned for Hailey to sit beside her on the bed.

"What are you doing?"

"Going through some old family photos. I thought I'd try to put them in albums since I'm home a lot right now."

Hailey picked up an aged black-and-white picture of a man and woman standing in front of an old car. "Who is this?"

"Who do you think it is?" Gran raised an eyebrow.

Hailey shrugged. The man and woman both looked so young. And so happy together.

Gran put her hand on her hip. "That's Harry and me."

Hailey pulled the photo closer to analyze it. "You were beautiful, Gran."

"You sound shocked." She blinked.

"No, I . . . I . . ."

"I wasn't always an old grandma, you know. I used to be young and vivacious." She ran her fingers through her short, silver hair. "I still feel that way. When I look in the mirror I don't recognize that old woman looking back at me." Gran gazed out the window at nothing in particular. "I don't know where the time has gone."

Hailey put her hand across Gran's wrinkled and veined hand.

"Now we're old. And," Gran stopped. Tears slipped down her cheeks. "I don't know what I'd do without that old coot. He scared me to death having that stroke."

Hailey reached her arms around her grandmother.

"When did we get this old? I'm not ready for my life to be over." In a thick voice, she continued, "There's still life left to be lived."

"Gramps is going to be fine," Hailey said, trying to reassure her grandmother. And herself.

"What if he's not? What if he never speaks again? Or worse, what if he has another stroke? What would I do without him?" Her voice quivered with emotion.

"Let's not worry about that." Hailey rubbed Gran's shoulder. "He's making progress in his speech, and there's no reason to suspect he'll have another stroke. I'll be here for however long you need."

Gran leaned her head against Hailey's. "I appreciate your help, but you have your own life. You can't stay here forever."

"Maybe I'll do just that." Hailey smiled. The idea of moving to Florida kind of intrigued her.

"Don't be silly." She patted Hailey's knee. "You have a career back in Colorado. And a life."

"Maybe a career." Hailey let out a long breath. "But certainly not much of a life."

"You'll find another boyfriend."

"Please don't suggest I date Roger." Hailey crinkled her nose.

Gran laughed. "He was kind of a goof, wasn't he?"

"Yes." Goof was a perfect description.

"But my other friend—"

"Stop right there." Hailey held up her hand. "What is with you? You don't have some secret matchmaking service I should know about, do you?" Hailey asked flippantly.

Gran clutched at her chest. "Why, of course not. Don't be ridiculous. A matchmaking service?" Gran chuckled. "What a silly notion."

"Gran?" Hailey stared at her, suddenly wondering why Gran was so defensive.

"Hailey, dear. Her grandson is handsome and—"

"Gran, I only want to hang out with you and Gramps." She peered at her grandmother with serious eyes. "Really."

"I just hate to see you sit night after night with a couple of old fogies."

Hailey had to smile. *Fogies?* "Is it okay if I love being here with you?" Hailey felt safe and secure with her grandparents. It reminded her of being a kid, when life was less complicated.

Gran squeezed her. "Sure it is."

Hailey picked up a batch of photos. "Let's see if we can organize these."

Chapter 8

Friday evening, after a couple of stressful therapy sessions, Peter pulled into his mom's driveway. Technically, it used to be his driveway since his mom still lived in his childhood home. The drive to Orlando was about an hour—enough time to clear his head after a long week at work.

"Hey, mom," he said as he opened the front door to the beige stucco home.

"In the kitchen," rang out his mom's cheerful voice.

He followed the garlic and onion scent that beckoned him. "Smells delicious, as usual."

"I know lasagna is your favorite," she said, her gray hair a little mussed.

"And garlic bread." He leaned down and gave her a kiss on the cheek. "You spoil me."

"I don't get to cook much anymore. Not since . . ."

"I know, Mom, I miss him too." He wrapped his arms around her. It had been a little over a year since his dad collapsed with a massive heart attack while he was in the backyard.

"I'm so glad you come to see me. Otherwise I'd be very lonely."

Peter pulled a stool up to the familiar but dated Formica breakfast bar. "I've been meaning to talk to you—"

She held up her hand. "If this is about moving again, you know I can't."

"But if you moved closer to Daytona Beach I'd be able to see you more often and make sure everything is okay. Plus, Laura and Benji are there now."

She turned and leaned against the counter. "You know I can't leave here. This is where my life has been for the last forty-nine years."

Peter let out a breath. He didn't want to ask his mom to leave the home she loved, but she wasn't getting any younger and he worried about her falling or having a health issue and being there alone. "I know, but I'd love to have you closer. You know, to help me cook."

She gave him an I-can-see-right-through-you look with her pale blue eyes. "You think I'm getting too old and decrepit."

"That's not it." He didn't think she was ready for a rest home or anything like that, but he wanted to keep a better eye on her.

She reached out and squeezed his shoulder. "You are a good son. I waited a long time for you, and you were definitely worth the wait." She smiled.

Realizing this was a losing battle, he asked, "How can I help with dinner?"

"I think it's all ready." She placed the dish loaded with lasagna on the table. "Let's thank the good Lord for this food and then dig in."

After a generous second helping, Peter leaned back and said, "I need to work this off. How about a walk?"

The late spring sun hung low in the sky and the warm, thick air surrounded them as they strolled leisurely along the street.

"The neighborhood hasn't changed much," he said. "At least the houses still look the same as when I was a kid."

"I think I'm the last original owner. Mr. Shaw died last month."

"I remember you telling me. He was ancient when I lived here. He must've been at least a hundred and twenty." He laughed.

"So tell me about your job. Any new patients lately?" She looped her arm through Peter's.

His mind went directly to Hailey. "Uh, not really. No. Not anyone to tell you about." He shrugged a shoulder, then cleared his throat.

"Hmm." His mom looked at him with a dubious eye. "Obviously."

"Mom, I work with elderly people. Are you implying I met an older woman or something?" He feigned shock.

"Or something." There was a hint of suspicion in his mom's voice.

Peter scratched at the back of his neck.

"Want to tell me about her?"

"What makes you think . . . "

She touched his arm. "I'm still a great listener."

"It's really nothing." He ran his fingers through his hair. "A new gentleman, Harry, came in. He had a stroke. "

"And?"

"His granddaughter brought him in." Hailey's captivating smile flashed through his memory.

"I see." She nodded.

"And I don't know. I haven't been able to stop thinking about her since I met her." Peter had always been able to talk to his mother about life, girls, and relationships.

"Why don't you ask her out?"

"That would be completely inappropriate." He gazed ahead of them. "Besides, for all I know she's married with six kids." *I sure hope that isn't true.*

His mom laughed. "Sounds like you need to find out."

"I can't. It wouldn't be professional." He didn't want to appear unprofessional in any way, shape, or form.

"You never know what might happen," she said in an upbeat manner.

"And . . ."

His mom leaned her head against his shoulder. "Don't you think enough time has passed?"

Peter drew in a breath. "Some days, yes. Other days, no."

"You're a good man and you need a good woman."

"Maybe . . . someday."

They walked arm in arm for a few minutes as the sun descended lower and the cirrus clouds took on pink and orange hues while children laughed in the distance.

"How about some dessert?" his mom finally said.

"I might have a little room left." He patted his stomach.

"You always have room for dessert." She tugged at the collar of her white blouse.

Peter laughed. "You know me too well."

As they made their way back to the house, Peter reflected on his mom's words. *You're a good man and you need a good woman.* Maybe she was right.

Chapter 9

A couple of days later, Hailey spent the morning working. She spoke with a client, Renee Thompson, who owned two hair salons, trying to get information about several business expenses. Once she had the information, Hailey entered it into her spreadsheet. She had a conference call with the owners from Crandall Automotive, then answered some emails from Mrs. Saunders. Finally, she wrapped up her work and went into the living room where she found Gramps in his recliner.

"It's time to practice your sounds and words. Today we're going to work on the B sound," she said with enthusiasm.

Gramps waved her off.

"I know, Gramps." Hailey patted his hand. "This seems silly, but the therapist said we needed to practice." She batted her eyelashes at him. "Please?"

He gave her a defeated look.

"The more we practice, the sooner you can tell your super-awesome and always-so-funny jokes. Right?"

He made a face at her.

"Come on. Let's practice and then I'll take you to the barber to get your hair cut." She pointed at him. "You could be a hippie with all that long gray hair. I can practically braid it."

Gramps rolled his eyes.

Hailey encouraged Gramps to put his lips together and then push the air out with a voiced B sound. She modeled how to say bye, bee, and boo. Gramps worked hard to make the right sounds and it wrenched Hailey's heart to see her once strong and verbally expressive grandfather reduced to making simple sounds like a small child. She had to do her best to help him recover all of his speech. There was no other option.

"You're doing a great job." She gave Gramps a high five.

After thirty minutes of practice, Hailey drove Gramps to a barber that was around the corner from the retirement community.

They walked into the barbershop and Hailey gave instructions to the balding man wearing a black polo shirt. "He doesn't like it too short," she said.

The man simply smiled, then showed Gramps to a chair.

She sat on a bench along the white-painted wall and started thumbing through a magazine. Hailey stopped on a photo of a celebrity. "Wow, she should sue her plastic surgeon." Hailey continued to peruse the magazine, getting lost in a story about Harrison Ford, who was still attractive even though he was pretty much prehistoric.

"He's my favorite *Star Wars* character," a male voice said.

Startled, Hailey looked up to see Gramps's therapist standing near her. "Oh, hi, Mr. Stafford." She shut the magazine and then dropped it on the floor.

"Mr. Stafford makes me sound so stuffy. And *old*. Remember, my name is Peter." He bent down, scooped up the magazine, and then handed it to her.

"All right. Peter it is." She took the magazine from him. "Thanks."

"I see you found my barber."

Did he think she was following him or something? "*Your* barber?"

Peter laughed.

"Gramps needed a haircut. He directed me over here," she said, trying to explain why she was there, so he wouldn't think it had anything to do with him.

"I'm not surprised." He put his hands in his pockets. "George is the best."

"You're on a first name basis with the barber?"

"Oh, yeah." Peter shrugged. "He's been cutting my hair since I moved here."

Peter didn't look like he needed a haircut. His thick blond hair barely touched his ears and fell perfectly across his forehead. "I don't think he'll understand Gramps."

"He doesn't need to." Peter sat next to Hailey and her muscles began to twitch. *Why does this man make me into a puddle of nerves?* "George is a master at knowing exactly how to cut hair," he said.

Hailey crossed her legs. "Do you live around here?"

"A couple of miles up the street."

She searched for something to say—something that didn't sound stupid. "My grandparents live in the Starlight Retirement Community."

"I'm familiar with it." He nodded. "I have several patients who live there."

"Lots of people with strokes?" Hailey had never thought much about strokes until Gramps had his.

"Yeah. I love working with older people," he said with sincerity.

"Really?" She'd always had a strong relationship with her grandparents, but most of her friends didn't have much to do with old people.

"Getting to see them in their older years, when they've accumulated so much wisdom, is enlightening." Peter laced his fingers and placed them in his lap. "As a society, we tend to discard people when they're senior citizens, but they're the ones who've lived lives and have all the experience." He smiled and a dimple on one side of his mouth appeared, right next to his full lips. *Stop looking at his lips. His attached lips that belong to another woman.* "Plus, they're usually pretty uninhibited, which makes it entertaining to work with them."

"Sounds like you love your job." *Good recovery.*

"I do." He looked at her with his magnetic blue eyes. "So you're from Colorado?"

"You remember." A tingle slid down her back.

He tapped his forehead. "Photographic memory."

Is he serious? "I'll keep that in mind."

"Did your husband stay back there?"

A strangled laugh fell out of Hailey's mouth. "I'm not married." *Not even close.*

He gave her a look, but she wasn't sure what it meant. "Did you leave a job?"

"I'm an accountant. I work for a big firm in Colorado Springs. Since we're past tax season, and I've earned quite a bit of vacation time, my boss let me take a leave of absence to help my grandparents. I'm still taking care of some clients long distance." She sounded calm and professional, so Hailey mentally patted herself on the back. Maybe she could carry on a conversation with this man without thinking about his mesmerizing eyes or his full lips or what it would be like to see him socially—if he were single. Which he wasn't. The image of the woman and the young boy flashed through her mind.

"Then you'll have a job to go back to?" he asked, jolting her out of her thoughts.

"Oh, yeah. It's a great job." She was grateful she'd have one when she returned to Colorado Springs.

Peter crossed his ankles and leaned back. "How long will you stay?"

"I'm not sure. However long it takes to help Gran and Gramps." And, hopefully, heal her heart. Because it was still broken. By . . . that one guy she used to date.

"I bet it's a huge relief for them to have you here."

"I hope so. I love being able to spend time with them. It's been a while. I used to see them all the time when I was a kid. They lived in Denver, not too far from us."

"Oh yeah?"

"Gramps was a policeman and Gran worked at an elementary school as the librarian for years. When they retired, they wanted to get away from the snow and cold so they came here to Florida."

"I'm a Florida native myself. Grew up in Orlando. My mom still lives there."

Hailey felt a hand on her shoulder and jumped. "Oh, Gramps. Are you done already? That was a quick haircut."

She'd been so focused on Peter that she hadn't even noticed that Gramps was done. Gramps smiled at her, then looked at Peter. Hailey was glad for a moment that Gramps couldn't say what she knew he wanted to.

Hailey stood. "Nice talking to you."

"See you at our next appointment. I think it's an in-home visit," Peter said. *Why does his smile sparkle like that?* She chastised herself for being attracted to this man, especially because he was off limits.

Hailey ushered Gramps out of the barber shop while he said garbled words. "I may not know exactly what words you're using, but I know what you're trying to say. Peter is a nice man. A nice *married* man. We were simply having a conversation while I waited for you to get your haircut. Nothing else. He's married and has a child."

Gramps wore a disappointed expression.

"Besides, even if he were single, I'm only here temporarily, and I haven't recovered from my jerk ex-boyfriend yet."

He squeezed her hand.

"Not all guys are wonderful like you." She reached over and kissed him on the cheek.

George motioned Peter over to the barber's chair and draped a black cape across him.

While Peter sat, getting an unneeded trim, he hoped Hailey didn't suspect he'd only shown up there because he'd seen her in the parking lot as he was driving through it. The moment he'd spotted her, it was like his mind lost control of his body. Before he knew it, he'd parked and walked into the barbershop with no idea what he'd say to her.

"Pretty girl," George said, looking over the top of his glasses.

"Huh?"

"The woman with her grandfather," George cut some hair on top of Peter's head.

"What do you mean?"

George gave Peter a do-you-think-I-was-born-yesterday look in the mirror. "We both know you don't need a haircut."

"Of course I do. It was getting too long around my ears."

"Whatever you say," George said. "The customer is always right, after all."

"Aw, come on. Was I that obvious?"

"Only to those of us with eyes." George laughed.

"You're hilarious, my friend." Peter shook his head.

George took off the black cape from around Peter's neck. "All done."

Peter pulled out his wallet, but George held up his hand. "No charge."

"But you trimmed my hair," Peter reasoned.

"It's on the house."

Peter blinked. "But—"

"Save your money. You may need it." George started laughing, obviously amused at his implication.

"Thanks, George. I'll be back again . . . I think."

Peter left the barbershop hoping Hailey wasn't as suspicious as George. It really had only been accidental that he'd seen her. It wasn't quite as accidental that he'd gone into the barbershop. Actually, not accidental at all.

He suspected that she was attracted to him as well. It wasn't just that she'd inadvertently said, "*sounds attractive,*" though that was entertaining, especially when her face turned bright crimson, but it was how she responded to him and the way she looked at him. For the first time in a long time, he was genuinely interested in a woman. Unfortunately, the situation dictated that he couldn't do anything about it.

Chapter 10

The next day, Hailey took her grandparents over to the social hall, as Gran called it, for the Tuesday afternoon gathering. It was a large building where the residents of the area met for dances, meetings, and activities. Today was a get-to-know-you day to help new residents feel welcome. Gramps wasn't thrilled about going, but Gran insisted he get out and say hello to folks.

Gran said the two of them would be fine there without Hailey and sent her back to the house. Hailey wanted to argue, but she was looking forward to taking a nice shower, then getting caught up on some work.

As she stepped out of her bedroom still sporting a towel on her head, someone rapped on the door.

She rushed to it, hoping it wasn't an emergency involving her grandparents. On the porch stood her aunt, Regina, her dyed black hair in a scraggly ponytail and her mid-section hanging over the top of her too-tight jeans. Other than her ex, Kevin, Regina was the last person Hailey wanted to see—there was far too much history there.

Regina stared at her. "Are you gonna let me in or what?"

Her aunt deserved the *or what*.

Regina pushed the door open and brushed past Hailey.

"Aunt Regina, I didn't know you were coming," Hailey said as calmly as possible.

"Didn't think I needed your permission to visit my own parents." Regina surveyed the room.

"They'll be surprised, that's all." That was a nice way of putting it.

Regina arched one of her too-thin eyebrows. "Are you tryin' to say that I don't come see them?"

"No. They hadn't said anything so I'm sure—"

Regina waved her hand at Hailey. "Never mind. Where are they?"

Trying to keep her anger under control, Hailey said, "They're at the community center."

Regina nodded, her long, silver earrings swaying.

Hailey reminded herself that even though Regina deserved a big kick in the rear, she was still her aunt, and her parents had taught her to be respectful. "Do you want to sit down?"

"Don't mind if I do." Regina sat with an ample thud on the couch.

Not really wanting to know the answer, but being polite, Hailey asked, "What have you been up to?"

"Travelin' the country with Jake."

"Jake?" Regina had such a long list of boyfriends it was hard to keep track.

"Don't matter. He's yesterday's news." Regina stood and walked to the kitchen where she rummaged through the refrigerator. "Anything in here to eat? I'm starving."

"I think there are leftovers from dinner last night. You can have all the meatloaf you want." Hailey smiled inwardly.

Regina pulled out a container, lifted its lid, and took a whiff. She jerked her head back. "You make this?"

"Yeah. It's a—"

"Don't give up your day job to be a cook." Regina laughed at her stupid joke.

"How long are you planning to visit?" *Please say it'll only be a day or two. Please. Please. Please.*

Regina let out a snort. "I'm not plannin' to visit. I'm movin' in."

"Oh." *Moving in? I can't even.* Hailey wanted to burst into angry tears.

"You're looking at me with some kind of shock on your face." Regina narrowed her eyes, then walked past Hailey back into the living room.

"You have heard that Gramps had a stroke, right?"

Regina whirled around and stared at her. "No. Hadn't heard that. I don't seem to be in the family news group." She laughed.

"Would you like to know if he's okay?" Regina's lack of sensitivity was appalling.

"You know," she set her hand on her plump hip, "I don't think I like your tone."

Hailey drew in a long breath. "Excuse me?"

"These are my parents. Don't act like I don't care about them."

"I wasn't," she lied. Regina only cared about Regina. Period.

"Why are you here anyway?" Regina plopped back onto the couch.

"To help Gramps." *Obviously.*

"I see." Regina kicked off her boots and sat back, shoveling food into her mouth. "It don't matter now," she said with her mouth full. "I can take care of them. You can go on home."

A noise sounded at the door. Hailey looked to see her grandma opening the door. She rushed over. "Gran, I thought you weren't going to be done for another thirty minutes."

"Harry got too tired, so Dee brought us back." She lowered her voice. "Is she here?"

Hailey nodded.

"Momma, Daddy," Regina said, standing "I'm so happy to see you." She wore a sickly smile.

Gramps looked at her and smiled.

"Regina, what are you doing here?" Gran's voice was monotone.

"Momma, is that any way to talk to me? I haven't been home in—"

"Two years," Gran said in a sharp tone. "No word from you in over six months."

"I know. I know." Regina engulfed Gran in a hug. "And I'm sorry. But I'm here now. When I heard about Daddy's stroke I knew I had to come."

Hailey rolled her eyes. Regina was something all right.

"How'd you hear about that?" Gran asked. One thing Hailey loved about her grandmother was how she never let anyone get away with anything.

"Cousin Barb told me."

Gran nodded, but Hailey could tell she didn't buy it.

Gramps made some sounds, then reached his arms out for a hug. Regina snuggled up close to him.

"Always was a daddy's girl," Gran said quietly.

"I'm going to stay and help for as long as you need me." Regina grinned. Hailey wanted to smack that fake smile right off her aunt's face.

"Hailey is already—" Gran started.

"Now that I'm home, she can go back." Regina helped Gramps over to his recliner.

"I can make up the other bedroom," Gran said with resignation.

Hailey wanted to scream. Regina was so pushy and bossy. And she didn't care about anyone but herself. In all of Hailey's growing up years, Regina had visited a couple of times and it always ended badly. And usually with some cash missing. She couldn't be more opposite from Hailey's dad, who had worked hard in his career, put down roots, and raised a family. Regina liked to call herself a free spirit, but more accurately, she was lazy and irresponsible. And if she thought she was going to run Hailey off, she had another thing coming.

Chapter 11

Peter knocked on the door and it whipped open. Benji stood there with a wide grin. "Uncle Peter." He took a stance in his red T-shirt with SpongeBob standing next to Patrick. "Want to see what I learned in karate this week?"

"I'd love to." Peter stepped inside, an oven-roasted chicken scent floating in the air, making his stomach growl.

Benji kicked his leg out, then pulled his arms in. "Mom and her friend are in the kitchen."

"Friend?" Laura hadn't mentioned anyone else would be joining them for dinner. Peter adjusted his gray dress shirt.

Benji nodded. "Mom says she's beautiful and you'll like her."

"Oh, she did?" *Not again.*

"But I'm not supposed to say anything." He covered his mouth.

"I won't tell her," Peter said as he tried to decide if he should turn around and leave.

"Peter, is that you?" Laura's voice carried into the entryway.

"Yeah, Mom, he's here," Benji shouted.

The decision was made. Now he had to go meet Laura's friend. Reluctantly, he walked into the cozy kitchen. He made eye contact with his sister. Another woman, with short black hair and wearing a cream-colored pantsuit, turned around.

"Peter, this is my friend, Fiona." Laura beamed as if she'd solved world hunger.

"Hello," Fiona said, then extended her hand. "Nice to meet you."

Peter shook her hand, noticing her manicured nails, and said, "Hi." He wished Laura had told him she was having a friend over. He might have come anyway, but at least it would've been his choice. Now he felt pressured.

"Laura tells me you are a speech therapist," Fiona said.

He nodded and smiled, feeling almost as if he were back in middle school.

"I think that's fabulous. What an interesting career." Fiona looked at him with her dark brown eyes.

"I enjoy it." The room felt warm and small.

"Peter works mainly with senior citizens," Laura said, offering Peter a glass of water. For a moment, he thought about dumping the glass on her head for putting him in this precarious position.

"I bet that's fascinating." Fiona moved in closer.

Peter loosened his collar. "I have some great patients."

A phone chimed and Fiona reached into her pocket. "I'm sorry. I have to get this. It's a client." She stepped into the other room.

"She's a real estate agent. Isn't she beautiful?" Laura said with way too much enthusiasm.

"Why do you do this?" he said gruffly.

She gently tapped him on the shoulder. "You need to date, Peter."

"Says who? Is there some unwritten rule that every single man has to date?"

"You've been divorced for how many years now?" She held up a hand and started counting her fingers.

"Your point?" Sometimes his sister was exasperating.

"You need a companion."

"So do you." He regretted it as soon as he said it. "I'm sorry. I didn't mean to—"

"No need to apologize." She shrugged and shook her head. "I know I sprung this on you. I just thought you'd like to meet someone." Laura began tossing the salad.

"Maybe. But I'd rather do it on my own. Remember the last time you tried to set me up? It was a disaster. I'm lucky I survived."

"How was I supposed to know her jealous ex-boyfriend would show up and threaten you with a knife?" Laura whispered.

Fiona walked back into the room. "I am so, so sorry, but I'll need to take a raincheck. I have a buyer for this property that needs to meet me right now."

"Don't worry about it," Laura said.

Fiona turned to Peter. "I do hope we'll get another chance to get acquainted. Laura has told me so much about you. I'd love to get to know you better."

Peter smiled.

With that, Fiona left.

Laura started laughing uncontrollably.

"What is so funny?" Was his sister having a breakdown?

When Laura pulled herself together, she said, "I'm the worst matchmaker ever."

"I agree." He laughed.

Laura dished up some chicken and salad, then handed Peter his plate. "Oh, before I forget, can you pick up Benji from his afterschool program on Thursday? I have a meeting."

"Sure. We can go get some dinner." Peter grabbed a crescent roll.

"Yes!" Benji said, pulling his arms through the air and down to his side in a satisfied gesture.

"Where would you like to go?" Peter asked.

"We have our spirit night at Smitty's Barbecue," Laura said. She poured her son a glass of milk. "Smitty's pays a percentage to Benji's school for everyone that eats there."

"And the class with the most kids that go gets T-shirts." Benji shoved in a big bite of chicken followed by a roll, giving himself chipmunk cheeks.

"Benji, don't stuff your mouth, please. Remember your manners." Laura turned to Peter. "I can meet you there."

"It's a date," he said.

Chapter 12

The next day, after running a few errands and taking a little more time than she needed so she could avoid her aunt Regina, Hailey returned and found Gramps snoozing in his chair. He looked so peaceful. For a moment, Hailey worried that maybe he was too peaceful, so she sidled up close to him to make sure he was breathing. He was, and she gave a sigh of gratitude.

It was painful to see him like this. He'd been such a strong man all her life. He was a decorated police sergeant who'd spent his life protecting others. It was wrong, somehow, that now he needed her because it had always been the other way around. Next to her dad, Gramps was her hero.

Watching someone she loved become weak and needy sent a deep ache into her bones. What if Gramps didn't fully recover? What if he never told his corny jokes again or his fantastic tales of meeting aliens late at night? What if he simply withered away? What if . . . She didn't want to think anymore.

Gran and Regina came out from the back bedroom.

"Hi, Hailey," Gran said. "We've been getting that room ready."

"Oh," Hailey said. Gran seemed to be happy. Even though Regina wasn't one of Hailey's favorite people, maybe having her back would heal some old wounds with Gran. At least that's what Hailey was telling herself.

"I think Hailey can go back home now." Regina gave Hailey a smirk.

Gran looked at Hailey. "It's up to you. If you need to get back—"

"I don't." Hailey said with emphasis. Regina was trying to strong arm her away from her grandparents and she didn't like it. Hailey wasn't sure what purpose her aunt had in being here right now, but she didn't want to leave her grandparents at Regina's mercy.

"There's room for all of us here." Gran smiled.

"Sure, I guess," Regina said. "I'm hungry. What's for dinner?"

"Pasta salad." Gran said.

Hailey glanced at the large gold clock on the wall. "Gramps has his therapy appointment in thirty minutes."

"You go ahead and take him," Regina said, sitting on the couch. "I've got an appointment with the TV and *Judge Judy*."

"Actually, it's a home visit. The therapist will be here." Nerves rippled across Hailey's stomach at the thought of Peter coming to the house. She assured herself it wasn't because she was attracted to him. Because that would be wrong. Very wrong. She was nervous because . . . well, it wasn't because she liked him in any kind of romantic way.

"Oh. Uh, I forgot I had an appointment." Regina jumped up. "I gotta go."

Hailey nodded. *Of course.* Regina wouldn't want to be involved in therapy so she could help her own father regain his speech. That'd be too hard. Hailey didn't want to be cynical, but she didn't like this whole situation with her aunt barging in on her time with her grandparents. Regina was upsetting everything.

A knock sounded at the door and Hailey tried to ignore her quickened heart rate. She smoothed her hair and took in a deep breath.

Opening the door, she said, "Hi. Come in."

"Thank you." Peter smiled, but Hailey had rules about flirting with married men and she'd almost crossed the line before at the barber shop. It would be business-only today.

Peter walked over to Gramps. "Hello, Harry. How are you today?"

Gramps gave a nod.

"You have a nice home. This must be your favorite chair." Peter rested his hand on the recliner. "I bet you've watched many a football game sitting in this chair."

"And basketball. Denver Nuggets all the way. Right, Gramps?" Hailey said, recalling the many times she and Gramps had watched games together.

Gran walked into the room wearing a bright multicolored apron.

Peter turned to her. "Hello." He reached out and shook her hand. "I'm Peter Stafford. Good to meet you."

"I'm June. Please excuse the way I look. I've been baking some bread." Gran had a dusting of flour on her chin.

"Nothing better than home-baked bread."

"You'll have to enjoy some with us," Gran said. Hailey hoped she was being polite and didn't really mean it.

"Thank you for allowing me to come to your home," he said. "It's very nice. I especially like your display of family photos."

Gran beamed as she pointed to various photos and explained who was pictured. "And this is one of Hailey when she was in seventh grade. She won the Spelling Bee for the all the schools in the area. It was sure a proud day."

Peter glanced at Hailey and fire licked her cheeks. Puberty had hit her hard that year and this photo was the epitome of how unattractive she'd looked with her greasy hair, thick eyebrows, blotchy skin, and mouth full of braces.

"That's a great achievement," he said.

"Thanks." What else could she say? Except that once he left, she was going to burn that photo once and for all.

"Thank you for coming," Gran said, interrupting Hailey's silent pity party.

"I find that doing a session in the home helps me to better understand my patients and their needs. And it allows the patient to feel more comfortable in his own surroundings."

Gran put her arm around Hailey. "We can get out of your way."

"I prefer if you stay so you can see what we work on. That way you'll know what to do afterwards."

"Certainly," Gran said.

Hailey watched Peter work with Gramps. They seemed to fall into a comfortable routine and she was impressed by the way Peter interacted so respectfully with Gramps.

Peter gave Gramps a few words and Gramps struggled to pronounce them. After a few minutes, Gramps pushed out a breath, then let out an expletive. Hailey could see the frustration and discouragement in his eyes. She couldn't imagine the difficulty of trying to communicate and being unable to. She wanted to throw her arms around her grandfather and reassure him that everything would be fine.

"Harry is making progress," Peter said with confidence. "He'll get there."

Gramps clucked his tongue in frustration.

Peter touched him on the shoulder. "I know it may seem like it won't happen, but I've worked with many in your same situation who are telling jokes again like they used to. And I suspect you tell some pretty good ones."

Gramps studied Peter.

"Am I right, Harry?" Peter said. "You strike me as a fun-loving, corny-joke-telling kind of a guy."

Gramps shrugged with a slight grin.

"Keep working with me and you'll be telling them again." Peter's confidence made Hailey feel confident too. He sure had a way with words. And with people. He seemed to have a gift.

They spent a few more minutes going over some common phrases, and Hailey wrote them in her notebook to use when she worked with Gramps.

After the session, Gramps gave Peter a nod that Hailey recognized meant he liked his therapist and trusted him.

"I'll see you at our next appointment, Harry," Peter said warmly.

"Thank you so much," Gran said.

"Yes, thank you," Hailey said, her interest in this man piqued even more. *Remember, he's not available.*

"My pleasure."

"He likes you," Hailey said as they walked toward the door.

Peter laughed. "I enjoy him. I'm looking forward to hearing his jokes." Peter opened the door and paused as if waiting for Hailey to walk out ahead of him.

Hailey stepped outside and asked, "How'd you know he liked to tell jokes?"

"I've got a sense about those things." He smiled and it grabbed at Hailey's stomach against her will.

"Oh." She couldn't think of anything else to say.

Peter cleared his throat. "Have you had a chance to go to the beach?"

"Not yet. I've been so busy helping with Gramps." Hailey hoped she'd make it to her favorite spot down by the Oceanwalk before she left.

"There are a lot of great things to do here. Like the Tiki Lounge. Or the Oceanwalk. Great shopping and restaurants. Bubba Gumps is one of my favorites." He almost seemed to be rambling on.

"Okay." She'd been to most of those places many times.

Peter paused for a moment as if he wanted to say something. Awkward silence fell between them. "I guess I better head back," he said finally.

"Thanks again for coming," she said, unsure of why things had turned weird.

Peter plunged his hands into his pockets. "See you at the next appointment."

"I'll be there." Hailey nodded. She wanted to say she was looking forward to seeing him, but that would be inappropriate. Wouldn't it?

Hailey watched him drive away. Their exchange left her wondering, even confused. It was almost as if he was going to ask her out or something. But that made no sense.

She was certainly not the kind of woman who flirted with attached men. Even an extremely attractive, kind, gentle man. Married or attached men were off limits. No questions asked.

Inside his car, Peter gave himself a face palm. He sounded like a prepubescent teen with a tangled tongue. He was this close to asking Hailey on a date. *This close.*

Being around her made him feel things he hadn't felt in years. His stomach quivered and his pulse sprinted when he was near her. What was wrong with him?

He didn't need to ask that question twice.

Peter knew exactly what was wrong.

He was attracted to her. There, he admitted it. And it was more than her beauty. The way she interacted with her grandparents and how she'd dropped her life to come and help them spoke volumes about her as a person. He enjoyed talking to her and simply being in the same room with her.

Admitting it or not, it was still ill-fated. She'd be returning to Colorado, and he was in a professional position of trust. He couldn't cross the line and ask her out. Could he?

Of course, a specific policy prohibiting him from dating a member of a patient's family didn't exist, but it felt off. Like he would be invading her privacy or something.

Besides, what if she wasn't interested in going out with him? That would make the upcoming appointments uneasy, and it would be nearly impossible for him to work with Harry. He didn't want to make anyone feel uncomfortable. His number one priority was to help Harry regain his speech. Peter had to keep everything professional and impersonal with Hailey.

Except that wasn't at all what he wanted to do.

Chapter 13

After thanking Peter for doing the home visit, Hailey walked back into the house.

"He sure is a nice young man," Gran said as she started setting the table for dinner.

"Who?" Hailey played dumb. She grabbed some silverware from the drawer.

"You know." Gran placed some glasses on the table. "And, my lands, he's handsome to boot."

Hailey gave her grandmother a look of confusion even though she knew exactly who Gran was talking about.

Gran peered at Hailey. "I think he likes you."

Hailey held her hand up. "Whoa. Hold on, Gran. Peter—Mr. Stafford—is Gramps's therapist. He was here to help Gramps. There is nothing going on between us."

Gran lifted an eyebrow.

"Seriously."

"Hailey, I—" The phone rang, interrupting their conversation. Gran answered it and said, "Hello? . . . Oh, hi, Lila." She pulled the phone away from her. "It's Lila," she said to Hailey.

Hailey nodded, grateful for the reprieve.

"Oh, I don't know about bingo tonight."

Hailey mouthed, "Go and have some fun, Gran."

Gran shrugged. "Maybe I'll see." Gran turned her back to Hailey and took a few steps into the hallway cupping her hand over her mouth and the phone.

Even though it was rude to eavesdrop, Hailey couldn't help herself. She strained to listen to Gran. "I made a . . . connection . . . yes, David's grandson . . . we're thinking Tuesday possibly . . . I can work on that for tonight. Leave it to me."

Regina came bounding in the front door wearing too-tight jeans and her scraggly hair hanging limp. "Do we have some food to eat? I'm starving." She kicked off her sandals.

Hailey bit her tongue. Her aunt was so self-absorbed. And rude. Hailey wanted to tell her to leave and never come back, but she couldn't. As much as she disliked Regina being in the house, Regina was still her aunt and she knew that Gran and Gramps loved her. Somehow, Hailey needed to learn to see the good in her aunt, even if it was hidden underneath twenty-five layers of obnoxiousness.

Gran walked back into the room and said, "I have to get off the phone, Lila. Regina is home and we're about to eat dinner." She hung up.

Regina dropped her abundant self onto a chair at the table.

"Glad you made it home in time to eat." Hailey tried to sound sincere, but it didn't come out that way.

Regina threw a sharp look at Hailey.

"What were you saying about a connection, Gran?" Hailey asked. "And what about tonight?"

"Oh, that was nothing." She motioned to Gramps. "Come on in to eat."

Gran was stonewalling, but Hailey didn't know why. She also knew it was useless to keep asking, so she joined her grandparents and Regina at the table.

At dinner, Hailey said, "What time do you want to go to bingo?"

"I don't know. Maybe I shouldn't." Gran used her fork to push the chicken and rice casserole around on her plate.

"I want you to go," Hailey insisted. "Maybe Regina would like to go with you."

"Me? Bingo? Uh-uh. Too boring. Besides, I wanna watch me some *Wheel of Fortune*. Then Daddy and I are gonna watch a movie."

Gramps blinked a few times, then shrugged as if that was the first time he'd heard about it.

Gran turned to Hailey with a hopeful look in her eyes. "Maybe you'd like to come with me?"

"Sure. Why not? I've never played bingo before. I need to check my email before we leave, but I don't think there will be anything urgent." Going with Gran would be better than spending the evening working and much better than hanging out with Regina.

After they cleaned up the dishes, Hailey sent off a couple of responses to some clients. She and Gran drove over to the community center, parked the car, and then went inside, where miniature palm trees in red pots adorned the doorway. The temperature dropped more than twenty degrees and windows lined the opposite wall of the large building. Rows of tables ran across the expanse of the room. People, most of them with gray or white hair, congregated around the tables, conversing with one another.

"Oh, look, there's Lila." Gran pointed to her friend at a table with several other women.

Hailey and Gran made their way over. Lila wore a stylish green-and-navy outfit. Hailey imagined she was breathtaking in her younger years. Lila acknowledged them with a genuine smile when they approached.

"Hi," Lila said.

"This is Hailey's first time. She's never played bingo before."

"Never?" The shock in Lila's voice was evident, as if everyone had played bingo and Hailey was some anomaly.

"Never," Hailey said. "I guess you'll have to explain it to me."

Hailey glanced around the room. When she looked back, Gran and Lila had their heads together and they were whispering. As soon as they noticed Hailey watching them, they stopped.

"What's going on?" Hailey asked. If she didn't know better, she'd think her grandmother was some kind of secret agent with her clandestine calls and covert meetings.

"Nothing." Gran exchanged looks with Lila. "We're not doing anything. Or talking about anything."

"I think you're up to something. You've been acting strange, Gran." Hailey was certain Gran and her friend were knee deep in some scheme together.

Gran blinked. "Me? I've been acting as normal as ever. Don't you agree, Lila?"

Lila nodded. "Normal as ever." She gave a cheesy smile that only made Hailey more suspicious. "June and I like to visit, that's all. We're BFFs. Isn't that what you call good friends these days?"

"Yes, but—" Hailey started.

"I must say, I don't know what you mean." Gran acted as if she'd been accused of a crime.

"Oh, here comes my grandson, Darren," Lila said with excitement.

Suddenly, it was quite clear. Gran and Lila were up to something, all right—matchmaking. Irritation settled on Hailey's shoulders. She could only imagine what Lila's grandson looked like. Probably like Roger. On steroids. Gran needed to stop with the setups.

As Hailey prepared herself for Mr. Homely, she turned and watched a man with wavy dark hair and a day's worth of stubble sit down. When his gaze settled on Hailey her breath hitched.

This can't be Darren. Can it? He wasn't at all what Hailey expected. For some reason, every Darren she'd ever known wasn't the least bit attractive. But that wasn't the case with this one. His brown eyes were the color of Dove dark chocolate, and from the size of his biceps, he obviously worked out regularly.

"Hi. Nice to meet you," he said in a husky voice.

"Yeah," was all Hailey could say. *Are you sure your name isn't Adonis?*

"Will you be playing bingo tonight, Darren?" Gran asked, obviously pleased with herself.

He nodded and slipped another glance at Hailey.

"Maybe you can teach my granddaughter. She's never played before." Gran was as transparent as a window, but Hailey had a hard time being angry about it.

"Is that so?" Darren said.

Maybe bingo would be a lot more fun than Hailey had anticipated, even if Gran had completely ignored her request for no setups. "She's right. Never played." She shrugged.

"Darren loves bingo," Lila said with a smile that engulfed her face.

"It's simple," he began. "The caller will say a letter and a number. If you have it, you cover it up with one of these." He handed her a small disk, his fingers leaving a hot spot where they brushed her hand. "Once you get five in a row—down, across, or diagonally—you win."

"And you yell out bingo so we all know you've won," Lila added enthusiastically.

"What do I win?" Hailey asked.

"Depends. Sometimes it's money and sometimes it's prizes," Gran said.

"Sounds easy enough." Hailey unconsciously began twirling her hair. She never expected to meet a gorgeous man at a senior citizens' bingo game, and she had to remind herself she wasn't interested in dating anyone, but Darren made that difficult, especially with a face like his. *Maybe I could make an exception. After all, a few fun, no-strings-attached dates never hurt anyone.*

Gran paid for Hailey's bingo cards and the caller began the game.

"I-nineteen," the man in the emerald-green polo shirt with a large belly said into the microphone. "I-nineteen."

Hailey searched her card, and sure enough, she had the number nineteen listed under the I. "I have it," she squealed.

Gran laughed. "Now get four more in a row and you win."

The caller yelled out another letter and number, but Hailey didn't have that one. The game continued for a few more minutes.

Darren had several of his spaces covered. Hailey looked at her card. She needed only one more to make five across.

"G-fifty-one."

"I got it," Hailey yelled out. "I have a bingo. At least I think I do." She started waving her hands. "Bingo, bingo, bingo."

Gran clapped. "Good job."

Darren flashed her an encouraging smile and she almost forgot what she was doing.

The caller said, "Please read off your card so we can verify."

Hailey looked at Gran, unsure of what the man meant. "Read off the ones you have in a row so he can be sure you won the game," Gran said.

Hailey proceeded to read the numbers.

"Ladies and gentlemen, we have a winner," the man said into the microphone.

"I won?" Hailey said with excitement and her fair share of disbelief. "I won. I really won."

A woman with poofy gray hair and a large, purple-beaded necklace handed her a ten-dollar bill. "Here is your prize."

"Thank you." Hailey held the money in her hand and stared at it. She'd never won anything before. Ten dollars wasn't much, but maybe it signified that her luck was about to improve.

"Congratulations," Darren said. "I think you're a ringer."

"A ringer?" What did he mean by that?

"A bingo professional."

Hailey laughed. "Is that even a thing?"

He shrugged and they both laughed.

A short woman with curly blonde hair approached the table and handed Gran a photo. "This is my Deirdre," she said in southern accent. "I already gave her bio to Lila."

Gran slipped a look at Hailey. "Uh, thank you, Shirley." She shoved the photo into her purse. "I'll get back to you."

"We already have someone in mind," Lila whispered, but Hailey overheard her.

"Oh, good. She'll be here in three days," Shirley said.

Gran cleared her throat. "It's time for another game, Shirley. It was nice to see you."

The woman walked away, leaving Hailey dumbfounded. *What in the world is going on?* Before she could say anything, another game started, but she vowed that she'd find out what all this intrigue was.

They continued to play for thirty more minutes, but Hailey didn't win any games. She was too preoccupied trying to figure out what Gran seemed to be involved in.

"This is the last game of the evening, folks, and we're playing for the grand prize. A gift card to Smitty's Barbecue," the caller said.

As the game went on, Hailey had a smattering of numbers. She glanced over at Gran's card, but she didn't have any in a row, either. When she looked at Darren's card, he had two possibilities of winning.

"O-seventy-five."

"Bingo," Darren said. He read off his numbers to verify that he'd won and the same lady came over and handed him the gift card.

"You and your girlfriend can go out to dinner," she said with a smirk.

Hailey didn't know what to say. Of course, she wouldn't say no to a dinner invitation from the handsome man who sat across from her, but she didn't want him to feel obligated.

After the woman walked away, Darren looked at Hailey. "That was awkward." He leaned in toward her. "But, not a bad idea."

Hailey gave him a half smile. She'd insisted that she wasn't interested in dating Lila's grandson because she figured he was another Roger. Fortunately, he wasn't at all like Dee's goofy grandson.

"Are you free tomorrow night?" he asked.

"Yes, she is. And she'd love to go out with you," Gran inserted.

Hailey made wide eyes at her grandmother, whom she still planned to interrogate later.

"He's a good-looking young man with a nice physique. You should go out and paint the town red. Have some fun," Gran said as she patted Hailey's shoulder.

Hailey's cheeks raged with heat. She wiggled her fingers, anxious to place them around Gran's neck. With a slight nod, she said, "I'd enjoy going to dinner with you."

"I'm looking forward to it," he said with expressive eyes.

Lila put her arm around Darren's waist. "See, I told you my Darren would be a good date."

"Thanks, Nana." He glanced at Hailey and an unspoken understanding passed between them.

"Lila, I'll take you home and we can let the kids ride together," Gran offered.

Kids? Did Gran just call me a kid? Hailey drew in a deep breath. Her grandmother was seriously asking for it tonight.

"I'd love to give you a ride home," Darren said. "Maybe we could go out for dessert on the way."

"Is dessert on our way home?"

"Oh, go on and have dessert with him," Gran prodded. "We won't wait up." And with that, Gran and Lila were off, arm in arm.

Hailey clenched her jaw. "I'm sorry. My grandma is relentless."

"No worries. Mine is the same. Always asking me when I'm getting married and telling me how I need to find a good wife and settle down and have a few kids."

"No wonder they're such good friends." Hailey laughed.

"I think they mean well."

"But Gran has no filter. None whatsoever. Anything that pops into her head has to come out of her mouth."

Darren grinned and a dimple appeared. "I guess that's one of the perks of getting older—you can say whatever you want."

Hailey laughed. "But please don't feel obligated."

"I don't. I never do anything out of obligation, believe me."

They walked outside into the dusky warmth. Even though the sun had almost set, the air wasn't any cooler. "The car is over here," Darren said.

As they drove over to a nearby restaurant the conversation was easy. Inside, they sat at a booth toward the back and ordered a Brownie Explosion to share.

"How long are you visiting?" Hailey asked.

"I'll be here another week or so. I transferred jobs and decided to take a few weeks off to visit Nana. How about you?"

"Gramps had a stroke so I came here from Colorado to help until he recovers." Hailey took a bite of the gooey goodness.

"How long do you think you'll be here?"

Hailey shrugged. "I'm not sure."

Darren seemed surprised at her answer. "What about your life back in Colorado?"

"It consisted of working, working, and more working." Sounded kind of pathetic, in a non-loser way, of course. Maybe it made her sound ambitious, which was a desirable trait, she reasoned.

"What do you do?" Darren spooned some ice cream into his mouth.

"I'm an accountant."

"You like it?"

"Numbers are easy for me." Hailey sipped some of her water. "What do you do?"

"I'm an engineer. I've been working in Dallas." He had a spot of chocolate right below his bottom lip.

"But you didn't like it there?" she said, wanting to hand him a napkin.

Darren sat back and licked his lips, finding the wayward chocolate. "A better job offer came up in Arizona. It starts the first of June."

"I'm sure Lila will enjoy having you here to visit." *I wouldn't mind spending more time with you too.*

As if reading her mind, Darren said, "Maybe we can see some

sights together while I'm here."

"Sure." What did she have to lose? He wasn't going to be here long, so she didn't have to worry about getting attached and risking another broken heart. She could have some safe, carefree fun with an attractive man. *Win-win*.

His eyes perked up. "Starting with dinner tomorrow night?"

Hailey smiled. "I'm looking forward to it."

They continued to chat until Hailey said, "I need to get back and check on Gramps."

Darren nodded. "Nana is probably wondering what happened to me. Despite what she says, she likes to wait up for me."

When they got back to the house, Hailey said, "Thanks for the dessert."

He grinned. "I'll come by tomorrow night about six o'clock."

"I'll be ready."

Hailey stood on the porch for a few minutes after he drove away. Who knew she'd meet a handsome, interesting man at bingo? Of course, she wasn't interested in anything long-term, but it'd be fun to spend some time with Darren. Maybe.

Hailey went inside the darkened house. Gran and Gramps were already in bed. She stopped next to their door and listened. She could hear two distinct sets of snoring sounds. Both of them were sound asleep. She walked past Regina's room. The door was slightly ajar, and Hailey couldn't resist, so she pushed it open a bit. Regina was all splayed out on the bed with one of her legs hanging over the edge. For a moment, Regina looked almost peaceful, until she started babbling something in her sleep and kicked her leg out. Hailey backed away from the doorway and went to her room.

In her bed, Hailey stared at the ceiling. A fan gently whirred, moving the warm air around her room. She was grateful she could be here with her grandparents and help them, even if she did have to endure her aunt's presence. And, Hailey noticed, she'd gone all day without even thinking about Kevin. Maybe her heart was finally healing.

Chapter 14

The next morning, Hailey was jolted awake by loud voices arguing in the living room. She hurriedly put on her robe and rushed down the hall.

A shirtless man wearing a leather vest and black leather pants stood face-to-face with Regina, who was wearing a large, neon pink nightshirt. His mousy-brown ponytail swung as he spoke. "I want you to come home with me. I've been lookin' all over for you," he said with a rough voice.

"I told ya, it's over. I ain't coming back." Regina looked over at Hailey. "You mind? This is private."

"I'm sorry, but I wasn't sure what was going on. You woke me up," Hailey said, hoping for an apology, but not expecting one.

Regina glared at her. "Never you mind what's going on here."

Hailey spotted her grandparents in the kitchen. "Don't you think you should take this outside so you don't upset—"

"This is none of your business." Regina jerked out her chin. "And I will talk to Phil wherever I please."

Regina was too much. She had no respect for anyone, not even her own aging parents. Hailey wanted to yell at her to stop being so selfish. Instead, Hailey clenched her jaw then said, "I don't think—"

"Yeah, you shouldn't," Regina said, cutting her off.

The man took a step closer to Regina. "Come on home, baby. I miss you."

Regina recoiled. "Don't touch me."

"I'm not leaving," he said with defiance.

"Oh, yes you are." Regina pointed at him.

He outstretched his arms. "I love you, baby."

"Love? Ha. That's a big joke," Regina shouted, then pushed him.

This was getting worse by the second. Hailey wanted them both to leave, but she knew she had no power to make them. She walked over to her grandparents, who were seated at the table. Maybe she could distract them, even shield them, from the drama going on a few feet away in the living room.

"Can I get you some breakfast?" Hailey asked with a painted-on smile.

Gran said nothing. Gramps was breathing hard as if he were summoning up enough strength to deal with Regina and her ex-whatever.

"I can make some eggs. Or waffles. I love waffles. I can add some chocolate chips." Hailey tried to sound upbeat despite the dark, angry energy that hung in the air.

Gran shook her head and cast her glance toward the ground. She seemed so defeated. Sad. Gramps, on the other hand, had fire in his eyes. If Hailey had to guess, he wanted to literally kick the guy out of the house. How long would they have to cower in the kitchen while Regina had it out with the lovesick loser?

"Look, Phil, it's been over for a while."

"I'm willing to do whatever you want, Genie."

He sounded pathetic as he kowtowed to Regina.

"Nah. I'm done. I told you if you didn't give up gambling and spending all the money, I was outta there."

Hailey wanted to protect Gran and Gramps from all this ugliness, but she had no idea how. She felt helpless. She sat next to Gran and placed her hand on Gran's.

"I'm not gambling anymore, baby."

"Liar. All men are liars," Regina spat out. "Get outta this house and don't never come back."

Phil let out a grunt, then stomped out of the house, cursing as he left.

"Good riddance," Regina bellowed after him. She marched down the hallway back to her room and slammed her door, making Hailey jump.

For several minutes, Gran, Gramps, and Hailey sat around the table and said nothing. Finally, Gran said, "Where did I go wrong with Regina? How did I fail her?"

Hailey put her arm around her fragile grandmother.

"Regina was my sweet little angel girl with ringlets. She used to follow me around the house and tell me how much she loved me. She'd help me with the housework and tell me how much she wanted to grow up and be a mommy and have her own babies. What happened to that little girl?" Gran cradled her face in her hands.

Gramps let out an audible sigh.

Gran sat back with a crestfallen expression. "We gave her everything. And she went off to college and was never the same. She got involved with drugs and has gone from one man to the next since then. We tried to reason with her, but she refused to listen. One of these days I'll get that dreaded phone call that she's dead in an alley somewhere." Gran began to cry.

Hailey hugged Gran tightly, wishing she could say or do something to take the pain away. Regina was so self-centered. She refused to see what her choices were doing to her parents. "I wish I could do something."

Gran wiped at her eyes. "I don't think there's anything anyone can do. If your dad was still alive, maybe things would be different. He and Regina were close." Gran flicked a tear from her cheek. "I miss him."

"I do too." Even though time had dulled the pain, Hailey still ached for her father. Not a day went by that she didn't miss him or wonder what it would be like if he were still alive.

Gran stood. "I need to go splash some water on my face."

After Gran left, Gramps blurted out, "I'm mad."

Hailey looked at him with mixed emotions. She felt bad that he was mad, but elated that he'd spoken a short sentence. "Gramps!"

"I'm mad," he said again as he shook his fist.

"Can you tell me why you're mad?" She wanted to prod him to say more.

Gramps uttered some more nonsensical sounds. His eyes pleaded with Hailey to understand, but she didn't. Her heart hurt. She wanted Gramps to speak more than anything.

"You're mad at Regina?" she guessed.

Gramps nodded.

"Because she was yelling at that guy?" That seemed the obvious answer.

Gramps shook his head.

Hailey searched her mind for another reason. "Because she's made a mess of things?"

Gramps drew his brows together and shook his head again. He pointed at Hailey.

"You're mad at me?" *I should've handled the situation differently. Now I've upset Gramps.*

Gramps rested his face in his hand, then pointed at Hailey again. "I'm mad," he said again. "She was . . . m-m-mean."

Hailey studied Gramps. "Because Regina was rude to *me*?"

Gramps's eyes lit up and he nodded, his body language communicating relief that Hailey understood him.

So that she clearly understood him, she said, "You're mad at Regina for how she treated me?"

"Yes."

"Oh, Gramps." She slung her arms around his neck. "It's okay."

"No."

Hailey peered at Gramps, tears brimming. "I can handle Regina. Don't you worry about it." She grabbed his hand. "In fact, I'm happy this happened."

Gramps gave her a puzzled look.

"It got you talking and we had a real conversation. That is huge progress." She could barely contain her exuberance.

Gran came back into the kitchen. "What's going on?" She glanced between Hailey and Gramps.

"We had a conversation," Hailey sang out, her feet dancing under the table.

"Who?" Gran wrinkled her forehead.

Hailey leaned her head toward Gramps. "The two of us."

"You did?" Gran clasped her hands together.

"He's going to be talking up a storm in no time." Hailey hadn't felt this hopeful since the stroke.

"From your lips, Hailey, from your lips," Gran said, hugging herself.

❦

Late that afternoon, Hailey picked through her clothes trying to decide what to wear on her dinner date. Regina had lumbered out of the house earlier without a word and had ridden away on her motorcycle. Her aunt was a master at the disappearing act.

"May I come in?" Gran asked as she knocked.

"Sure. I can't figure out what to wear and Darren will be here in an hour." She grabbed a pink print shirt and held it up to her chest before tossing it on the bed.

"You always look so pretty in that white skirt and lavender blouse."

"I think that's too dressy." Hailey rummaged through another few shirts. "I don't want to give him the wrong impression."

"That you like him?" Gran crinkled her nose.

"Yeah, I don't want him to think I do."

Gran shook her head. "My lands, girl, isn't that why you date? Because you like the young man who asked, or at least are interested in him?"

"Yes, but . . . it's complicated these days."

"I guess so." Gran sat on the bed. "I remember my first date with your grandpa."

"Oh yeah? Tell me about it." Hailey sat next to Gran, eager to listen to the story.

"It was 1955, and I was only eighteen."

"That's young." It was hard to imagine Gran as a teenage girl. She'd always been so Gran-ish.

A smile spread across Gran's face. "I met him at a community dance. He'd come with his cousin, Clyde. He was older, already out of high school, and I was about to graduate." Gran paused. "He had this thick, dark hair that was slicked back. He asked me to dance and the moment his hand touched mine, it made my heart go pitter-pat."

Hailey watched Gran as she recalled the memory and seemed to be lost in a time far gone.

"I'd been dating this handsome boy, Bill, during our senior year. He was on the football team, and he lived a few streets over from me. Everyone, and I mean everyone, thought we'd get married. He was supposed to be at the dance that night, but had to work at the last minute. My friend, Betty, insisted I go with her, so I did." Gran let out a long breath. "The moment I laid eyes on Harry, I was smitten. He asked me to dance and I accepted. Oh, my, Harry was such a smooth dancer." Gran rested her hand across her chest. "We danced to several songs and then went outside and talked. It was such a clear night. The stars were so bright, and the moon was almost full. As Harry talked, I felt like I was falling under a spell. He asked me for a date, and I said yes." Her mouth curled up.

Hailey blinked. "What about Bill?"

"I didn't care." She shrugged a shoulder. "I only wanted to spend time with Harry."

Hailey studied her grandmother, whose face almost seemed to have transformed into that young girl in love. "Where did you go on your date?" Hailey asked, mesmerized by her grandmother's recollection.

"He took me to dinner and we were supposed to go to a show, but we ended up talking instead." She laughed. "Even back then he told the silliest jokes. And puns. Oh, that man and his puns."

Hailey rested her head on Gran's shoulder.

"From that night on we were inseparable. My folks thought I was too young, but all I wanted to do was marry him. So I did." Her voice cracked. "And here we are all these years later, and I love him even more." She looked at Hailey. "Maybe it will be the same for you."

Hailey waved her hand because she definitely wasn't looking for love. "I don't know about that, but I think it will be fun to go out tonight."

"And maybe it will help you forget about your ex-boyfriend . . . what's his name?"

"Yes." Hailey nodded with a smile. "What's-his-name."

Chapter 15

Peter closed the file on Hilda, a sweet woman originally from Germany and a patient for the last two months, and moved it into the *Deceased* folder on his screen. It was becoming too common to move files into this folder, and each time it made Peter remind himself that this was why he needed to remain detached, or at least try to. Working with elderly people was particularly difficult at times because they passed away often. Sometimes he wondered if he'd be better off helping children. But then he thought back to his grandma, Pearl, and how she'd struggled to regain her speech after her stroke.

Another therapist, Pam Shirley, stopped at his door. "Peter, I've had a family emergency come up. I don't think I'll be back until Tuesday. Could you fit in a few appointments on Monday so I don't have to reschedule all of them?" she asked.

"I can have Joyce check my schedule, but I'm sure we can make it work."

"Thanks, Peter. I appreciate it." She rubbed her eyes.

Peter could see her obvious emotional state. "I hope it isn't anything too serious."

"My brother had a car accident and is going in for surgery. I want to be there for my sister-in-law and my nieces," Pam said, running her fingers through her short blonde hair.

"I'm sorry to hear that." His heart felt heavy for her. "Whatever I can do to help out."

"I should be back Monday night." Pam exhaled. "I'm still in shock. I talked to him on the phone a few days ago. I guess he was driving through an intersection and another car ran a red light and T-boned his car. It was nasty, but he should make a full recovery. I feel like I need to be there." She shook her head. "Life can change in an instant."

"Don't worry about anything here." Peter tried to think of something else he could do to help.

"I knew I could count on you. Thanks." Pam turned and left.

Peter parked his car in the elementary school lot and made his way to the entrance of the white brick building.

"Hi, I'm here to pick up Benji Reynolds," Peter said to the unfamiliar woman with short gray hair at the front desk.

After she looked through some papers, she asked, "What's your name?"

"Peter Stafford."

"You're his father?" she asked, looking over the top of her thick, black-rimmed glasses.

"No. His uncle." He set his hand on the counter.

She pinched her eyebrows together. "I don't think we have permission for you to pick him up."

Trying to remain patient, Peter said, "I've picked him up before."

"That may be true, but without the right paperwork I can't let you take him," she said in her nasal voice.

Peter drummed his fingers on the counter. "I'm sure it's here. Laura said she was sending an additional note in his backpack."

"I'm sorry, but I don't see anything." She shrugged.

Maybe if he explained the situation the woman would allow him to take Benji. "My sister, Laura Reynolds, won't be picking him up because she has a meeting. I'm the one who is supposed to get him today."

The woman stared at him without saying anything.

"So I need to be able to take him with me. We're meeting her at Smitty's because it's a spirit night tonight." *That should convince her I know what I'm talking about.*

The woman still said nothing.

Trying to push the rising frustration down, Peter calmly said, "Can you ask Benji if I'm his uncle?"

She quirked an eyebrow. "I don't think so."

What is this, a prison? This woman is being so difficult. Is it in her job description to be a pain in the neck? Peter wanted to tell her how ridiculous this was, but opted to try another approach. "Is there someone else I can talk to?"

"I'm the only one here," she said with overstated authority.

"In the building?" *There must be someone with some common sense in here somewhere.*

"Of course not. But I can't leave this spot to go find anyone, and I can't let you inside the building."

Peter ran his fingers through his hair. He understood the reasoning behind the policy, but it was infuriating. "So where does that leave us?"

She shrugged.

"Can you call someone to come up here?" He was losing his patience with this woman.

"I don't know. I'm new."

Peter nodded, the irritation bubbling up inside. "We need to do something because I'm going to have an upset nephew and an angry sister if we don't resolve this."

"I can check his file again."

"Thank you."

After a couple of minutes clicking on the keyboard, she said. "I still didn't find anything."

"Could the permission slip be in a file cabinet instead of on the computer?" Peter needed to solve this problem now.

"I don't think so. Everything we have is on the computer."

Another, younger woman wearing a Richardson Elementary T-shirt and black pants, walked into the front office. "Is there a problem here?"

Feeling a sense of relief and hope, Peter said, "I need to pick up my nephew, Benji Reynolds. I've picked him up before, but she can't find the permission document from my sister."

The woman clicked through a few screens on the computer. "Here it is."

Peter let out a breath, grateful for this second woman. "Thank you."

"I didn't know I had to go to that screen," the other woman said.

"Check his driver's license against the one that is listed."

Peter handed over his license.

"You can go back and get your nephew," the irritating woman said sheepishly.

Peter found Benji in the back room working on an art project. He had blue and yellow paint on his hands and a spot of white on his cheek. "Uncle Peter. Look at my painting. It's when we went to the beach last summer."

Peter leaned down to get a better look. "It's great. I think maybe you'll be a famous painter someday."

"Really?" Benji's blue eyes twinkled.

"Sure. If that's what you want. The sky's the limit." He wanted to encourage Benji to be free to do whatever he wanted.

Benji hoisted his large camouflage backpack on his shoulder, and they walked out to the car. "Thanks for coming to get me."

"I'm excited to try this barbecue place." Peter pulled the backpack from his nephew's shoulder and put it in the trunk of the car.

"We need to sign in so my class gets credit for us eating there." Benji's excitement was endearing.

"I'll make sure I have my driver's license ready," Peter said under his breath.

Benji scrunched up his nose. "Huh?"

"Never mind." He told himself to forget about the run-in with the aggravating woman and focus on his nephew.

Once they arrived at the restaurant, they sat in a booth toward the back. Country music played in the background, and the walls were covered in old wood that made the space look and feel like a barn. Spurs hung on the wall next to a shelf with two pairs of old cowboy boots.

"What's good here?" Peter asked as he looked over the menu, the sweet and spicy scent of barbecue sauce making his stomach demand nourishment.

Benji shrugged.

Peter checked his watch. "Your mom should be here pretty soon. Do you want to wait for her before we order?"

"Sure."

"I was afraid you'd say that."

Benji gave him a perplexed expression.

"I skipped lunch today." As if on cue, his stomach let out a loud growl.

Benji started laughing.

Peter patted his tummy and said in a Yoda voice, "Behave you must, Mr. Stomach. Feed you soon, I will."

"You're funny," Benji said with a grin.

"Mostly, I'm starving. I hope your mom hurries." He glanced at his watch.

They continued to talk about karate, swimming, and taking a trip to the beach while they waited forever for Laura to arrive.

Hailey finished her makeup and finger-styled her hair. "This is as good as it gets," she said to herself in the mirror.

She walked out into the living room where Regina was sprawled on the couch. "Hey, hey. Look at you. Where you off to?"

"She has a date," Gran said as she sat on the chair thumbing through a *Knit Simply* magazine.

Regina whistled. "Maybe you'll get lucky."

"Regina!" Gran said, shaking her head. "Mind your manners, please."

Hailey brushed off Regina's crude remark. She and Regina had nothing in common. Part of her regretted leaving Gran and Gramps with her aunt. She was an adult, but she acted more like an irresponsible, hormonal teenager.

"Aw, come on, Momma." Regina laughed, but it sounded more like a cackle.

"I hope you have a nice dinner tonight. You look so pretty. I'm glad you decided on that outfit. The lavender blouse looks so nice with your skin tone," Gran said, looking over the top of her magazine. "Did he say which restaurant?"

"I think some barbecue place." Hailey brushed at her white skirt. "I can't remember."

A knock sounded at the door, so Hailey turned and answered it. Darren stood on the porch in plaid shorts and a yellow polo shirt that complemented his olive skin and highlighted his toned body. He was handsome all right. "Hi, Hailey. Are you ready to go?"

Hailey stepped outside in the heat because she didn't want to expose Darren to her rough-and-tumble aunt. *Who knows what might come out of her mouth?*

"Nice to see you," she said as they started walking toward the white Toyota Corolla.

On the drive over to the restaurant, they chatted easily about music and movies while the air conditioner blew cool air over her warm skin.

"I've never been to this restaurant," Darren said.

"What's the name of it again?"

Darren pointed to the sign as they drove into the parking lot. "Smitty's Down Home Barbecue."

"Sounds like a good place."

They pulled up to a faded, wood-sided building with some sheet metal accents and an iron statue of a horse in front. "Looks authentic," Darren said. "Must mean they have good barbecue."

They walked inside and waited to be seated. The restaurant was noisy and the scent of roasted meat, onions, and tangy barbecue sauce sifted through the air. It reminded Hailey of backyard cookouts with her family.

A woman with short, bleach-blonde hair and a tattoo of a sunflower on her wrist guided them through the crowded dining room to a booth and they both sat.

"Seems to be a popular place," Hailey said, glancing over the menu. She decided to order the smoked turkey platter with a salad bar.

A tall, thin man with receding brown hair took their orders and then said, "You can get your salad whenever you're ready."

"Thanks," Hailey said. "I'll go get my salad and be right back."

Darren smiled and gave her a nod.

Hailey began loading up her plate with lettuce, carrots, tomatoes, mushrooms, and cucumbers, then added a generous helping of salad dressing. She had the plate in her hand when she turned quickly without looking and accidentally hit someone, spilling some of her salad down the front of the person.

"Oh, no. I'm so, so sorry," she said trying to steady the plate. "I don't know how—" Her sentence cut short and her heart clenched tight when she saw who stood before her. "Peter?"

"Hi," Peter said, wiping at his black dress shirt.

Hailey stood there mortified, suffering from shame-induced paralysis. She'd just spilled vegetables coated in Thousand Island dressing all over the front of Peter Stafford, of all people.

He gazed at her. "Usually, I'm not a big fan of salad. Maybe it's because I've been trying to eat it all these years instead of wearing it." He laughed.

Her mouth gaped open. "I am so sorry. I should've looked before I turned." What else could she say?

"It's no big deal, really," he said. "It's only a shirt. I mean, it *is* my favorite one that I wear all the time and was planning to wear it tomorrow to an important meeting."

"Oh, no. I'll pay to have it cleaned. Or buy you a new one." She grabbed some napkins and wiped at his shirt.

He laughed again, and she could see the glint in his eyes—he was teasing her.

A woman that resembled Reese Witherspoon walked up to them. Hailey thought it was the same woman she'd seen with Peter before. She quickly stopped wiping at Peter's shirt front. *I hope she doesn't think I was flirting with her husband.*

"What happened to you?" the woman asked, eyeing them.

"I said something to this woman, and she responded by throwing her salad at me," Peter said with feigned innocence.

"You probably deserved it," the woman said, slugging him in the arm.

Peter shrugged, then said, "Laura, I'd like you to meet Hailey. Her grandfather is one of my newest recruits."

"Hi. Nice to meet you," Laura said politely. But underneath her manners, she seemed to be scrutinizing Hailey, making Hailey want to duck under a table. *Does she somehow know that I think—thought—Peter was attractive? Before I knew he was married, of course. But still.*

"Nice to meet you too," Hailey said so she wasn't rude. *Can I evaporate now?*

A boy came running up to them. "Can I get an ice cream now?" he asked Peter.

"You need to ask your mom." Peter pointed at Laura. "Not me. Remember?"

"But she says no." The boy made a face. "You always say yes."

"Go ahead and get an ice cream," Laura said and he ran off.

They seemed to be a typical family. It would be sweet if it didn't make Hailey feel a little disappointed somehow.

The woman looked at Hailey. "My brother loves to spoil Benji."

"Your *brother*?" It came out a little strangled.

"Benji is my nephew," Peter said matter-of-factly, obviously not realizing the revelation he'd shared.

Hailey let out a nervous laugh. *They aren't a couple. I had it all wrong. Completely wrong.*

"What's so funny?" Peter asked with his brows knit together.

Hailey wasn't sure what to say. *Oh, yeah. I was attracted to you, but saw you with a woman and a boy and assumed you were married. Yeah, that sounds terrible.* "Oh, sorry. Nothing," she said, the pitch of her voice higher than normal.

Peter studied her, making her cheeks feel like the sun sat atop them. "Are you here with Harry?"

"Uh, no." She cleared her throat. "I'm on a . . . date." Hailey tapped the underside of her almost-empty plate with her fingers.

"Oh." Peter took a step back. A quick something flashed across his face, but it was too fast for her to interpret it.

"Again. I am so sorry for spilling on you. I guess I should get, you know, back. To my date." Hailey took a few steps backward and ran into the end of the salad bar, making her stumble. Thankfully, she caught herself before falling to the ground and adding even more humiliation to the evening. "I don't know why I'm so clumsy tonight." She wanted to escape as fast as possible.

"I'll see you later." Peter smiled, seemingly clueless about the reason for her clumsiness.

Hailey nodded, then quickly retreated to her table.

Laura stared at her brother, and Peter couldn't take it anymore. "What?" he said with an air of indifference.

"What's with her?" Laura inclined her head in Hailey's direction.

"Who?" Maybe if he played dumb Laura would stop asking questions. He cast his gaze to his plate.

"The woman at the salad bar?"

"I don't know." He averted eye contact with Laura. "Is there something with her?"

"Don't play coy with me, Petie."

"You know I hate it when you call me that." He sat back. His sister was annoying at times, but never more so than when she inserted herself in his love life.

Laura slapped the table with both palms. "It all makes sense now."

"Okay, I give up." He peered at her. "*What* makes sense now?"

Laura smiled and nodded.

Peter pushed out a breath. "Am I supposed to read your mind or something?" This conversation was grating on his nerves.

Laura widened her eyes and said, "You're interested in her."

"I'm *what*?" He said it as if there weren't a grain of truth in it.

"No wonder you weren't into Fiona. I didn't understand it at the time, but now I do."

She grabbed a French fry from Peter's plate and shoved it in her mouth. "Are you going to ask her out?"

"Fiona?" Peter said, hoping to throw his sister off. "I'm thinking about it."

"Give me a break," Laura said.

Peter blew out a breath of exasperation. "No. I'm not going to ask Hailey out."

"First name basis, is it?" She gave him a smug look. "And why not? She's obviously interested in you."

"She is?" He said it too enthusiastically.

"Totally." Laura popped another fry into her mouth.

Peter reminded himself to be calm and nonchalant. "Even if she were, it'd be inappropriate. Her grandfather is under my care."

"There's a rule against dating a patient's family member?"

Now his sister was truly annoying him. "Laura, please stay out of it."

She wagged a fry at him. "I'm only pointing out the obvious."

"I think we're done here." He pushed his plate away, then stood. "I'm going to get Benji, so we can go home."

"Fine." She tossed a napkin on the table. "But I'm right."

Peter walked over to the ice cream area and snuck a glance around the restaurant. He spotted her. Over in the far corner. He didn't want to stare, so he looked away. Knowing she was with another man made him feel . . . something.

"Hey, Benji, are you done getting ice cream?"

"This is my second one." Benji took a long lick of the chocolate treat.

"Uh, huh." Peter glanced back in Hailey's direction. To his embarrassment, his gaze met hers. He quickly took a step back. He hadn't felt this awkward since middle school when a girl five inches taller than him asked him to dance.

He reached his hand out for Benji. "We're ready to go now."

"Are we going to see a movie?"

"I don't know, bud. It's getting late and I have a full schedule tomorrow." He hoped Harry wasn't one of the patients because, after tonight, he wasn't ready to see Hailey. He needed to process his feelings and reactions first.

They walked out to the car. Peter forced himself not to look back at the restaurant. For whatever reason, this woman had some kind of pull on him, but he didn't know why. What were the odds that they'd both end up at the same restaurant?

When Hailey returned to the table, Darren gazed at her plate with a puzzled expression. "What happened to your salad?"

"Oh, yeah." She glanced at the mess in front of her, trying to think of something to say.

"Looks like you really did toss your salad." He laughed at his joke.

Hailey gave him a courtesy laugh. "I kind of dropped it." She pushed the plate away because she was no longer interested in eating the salad. Seeing Peter had made her feel discombobulated.

"I think our meals will be here shortly."

After a few minutes of small talk, the waiter brought them their meals.

"My favorite *Mission Impossible* movie is *Ghost Protocol*. How cool to scale a building on the outside like that," Darren said, then took a bite of his potato salad.

Hailey's gaze kept being tugged in a different direction. Peter had been with his *sister*. Not a *wife*. Not a *girlfriend*. Of course, after the salad incident *and* her hyena-laughing reaction he must've thought she was a nut job. And maybe she was.

"Hailey?" Darren said.

"Oh, yeah. I love all the *Mission Impossible* movies. Peter Cruise is great."

Darren gave her a confused look. "Peter Cruise? Is that Tom's code name?"

"Oh." She laughed uncomfortably. "Did I say *Peter* Cruise? That's ridiculous. I meant Tom. I don't know why I said that." But she knew. Because her mind was on a speech therapist across the room. And why? What was wrong with her? Darren was great looking, easy to talk to, and fun. Why would she be thinking about Peter? *Focus on Darren.*

"Maybe we could watch a *Mission Impossible* marathon?" he said, breaking into her thoughts.

"That sounds fun." Hailey felt pulled to see if Peter was still in the restaurant, but she resisted.

"Except I'm not sure where." He sat back. "I don't know if Nana even owns a DVD player. She's never been fond of electronics. We watch cable."

"Gran and Gramps have a DVD player, but they also have a Regina."

"Huh?"

"My aunt." Hailey refrained from making a sour face. "She's camping out at their place right now, and I guarantee we don't want to spend the evening with her."

"We could try to find a movie tonight. If you're up for going to a theater."

"Honestly, I'm pretty tired." It was the truth. At least most of it. More than anything, she needed some thinking time to straighten out her befuddled thoughts.

"Okay." Darren didn't hide his disappointment.

"This is a great barbecue place. I'd like to come back sometime." Hailey wanted to let Darren know she'd enjoyed the date, even if seeing Peter rocked her a bit—a tiny bit.

"You would?" He perked up.

"Yeah. And let's do the movie marathon." It was much safer to spend time with Darren. He was leaving in a week, after all.

"All right."

They left the restaurant and Darren took her home.

"Thanks again for dinner. It was yummy. And the company was the best part," she said with emphasis.

Darren smiled.

Hailey got out of the car and went inside where her grandparents were watching TV.

"Come watch this with us," Gran said. "It's one of those talent shows."

Gramps pointed at the television. "S-s-sin-g-g-ger."

Hailey gazed at him.

"Harry likes this singer," Gran said. "Only because she's a beautiful blonde with nice assets, if you know what I mean. She really has no talent whatsoever." She went back to her knitting.

Gramps waved his hand, then nodded at Hailey, who took a seat next to Gran. "He's saying more and more words," Hailey said. A warm feeling enveloped her. Gramps was on his way to recovery for sure.

Gran agreed.

"This is exciting." Every word meant progress. Hailey couldn't wait to tell Peter—er, rather, his speech therapist—she mentally corrected herself.

"How was your date? He's a good-looking young man, isn't he?" Gran asked as she flipped blue yarn around her fingers.

"It was fun. We went to a barbecue place. Darren is a really nice guy."

Gran gazed at her. "Uh oh."

"What?"

"That sounds like you aren't interested." Gran picked up her glass to take a drink, but it was empty.

"Not true, Gran." Hailey grabbed the ball of yarn that had slipped to the ground and handed it back to her grandmother. "I am as interested as I'm ever going to be while I'm here in Florida." Although things had changed now that she knew Peter wasn't attached, it still didn't alter the fact that she'd be heading back to Colorado as soon as Gramps was healthy enough.

Gran quirked her eyebrow, but didn't say anything.

"So is Regina home?" Not that she cared much, but Hailey wanted to divert the conversation away from her dating life.

Gran's mouth tightened.

"She didn't go back out with that guy, did she?"

"I didn't ask where she was going. It's better I don't know." Gran's needles clicked together.

Poor Gran. She had such a hard time dealing with her rebellious and ungrateful daughter. Hailey wished she could knock some sense into her aunt and make Regina see how she was hurting Gran and Gramps.

Hailey's phone vibrated. She grabbed it from her pocket. "Hi, Mom."

"Hey, honey. Brit had the baby."

"She did?"

"Yes. He's beautiful." Hailey could hear the delight in her mom's voice. "They named him Thomas."

"Aw, after daddy?" Her throat thickened. "That's so sweet. How are they doing?"

"The baby is fine, but . . .," her mom paused. "Brit started hemorrhaging."

"Oh no." Hailey touched her cheek. "What does that mean?"

"They had to give her some blood and they're watching her closely. She'll be fine, but she'll need some extra time at the hospital. Which means I'll need to stay here longer."

Hailey felt torn between taking care of her grandparents and going to see her sister. "What should I do?"

"Tell me how Harry is doing," her mom said.

"Much better." Gratitude surged through Hailey.

"Is he talking again?"

"A little." Hailey wished he were saying more, but she was willing to be patient for his full recovery.

"I think you need to stay there. Maybe after Brit goes home and gets settled, you can come see her."

"Tell her congratulations. I can't wait to hold my nephew."

Hailey ended the call.

"Brit had the baby?" Gran asked with bright eyes.

"Yeah. They named him Thomas."

Gran's eyes moistened. "That makes me happy." She turned to her husband. "Did you hear that, Harry? We have a new great-grandson. And his name is Thomas."

Hailey considered telling her grandparents about Brit's complication but decided against it. She didn't want to worry them, especially because her mom said Brit would be fine.

Gramps stood, walked over to Gran, and kissed her on the cheek. He patted her on the shoulder and then slowly walked into the kitchen. He returned with a glass of lemonade for Gran and one for Hailey.

"You read my mind," Gran said. "Thank you, dear."

"Thanks, Gramps," Hailey said. "You're the best."

Gramps sat back in his recliner.

Hailey spent the next hour sitting next to Gran on the couch. As much as she wanted to see her nephew, she knew that she was where she needed to be. Once Gramps had recuperated enough, she'd go back to Colorado to see her sister and the new baby.

Chapter 16

Laura had successfully talked Peter into coming back to her apartment after dinner. "Do you want something to drink?" she asked as she walked into the kitchen.

"No, thanks." Peter sat on the couch and gazed out the window while conflicting emotions whirled around inside him.

"Can I get you something else?" Laura peeked around the wall.

"I'm fine." He wanted to sit and stare at nothing. He probably should've just gone back to his place, but sometimes it was too empty there.

Laura sat on the couch next to him. "Thanks again for getting Benji."

"Sure." Peter watched the last few shards of dusk disappear.

Laura popped the tab on her soda can and the carbonation bubbled out. She wiped her hand on her pant leg. "I still say you should ask her out."

Peter knew exactly who she meant, but he wasn't interested in a long discussion with his sister about his love life, or lack thereof. He needed to set her straight. Again. "Look, I already told you she's a patient's granddaughter."

"Who cares?" Laura crossed her ankles and leaned back.

"I'm not going to ask her out. It wouldn't be professional. Besides, she was with a guy." The memory of her with that man sent a jab of irritation through Peter, but he knew it was irrational for him to feel annoyed, or anything else for that matter. Hailey was Harry's granddaughter. There was nothing between them.

"Oh."

He could tell by the tone of Laura's voice that she was trying to imply something, but he hesitated to ask. Finally, he said, "Okay, what?"

Laura sipped her drink. "This is the first time I've seen you remotely interested in a woman since Sara."

He didn't say anything, because it was true. After Sara left him, he was broken, and he wasn't about to allow another woman to hurt him that deeply, so he'd withdrawn and thrown himself into his career to avoid a social life.

"Are you going to be a bachelor forever?" Laura poked him in the leg.

He scratched his throat. "Maybe."

"That isn't a solution, and you know it."

"I think it is." Not having a woman in his life meant no chance of another broken heart. His life was his own. He could do what he wanted, when he wanted, without interference. Peter liked the way he lived and didn't need a woman to complicate it. He was happy and content.

Laura shook her head. "You are so difficult."

"I appreciate your concern for my love life, but I'm fine. You don't need to worry about me. I'm happy. Besides, I need to focus on my career and opening my own therapy practice." He had his eye set on his goal and he wasn't going to let anyone distract him.

"You're going to be a lonely old man." Laura let out a loud burp, then covered her mouth. "Excuse me."

"I have you and Benji," Peter said. "I'm not lonely."

"It's not the same as having a relationship." Laura set her can on the table.

Peter decided to turn the conversation back on his sister. "What about you? It's been almost three years since Sam passed."

She adjusted her weight and leaned back against the couch. "That's different."

"How?" He genuinely wanted to know.

"I have a son to worry about, and I was already married to the love of my life." She put her feet up on the coffee table. "I'm not looking for another one."

"Same." He'd thought he'd married the woman he'd spend his life with, but he'd been wrong—very wrong—and he didn't want to take that chance again.

"Fine." Laura stood up and walked to the kitchen. "This conversation is going nowhere."

"Mom," Benji said as he rushed into the room wearing a Spiderman costume. "Can we go get a movie at Redbox?"

"School night, remember?" Laura said. "It's time for bed."

Benji collapsed to the floor. "Aww, Mom," Benji wailed.

"I better get home myself." Peter stood.

"What if your uncle reads to you before bed?" Laura said, casting Peter a hopeful glance.

Benji lifted his mask and eyed Peter.

"Only one book. That's all." Peter reached out his hand to Benji.

Benji reluctantly placed his hand in Peter's and stood. "Okay."

"Let's hear some enthusiasm," Peter said as he took off Benji's mask and rumpled his hair.

"I get to pick the story?" Benji asked with wide eyes.

"Sure."

Peter and Benji walked down the hallway together.

After he'd read a much longer book than he anticipated, Peter said goodbye to his sister and left. He drove back to his place. His thoughts centered on running into Hailey at the restaurant. She'd only come to town recently, so he guessed her date wasn't too serious.

Something about her grabbed him. A part of him wanted to

explore it, but the sensible part reminded him that her grandfather was under his care and any kind of attempt to ask her out would be awkward at best.

Besides, he was still convinced that one broken heart was enough. He didn't need, or want, to risk that pain again. Better to remain a bachelor and keep control of his life and his heart. Even if that meant no bedtime stories with children of his own.

Chapter 17

The early morning sun rays peeked through the blinds in Hailey's room. Was today Thursday or Friday? She wasn't sure. Since coming to Florida, she'd lost track of time. She'd need to check her email and do some work this morning, but first she'd go for a run. It'd help clear her head.

Since Gran and Gramps weren't up yet, she dressed in her shorts and tank top and then slipped outside to begin her swim through the air. It took less than five minutes for her shirt to become soaked with perspiration.

Hailey had come to Florida to help her grandparents, not to find a man. She had to admit, though, Darren was handsome. He was fun and easy to talk to. He wasn't permanent, and she could enjoy a few dates with him—no attachment or entanglements.

Her mind shifted to Peter. For some reason, he made her heart pound, her nerves tingle, and her knees wobble. Seeing him in the restaurant made her mouth forget to work and her brain go on hiatus. Then there was the incident at the salad bar and the laugh that fell out of her mouth when he told her that woman was his sister. His *sister*. Yep, being around him made her into a ninny, as Gran would say.

Hailey picked up her pace and fell into a nice run. She would for sure have to shower before taking Gramps to his appointment. She'd have to get Gran to come with them so she could avoid talking to Peter. She didn't want things to be any more awkward than they already were. Admittedly, she was attracted to him, but it wouldn't—couldn't—go anywhere. It was much better to go on dates with Darren. He was safe.

After forty minutes, she returned to her grandparents' house, breathing hard, but happy she'd exercised and cleared the muddy waters in her mind. She would go on some fun dates with Darren, if he asked. And she'd forget about Peter. It was simple.

Hailey showered, then spent some time going through expenses for Crandall Automotive. She ran the report that showed where the budget for the previous month had been exceeded and emailed it directly to Mr. Crandall. She answered a couple of emails and updated the spreadsheet for Renee Thompson's hair salons. She also sent a new bio to Mr. Michaels for the company website that was being overhauled.

After finishing her work, Hailey dressed in her black shorts and a turquoise shirt. She walked out into the living room.

"You look lovely today, dear," Gran said. "That shirt really brings out the blue in your eyes."

"Thanks." Hailey adjusted her shirt and convinced herself she wasn't wearing it to impress anyone. "You're coming with us today, right?"

Gran rummaged through her purse. "I need to run some errands."

"Great. I'm happy to take you after the appointment. You can learn more of what to do so you can help Gramps after I go back home." Seemed reasonable and made perfect sense to her.

Gran frowned. "I don't want to think about that. I'm enjoying having you here too much."

"I plan to stay a while longer, but, eventually, I have to go back to my life. What's left of it anyway. And I have a new nephew."

"Your mom called while you were gone and gave me all the details." Gran applied some red lipstick. "I'm sure he's adorable."

"I can't wait to see him." A part of Hailey was disappointed that she wasn't there with her sister, but she knew Gran and Gramps needed her, and it was nice to feel needed.

Gran wrote a few things down on a piece of paper and put it in her large flowered bag. "I have to write myself notes so I don't forget what errands I need to run."

Hailey glanced around. "I haven't seen Regina today."

"She left while you were out exercising. Said she was going to do some things. I don't know what that means." Gran gazed at Hailey with melancholy eyes. "I don't think I want to know."

Hailey gave her grandmother a slight smile. "I'm going to fill my water bottle before we leave." She made her way over to the refrigerator. While she was filling her bottle, she noticed a binder on the counter next to the refrigerator and started thumbing through it. Her eyes widened as she saw photos and what appeared to be biographies of men and women of all ages in page protectors. *What in the world?* She finished filling her bottle and looked through more of the binder. She found a page about her. In the back was what looked like a chart, with names and dates, check marks, stars, and big Xs next to some of the names. *What is going on?* When she found her name and Roger's name intersected with a big red X, she sang out, "Gran!"

Her grandmother turned, and when she saw that Hailey held the binder, the color drained from her face and she dropped her purse.

"What is this?" Hailey suspected what it was, but wanted to hear it from Gran's own lips.

Gran rushed over and grabbed the binder. "Never mind. It has nothing to do with you."

"Uh, I beg to differ. There's a photo of me from a few years ago and a page about me with lots of details." Hailey wasn't sure if she should be angry or what.

"Oh." Gran pursed her lips. "I . . . uh . . . this is just a collection of memories. That's all. I thought I put that away." Gran went to grab the binder, but Hailey moved it out of her grasp.

Hailey stared at her grandmother. "I don't believe you. I want you to tell me exactly what this is." Hailey waited for Gran's response.

"It's really nothing." Gran waved her hand.

"You're lying to me. You want to know what I think it is?" Hailey said, holding the binder with one hand and her other hand perched on her hip.

"Not really." Gran grabbed the binder from Hailey and cradled it to her chest.

"I think you and your friends are running an escort service." It sounded outlandish, but it seemed like the obvious answer.

An indignant expression crossed Gran's face. "My lands, girl, we certainly are not madams, if that's what you think. This is all perfectly innocent."

"Why don't you explain it to me then?" Hailey tapped her foot.

"Fine." Gran sat on the sofa and set the binder on her lap. "Lila and I, with a few others, help our friends find dates for their kids and grandkids. And sometimes we help others in our community find dates. It's all very innocent, I assure you."

Hailey rubbed her forehead. Gran was running a dating service out of her retirement community? When Hailey had accused her grandmother of matchmaking, she didn't actually think it was a real thing. But the binder said otherwise. Hailey couldn't even wrap her mind around Gran being a professional matchmaker. "This is a business?"

"Not technically a business. We don't charge any money."

Hailey sat next to Gran. "So you fix people up and keep track of it in your binder?"

Gran nodded. "We have regular meetings to discuss possible matches."

A realization hit Hailey. "That's why you were acting so weird at bingo. And that woman handed you a photo. It was for this."

Gran nodded. "It's harmless."

"I'm not sure that messing with people's hearts is harmless, Gran."

"We only introduce people. That's all." Gran opened the binder.

"People are lonely or they have family members who are." She pointed at a photo. "This is Amelia's granddaughter, Kirsten. She was engaged but her fiancé was killed in a motorcycle accident."

Hailey laid her hand across her chest. "That's so sad."

"Kirsten hadn't dated for a couple of years. We introduced her to Wanda's nephew and they liked each other." Gran flipped through pages to the end of the book where there were photos of couples. She pointed to a picture of a red-haired woman whose arms were wrapped around a man with curly black hair. "Got married last year."

Hailey studied Gran. "How long have you been doing this?"

"About eight years now."

"Wow." Hailey raised her eyebrows. "And you thought Roger and I would be a good match?"

Gran laughed. "Oh, goodness, no. But Dee was insistent. Poor Roger."

"I guess it's not a big deal. Except for me. I do not want to be included in this." She raised her index finger. "And I don't want you to try to pair me up with anyone. At all."

"But—"

"No buts. Seriously. I am off limits." She gave Gran her stern face.

Gran let out a long breath. "I suppose. But I worry about you being alone."

Gramps shuffled into the living room and gave Hailey a smile. She stepped over to him and kissed him on the cheek. "Are you ready to work today?" she asked.

Gramps shot her a do-I-have-a-choice look. He went over to the kitchen table and grabbed something, but Hailey couldn't see what it was.

"The therapist says you need to keep working hard to regain your speech. The world needs your corny jokes," she said, trying to be cheery.

Gramps shrugged as if dismissing the idea.

"Harry, you have to listen. You can't be so bullheaded if you want to be able to talk again," Gran said.

Gramps nodded, then walked over to Gran and extended his hand, exposing the carnation he'd taken from the vase on the kitchen table. "F-f-for . . . you."

"The flower?" she asked.

"All . . . of . . . it."

Gran stood then hugged him. She looked directly into his eyes. "I know this is hard for you."

He gave her a tight smile. It didn't take words to understand his meaning. He was doing his best and working hard to please Gran because he loved her.

Hailey swung her arm around him. "Let's get you into the car."

The three of them arrived at the clinic. The apprehension of seeing Peter intensified with each step Hailey took, and her stomach roiled in anticipation. "Maybe you should go in with Gramps this time, and I'll wait for you in the lobby."

Gramps frowned at her.

"I'm sure we'd be fine," Gran said. "But I'd feel better if you went in with us. Then you can hear what he says and help me understand it all."

Hailey let out a breath. She was being ridiculous anyway. Peter probably wouldn't even remember running into her—actually, she'd literally run into him—and the high-pitched laugh that escaped her lips when he introduced his sister. "Okay, I'll come with you."

After a few minutes in the waiting room, a nurse showed them to a back room. While they waited, the room seemed to shrink around them, making it hard for Hailey to breathe. The door swung open and Peter stepped inside. Hailey's heartbeat kicked up a hundred notches, and the back of her neck warmed.

"Good to see you again," he said as he looked at Hailey.

She gave him a forced smile.

He turned to Gran. "And you too. I'm glad you came today."

"Harry has really started to improve." Gran paused and glanced at Hailey, then back at Peter. "You are a wonderful therapist."

Hailey fidgeted in her seat. *Gran better not say anything else.*

"Thank you. I have a great patient."

Peter began working with Gramps and even coaxed some new words out of him. Hailey watched the easy interplay between Peter and her grandfather, marveling at how well they got along. Each time that Peter pronounced a word and Gramps tried to mimic it, though, sadness pricked Hailey's heart. Learning to speak again was a struggle for Gramps and a stark reminder that he'd had a stroke. With his advancing age, she had to face the harsh reality that she might not have many more years with him. Add to that her demanding work schedule and suddenly her throat began to swell with emotion. Time was her nemesis.

"Put your lips together like this," Peter said to Gramps. Hailey found herself trying to do the same with her own lips. She watched Gramps work hard to say even the simplest words and wished she could somehow help him more. The least she could do was to make it a priority to visit more often after this. No matter how much Mr. Michaels expected from her, she'd have to ask for more time off to make regular visits.

"Excellent, Harry. You're making great progress," Peter said with enthusiasm. Hailey's gaze shifted to Peter and the way he peered at Gramps with laser-focused attention. It was easy to tell that Peter not only loved his job, but truly cared for his patients. The way he spoke with such kindness and gentleness touched Hailey. His sincerity and genuine concern were very attractive qualities in a man. If she were looking for such qualities. Or a man. Which she wasn't.

After the session, Peter patted Gramps on the shoulder and said, "Fantastic session today."

He turned to Hailey and Gran. "Keep encouraging him to use common words. He doesn't have to say things in a way that's grammatically correct, but you can model proper sentence structure for him so his brain begins to recognize it again."

"Hailey practices with him. She's been such a big help." Gran patted Hailey on the leg.

"I can see the improvement already," Peter said to Gran.

Hailey held her breath, hoping Gran wouldn't spring into action and try to embarrass her any more.

"I sure appreciate your help. It was such a shock when he had the stroke." Gran laced her fingers in her lap, then absently rubbed her thumbs together.

"It's amazing how the brain can compensate, and with some work we can restore your speech, Harry."

"Are you from around here?" Gran asked and Hailey stiffened. *Do not ask him any personal questions.*

"I grew up in Orlando, but I've been living here for four years." Peter leaned back in his chair.

"You know, Hailey has been wonderful taking me to bingo and spending time with us old folks, but I'd like her to do some things young people do. I hear there's a Latin festival at the Oceanwalk this weekend."

Hailey shot Gran a warning look, but Gran paid no attention.

"Ah, yes. Mar y Sol. There will be lots of food and music," Peter said brightly.

"Maybe you could take Hailey?" Gran said.

Hailey's face blazed with fire and she wanted to shove her grandmother out of the room before she said anything else. *I cannot believe you just said that. I am so going to strangle you.* "Gran, I'm sure that he has another appointment right now," Hailey said, keeping her hands at her side so she didn't slip them around Gran's neck.

Peter cleared his throat and shifted his weight, then snuck a glance at Hailey. "Uh, sure . . . I'd be happy to take you . . . Tonight . . . If you're interested."

A smile stole across Gran's face and Hailey wanted to scream at the obvious way Gran cornered the poor therapist into a mercy date.

"You don't need to do that." Hailey shook her head. "I'm pretty busy taking care of—"

"We don't need her at all tonight," Gran offered quickly.

Peter blinked, then said, "Okay. I'm free . . . if you are."

What could she say? Do? Gran had thrust her into an embarrassing situation from which she had no escape.

"She's free," Gran said with a much too cheery tone.

Having no other option, Hailey said, "I'd love to go." She fumed. *Gran is outrageous. She's been bold before, but never like this. As soon as we are out of the office, I'm going to let her have it. Until then, I need to be polite and smile.*

"I'll be by about six o'clock," Peter said.

"I'll see you then." Hailey smiled with gritted teeth.

They walked out of the office. Gramps wore a silly grin and Gran walked like a proud peacock. When they got to the car Hailey said, "Gran, how could you?"

"What do you mean?" She wore an oblivious expression as if she had no idea that she'd practically held a gun to Peter's head to force him to take Hailey to some festival.

"That was so inappropriate." Hailey tried to keep her voice down, but she wasn't being very successful. "I don't even know where to start."

"You could say thank you."

This woman is maddening. "Gran, I told you my dating life was off-limits. I'm not part of your matchmaking book." She rubbed her temples.

Gran got into the car and shut her door. Hailey helped Gramps into the back and then got in herself.

"You don't think he's attractive?" Gran asked.

"That is beside the point." Hailey secured her seatbelt, then sunk the key into the ignition. "You totally disregarded what I said."

"But you *do* think he's attractive?"

"Gran!" Hailey stared at her grandmother. "He is Gramps's speech therapist. He shouldn't be going on dates with—"

"Harry? Because *you* aren't his patient. Your grandfather is. Nothing wrong with you going out with him." Gran gave a certain jerk of her chin.

Hailey pushed out a breath. This was hopeless.

"Just see what happens, dear," Gran said.

"Like either of us had any choice," Hailey said. They'd both been hoodwinked into a date.

"I know people." Gran nodded. "I have intuition about these things. He's a good man, and you need a good man."

"I don't need a man." Hailey started the car and backed out of the parking space. She drove through the parking lot. "And you didn't even know if he was single."

"I could tell by the way he looked at you that he was single."

"What?" She put on the brake and jolted the car. Hailey looked over her shoulder. "Sorry, Gramps."

"You heard me." Gran kept her gaze straight ahead. "He is surely sweet on you."

Hailey shook her head. Gran was making outrageous claims. "He was being a good therapist. That's all."

"No, no." Gran shook her head. "Much more than that. I know these things."

Hailey drew in a deep breath of frustration. It was a losing battle.

"You should wear that pretty blue dress you have."

Hailey glanced at Gramps in the rearview mirror and he winked at her. They were both plotting against her. "I'll go out to this festival thing with him, but then you have to promise to drop it. And no more matchmaking for me. I mean it."

"I will." Gran settled back in her seat, wearing a confident smile. "I promise."

They drove to the house in silence and Hailey went to her room. How could this have happened? Yes, she admitted it. She was attracted to Peter. Yes, she would like to go on a date with him.

But now it was like he'd been forced at gunpoint, or at least Gran point. He probably wasn't even interested in going out with her but did the honorable thing when Gran put him on the spot. Sometimes, she really wanted to throttle her grandmother.

She retrieved her blue dress from the closet and gazed at it. As a sign of rebellion, she tossed it on the bed, refusing to wear it. Instead she found her white lace shorts and a flowing peach blouse—casual and easygoing.

I hope I don't regret this.

Chapter 18

Peter finished his last appointment. His mind kept jumping ahead to Mar y Sol. Although he would have preferred to ask Hailey on a date in his own way, he had to laugh at her grandmother's insistence. Or was that audacity? And the blush that colored Hailey's cheeks made him smile. It was the same color as when she spilled her salad on him.

He hoped he wasn't crossing some sort of line by taking a patient's granddaughter on a date.

"So what are you up to tonight?" Joyce said as she leaned against the doorjamb.

"Uh, not much."

"A few of us are going out for drinks and dancing. You should meet us there." Joyce ran her fingers through her hair. It was probably meant to be enticing, but it only made Peter want to run as fast and as far away from her as possible.

"Actually, I can't." He wrote a few notes, hoping Joyce would think he was busy and leave him alone.

"Why not?" He could hear the pout in her voice.

"I already have plans." He suddenly felt grateful for Hailey's grandmother.

"I'm sorry to hear that." She licked her lips. "Maybe next time."

He had no desire to spend a social evening with Joyce, especially dancing with her. *No thank you.* Peter didn't want to offend her, so he said, "Maybe." He clicked off his computer and grabbed a file folder. "Can you take this to the front?"

Joyce begrudgingly held out her hand and took the folder. "Sure."

Peter stood and said, "Thanks for all you do, Joyce. I appreciate it." Before she could say anything laced with innuendos, Peter stepped past her into the hall and made his way out the back door.

In his car, he took a few moments to contemplate. Was it wise to go on this date with Hailey? He'd been adamant about avoiding any complicated relationships at work because he didn't want any problems, and especially because he didn't want to get involved with Joyce. She wasn't his type. She was the opposite of his type.

It was different with Hailey. He'd been drawn to her the first time they'd met. Her sweet smile and natural beauty appealed to him, but more than that, the way she loved her grandfather showed him how kind and caring she was.

His phone vibrated and he pulled it from his pocket.

Benji wants you to come over for a movie tonight.

He pondered what to text back so he didn't let on that he had a date with Hailey. *I'd love to, but I can't.*

Why not?

What should he say? He didn't want to lie to Laura, but he didn't want her to hit him with a bunch of questions either. *I'm going to Mar y Sol.*

That festival?

Yeah.

What time? Benji and I can meet you there.

Now what? He tapped out, *I'm not going by myself.*

Who with?

He didn't want to answer. What if he didn't text back? He knew that wouldn't work, because Laura would start calling him. Over and over and over again. Because she wouldn't give up until he talked to her.

Maybe if he said he was going with a friend that'd work. Because he and Hailey were friends. That was all. A *friend*.

A woman?

Why did his sister have to be so nosy? *Yes.*

His phone started ringing. *Great. Exactly what I didn't want.* But Laura wouldn't give up, so he reluctantly answered. "Hello?"

"Are you going on a *date?*"

He forced out a puff of air. "Yes."

"With who?" his sister asked eagerly.

He might as well tell her and get it over with. "Hailey." There, he'd said it.

A long silence passed, and then Laura asked, "The woman at the restaurant?"

"Yes."

"How did *that* happen?" He could picture his sister's face filled with anticipation.

He didn't have time to tell her. "It's a long story, but I need to go."

"I want the details," she demanded.

"Okay."

"Text me later. After the date. I want to know all about it." Laura was probably jumping up and down that he was finally going on a date.

"I will."

"Peter?" she said softly.

"Yeah?" What was she going to say now?

"I'm happy to hear this. Go out and have fun."

"Thanks." He ended the call.

He dropped the phone in his lap. He'd been playing it safe for years. Ever since Sara. Maybe it was worth the risk to get to know Hailey.

After all, he still wanted the dream—a house, wife, kids with bikes strewn on the front lawn. He thought he'd had it, but it had slipped through his fingers like grains of sand.

He could keep protecting his heart, but that would leave him empty and alone. Like Laura said last night, he'd be a lonely old man, and he didn't want that. Hailey seemed to be the kind of woman he'd want to date.

Maybe even the kind of woman he'd want to love.

Chapter 19

Hailey sat in the living room, her right foot shaking and her heart playing leapfrog with her lungs. This was dangerous. Peter wasn't at all like Darren. He wasn't safe, and she was taking a big risk going out with him. Of course, maybe he wasn't interested in her but was simply being a gentleman after Gran backed him into the date.

Gran walked into the room, her floral scent close behind her. "Wow, you look beautiful. I like that blouse."

"Thanks." Hailey still wasn't pleased with Gran's earlier antics.

Gran stepped over to Gramps and slung her arm around him. "We'll get her married off one way or another, right, Harry?"

They both laughed, which made Hailey's blood burn. "The two of you are incorrigible. This is only a date that Gran pressured him into. Nothing else." Her voice had an edge to it.

"My lands"—Gran slapped her knee—"you are blind if you think that."

A knock sounded and Hailey's heart plummeted to her stomach. She hadn't been this nervous since she had to tell her mom that she'd backed their new car into the neighbor's mailbox.

Gran rushed over and opened the door. "Hello. Please come in."

Her tone was much too enthusiastic.

Peter stepped inside and Hailey's breath hitched. He wore khaki shorts and an aqua V-neck T-shirt that hugged him in all the right places and made his eyes even bluer—if that was even possible. She had to slyly let out a long breath to calm her sizzling nerves.

"Hi," Peter said. "You look nice."

"Thank you," Gran said with a smile as she smoothed her hair. "You look quite dashing in that blue shirt."

Peter's cheeks colored and he shifted his weight.

"Aw, now, don't be embarrassed." Gran touched him on the arm. "I know you meant Hailey."

"Oh, well, you also look nice, too, June," he stammered.

Hailey shot Gran a sharp look. *Poor man.* "Thank you, Peter," Hailey said.

He turned to Gramps. "How are you this evening?" He reached out his hand.

Gramps shook it and said, "G-good . . . . You?"

Peter smiled. "Glad to hear you talking."

"I'm all ready to go." Hailey said. She wanted to hurry out before Gran asked him something preposterous, like if he planned to propose tonight or something, because she wouldn't put it past her.

"We won't wait up for you, Hailey." Gran elbowed Gramps, and she smiled like she'd won the lottery. Hailey wanted to bop her.

Outside, Hailey said, "Sorry about that. Gran can be a little outrageous."

"No worries." He opened the passenger door of his black Audi and she slid into the seat.

When he got inside, Hailey said, "Are your grandparents still alive?"

"My dad's parents are, but my mom's father passed away more than forty years ago. And her mother had a stroke when I was a teenager and came to live with us."

Hailey tried to pull her gaze from Peter, but found it nearly impossible. "Did you help take care of her?"

"Yeah. Actually, I practiced her speech with her every day until she died." Peter started up the car.

"Is that why you decided to become a therapist?" Hailey was interested in knowing more about this man—purely because it would be good to know about Gramps's therapist, of course. No other reason.

He nodded. "I loved working with Grandma Vera and seeing her verbal skills improve. When I got into college, I found the concept of language and speech fascinating, so I decided to study it."

"How long have you been working at the rehabilitation hospital?" Hailey watched him, noticing his well-defined jaw line. *Is it hot in this car? I think I need some more AC. Full blast.*

"About four years. And I really enjoy it." Peter rested his right hand on his thigh and Hailey couldn't help but wonder what it would be like to feel her hand encased in his. *Stop. Right now. Get control of yourself.*

She finally tore her gaze from him and looked ahead at the spattering of clouds across the deep blue sky. "Gramps sure likes you."

"Harry is a fine man. I often think about my patients and wonder what they were like before I met them." His voice had a tinge of sadness.

"Gramps was a police sergeant. He was on the force in Denver forever. I used to love to see him all ready for work." An image of Gramps fully decked out in his uniform flashed through her mind. "He was so strong and vibrant," she said wistfully.

"It's hard to watch those we love become weak and unable to do the things they used to do." Peter said it in such a tender way that it made Hailey's heart swoon.

"Very hard." Hailey gazed at the palm trees along the road. Florida scenery was certainly different than Colorado.

"Are Harry and June your mom's parents?"

"No. My dad's. He died when I was a girl, so my grandparents were super involved with me and my sister Brittany when we were growing up. Until they retired and moved to Florida." The memory of the day they left still made her throat thick.

Peter glanced at her. "Florida is a popular place to retire."

"Well, Gramps is a NASCAR fanatic. He loves the Daytona 500. Came here one year in the nineties to watch it and decided they'd move here when he left the force." Hailey tried not to notice how Peter's cologne wafted through the car and made her want to snuggle up to him.

When they turned down a side street, cars were parked all over. Several signs indicating public parking lined the road. They pulled into a lot and Peter paid the man standing there.

"Looks like there's a big crowd," Peter said as they parked.

Peter opened her door and extended his hand to help her out. The minute her hand touched his, warmth traveled up her arm, sending ripples of energy across her back. "Thank you," she said as she let go.

Latin music rang through the air, catching her attention. She looked in the direction of the pulsating sounds.

"The festival is on the boardwalk over there," Peter said.

Throngs of people moved along the boardwalk while several hotels stood behind them. Peter and Hailey made their way over to the stairs that led up to the boardwalk. Booths with food and drinks lined either side, while people, most speaking in Spanish, walked along. "Is it like this all the time here?" Hailey asked.

"There always seems to be one festival or another going on. Always some big celebration." Peter smiled, making the skin around his eyes crinkle.

"Sounds fun." The rhythm of the music and the delectable smells of the food booths made Hailey want to let go and enjoy every moment of this night, but she reminded herself that she needed to stay in complete control. *This is a mercy date. Nothing else.*

"I should get out more," Peter said as he scanned the crowd.

"You should." Hailey fanned her arms out. "This is a beautiful place."

"You're right. I don't think I appreciate it like I should. Sometimes

I get so caught up in work, I forget to take time to smell the roses, as my grandma would say." He laughed.

"I think that happens to all of us. When it's tax season I can barely breathe, let alone enjoy the mountains or skiing or any of the things that people come to Colorado to experience." Hailey couldn't remember the last time she'd gone skiing.

They walked past a booth selling tacos. The fragrant scent of oil and onions made Hailey's stomach growl. Peter must've noticed her ogling the authentic food because he said, "How about we get something here?"

"Sure." Hailey loved Mexican food. She could easily subsist on tacos and burritos for the rest of her life.

Peter ordered some tacos and they took them over to a grassy area. There weren't any chairs or tables, so Hailey sat on the ground. Peter followed suit.

Hailey bit into the fried tortilla and spicy meat. It was the best taco she'd ever had.

"Like it?" Peter asked, his sparkling blue eyes watching her.

"It's delicious." She wished she'd grabbed a napkin because some of the taco juice slid down her chin. She used the back of her hand to wipe it up, hoping Peter didn't notice.

"Do you like being an accountant?" Peter said, handing her a napkin.

Great. He saw me drool. She wiped her chin and then tried to focus on his question, so she could say something reasonably intelligent. "I like that numbers make sense. They're black and white. You don't have to interpret them. They just are. People are so many shades of gray."

"And that's exactly what I enjoy about my job. Learning about people. I see many of them toward the end of their lives, but each of their stories is unique. Take Harry's, for example. I didn't know he was a policeman. He must've seen so much when he was on the force."

"Oh, yeah. He has lots of stories." She picked an olive from her taco and popped it in her mouth. "Some of them are pretty heartbreaking, but a few were wonderful. He's had a full life."

"I bet you've spent hours listening to him." Peter bit into his taco.

"I have, but now I wish I'd spent more time." Hailey tried to push the regret away.

Peter used a napkin to wipe his mouth. "Time is the one thing that keeps on ticking no matter what. Once it's gone, it's gone. No rain checks and no refunds."

"I've realized that this trip more than any other." Hailey let out a long breath. The reality that both her grandparents were getting older pierced her heart. *How many more visits will I have with them?* She thrust that question from her mind.

Peter studied her.

"What?" Her cheeks warmed. *Do I have something on my face?*

Peter's eyes shone. "You really love him. And your grandmother."

She nodded. "Yeah, I do." It was hard to describe the deep feelings she had for Gran and Gramps, but somehow Peter seemed to understand. She took the last bite of her taco and hoped she wouldn't drool anymore.

"You're so compassionate with him. Some family members can be difficult to deal with. Some are even downright mean to their loved ones." He took a bite of his taco. When he finished chewing, he said, "It makes me feel bad when patients aren't treated well by their families."

Hailey was touched by Peter's sincerity. "I just want Gramps to be like his old self."

Peter nodded and finished his taco. He stood, then extended his hand. Hailey took it, but this time Peter held onto it. They began walking, and as they neared the outdoor theater, the music became too loud to talk over. They stood inside the area, still holding hands, and listened. Hailey liked how her hand felt so comfortable inside Peter's. She immediately reminded herself to be careful, but she didn't remove her hand.

Since Hailey didn't speak Spanish, she didn't understand the words to the song, but the beat was still catchy, and she tapped her foot in time. She snuck a glance at Peter and he was rapping his other hand against his thigh. Adults and children began dancing. Before she knew it, Peter led her out closer to the band. He started to dance, and, against her better judgment, she fell into the rhythm, letting her body—from the top of her head to the tips of her toes—feel the music. She tossed her head back, and then Peter pulled her to him. The sounds of the guitar and drums rang all around her. Several little girls started to circle them, smiling and laughing. Hailey began clapping to the beat, the corners of her mouth curling into a wide grin. She hadn't had this much fun in a long time. Being with Peter and dancing under the twilight sky with puffs of colorful clouds overhead was a perfect combination. They danced to several fast songs, and she found herself wanting to keep dancing like this all night.

When the music slowed, Peter pulled her close. Too close for her to think clearly. With his hand on the small of her back and his other hand clasped around hers, they swayed to the Latin sounds. Her heart threatened to dive out of her chest when he rested his warm, smooth cheek on hers. A tug-of-war raged between her heart and her head as she struggled to keep her thoughts on the music instead of on the man that held her, but it was a losing battle.

She was grateful when a Hispanic man with a brightly colored shirt approached the microphone and said in a heavy Spanish accent, "Gracias. The band is taking a break now."

The crowd started to disperse.

Peter smiled. "Probably a good time for us to take a break too. We could go get some dessert."

"I'd like that." A break would help her clear her mind. Before they could move, Hailey looked beyond Peter and saw a woman with a sour expression dressed in heels, black leggings, and an extremely low-cut leopard print shirt walking toward them. Hailey recognized her from the therapy office.

"Uh, oh," Hailey said. "She doesn't seem happy."

"Huh?" Peter gave her a puzzled look.

The woman extended her hand and placed it on Peter's shoulder. He turned. "Uh, Joyce. Hi. Good to see you here." His words were stilted.

Joyce eyed Hailey up and down. "So this is what you meant when you said you had plans."

"Oh." He looked between Hailey and Joyce, obviously uneasy. He stammered, "I . . . uh . . ."

"Actually," Hailey interjected, "my grandmother asked Peter to bring me here, so I could experience some, what did she call it?" Hailey glanced at Peter. "Young people activities?"

"Yeah, I think that's what she said." Peter nodded.

"Peter was kind enough to agree. Although, he really had no choice." Hailey laughed. "Gran was quite insistent."

"I see," Joyce said, a muscle under her eye constricting almost imperceptibly.

"Would you like to join us?" Hailey asked, trying to diffuse what seemed to be an uncomfortable situation.

"You're welcome to," Peter said, the muscles in his neck tightening slightly.

Joyce's scowl relaxed a bit. "Sounds like fun, but I need to get back to my friends."

"Oh, we understand." He nodded. "It was good to see you."

Joyce gave a jerk of her head, then sashayed away.

"I take it she wasn't happy to see you here," Hailey asked with a lift of her brow.

Peter's mouth tensed.

"Want to tell me about it?" Hailey said, curious for his response.

Peter massaged the back of his neck. "Joyce hasn't made it much of a secret she'd like me to take her out."

"But you don't want to?" She peered at him.

"No." His eyes widened. "She's a nice person, but not my type."

Hailey watched Peter. Wanting more details, she asked, "What did she mean about tonight?"

"Joyce wanted me to come dancing with her." He shifted his weight. "I told her I had plans."

Interpreting the meaning behind his words, Hailey said, "But you haven't told her you aren't interested?"

"Not exactly."

"You should tell her. Women would rather know a man isn't interested than think he is."

Peter's gaze caught hers. "What about when a man *is* interested?"

Hailey swallowed quickly and her heartbeat quickened. "Women like to know that too."

He started walking and she followed. They stopped and stood near the railing that overlooked the beach. The almost-full moon was rising over the sea, its reflection bouncing on the ripples of the water.

Changing the direction of their conversation, Hailey said, "What was it like growing up in Orlando? Were you at Disney World all the time?"

Peter laughed and his shoulders eased. "Orlando seems to be synonymous with Disney. I worked there for about a year to save money for college."

"Oh yeah? What did you do?" She imagined he was in customer service because he was so good with people. Or maybe Prince Charming. *Are you serious? Stop thinking things like that.*

"I was a Jungle Ride Skipper."

She blinked. "You told all those lame jokes?"

"Yes, yes I did." The corners of his mouth lifted.

"I'm surprised." This man intrigued her.

He pointed to himself with mock indignation. "You don't think I can tell corny jokes?"

"I didn't picture you as a skipper, that's all."

He leaned back against the railing and gave her a sideways glance. "Where did you think I worked?"

"I'm not sure, but something . . . less flashy." She was tripping all over her words.

He gave her a confused expression. "Skippers are flashy?"

She searched for a different description. "Gregarious is a better word. You seem more reserved."

He straightened. "I'll have you know that I had crowds of people laughing at my jokes. The same jokes. Over and over and over again."

Hailey chuckled at the thought of Peter telling silly jokes to a boatload of people. "I would like to have seen that."

"Have you been to Disney World?"

"After Gran and Gramps moved out here we came to visit a few times and did the whole Disney thing." The memories made her smile. "I haven't been for six years or so."

He gazed at her. "Maybe we should remedy that."

Her heart skittered and her mouth went dry. "Maybe we should."

Peter cleared his throat. "Let's get dessert. I saw some churros over there." He pointed down the boardwalk.

They walked over to a booth, and Peter bought two of the long, skinny pastries and handed one to Hailey. They walked further down, away from the crowd. The moon rose higher in the sky and twilight began turning to darkness.

Hailey took a bite of her churro, the cinnamon sugar dancing on her tongue. "Mmm, this is yummy."

"I'm glad you like it." Peter gazed ahead. "And I'm glad we came here."

"Even if you were coerced?"

He didn't say anything for a few moments. "Coerced is a strong word." His smile gleamed even in the moonlight. "Maybe encouraged."

"No, I'd definitely say coerced. My grandmother is relentless." Hailey took another bite of her churro. When she finished, she said, "She runs a dating service, you know."

Peter jerked his head back. "What?"

"Yep. Gran and some of her friends have this big book filled with photos and bios of single people, and they match them up. Regularly."

Hailey was still trying to wrap her head around it.

Peter started laughing. "You're kidding, right?"

Hailey slipped another bite into her mouth. "No. Not kidding. That's why I say you were coerced into tonight. Gran was at her finest today. You literally had no choice. She's a professional." It was all true, but Hailey had to admit she was fishing a bit.

They walked along a pathway next to the ocean without saying anything, every step convincing Hailey that Peter felt compelled to be with her because of Gran's insistence and for no other reason. The longer they walked, the more she wanted to jump into the water and swim away.

Finally, Peter said, "Coerced is definitely not the word I would use."

Hailey's heart skipped a couple of beats. "It's not?"

"No." He gently placed his hand in hers.

Warmth coursed through Hailey and tempting thoughts swirled in her mind. Not only was Peter handsome, but he was interesting and fun. She hadn't felt this relaxed or at ease in a long time. Not even with Kevin, which meant she was treading in dangerous waters. She reminded herself that she couldn't afford to get her heart involved because it would only lead to anguish. Wouldn't it? It was much smarter to keep things uncomplicated between them—even if that wasn't what she wanted—because that made the most logical sense. "Uh, I should probably get back. I want to check on Gramps." It sounded like an excuse—which it was—but she needed some space so she could gain control over her disobedient feelings.

They made their way back to the parking lot still holding hands. Hailey knew better, but she couldn't convince herself to let go of his hand until he opened her door. Inside the car, Peter reached for her hand again and she complied. His soft fingers gently closed around hers and he caressed her thumb. The simple gesture captured her attention and she stared at their intertwined fingers, awed at how natural it all felt. A little voice inside her head tried to remind her that this wasn't the best idea, but she ignored it for the moment.

As they drove, the cooled air from the AC filled the car, but it did little to counteract the heat that inched its way up Hailey's arm. They drove in silence for a few minutes, but it wasn't awkward or uncomfortable. In fact, it felt peaceful.

When they passed by the Daytona International Speedway, Hailey's thoughts shifted to her grandfather. "You know, of all the things that could've been affected by his stroke, speech was the worst one for Gramps. He loves to talk and joke around. He would've been an excellent Jungle Boat Skipper." The image of Gramps on a boat telling stories made Hailey smile.

Peter squeezed her hand. "I'd like to see that."

"Me too." Without warning, fear wrapped around her and anxiety set in. "I sure hope . . ." She didn't want to finish the sentence.

"I've seen people like Harry regain a lot of their speech. I'm very hopeful. And with you helping him, he'll get there," Peter said with certainty.

"Thanks." Hearing his confidence helped settle Hailey's nerves. Maybe Gramps really would be his old self again.

They drove up to the house. Peter opened her door for her. *He's such a gentleman, which is so rare these days.*

"Thank you. It was a lot of fun." She meant it more than she should. *Remember, you're going back home. This can't go anywhere. It can't.*

"I enjoyed it very much. Thank you." Peter lingered for a moment.

Her chest constricted. *He's not going to kiss me, is he? I don't want him to. Do I? No, I don't. That would complicate things way too much. No kissing.*

"I had a great time." He seemed to be stalling.

"Me too." *Maybe a little kiss wouldn't hurt. Stop. No kissing! Back away and stop looking at his lips.*

He took a few steps backward. His foot caught the edge of an ornamental rock and he stumbled. Hailey tried to reach out for him, but before she knew it, he was on the ground in a heap.

Her eyes grew as wide as the plains of Colorado while she stared at him, her mouth gaping open. She wasn't sure what to say. Or do. The obvious mortification colored his cheeks, and she didn't want to make it worse by reacting, but she was worried he'd hurt himself. "Are you okay?" She wanted to reach out for him, but instead she stood there motionless, unsure of how to temper the situation.

Peter jumped to his feet and brushed grass clippings from his shirt, a look of pure disgust on his face. "I'm fine."

"I think you scraped your elbow." She pointed to a spot on his arm. "Can I get you a bandage?"

He waved his hand. "No, it's okay. I'll see you later." He turned and hurried back to his car.

Hailey wanted to tell Peter it was no big deal, but she'd been in a similar situation on a date in high school when she'd tripped over a curb and ripped a hole in her pants. She remembered wishing she'd evaporated on the spot and never wanting to see that boy again. *I hope that doesn't happen with Peter.*

Hailey gazed at the empty street after he'd driven away. A thousand thoughts tumbled in her head. The best idea was to "nip this whole thing in the bud," as Gran would say, before it went too far. Yes, that's what she needed to do. Nip it, and nip it fast.

She glanced at the hand that had held Peter's and clutched it to her chest. *Nipping it is the right thing to do. Isn't it?*

Chapter 20

Right in front of her! Peter wanted to disappear and never see Hailey again. His neck still burned from the shame. *Who falls backward in front of a woman on the first date?* He shook his head in disgrace.

He didn't think he could ever face her again. He pushed out a breath and hit the steering wheel. *Great impression, Pete. Way to go.*

He parked his car, then went inside his apartment and fell onto the couch. The night had been awesome. Walking along the boardwalk, getting to know Hailey, even the churros were delicious—everything had been going so well. Until he took her home. He planted his face in his palms.

His phone vibrated. It was a text from Laura.

Are you home yet?

Yep. He sent back.

How was the date?

He paused, then tapped out, *Great. Terrible.*

Huh?

Never mind. He didn't want to explain, especially over a text.

Almost immediately his phone lit up.

Not at all surprised, he answered, "Hi."

"What do you mean it was great *and* terrible?" He could hear the confusion in her voice.

Peter sat up. "We went to the boardwalk for the Mar y Sol festival."

"Was that the great part or the terrible part?"

"Great." He couldn't help but grin at the memory of the evening.

"Am I missing something? What was terrible about it?" Peter didn't have to see the expression on his sister's face to know she didn't understand what he meant.

He rubbed his forehead. "When I took her home."

Laura let out a gasp. "You didn't try to kiss her or something, did you? On the first date?"

"No. Of course not. As much as I wanted to kiss her, and even considered it for a minute, I didn't. I wanted to be a gentleman."

"Then *what?*" Her voice rose.

Peter closed his eyes, wishing he could erase what happened. "As I was saying goodbye, I backed up and . . ."

"Yeah?" she said expectantly.

"Fell." There he said it.

Laura started laughing. Peter tapped his leg while he waited for her to finish. "Are you done?"

"You actually fell down? Like really fell?"

"Yes. Right in front of her. Spread eagle on the ground and everything." He cradled his head.

"Smooth move." She started laughing again.

"Any words of actual encouragement? Like, 'She probably didn't even notice,' or 'Don't worry, everyone does that on the first date.' You know, something helpful."

Laura stopped laughing. "I'm sure it wasn't that big of a thing. Really." She let out a snort. "Sorry."

"I can't ask her out again. I'm too embarrassed." He couldn't, could he? "The rules of the universe dictate that I never return to the site of, nor persons involved in, said humiliation." He tried to sound businesslike, as if such rules existed.

Laura chortled. "Oh, please. That's stupid," she said. "And a lame excuse." A vision of her rolling her eyes popped into his mind.

"It's a waste of time anyway. She's going back to Colorado." That sounded reasonable, even if he wished it weren't true.

"And you can't go out and have fun while she's here?" Laura was beginning to annoy him.

"What's the point?" He wasn't interested in a fling, and he didn't want to tangle his heart strings with someone who would only be here temporarily. This whole thing was ill-fated from the beginning. He should've gracefully declined when her grandmother suggested it.

"You have been out of the game for way too long."

"I know. Purposely. Dating is the worst." Why did he have to date anyone? He was happy living on his own. He didn't have to answer to anybody. He could come and go as he pleased. He didn't want or need anyone to complicate his life. Or worse, to trample all over his heart.

"I think you should ask her out again. She doesn't seem like the type of girl who would hold your clumsiness against you." Laura was insistent.

He didn't want to argue with his sister, so he said, "I'll see her when she brings her grandfather in. And go from there. But I'm hanging up now because I need to get some sleep."

"Talk to you later."

Peter went into his bathroom and looked at himself in the mirror. Sure, Hailey was fun and easy to talk to. And beautiful. And she smelled nice. Very nice. The date was great, except for the whole falling episode. He pointed at himself and said with conviction, "You don't need the aggravation." He nodded. Keeping it professional was the best plan.

Chapter 21

Gran and Gramps had been asleep when Hailey got home, so she'd gone back to her bedroom. After she changed into her pajamas and brushed her teeth, she went into the kitchen for a drink of water. She didn't bother to turn on the light when she filled her glass at the refrigerator.

"How was your date?"

Hailey jumped back and grabbed at her chest. "Gran, you scared me to death."

"I'm sorry. I didn't mean to, but I wanted to hear all about your night." Gran flipped on the kitchen light.

Hailey took a few breaths to calm her heart rate, then sipped her water. "It was good."

Gran studied her with a discriminating eye. "That seems vague."

"Okay." She leaned against the counter and swirled the water in her glass. "You win. I had a great time."

"I knew it," Gran said with a smug tone.

"You're still not off the hook for pressuring him into asking me." Hailey had to wonder how many unsuspecting people in Gran's binder were tricked into going out.

"Who cares how it happened. The important thing is you went.

When is your next date?" Gran's eyes lit up.

"Let's not get ahead of ourselves here." She took a swig of water. "Remember, I'm eventually going back to Colorado."

Gran peered at Hailey. "You might as well enjoy your time here with a good-looking man."

"I could go out with Darren again. That *is* what you and Lila cooked up, right?" It was only fair to use Gran's conniving against her.

"Pish, posh. Lila and I were hopeful, that's all. And Darren's nice." Gran grabbed a glass from the cupboard and filled it with water. "But no crackle and sizzle like between you and Peter."

Hailey tried not to smile at her grandmother's enthusiasm. "Crackle and sizzle? That's ridiculous."

Gran held up a finger. "Matters of the heart are never ridiculous."

"You're making way more of this than there is. We went on one date." *A fantastic, fun, memorable date, but still just one.* Gran practically had them married off and living in a house with five kids.

"You need one date before you can have two, and then three and so on." Gran walked into the living room and Hailey followed her.

"Let's see what happens." Hailey put her hand on Gran's shoulder. "And for all that is good in this world, please, please do not say anything to him."

"Me?" Gran shrugged with an innocent expression. "I would *never* do that."

Hailey gave her grandmother the yeah-right-I've-already-seen-you-in-action look.

"You can't blame me for wanting to see you happy."

Someone rapped loudly on the door, making Hailey jump. She didn't have to wonder who it was. Hailey opened the door, and Regina stumbled inside. The stench of cheap alcohol oozed out in a cloud that surrounded her. "Hey, what're you two doing?"

"Oh, Regina," Gran said, her tone dripping with disappointment. "Why?"

"What, Momma?" Regina hiccupped.

Gran clucked her tongue. "You're drunk."

"Yeah, yeah I am." She cackled with a raspy voice.

"If you want to live here you can't come home like this." Gran put her hands on her hips.

"Why not? I ain't hurtin' no one. An' I only had a couple drinks. After I had a few beers." She laughed.

"Is this what you want do with your life?" Gran said softly, pain evident in her eyes.

"What I do with my life is none of your business," Regina said in a cold tone. She stepped close to her mom, dwarfing Gran with her girth.

"Regina, maybe you should go to bed," Hailey said. She couldn't stand how her aunt treated Gran and Gramps.

"Don't tell me what to do." Regina's eyes were bloodshot, and her breath was lethal.

"Don't talk to Hailey that way," Gran said.

"Why? Because she's Tommy's daughter? He was always your favorite. Maybe if you'd been nicer to me I mighta turned out different. It's your fault I'm like this."

Hailey knew she should stay out of it, but she'd had enough. "You can't blame Gran."

Regina turned toward her and took a few shaky steps. "Why not?"

"You are a grown woman." Hailey drew in a breath of courage. "You should be taking responsibility for your own actions. Your own choices. Stop blaming other people."

Regina narrowed her eyes and took an imposing stance. "Listen to Miss Hoity Toity over here. Like you know anything."

Hailey squared her shoulders. "I know that Gran and Gramps love you."

"Oh, please." Regina rolled her eyes. "They loved your daddy. Not me."

Gran's mouth dropped open. "What are you talking about?" Her voice shook. "That's not true."

Regina took a defiant stance. "Yeah, it is."

"You know we never treated you differently than your brother." Gran breathed heavily with emotion. "We loved you both. Equally."

"Sure didn't feel like it. You gave him all the good attention and were always on me about something or other." Regina held up a finger. "I was never good enough or smart enough. And definitely never pretty enough." Regina let out a burp.

"You aren't being fair. We only wanted what was best for you," Gran said.

"Nah." Regina took an unsteady step. "All you wanted was for your perfect son to have a perfect life."

"Regina!" Gran's cheeks flushed red. "Where is this all coming from?"

"Guess I been holdin' it in all this time. Who knew?" She chuckled. "Must be from watchin' all them Dr. Phil shows."

"How dare you hurt Gran like this," Hailey said, her blood burning.

Regina's face hardened, and she wagged her finger at Hailey. "How dare you talk to me."

"Someone needs to." It was time to stand up to her aunt's bullying.

"Well, it ain't you." Regina smoothed her wild hair. "You got nothin' to say to me."

"You're so busy feeling sorry for yourself, you can't even see how much your parents love you. How much they've done for you. Woman up and take control of yourself. Your life is what *you* make it. You don't have to live this way." Hailey stood firm, her courage making her legs wobbly.

"Look, if I wanna go get drunk every night, that's my business." Regina pointed at herself with her thumb.

Hailey stepped closer to her aunt. "But you're bringing it here, making it our business."

Regina waved her hand. "I'm going to bed." She stomped off.

Hailey wanted to slap some sense into her, but she knew it

wouldn't do any good. Hearing Regina say such cruel things to Gran broke Hailey's heart.

Sure, Gran and Gramps weren't perfect parents, but they loved Regina. And Regina was there because she didn't have anywhere else to go, so Gran and Gramps took her in. They weren't fools—they knew why she was there.

Hailey's heartbeat thudded in her ears and her face burned. Regina made her so angry she could spit fire.

Gran was on the couch, sobbing. Hailey went to her and put her arms around her. "I'm so sorry."

"I don't know why she's saying this. We were never mean to her." Gran sniffed. "We tried to encourage her to be something. To be better. To do good things with her life."

"Regina wants to blame you so she doesn't have to take responsibility for herself." Hailey caressed Gran's back.

Wiping at her eyes, Gran said, "Instead of encouragement, all she saw was us being critical?" Gran glanced up at the ceiling. "Maybe we are to blame."

"No, you're not." Hailey pulled Gran close. "She's lashing out at you because she's unhappy."

"What am I going to do with her?" Gran slumped against Hailey.

"I don't know." Hailey wished she had some wisdom to share with her grandmother, but she was at a complete loss. Her insides twisted at the thought of going back to Colorado and leaving Gran and Gramps to deal with Regina. She wasn't sure she could do that.

Chapter 22

Gran stood at the sink looking out the window as the morning sunlight streamed in when Hailey walked in.

"Regina is gone," Gran said in a thick voice.

"She is?" A wave of relief cascaded over Hailey.

"I checked her room." Gran faced Hailey. "All her stuff is gone. Just like that."

Hailey could see the anguish etched on her grandmother's face. "Any idea where?"

"I never know where." Gran cradled her head. After several moments, she said, "When I first held Regina in my arms, I had so many hopes. So many dreams for her." Gran's eyes glistened, and she seemed to be lost in another time. "She wanted to be a ballerina. Begged us to put her in ballet. She wasn't very graceful, but she tried hard." A slight smile crossed her lips. "Then she wanted to play the piano, so we gave her lessons. In high school, she was interested in several things, like theater and choir, but it wasn't easy for her like it was for your dad." Gran let out a breath. "I thought I was encouraging her and helping her. Instead . . ." her sentence trailed off.

Hailey put her arms around Gran. "I don't think—"

"You heard her. She thinks we favored your father. That we loved him, and we didn't love her." Gran stepped back, wiping at puffy eyes.

"We all know that isn't true."

"I gave her everything. I worked myself to the bone so she could have what she wanted. When she turned sixteen, we bought her a car. I don't understand." Gran collapsed into a kitchen chair.

Hailey sat in a chair next to Gran. "I don't know if she even understands. But I do know you can't blame yourself."

"Who else is there to blame?"

"Regina. She's a big girl. Has been for years." Hailey laid her hand on Gran's. "She's made choices and now she has to live with them."

"It's so hard to watch her live like this. I want to save her from herself." Gran seemed so defeated.

Hailey squeezed Gran's hand. "I don't think anyone can save Regina, *but* Regina."

They sat in silence for several minutes while Hailey tried to ignore the thoughts that darted through her mind about her own life and its lack of direction lately. It was easy to point fingers at Regina and see that she'd wasted years of her life without much to show for it, but what about Hailey? What did she have to show? A decent job. An average apartment. A car. She thought she'd been moving toward the next chapter of her life with Kevin, but that didn't pan out. So, where was she headed now? For sure she didn't want to end up like her aunt, twenty or thirty years down the road with a string of old boyfriends and nowhere to call home.

When was she going to take her own advice and live the life she wanted, instead of floundering and allowing herself to be a victim of Kevin's choices? Working all the time and watching Netflix while she hid out in her apartment to avoid Jimmy Vaughn and the rest of the world wasn't the life she'd pictured for herself. All she needed to do now was figure out what, exactly, she wanted.

"I'm glad you're here," Gran said, jolting Hailey back into reality. "I know you can't stay forever, but for now, I'm happy to have you. Thank you."

Hailey hated seeing the sorrow in Gran's eyes. She wanted to take it away. All of it. But she couldn't. "I love you, Gran." It was all she could offer.

Hailey finished checking over a few reports and making some notations in the file for Crandall Automotive. She fought the disappointment that she'd spent the last four hours working on spreadsheets and entering expenses for her clients instead of spending that time with her grandparents. She rubbed her eyes to counteract the strain from staring at the computer screen for so long when she heard a knock at the door. "I'll get it," Hailey said from her bedroom, eager for a break, but bracing herself in case it was her abrasive aunt returning for more carnage.

She opened the door to Darren. "Hi," he said, sporting a closely trimmed beard.

"Hi. How are you?" She hoped she didn't sound too surprised. He looked good in his cargo jean shorts and pale green polo shirt.

"Would you like to catch a movie later?" He raised his eyebrows and smiled.

"Yeah, I would." It'd be good to get her mind off the mess Regina had caused, and she needed a distraction from her confusing feelings about Peter.

"Great. I'll be back about seven o'clock?"

"Sure." A movie with Darren might be exactly what she needed to have some light-hearted fun.

"See you then." He gave her a wave.

Hailey shut the door.

"Who was that?" Gran asked from the kitchen.

"Darren. He's taking me to a movie." Hailey stepped up to the counter and helped Gran put clean dishes away.

"I'm glad you're getting out. Even if you don't like him much."

Gran put a glass in the cupboard.

"Not true." A mischievous smile spread across Hailey's face, and she filled a glass of water. "He's hot. I mean, so hot he's on fire." She fanned herself. "Whew!"

Gran shook her head. "In my day, we would've called him a dreamboat. Doesn't that sound better?"

Hailey laughed and decided to play along. "Okay, Darren is a *dreamboat*. Happy?"

"Yes." Gran removed her brightly colored apron and smoothed her neon-pink blouse.

"He's super nice too. A perfect date." Hailey took in a gasp of air and laid the back of her hand across her forehead. "Maybe even marriage material. Why, Gran, I think you might've found me a husband," Hailey teased dramatically.

Gran rolled her eyes.

"Isn't that what you and Lila wanted? To have us date and then marry us off together?" Hailey began drinking her water.

Gran sighed. "That might have crossed our minds." She held her hand up. "But that was before I realized you carried a torch for the speech therapist."

Hailey sputtered and coughed. "I *carry a torch* for him?" She set her glass down and wiped her mouth.

Gran faced Hailey squarely. "That's not quite right. Carrying a torch for someone means unrequited love, and that's not true. He most definitely returns the favor."

"Is that right?" Hailey leaned against the counter and crossed her arms in front of her chest.

"Absolutely. Like I said before, I know these things." Gran gave Hailey a confident nod.

No longer interested in teasing, Hailey shifted her weight. "Remember when I said I wasn't interested in a relationship?"

"That *is* what you said." Gran walked into the living room.

Hailey followed her and said. "But you don't believe me."

Gran shook her head.

Hailey wanted to convince her, but Peter was making her think things she didn't want to think and feel things she didn't want to feel. It wasn't that she never wanted a relationship again. She did. Eventually. But right now, she needed to focus on her grandparents. Besides, what would happen when she returned to Colorado? She absolutely did not want to return home only to nurse another empty, aching heart.

After some silence, Gran said, "I haven't heard a word from Regina. Not that I expect to." She fluffed a pillow on the couch and adjusted a picture frame near the table lamp.

"I bet she'll be back." Hailey wasn't sure which was better—that Regina stay away or come back, which would inevitably lead to more trouble.

Gran's eyes watered. Hailey wrapped her arms around her fragile grandmother. "Things will be okay."

"I hope so, dear."

When Gramps walked into the living room several minutes later, Hailey glanced at the gaudy gold clock on the wall. "Hey, Gramps, how about we work on some of your words?"

Gramps bristled at the idea.

"Please? It'll be fun." Hailey gave him an encouraging smile. She felt pressure to work with Gramps as much as possible because the more she worked with him, the sooner he'd regain his speech, and that was the reason she was here.

He gave her a softened look, indicating that he'd comply.

Hailey grabbed the worksheets as well as some flashcards she'd made from index cards from the list of common words they'd been working on.

They began their impromptu therapy session. Gramps struggled to make sentences, but he was saying some of the words more clearly. Hailey wanted to keep pushing him, but she could see he was becoming fatigued.

"You've done great today, Gramps." She gave him a hug. "I'm so proud of you for working hard. I know it isn't easy."

"Th-th-thank you," he said.

"You are so welcome." She gathered the index cards together.

Gramps pointed at the middle of his chest, then pointed at Hailey. "L-l-love."

"I love you too, Gramps."

Hailey brushed through her long hair and then added some lip gloss. Going out with Darren would be fun. *It would.* She adjusted her pastel yellow shirt and added a pair of gold earrings. She decided to wait in the living room where Gramps was watching a movie.

"May I join you?" Memories of snuggling up with Gramps and watching movies filled Hailey with nostalgia and, once again, she was grateful she'd come to Florida to help her grandparents and make some new memories.

Gramps straightened in his chair and brushed at his brown plaid shirt.

Hailey sat on the couch near Gramps and said, "I have a date pretty soon."

He gave her a knowing smile and touched his mouth.

Hailey knew exactly what he meant, but refused to acknowledge it. "Does your mouth hurt?" she asked with mock concern.

He shook his head.

"Oh, I know. You're hungry."

Gramps rolled his eyes and gave her an irritated look.

Hailey didn't want to upset Gramps, so she said, "My date is with Lila's grandson, Darren."

Wrinkling his nose, Gramps shrugged a shoulder.

Her grandparents were both plotting against her. They meant well, but she preferred they stay out of her love life, such as it was. Or wasn't. "What are you watching?" she said.

Gramps tried to say a few words but they didn't make any sense. He tried again, but they were all gibberish. After another attempt, he let out an expletive.

"Harry, why are you cursing at Hailey?" Gran said sharply as she walked in, her perfume filling the room with a fragrant gardenia scent.

Gramps pushed out a breath of aggravation.

"He wasn't swearing at me, Gran. He's frustrated that he can't tell me what movie this is."

Gran glanced at the TV. "Oh, that's Cary Grant in *North by Northwest*. Handsome fellow that man. I loved him in *An Affair to Remember*. One of my favorite movies."

Gran sat on the couch next to Hailey and grabbed her knitting. "You're waiting for Darren?"

"Yeah. He should be here any minute." Hailey fumbled with the buttons on her shirt.

After fifteen minutes, Gran looked up from her knitting and said, "I wonder where he is."

"Must be running late." Hailey was losing interest in the date as each minute passed.

"I could call Lila to see where he is," Gran suggested.

Hailey crossed her legs and sat back against the couch, absently fiddling with the earring in her right ear. "No. I'll wait." She had to admit she wasn't in any particular hurry to spend time with Darren. Sure, he was handsome and nice, but Gran was right—no *crackle and sizzle*, as Gran had said, between them.

Another ten minutes passed.

"Odd that he hasn't come." Gran turned her knitting and started a new row. "Maybe he isn't a punctual sort of young man."

"Or maybe he decided he didn't want to go out after all." Hailey was a bit miffed now. Was he standing her up?

They finished watching the movie. If she'd been born a hundred years or so earlier she would've found Cary Grant attractive with his dark hair and brilliant smile.

"We can watch another one. I'll make some popcorn in the microwave," Gran offered. "I'm sure something came up. He didn't strike me as a man who wouldn't keep a date."

"Whatever." Hailey wasn't that invested, but she was still bugged. She didn't want to talk about it, and Gran seemed to be avoiding the subject Hailey was sure was on her mind: Regina.

"Look, Harry, *Rear Window* is on." Gran turned to Hailey. "Your grandfather has always been sweet on that Grace Kelly."

Gramps didn't even try to hide his smile.

"Such a beauty. Real shame how she died in that car accident. She was a princess, you know."

Hailey nodded. She had no idea who Gran was talking about.

After watching the movie, eating some popcorn, and downing a bowl of ice cream, Hailey said, "I better get some sleep. If I stay out here any longer, I'll have to roll myself down the hall to my bedroom."

"Good night," Gran said. "I'm sure there's a reasonable explanation for Darren not coming."

"I guess." Darren wasn't the first guy to choose something, or someone, else. Kevin came to mind immediately, but Hailey shooed him right back out of her head.

Chapter 23

Hailey awoke to her phone playing a clip from Adele's song, *Hello*. Wasn't it too early in the morning for a phone call? Especially on the weekend. She glanced at the caller ID. *Oh great.* "Hello?" She tried to sound chipper—like she'd been up for hours.

"Hailey?" his voice was gruff.

"Mr. Michaels." Hailey rubbed the sleep from her eyes and tried to get her bearings.

"Did you get my email?"

Hailey sat up in bed. "Yes," she lied. She hadn't even looked at her email before going to bed last night.

"Can you get me the information?" He sounded anxious.

"Yes." Whatever it was, she could get it. She'd have to.

"And what about the Carver account? The new one I sent you. Have you filed the reports?"

"I was planning to do that today." At least she was planning to do that right after this phone call, even though it was Sunday. When it came to business, Mr. Michaels didn't care what day of the week it was. Or how early. *Does he ever take a day off?*

"I'll look for your email." He said it in a way that left no doubt she had to get back to him ASAP.

"Yes, sir."

Hailey ended the call and immediately went to her phone settings to give her boss a customized ring so she'd know it was him next time. She'd been trying to keep up working on her accounts, but Mr. Michaels was quite the task master, even from across the country.

Hailey found her laptop and logged on to her email. She searched through her files to find what Mr. Michaels needed. She breathed a sigh of relief when she found it and sent him the information. Then she began filing reports for the Carver account.

"Hailey?" came Gran's voice through the door.

"Yeah?"

"Darren is here."

What? Was he coming to give her some excuse why he ditched her last night? "I'll be out in a minute."

She grabbed some shorts and a T-shirt, then ran into the bathroom to brush her teeth and put her hair in a messy bun. No time for make-up. *This is as good as it gets, especially after being stood up last night.*

When she walked out into the living room it was somber. Darren stood by the front door wearing a wrinkled shirt. His hair was disheveled and his normally vibrant eyes were bloodshot and sad. *He looks awful.*

"What's going on?" Hailey asked, feeling concerned.

"I wanted to come by and let you know what happened." Darren's voice was heavy.

Obviously, something was off. "What's wrong?"

Darren glanced at the ground. "I left here yesterday and went to my grandma's. Apparently, she'd fallen while I was gone and hit her head. She was disoriented when I found her."

"Poor Lila." Gran covered her mouth.

"Is she okay?" Hailey asked.

"I took her to the hospital and she seemed fine. But then . . ." He paused and ran his fingers through his hair. "She passed away during the night."

Gran gasped. "No, no. Not Lila. She was so vivacious. And one of my dear friends. She can't be gone. She can't."

Hailey was stunned by the news. "I'm so sorry."

"Me too." Darren nodded. "It doesn't feel real."

"What can we do to help?" Gran asked, her voice shaky. She moved closer to Darren and rubbed his shoulder.

"My parents are on their way." He looked at Hailey. "I didn't want you to think I'd blown you off."

"Don't even worry about that," she said, feeling guilty for her accusatory thoughts.

"I better get back," Darren said. He shuffled over to the door and let himself out.

Hailey hugged Gran. "I'm so sorry about your friend."

Gran took a few steps back and wiped at her face. "My friends keep dying. First, it was Edith back in March. She was younger than I am. Then JaneAnn and Brenda both passed just days apart last month. My heart can't take it."

Hailey caressed her grandmother's back. It must be so hard for Gran to lose her friends and see so many around her die. *As long as Gramps isn't one of them.* Hailey thrust that thought from her mind immediately. "What can I do?"

"I don't know. I still have Lila's book about container gardening." Gran shook her head. "I guess she won't need it back." Tears slipped down Gran's cheeks.

Chapter 24

A few days later, Hailey accompanied Gran and Gramps to Lila's funeral. Gran had toned down her normally bright wardrobe and wore a simple dark green dress. Gramps sported a charcoal suit with a forest-green striped tie, which complemented Gran's dress. Hailey hadn't packed any outfits for a funeral. She hoped she didn't stand out too much in her blue summer dress.

The service was held in a small church a mile or so from the retirement community. Lila and her husband, Don, who'd died more than five years ago, had lived in the area for forty years, so the church was filled with her family and friends.

The strong scent of cut flowers enveloped Hailey as she sat on a pew toward the back. She hadn't known Lila long, but it struck her how this woman was vibrant and full of life last week. Lila had been so eager to introduce Hailey to Darren, and her smile had sparkled when she spoke of her grandson. Then, without warning, she was gone. Life was so fragile. *Too fragile*. Hailey wanted to drink in every drop of her time with her grandparents instead of spending so much time working while she was there.

This week had almost felt like she was back at the office with all the extra requests from Mr. Michaels. He'd added another client to her workload, and she'd spent nearly all day yesterday going through expense records and populating a new spreadsheet with all the numbers. The more time she spent with her grandparents, the more she realized that numbers were constant, dependable, and black and white, but they failed to give her the same satisfaction she'd once had—the satisfaction she now felt helping Gran and Gramps. People might be various shades of gray, but maybe the beauty of life was experiencing those shades.

A group of women sang a song, and Lila's oldest daughter offered the eulogy. Lila had lived a full and interesting life. When Hailey was a teen, she'd thought old people were kind of creepy with their wrinkled hands, strange ideas, and old-fashioned vocabulary. She loved her grandparents, but other old people freaked her out. As Hailey had grown older, she realized that these people were more than baggy skin and thinning hair. They had lives. They'd lived and done things. They'd been happy, sad, angry, hurt. They had talents and dreams.

Something Peter said popped into her head and she smiled. He was right. The older generation had wisdom and were sometimes, maybe even many times, marginalized by the younger generation. The millennials didn't seem to have much use for the baby boomers, who'd experienced so much and learned from those life experiences.

Hailey hadn't heard from or seen Peter since their date at Mar y Sol on Friday night. It wasn't that she expected to hear from him necessarily, but it would've been kind of nice. Even though they'd had a fantastic date, each day that passed with no contact reinforced what she suspected: he'd taken her out simply because he'd been trapped into it, which was fine. *Really*. Gramps had an upcoming appointment and she planned to act like nothing had ever happened. It'd be easier that way.

After the service, Gran and Gramps extended their sympathy to Lila's family.

Darren approached Hailey and said, "It was great getting to meet you." He sunk his hands into the pockets of his navy dress pants.

"What are your plans?" she asked.

"I'm flying to Phoenix tomorrow. I'm starting my job next week." He rolled his lips inward.

Hailey looked at Darren. "I'm so sorry about your grandma."

"Thanks." He tried to smile but it didn't reach his eyes.

She touched him on the arm in a sympathetic gesture. "I'm sure she appreciated you being here."

"I'm glad I came." He shrugged.

Feeling a little awkward, Hailey said, "Good luck in Phoenix."

He nodded and walked away. Besides being good-looking, Darren was a decent guy. If things had been different, maybe they would've dated. Or not. Regardless, it was nice to know a good guy existed out there in the wicked world of dating.

"I think we're ready to go," Gran said when Hailey approached her and Gramps.

They walked out to the parking lot behind the small, white church. The noon air was heavy with moisture and the hot temperature caused perspiration to bead along Hailey's hairline.

"Eat," Gramps said.

Hailey smiled. Gramps was doing fairly well communicating with his limited vocabulary. "Where should we go?" Hailey asked, dabbing at her forehead.

"Harry likes Red Lobster." Gran smiled at Gramps and looped her arm through his. "He likes to take me on dates there. Isn't that right?"

Gramps patted Gran's hand, then leaned his head against hers, wearing a sincere grin.

"He's still a catch, my Harry," Gran said.

Hailey watched them walk, arm-in-arm, across the parking lot, the moment tugging at her heart. *How much longer will they have each other? How much longer will I be able to spend time with them?* She pushed these questions aside because considering the answers was too daunting.

They arrived at the restaurant and sat next to a large window, the scent of garlic and seafood wafting through the room. After they placed their orders, Gran said, "I haven't heard at all from Regina. I'm afraid . . ."

"There's no reason to worry. I'm sure she's fine. Probably off exploring the world again." Hailey didn't care much where her aunt was, but she didn't want Gran to worry.

"But look what happened with Lila. She was fine one day, then gone the next. What if something happens to Regina?"

"I bet she'll show up again—"

"In a month? A year? Who knows when she'll come home again or contact us? I worry about her." Gran's eyes moistened.

Hailey held her grandmother's hand. "I know. It's hard to have her live like she does. But I know she loves you."

"She has a funny way of showing it." Gran's mouth twitched.

"Yes, she does." *Actually, she has a terrible way of showing it.*

Gramps shook his head. Hailey didn't need words to know he was disgusted with the actions of his daughter; she could see it painted all over his face. How could Regina hurt them like this?

They finished their meals without saying much and then made their way back to the house.

"I'm sure tired," Gran said as they stepped inside. "I think I'd like to take a nap."

"Gramps and I will find something to do." Hailey was sleepy herself, and the accounts she needed to attend to weighed on her, but she didn't want to leave Gramps alone.

Gran wagged her finger at them. "Don't get into any trouble."

"Us?" Hailey put her arm around Gramps. "We'd never get into trouble, would we?"

Gramps shook his head with an innocent expression.

After Gran left, Hailey said, "So what'll it be? A game of cards? A movie?"

Gramps pointed through the window to the car.

"A drive?"

He nodded.

Hailey blinked. She thought they'd stay home, but if Gramps wanted to take a drive she was more than happy to oblige.

Chapter 25

Peter spun his phone on his desk. He picked it up, then set it down. He leaned back in his chair. He wanted to take Hailey on another date, but he was still embarrassed that he'd fallen right in front of her. She probably thought he was a first-class idiot. He glanced out the window. *Am I making too much out of this?*

"Knock, knock," Laura said, interrupting his thoughts.

"I didn't expect to see you here at the office." His sister didn't usually come to see him at work.

"I brought you a sandwich from the deli." She handed him a sack. "It's your favorite. Italian with pepper jack cheese."

Peter pulled out the sandwich and took a whiff. "That was nice of you."

"Maybe." She quirked an eyebrow.

"Huh?" He peered at her.

"It's a bribe."

Peter shook his head. He knew where this was headed. "No."

"No, what?" Laura gave him a perplexed expression and tried to look innocuous.

"I am not going to come over for another blind date ambush."

"Blind date ambush?" She sat in the chair across from his desk.

"With your friend . . . I can't remember her name." The only woman's name that bounced around his brain was Hailey's.

"Oh, please. Like that was torture." She playfully rolled her eyes. "You had to spend some time with a beautiful, smart woman. Poor you."

When she said it like that it made him sound a little dramatic. But the truth was, he only wanted to spend time with Hailey. "I don't want to—"

"Relax." She waved her hand. "I'm not trying to set you up on a date."

"Oh." *That's a relief.*

"I came by to see if there's any chance you can grab Benji again for me tonight?"

"Sure." Peter loved spending time with his nephew. "You didn't have to bring me a sandwich, you know."

Laura blew out a breath, then said, "I hate asking you."

"Why?" That didn't make any sense.

"Because he's my responsibility and I should be the one—"

"Who juggles everything? I'm here to help." Peter admired his sister's strength and the way she sacrificed for her son.

"I appreciate it." She set her elbows on his desk, her blonde hair falling forward over her shoulders. "More than you know."

"You're welcome."

Laura pointed at his phone. "Please tell me you've called her."

Peter pocketed his phone, then unwrapped the sandwich.

"You haven't?" Her eyes widened. "It's been like five days. She's going to think you aren't interested." Laura sat back in the chair and pulled her legs up, crisscrossing them.

"I want to call, but I'm still embarrassed." The tips of his ears warmed.

Laura held out her hands. "Who cares that you fell?"

"I do. That was no way to make a good impression. In fact, it was the opposite."

"I'm sure she's totally forgotten about it," Laura said with conviction. "Call her and ask her out again."

He played with the sandwich wrapper. "I don't know."

"Oh." Laura sat up straight. "Take her to the Hilton. The restaurant there has a karaoke bar."

Peter leaned back in his chair and made it squeak. "She wouldn't want to do that." He looked at Laura. "Would she?"

"Sure! Show her that you're fun." She pointed at him. "And once she hears you sing, she'll melt into your arms."

"Melt into my arms? Really?" He shook his head. "That's a little over the top."

"It's true. A man that sings is soooo attractive. Trust me on this." She gave him a you-have-to-believe-me nod.

Peter appreciated his sister's confidence in his singing ability, but she was prone to exaggerate.

Laura reached over and took a chunk out of his sandwich and popped it into her mouth. "You know, if you weren't such a great therapist, I'd suggest you make a career of singing."

"That was a long time ago." A *very long time ago.*

Laura said with a wistful voice, "I wish you'd sing again."

"I haven't felt much like it since . . ." He shrugged.

"Maybe it's time for that to change." She pointed at the pocket that held his phone. "And it all starts with another date. Go on, call her."

Laura was a great sister, but sometimes she was way too pushy. "I'll think about it."

After she left, Peter took out his phone and stared at it. He was probably overreacting. They'd had a lot of fun on their date. His less-than-graceful exit wasn't that big of a deal, right?

He should call Hailey. Before he lost his nerve.

Chapter 26

Hailey slid into the driver's seat. She was familiar with the area but was still glad she had her phone with the map function. "Where to, Gramps?"

He said something, but she wasn't sure what it was. "The beach?" They weren't exactly wearing beach attire, but a drive to the ocean would be nice.

He shook his head.

Hailey tried again. "The grocery store?" Maybe he wanted to get some beef jerky. Ever since his cholesterol level became elevated, Gran started insisting he eat healthier and put his favorite snack on the endangered list. Of course, that didn't stop Gramps from sneaking some whenever he got a chance. Maybe today was one of those days.

"No s-s-store."

Where else would he like to go? "The mall?" she asked.

Gramps clucked his tongue, then said a few words that were hard to understand, but Hailey took another stab at it. "The Speedway?"

Gramps nodded and gave her a grin. "Yes."

"I guess I should've figured that first off since you are an official NASCAR fanatic." She looked at Gramps. "How about me and you going to the Daytona 500 next year?" She liked the sound of making future plans—it made her happy.

"Yes!" Gramps patted her on the leg. "A d-d-date."

Hailey tried to not think about driving past the Speedway with Peter last week because it made her chest constrict. It was obvious that he must not have felt the same connection she did on their date. Not wanting to linger on that depressing thought, she said, "Let me put that into my phone, and then we'll have the directions to get there, because I can't remember exactly."

Gramps let his shoulders slump. Hailey knew he'd prefer to give her the directions himself or, better yet, drive the car. "All in good time, Gramps."

He gazed out the window as they started down the street.

When they were crossing an intersection, Hailey's phone rang. "Can you answer it for me?" She wasn't sure who it might be, and she didn't want to be distracted while she was driving.

Gramps picked up the phone and fiddled with it, but the ringing stopped.

After the next light, Hailey pulled into a parking lot. She held out her hand and Gramps placed the phone in it. When she looked at the missed-call screen, she didn't recognize the number. "Maybe there's a message."

As soon as the message began, her heart shot to her throat. "Hi, Hailey. I'm sorry I missed you. I'll try calling again," Peter said on her voicemail.

She held the phone in her hand, her palm moistening.

Gramps looked at her expectantly. She didn't want to tell him it was a message from Peter because she was sure he'd read too much into it and somehow blab to Gran about it. Besides, Peter was probably only calling to check on Gramps. Nothing else.

"Who?" Gramps asked.

"Wrong number," she lied.

Gramps stared at her as if seeing right through her. "Who?" he asked again, peering at her intently.

Hailey glanced out the window, then back at Gramps. "Okay, fine. It was Peter."

A smile splashed across his face and reached all the way up to his eyes.

"Don't be getting any ideas. I'm sure it was to check up on you. That's all." She didn't dare hope it was for another reason—a personal reason—because, she reminded herself, that'd complicate things. She didn't need or want complications. Right? She needed to get ahold of herself and put this all into perspective. For Gramps. And for herself.

Gramps squeezed her knee.

"Peter is a nice man, but . . ." She bit her lip. *How to explain this?* "Even if I were ready to date someone, I'm going back to my life in Colorado. All this could ever be is a fun fling."

Gramps frowned at her.

"Not *that* kind of a fling. I simply mean that it couldn't go anywhere." She looked out the window at the bright blue sky. *Even if he is attractive, fun, and the most interesting man I've met in a long time.*

Hailey put the phone down and started driving again. She merged onto International Speedway Boulevard.

Gramps picked up the phone and gave her an encouraging smile.

Hailey held her hand up. "No, no. I'm not going to call him back." She'd made her mind up. "Even if he were calling for another date, that wouldn't be a good idea. I don't want to go out with him again," she said, knowing it wasn't true.

Out of the corner of her eye, Hailey could see Gramps shaking his head as if disappointed, which weakened her resolve.

After driving a few more miles with her insides twisted into knots, Hailey said, "All right. Maybe I *would* like to go on another date with him." She let out a breath. "There, I admitted it. Happy?"

"Yes."

They drove along, winding around in front of the Speedway. Palm trees lined the road and a huge modern building with colorful murals of race cars sat in front of the immense race track.

"I definitely want to come back and go with you to the 500," Hailey said, glancing at the complex.

Gramps kept his gaze on the building as they passed it. Hailey flipped the car around and they drove past it again.

"Never gets old, does it, Gramps? You've seen a lot of races in there."

"Yes," he said with happy eyes. Hailey looked forward to going with him to the 500 next year.

When they got back to the house, Hailey went to her bedroom and reluctantly logged onto her computer to get a few hours of work in. Her phone rang, and immediately her heartbeat echoed in her ears. Sure enough, it was the same number. *Peter.*

"Hello?"

"Hi. This is Peter." His voice was like velvet.

Sound casual and relaxed. "Hi. How are you?" She crossed her ankles, then uncrossed them.

"Good. You?"

"I just got back from a drive with Gramps." *There that sounded normal. And casual. And relaxed.*

"Where did you go?" he asked.

"To the International Speedway." She rolled the hem of her shirt between her fingers.

"Ah, yes. Because Harry loves NASCAR."

Hailey was touched that Peter had remembered their conversation. "Yeah. I'm going to come back next year and go with him to the Daytona 500." The tension in her shoulders began to ease.

"I'm sure he'd enjoy that."

"Gramps loves all things NASCAR. I think he secretly wishes he could be a driver." The image of Gramps behind the wheel of a race car made Hailey smile.

Silence hung over them for a few moments. Peter cleared his throat, then said, "I was wondering if you'd like to go out again."

"Sure." *Oh, great, I answered too fast.* "I mean, that sounds like fun."

Should she go out with him again? What about keeping things uncomplicated?

"I was thinking we could go to the Hilton."

A *hotel? What?* "Uh . . ."

"Wait, that sounded . . . No . . . I didn't mean . . . Can I start over?" He sounded flustered.

"I'd like that."

She could hear Peter exhale. "Inside the Hilton at the Oceanwalk is a karaoke bar that comes highly recommended."

"Oh, a karaoke bar." That was much better, except Hailey didn't sing. In fact, she sounded like a dying animal when she sang along to the radio.

"Unless you hate that idea."

She loved the idea, but wanted to play it cool. "No, but I'm not much of a singer." He wouldn't make her sing, would he?

"It's fun to go listen to people," he said. "I've been a few times."

"Do you sing?" Hailey tried to imagine Peter with a microphone in hand.

"A little."

"If you promise to sing, I'm in," she said. Being able to freely stare at him on stage was quite appealing.

"Deal."

"Sounds great." She shouldn't go on another date. She knew that. But her heart had overpowered her head.

"Tomorrow night? I can pick you up at seven o'clock."

"Looking forward to it." They ended the call. *Looking forward to it.* Did she have to say that? It sounded desperate. Like she didn't have a life. Which she didn't. But she didn't want to sound that way. *I should've said something else.* She tapped her forehead. *This is making me a little crazy.*

When she came out to the living room, Gran was sitting on the couch next to Gramps's recliner. Gran looked over her knitting at Hailey. "Well, well, well."

"What?" Hailey tried to act nonchalant even though her stomach felt like it was upside down.

Gran put her knitting down. "Your whole face is beaming."

Hailey's hands flew to her cheeks. "It is not."

"P-p-peter," Gramps said, then slapped his knee in exuberance.

"What?" Gran turned to Gramps and then back to Hailey with her mouth draped open.

Hailey gave Gramps the evil eye.

Gran looked at her expectantly, waiting for an answer.

"Fine," Hailey said. "He asked me for another date. No big deal." She wanted to play it off as something minor so Gran wouldn't get ahead of herself. Besides, she was still annoyed that Gran had forced him into the first date. But she was also a teeny, tiny bit grateful. Maybe more than a teeny, tiny bit.

"Oh, he did, did he?" Gran said with a smug tone and a tilt of her head.

"Tomorrow night." Hailey paused for effect and raised her eyebrows. "At the Hilton."

"What?" Gran wore a shocked expression. "He's taking you to a hotel?"

Hailey smiled, pleased that she'd gotten a reaction. She wasn't going to let Gran off too easy. "Gran. Really? There's a karaoke bar there. You know, where people get up and sing for the other people in the audience. It's at the Oceanwalk."

Gramps started laughing.

Hailey turned to her grandfather. "Hey, now. What are you implying over there?"

He waved his hand as if he meant nothing by his laughter, but his lips still wore a grin.

With a teasing tone, Hailey said, "Maybe the condition of the date is that you and Gran come with me." She put her hand on her hip. "I'd like to see you up there on the stage, Gramps."

He shook his head. "N-n-not me."

"I think it sounds like a fun date." If Gran's smile were any bigger it'd crack her face. "And pay no attention to your grandfather. You have a lovely voice."

Hailey knew much better than that. "We all know I don't sing. It's no big secret." She shrugged. "But it'll be fun to watch others. And Peter said he'd sing." A thrill ran up her back.

Gran turned to Gramps and touched him on the arm. "Did you hear that? He's a singer, too."

"Now don't go shopping for my wedding dress." Hailey wagged her finger to emphasize her point.

Gran feigned shock. "I would never jump to *that* conclusion, especially because your eyes don't light up and your smile doesn't stretch from ear-to-ear and your cheeks certainly don't turn rosy when you talk about him. It's obvious it's not going to go anywhere."

"Gran!"

Hailey hated that Gran could read her so easily.

Chapter 27

Hailey was up early Friday morning. She worked on a couple of her accounts for a while, then went for a run. It felt good to get her muscles working and it gave her time to focus on nothing but listening to Coldplay and running—definitely not thinking about her upcoming date with Peter.

When she returned from her run, she showered and got dressed. After noticing several new emails, Hailey spent time answering them and sending some files back to Mr. Michaels. Finishing up her work, she rummaged through her clothes. Gramps had his speech therapy appointment, and she wanted to look decent. That was a lie. She wanted to look amazing. Like take-Peter's-breath-away amazing, so he'd be excited about their date. She pulled out her blue dress and put it on. After fixing her hair and applying some mascara and lip gloss, Hailey walked out to the living room, but Gramps wasn't in there.

"Are you ready, Gramps?" she said down the hall.

"He isn't feeling well," Gran said as she came out of their bedroom.

"Oh. I hope everything is all right." Anxiety creased her forehead.

"I think he's tired. That's all." She slung her arm around Hailey and they walked down the hallway toward the living room. "It'd probably be best to skip this appointment and let him rest. Don't you worry. He'll be fine." Gran said it with such reassurance it made Hailey feel less stressed about Gramps.

"Sure." Hailey had to admit, though, she was disappointed she wouldn't see Peter this afternoon. Of course, they had their date that night, but she still felt let down. What was she saying? Thinking? This was crazy. She'd known him for a few weeks. And knowing was kind of an overstatement. They had only gone on one date. One fantastic, unforgettable, amazing date. *What is wrong with me? I need to get a grip.*

"Hailey?" Gran said, breaking into her thoughts.

"Uh, yeah?"

Gran studied her. "Did I lose you somewhere?"

"No, no. I . . . never mind. I can call and cancel his appointment."

"I can do that." Gran squeezed her shoulder. "I'm sorry."

Hailey stepped away from her and leaned against the back of the couch. "For what?"

"That you can't see him this afternoon." Gran said it so matter-of-factly.

"Don't be silly. It's no big deal," she said, unsure if she was trying to convince Gran or herself.

"Liar."

Hailey jerked her head back. "Excuse me?"

"You're disappointed." Gran peered at her. "I can see it all over your face."

"This is about Gramps, not me," Hailey said, trying to deflect the conversation away from her. "Do you really think he's ok?"

"I think he's tired and a good rest is what he needs. Don't worry." Gran walked past her into the kitchen. Over her shoulder, she said, "I'm going to bake some mint chocolate chip cookies. They're Harry's favorite."

While Hailey was going over some numbers on her spreadsheet in her bedroom, Gran walked in and said, "I cancelled the appointment and the woman rescheduled it for tomorrow."

"Tomorrow? It's Saturday."

Gran shrugged. "I guess they're open on Saturdays."

"We can go tomorrow, as long as Gramps is up to it." Hailey hoped he would be, especially if her date went as well as she anticipated with Peter tonight. For a moment, she lost herself in thoughts about Peter.

"I'll let you get back to work," Gran said.

"Oh . . . yeah . . . work." Hailey nodded, reminding herself to focus back on her clients. "Thanks, Gran." Somewhere along the way, she'd lost some enthusiasm for her job.

Gran left, and Hailey clicked over to her email. She found a frantic message from a client who needed immediate attention. Hailey called Mr. Lanceton.

"Hi, this is Hailey Baker from Michaels, Jensen, and Carter Accounting." She tapped her fingers on her leg.

"Ms. Baker. I've been notified by the IRS. I have an audit." She could hear the anxiety in his voice.

"Don't worry, Mr. Lanceton, everything will be fine." She wanted to reassure him.

"I've never been audited before. What if we're missing some paperwork?"

"We need to find out what is being audited exactly. Which part of your return is in question?" She opened his folder and scanned through the files.

"It's for two years ago."

She found the correct file and opened it. "I'll contact the agent and make arrangements to represent you." Hailey needed to stay calm so her client would feel confident in her ability to help him through this audit, even if her heart wasn't in it.

"Are you sure?" he said with a nervous edge.

"Yes, sir, that's my job."

"So what do I do?"

Hailey clicked through the various files. "I think we have all we need. I can get specific information from the agent, but I don't think there's anything to worry about. We have your receipts scanned and your expense reports appear to be in order."

"I've never had an audit," he repeated.

"I'll keep you updated." Hailey wanted to allay his fear because that was her job. "For now, don't worry. There's probably some information they want clarified. That's all."

She could hear Mr. Lanceton let out a sigh. "I feel better after talking to you."

"I'm glad. Now, enjoy your weekend. I'll take care of this."

"Thank you."

After she hung up, Hailey worried what this would mean for her personally. Audits were not her favorite part of her job. She hoped she could take care of it quickly and without having to return to Colorado right now, because she wasn't ready to leave her grandparents. Otherwise, she might have to ask her boss to have someone else represent Mr. Lanceton, which could pose a threat to her employment.

"Are you busy?" Gran asked, peeking her head into Hailey's bedroom.

Hailey sat back. "One of my clients is being audited."

"Uh oh."

"He's a little stressed, but I tried to reassure him." She hoped she had.

Gran stepped inside the room, her lime green blouse untucked. "Do you need to go back to Colorado?"

Hailey chewed on her lip. "I don't know."

"Oh." Gran hid her feelings poorly. "I know you have a life back in Colorado and need to go back," Gran said in a thick voice. "We'll be fine."

"Gran, you're getting all worked up for no reason. I'll take care of it. I'm sure everything will be fine." At least she hoped so. Audits could be stressful and time consuming, but Mr. Lanceton had been her client ever since she joined the firm, and she needed to take care of this for him.

Gran reached out and touched Hailey's flowing hair. "You look so pretty. Your dark hair has always highlighted your beautiful blue eyes."

Hailey hoped Peter would think the same. "Thanks. I need to get ready for my date before Peter gets here."

"Uh oh." Gran made a face.

Hailey braced for bad news, then said, "What?"

"He's here." Gran smiled.

"Peter is *here*? Already?" Her heart climbed up her throat and her stomach started to quiver. She wasn't nearly ready enough.

"Yes. He's talking to your grandpa."

"But he's early. I didn't think he'd be early." Hailey ran her fingers through her hair, then looked at herself in the mirror that hung next to the door. "I definitely need to refresh my make-up. And brush my hair. Oh, and my teeth." Hailey looked down at her dress. "Should I change?"

"No, no. This dress is a knockout. You look perfect," Gran said with a cheerful expression.

Hailey's nerves burned. "Tell him I'll be out in a second."

She rushed into the bathroom and worked to make her hair look full. She brushed her teeth. Twice. *I don't want bad breath.* She spritzed her favorite Dior perfume on her neck and her wrist. Hailey took several calming breaths and clasped her trembling hands. *Stop being such a nervous ninny.* She sounded like Gran.

"Hi," Hailey said as she walked into the living room. Peter was dressed in black pants and an emerald-green polo shirt that emphasized his trim frame. Hailey reminded herself to relax.

"Since I had a cancellation, I decided to make a house call." He winked and her stomach flip-flopped.

"I hope you kids have a good time," Gran said. "I'd love to hear you sing."

"Come with us," Peter said with sincerity.

Gran waved her hand. "No, no. You two go on. Us old coots will stay here."

Peter stepped over to Gramps. "I'll remember what you said." He shook his hand.

What does that mean? Oh, no. What did Gramps say? "I'm ready if you are," Hailey said. She turned to her grandparents. "I'll see you later."

"Stay out as late as you want," Gran said with way too much enthusiasm.

They walked outside toward his car, the sun descending in the sky. Peter opened her door for her. She slid inside and watched him walk around the front of the car. He was handsome, but he was so much more. He radiated kindness and a genuine concern for those around him.

Inside the car, Hailey was almost afraid to ask, but she wanted to know—had to know. "What did you mean you'd remember what Gramps said?"

"Sorry." He glanced at her with a twinkle in his eye. "It's only between us." He started up the car and began driving.

"Is that so?" She said it with a smile. "And you aren't going to tell me?"

He smirked, then shook his head.

"But, did he actually say something to you? Like a real sentence?"

"He did." Peter nodded, the slightly musky scent wafting through the car. "We had a real conversation. His speech is definitely improving."

Even though she wanted to know what he said, she was happy to know he was conversing. "I'm so relieved. I worry about him. And Gran. They're getting older, and I don't want to think about that." Sadness surged through her.

They didn't talk for a few minutes, but it wasn't awkward. It was . . . comfortable.

"I hope you're planning to sing," Peter said as they pulled into the parking lot of the Hilton.

"Uh, no." She held up her hands. "I don't want people grasping their ears and writhing on the floor in pain."

He laughed. "I'm sure it's not that bad."

"Oh, believe me, it is. I'll do us all a favor if I don't sing."

Once again, he was a gentleman and opened her car door. As they walked through the hotel and navigated through a crowd, he placed his hand on the small of her back and guided her to the restaurant near the karaoke bar.

Inside the restaurant, they sat at a small table near a window and ordered some dinner.

"Are you two here for the karaoke contest?" the waitress with short blonde hair asked.

"Contest?" Hailey said.

"Yeah. At the end of the night, we award the best singer with a prize." She nodded and the diamond stud in her nose glinted.

"Sounds interesting," Peter said.

"It's always entertaining. Are you and your wife here for vacation?" she said as she filled their water glasses.

"We live here," Peter answered without correcting her mistake.

After the waitress left, Hailey said, "I think this will be fun. Have you been here before?"

"No," he said. "I don't get out too often."

"Really?" Did that mean he didn't date much? It was hard to imagine that a man like Peter wasn't dating all the time. He had everything going for him—he was the total package.

"I'm pretty busy with my patients and my sister and nephew."

Hailey sipped her lemon water. "Your nephew is really cute."

"Benji is a bundle of energy. He lost his dad a few years ago in Afghanistan." A sad expression flashed across his face.

"Oh, I'm sorry."

"My sister has had a rough time, so I try to be there for her as much as possible."

"That must make it hard to date." She regretted it as soon as it left her mouth and wished she could call it back.

A slight smile played on his lips. "Dating hasn't been much of a priority, to be honest."

Changing the direction of the conversation, Hailey said, "Let's play a game."

Peter gazed at her with his striking blue eyes. "Okay."

"It's called Two Truths and a Lie."

"Sounds intriguing."

"We used to play it back in high school to get to know people. I'll tell you three things and you have to figure out which one is a lie."

Peter leaned in and smiled. "Go ahead."

"One. I set a record in cross country that still stands today at my high school. Two. I once met Jack Nicholson in Aspen when I was there skiing with my friends. Three. I can tune up a car." She sat back with a satisfied expression, certain she'd stump him. "There, go ahead and pick out the lie."

Peter strummed his fingers on the table while pensively studying Hailey.

The waitress returned and brought them their dinners.

Hailey cut into her sirloin. "So back to our game. It's hard, huh? Not to brag, but I always win." She smiled confidently as she waited for him to make a choice.

"I can believe you set a cross country record."

"Oh yeah? Why?"

"You are, you know, lean." He took a bite of his salmon.

"*Lean?* Is that a compliment?" she prodded.

He shifted in his chair. "You look like a runner. That's all."

"Thank you." She studied him, trying to decipher his meaning. "I think."

"Since you lived in Colorado, it isn't hard to believe you skied at Aspen. And plenty of celebrities go to Aspen."

"And the last one?" She spooned some creamy mashed potatoes into her mouth.

"I have a hard time envisioning you getting greasy and fixing a car."

"Why is that? Because I'm a woman?"

"No. I . . . that's not why." He licked his lips. "I don't see you as a mechanic. That's all."

She giggled to herself at how he became uncomfortable so easily. She smiled at him. "So which is it?"

"Now you have me all confused."

"That's the idea," she said, pleased with herself.

He leaned forward, seeming to regain his confidence. "Let's make this more interesting."

"Okay." *What does he have in mind?*

The corners of his mouth tugged up. "Whoever wins gets to pick a song for the other one to sing."

Hailey hesitated for a moment because she wasn't about to expose her dead animal voice to the world, but she agreed, confident she'd win. "You're on."

His eyes twinkled and he said, "I think the lie is meeting a celebrity at Aspen."

Hailey sat back, stunned. "How did you do that?"

"I'm pretty good at reading people. You have a tell." He stabbed a piece of broccoli and put it in his mouth.

"A tell?"

Peter nodded. "It gave you away."

No way did she have a *tell*. "That's not even true."

"It is." He took another bite of his salmon.

Hailey always won this game. She wanted to know how Peter figured out her lie. "Fine. What is it?"

"Your right eyebrow lifted almost imperceptibly, but I still noticed it, when you said you met Jack." He used a napkin to wipe his face. "But that one sounded realistic."

"My eyebrow?" Her hand went to her forehead. "Really? I had no idea. I guess I'll have to work on that."

"I'm impressed you can tune a car."

She sipped her water, satisfied that even though she'd lost the game, she'd impressed Peter. "Thanks to Gramps. He used to have me help him when I was a teenager. I liked that we could spend time together. We even worked on an old Toyota, and he gave it to me when I turned sixteen."

Peter smiled a warm endearing smile. "He's lucky to have someone who loves him so much."

"He's the best. And so is Gran." She leaned forward. "Your turn."

"All right. Let me think." He tapped the table.

"Come on." She was eager to learn more about him.

"You know you have to sing a song I pick now, right?" he said with a light tone.

"Yeah, yeah." Hailey brushed it off in hopes of avoiding it. "But if I win, you have to sing one I pick."

"Number one." He started. "I played Nathan Detroit in *Guys and Dolls* in high school. Two. I own all the Beatles albums. And three, I had heart surgery when I was a child."

"Wow. You're good." Now it was her turn to be impressed.

Peter gave her a self-assured smile.

This was tougher than she thought it would be. Maybe she'd met her match at this game. "I think the lie is number one." Hailey held her hand up. "No. I think number two."

His eyes sparkled. "What is your final answer?"

"Number two. You don't strike me as a Beatles kind of guy."

"I don't?" His eyes widened.

"No." Hailey looked him up and down. "More of an NSYNC guy."

He let out a derisive laugh. "Uh, no. Definitely not an NSYNC guy."

"So, am I right?"

"Buzzzz." Peter pointed at her. "You. Are. Wrong."

"I am?" How did she lose? Again. He was certainly throwing off her groove.

"I was never Nathan Detroit." He gave a jerk of his head. "I should've been, but I wasn't."

She noted a hint of resentment. "Still upset about that?"

He laughed. "So I pick a song for you. Again." He held up two fingers. "That makes *two* songs."

She let out a long breath. "Except I'm really, really not a singer. Like I said, for real, people will scream out in pain and the walls will tumble down in rebellion. We don't want all that ruin, do we?" She peered at him. "Do we?"

He shrugged a shoulder. "That was the bet."

"I know, and I'm never one to back out of a bet, but in the interest of world peace, I think it's for the best." Hailey gave him her best this-is-the-right-thing-to-do nod.

"But this is a karaoke bar. Singing talent isn't a requirement."

"Seriously. I should *not* sing." She pointed at him. "You'll thank me. Really."

"I don't know." He shook his head, then gazed at her with a playful expression. "Maybe you can offer up something in exchange."

"Like what?" She was enjoying this lighthearted banter.

He moved closer to her, making her heartbeat speed up. "What do you have in mind?"

"I can tune up your car," she offered.

"Hmm, that's quite tempting." The dim light in the restaurant couldn't hide the gleam in his eyes. "But I already have a great mechanic."

She thought for a moment. "Okay. Here it is. I'll make you dinner if I don't have to sing tonight."

"When?"

"You say."

"All right." He stuck his hand out over the table and as soon as she took it, sizzling energy bounded up her arm. "You have a deal." They finished shaking hands.

Hailey took a swig of her water and silently commanded her pulse to stop zipping through her veins. "You had heart surgery as a kid?"

"I was born with a hole in my heart." He nodded.

"That must've been scary."

"For my mom. I was too young to remember much of it. Apparently, it worked." He smiled.

"I'm glad." Did she say that out loud? She hurried to change the subject. "What's your favorite Beatles song?"

Peter drummed his fingers on the table. "That's hard. I enjoy all of them."

"And you sing."

A flash of humility crossed his face. "Yeah."

What else could this fascinating man do? "You play an instrument?"

"The guitar. Piano." He smoothed his hair. "And the violin in middle school."

"That's awesome." She had no idea Peter was so musically inclined. "I took piano lessons, but I think I'm tone deaf."

After dinner, they moved over to the bar and sat in some chairs to the left of the stage. A few people got up and sang. The first guy wasn't too bad, but the next one, a woman with spiky blue hair and an eagle tattoo on her arm, was terrible. Hailey wanted to cover her ears, but she didn't want to be rude, so she endured what sounded like the woman was being strangled. Maybe her own voice wasn't as bad as she thought.

She turned to Peter. "So, are you going to sing?"

Peter sat back. "I didn't lose the bet."

"But you could still get up there. For fun." Hailey wanted to hear him sing.

"Maybe."

She touched him on the shoulder. "Come on. Sing me a song." She tilted her head and gave him her best do-it-for-me-please look.

A smile edged around his mouth. "How can I refuse now?"

Peter stood and walked up to the side of the stage. After the next woman finished her song, he stood on the dark wooden platform, microphone in hand.

Speak to My Heart

A young man with a dark goatee stood in front of the crowd and said, "We now have Mr. Peter Stafford, who will be singing, *See You Tonight*, made famous by Scotty McCreery."

The music began and Peter started singing. Hailey's mouth curled up. Peter's voice was so smooth—like Dove dark chocolate melting on her tongue. He was good. Better than good. The more he sang, the more he got into the song. Hailey stared at him as he sang, her heartbeat thrumming to the beat of the song. She found herself wishing she'd be the girl Peter might be holding under the porch light tonight.

Toward the end of the song, the crowd started clapping with him. A couple of women whistled and shouted out at him to keep singing.

After Peter finished, the applause erupted. The DJ said, "The audience liked that. Stay tuned to see if you win the prize tonight, sir."

Peter waved at the crowd, then took his seat next to Hailey.

"That was incredible." She hadn't been prepared for the way his singing wound around her heart.

"Thanks." He scooted closer to her and his shoulder touched hers. "I haven't sung in front of anyone for a long time."

"Why not?"

"I guess," he paused, "I lost the music for a time."

"And Scotty McCreery?"

"Okay." He held his hand up. "I have a confession."

"This sounds interesting."

He cupped his hand over his mouth and whispered, his breath tickling her ear, "I watched *American Idol*. Every season of it."

"You did?" She looked at him with surprise.

He nodded, then lowered his head. "I hope I don't have to turn in my man card because of it."

"No way. Not after you sang like that. You should've been on *American Idol* yourself."

He laughed. "My sister said the same thing."

"So why didn't you audition?" She could see him singing on stage while the women watching him worked themselves into a dither. *Dither?*

There I go sounding like Gran again.

"I guess I was too busy with life." He played with the edge of the napkin. "And I didn't have enough confidence."

"Seriously?" Hailey held her hands out in front of her. "You sing like an angel."

"I do?" His grin sent ripples across her stomach as if a kaleidoscope of butterflies was trying to escape.

"Uh, did I say that out loud?" Sometimes her mouth worked faster than her brain.

"You did."

She didn't care if he knew she loved his voice. "Well, it's true."

When Hailey sat back, she noticed Peter's arm was draped around the back of her chair. Within a minute, his arm was around her shoulders. She settled in, liking how she seemed to fit perfectly there.

They listened to several more singers. Some were better than others and a few sounded like they were in pain. Hailey wished someone would put them out of her misery.

The DJ jumped up on the stage. He raised his hand and said, "We have a winner."

"It better be you," Hailey said as she elbowed Peter.

The DJ scanned the audience. "Peter Stafford, come on up."

"Woo hoo," Hailey shouted. She whistled.

Peter walked to the stage while the crowd applauded.

"You've won a T-shirt." The DJ handed him a bright yellow shirt. "You have a great voice, man." He clapped Peter on the shoulder.

"Thanks."

Peter came back to the table, shirt in hand.

"Congratulations," Hailey said. "You were obviously the best one here."

"Thanks." He inclined his head toward the door. "What do you say we go for a walk?"

"I'd like that."

They exited the lounge, dropped the T-shirt off at the car, and then headed toward the beach area. The air was warm and moist and a gentle wind caressed Hailey's face. The moon hung low in the sky and stars twinkled above them.

Hailey drew in a deep breath through her nose. "I love the salty air here."

"Don't get much of that in Colorado?"

"Nope. Not a lot." Hailey kicked off her sandals and held them in her hand. The cool sand felt like satin beneath her feet. "I love the ocean and listening to the cadence of the breaking waves. It's like listening to nature's music."

"The beach is my favorite place to come and think." He glanced at her. Even under the moonlight it was easy to see his appealing features. "I've spent a decent amount of time here."

"Had a lot to think about?"

Peter looked out toward the ocean. "You could say that."

"Anything you want to share?"

They continued walking on the silky sand, only the sound of the water lapping at the shore between them. After a few minutes, Peter said, "When I was a freshman in college, I met a woman. We dated for a couple of years and then got married."

He was married? *More importantly, is he still married?* Hailey remained silent and hoped Peter would continue.

He glanced up at the night sky. "By the time I earned my master's, she was gone."

Hailey clutched at her chest. "She died?"

"No." He shook his head. "She left me, but I felt like I'd died."

"I'm so sorry." She didn't want to pry, but she wanted to know what happened and hoped he'd tell her more.

"She wasn't a big fan of being a married college student. She particularly disliked not having much money. One day, I came home from school and her suitcase was packed. She said she was sorry, but getting married was a mistake. I think she liked the idea of being married more than she liked actually being married. At least to me."

Hailey's heart hurt. *Poor Peter.* "Wow. That must've been awful."

"It was pretty hard. I was in it for the long haul, but she wasn't." He drew in a deep breath. "That was about six years ago."

"Whatever happened to her?" She regretted asking such a prying question. "I'm sorry, I shouldn't have asked that."

"She married a wealthy attorney three years ago."

Hailey wasn't sure what to say or why Peter had chosen to share that with her, but she felt a stronger connection to him because of it.

"So, yeah, I've spent a lot of thinking time here. What about you?" He looked at her. "Did you have a thinking spot?"

Hailey nodded, remembering her special place. "Up in the mountains. I'd hike up to my favorite area right above this creek."

"I've never spent much time in the mountains."

"Oh, I love the Rockies, but I also love the beach. I've missed Florida over the last few years. Work has kept me in Colorado, and I haven't been able to visit."

"Have you ever thought about moving to the beach?" he asked in a quiet voice.

Was he fishing or merely curious? Regardless, she said, "I thought I'd always live in Colorado, but I'm not so sure anymore. Things haven't worked out exactly like I'd planned."

Peter laughed softly. "Life can sure throw us curveballs."

"Yes, it can."

He turned and peered at her. The moonlight streamed across his face and highlighted his strong jaw. "Here's to turning those curveballs into home runs."

"Sounds good to me." She loved his optimism.

They started walking closer to the edge of the water. A wave broke and water rushed around their feet. Hailey squealed, then jumped back, but she lost her footing and tumbled backward, landing on her backside.

Peter immediately extended his hand. She grabbed it and attempted to pull herself up, but was off-balance and fell back again.

She started laughing to cover her humiliation.

Peter took a few balancing steps and then fell next to her in the sand.

"We're a pair, aren't we?" she said wiping at the sand on her dress.

"Please don't remind me about how I fell the other night. I'm trying to forget that ever happened." He stretched out his legs in front of him. "I have another confession."

"Go on. I like your confessions." She was anxious to hear what he'd say.

"I was so embarrassed." He picked up a handful of sand and let it sift through his fingers. "I wasn't going to call you again."

"Seriously?" *He was so embarrassed he wasn't going to call me?*

"My sister convinced me."

She looked at him sideways. "I'm so glad she did." *Uh, oh. Did I say that aloud? Again?*

Peter smiled. He jumped to his feet, then pulled Hailey to hers. They lingered there for a moment under the night sky. "I need to get you home. I don't want June to be mad that I'm bringing you home late. I want to stay in her good graces."

Hailey laughed. "I don't think you need to worry about that." *Gran would love it if I ran off and married you right now.*

As they walked back toward the car, Peter reached his hand out and gently took Hailey's in his. Their hands fit together so naturally, as if they were a matched pair. *What's happening?* She bit her lip. *Who am I kidding?* She knew exactly what was happening. But was she prepared for it?

In the car on the way back, Hailey asked, "So you like to sing, you were in theater, and you had heart surgery. Anything else?" She wanted to know as much about this man as she could.

"I'm pretty good at cards."

"Oh, really?" She looked at him. "Ever play gin?"

"Yeah, among others. I play with my mom. She likes to play with some of her friends and practices on me." He laughed.

"Interesting."

"Why? Do you play cards?"

She turned in her seat toward Peter, wishing she wasn't wearing such a confining seatbelt. "I don't wanna brag, but I've been known to beat the socks off Gramps."

He tapped the steering wheel with his fingers. "I bet he lets you win."

"Are you kidding me?" Her voice rose. "He's as competitive as it comes. I win fair and square every time."

"Maybe we can play a game or two sometime with Harry."

"You're on." She playfully touched him on the forearm and before she knew it, his hand held hers.

"I'll warn you, though, I'm pretty good," he said confidently.

With a flick of her head she said, "I guess we'll see."

They drove past a restaurant with a sign offering the best gator in the area. "Have you eaten gator?" he asked.

"Not this trip, but I love it." A memory of the first time she had alligator with her grandparents rushed through her mind. "Well, I didn't love it the first time. Gramps convinced me to try it, and I spit it right out. Even wiped my tongue with the napkin and everything."

"Was that last year?"

"Very funny." She tapped his hand with hers. "I was much, much younger. I tried it again last time I was here, and now I'm hooked."

"We'll have to get some." He squeezed her hand. "I have a favorite restaurant."

"Sounds good." Hailey looked out the window. It sounded as if Peter were planning things to do in the future, like he planned to spend more time with her. How did she feel about that? She gazed down at their intertwined fingers. *Pretty good.* Actually, she felt better than pretty good—a lot better—about spending more time with him, even if her time in Florida would be up soon. She pushed that thought from her mind and refused to let it pop back in.

They arrived at the house and walked up to the porch.

"Thank you for going with me tonight. I had a great time," he said.

"Thanks for asking." She rolled the fabric of her dress between her forefinger and thumb like she was a nervous teenager on her very first date. "I hope you'll sing for me again."

"Since I have the voice of an angel . . ."

She slapped at his chest and he caught her hand, sending a torrent of flutters through her body. "I didn't mean to say that out loud," she said.

He smiled and her stomach knotted. The words from the song Peter had sung earlier echoed in her ears. Would he hold her under the porch light? Would he kiss her? Would she like it?

They stood there on the porch for several moments, their gazes locked on each other and electricity dancing between them. Hailey's heart somersaulted in her chest and the edges of her ears burned as she anticipated, even yearned for, a kiss. She could almost feel his lips on hers and taste his kiss as he leaned in toward her.

Suddenly, the door whipped open and Gran stood there. "I thought I heard voices."

Hailey stepped back, dazed. The *moment* with Peter vanished.

Gran looked from Hailey to Peter and then back to Hailey. "Oh. I'm sorry. I interrupted . . . something."

"No worries. I need to get home anyway," Peter said as he backed away. "Thanks again."

Hailey watched him walk down the pathway to his car and waved as he drove away. Disappointment welled up inside her. *If only Gran hadn't opened the door.*

"I'm so sorry. It's been ages since I've had someone go on dates. I opened the door because I thought it might be Regina. And I was glad to see it was you, but then I . . ." Gran stopped rambling. "Was it fun?"

Hailey stepped in the house and shut the door. "Yeah, it was fun." *More than fun. It was spectacular.*

"Are you going out with him again?" Gran asked with eagerness.

"I guess we'll see." She slung her arm around Gran's stooped shoulders. "Remember, though, I do have to go back soon to Colorado Springs. I have a life there."

"You could have a life here."

"As you would say," Hailey gestured with her hand, "that is putting the horse twenty miles in front of the cart."

Gran chuckled. "Putting the *cart* before the horse."

Hailey waved her hand. "You know what I mean."

Gran let out a long sigh. "So sue me for hoping for a happily-ever-after for you. And here in Florida by me."

Hailey pulled her grandma into an embrace. "I love you."

Right now, Hailey loved everyone. And everything. A smile ran across her face. Maybe her heart was finally ready to take another chance.

Peter lay in bed, his hands laced behind his head, staring at the ceiling. He hadn't felt so at ease and so alive with a woman in years. And Hailey didn't seem to mind that he'd been married. He'd found that was a turnoff for some women.

Warmth emanated from his chest and spread through his limbs as he replayed the night in his mind. He'd had more fun tonight than he could remember in recent months. Maybe even years.

Singing felt good.

Walking with Hailey felt good.

Holding her hand felt good.

It all felt good.

He turned to his side and fluffed the pillow underneath his head. A part of him feared it felt too good with Hailey—too good to be true. After all, he thought he'd spend his life with Sara, and that turned out worse than he'd ever imagined. It had been six years, but in some ways, his heart thought it was as recent as yesterday. Was he ready to take another chance and let Hailey all the way in, especially when she wasn't there long-term? Wasn't that foolish?

An image of her smiling flashed across his memory. Hailey was so easy to talk to. Easy to open up to. Easy to be around. He loved how she'd squealed when the cool water hit her feet. And how they fell onto the sand together.

It had been a great night, and he hoped there would be more.

Chapter 28

Hailey woke in the morning, glorious light streaming through the slits between the blinds in her window. She was eager to get dressed and take Gramps to his appointment, so she jumped out of her bed and went to the closet. Rummaging through her clothes, she found a green-and-white striped summer dress and held it up to herself in front of the mirror. *Perfect.*

Her phone started vibrating on the night stand. She hoped it was Peter. With a bounce in her step, she made her way over to her phone, but when Hailey saw the caller ID, her heart seized. Should she answer it?

It vibrated again.

She stared at the phone, her heart bouncing in her chest. Why was *he* calling?

Again, it vibrated against the wooden top.

With trembling hands, she picked up the phone and swiped the screen. "Hello?"

"Hailey?"

"Kevin?" *Stay cool, calm, and collected.* "Why are you calling me?" She wanted to be direct and get to the point.

"I went by your place to see you a couple of times, but you weren't home." He sounded the same.

"I'm in Florida." Hailey didn't need to explain anything to him. He was her ex-boyfriend. *Emphasis on the ex.*

"Why?"

She didn't want to be totally rude, even though he deserved it. "My grandfather had a stroke and I'm here helping him. I'm sorry, did you say why you were calling?"

Kevin cleared his throat. "I want to see you."

She started laughing, low and deep. "You want to see me?" That was a gem. *After almost three months of no contact and now he wants to see me? Priceless.*

"Yes. I've been doing some thinking and—"

"Like I said, I'm in Florida." Her tone was curt.

"For how long?"

"I'm not sure." No need to elaborate.

"Oh." He sounded shocked.

"Why do you want to see me?" What was the point? It was over. He'd made his choice and she'd made hers.

"I'd rather talk about it in person."

"What's done is done, Kevin." Hailey couldn't make it any clearer than that.

"Things have changed. I've changed." He sounded almost desperate. "If you'll hear me out."

Gran poked her head into the room. "We've finished breakfast and we're both ready to go when you are."

Hailey nodded. She pointed to the phone. Gran made an apologetic face, then shut the door.

"Look, I have to go right now. Gramps has an appointment." She wanted to end this call as fast as possible.

"Can I call you later?"

"I don't know, Kevin. I really don't know." Hailey didn't think she ever wanted to talk to him again. Not after his cheating and all his lies.

"I miss you."

"I need to go." With that, Hailey ended the call. She threw the phone on her bed. The last person she expected to call her was Kevin. Her stomach twisted and her head pounded. A mixture of feelings tumbled around her insides. She'd loved Kevin—wanted to marry him—but he'd hurt her deeply, and she'd spent the last few months healing her heart and making it forget about him.

"Hailey?" came Gran's voice through the door. "I can make you a quick breakfast before we go."

"Thank you, but I'm not hungry. I'll be ready in a few minutes," she said, then flopped on the bed in a heap. *I finally stop thinking about him and how much he hurt me, and then he has to go and call me. Why?* Her stomach felt like someone had taken a hand mixer to it.

On the way over to the appointment, Hailey's mind splintered in a million different directions. How did she feel about Kevin? Did she want to give him another chance knowing what he'd done? Could she ever trust him again?

Her thoughts shifted to Peter. She didn't know him well, but something about him made her feel safe, secure. And she wanted to spend more time with him, but should she?

Gramps reached over and tapped her leg. When she glanced at him, he smiled and nodded. They didn't need words, because Gramps had this knack of reading Hailey perfectly. "I don't know what to do."

"About what?" Gran asked, her knitting needles making a clicking sound in the backseat.

Hailey glanced at her in the rearview mirror. "Kevin called me."

Gran clucked her tongue. "That louse?"

"Yes." Louse wasn't a word Hailey used, but that accurately described him.

"When?"

"This morning. Right before we left."

"And what on earth did he have say for himself?" Gran's tone didn't leave Hailey wondering about Gran's opinion of Kevin.

Hailey blew some air between her lips. "He wants to see me again."

"Pfft," Gran said. "He should be so lucky. He was a terrible boyfriend. You deserve much better than that. You deserve someone like this man, Peter." Gran was never one to mince words.

"P-p-peter," Gramps said with some effort.

Hailey glanced at Gramps, then at Gran. "Apparently, you've both married me off to Peter all ready."

Gramps smiled.

"But I loved Kevin. I wanted to marry him. I planned my life around him. Maybe I need to give him another chance."

"Why? So he can prove he's a louse?" Gran didn't even attempt to hide the irritation in her voice.

"Gran, this isn't the fifties. We don't even use that word anymore."

"Doesn't matter what your generation calls a man like him. He's not worth your time." Gran said it with such finality.

"But maybe—"

"No maybes about it, Hailey," Gran said sternly. "He can't waltz right back into your life after what he did."

Hailey chewed on the inside of her cheek. Gran was right. Why was she such a doormat when it came to Kevin? She did deserve better. A lot better. But hearing his voice on the phone mixed her all up.

They pulled into the parking lot and then made their way into the rehab facility. While they waited to go back to a room, Hailey rolled her phone around and around in her hands. Why did Kevin have to call? She'd been doing fine. Make that *perfectly fine*. Now he had to go and call her and make her insides all twisty again.

When the nurse called them back, Hailey said to Gran, "I'll wait out here for you."

"Are you sure?"

"Yeah."

Gran wrinkled her forehead and grabbed her knitting bag. "Why?"

"You don't need me." That was true, but mostly, she wasn't prepared to see Peter. She needed some time to process what Kevin had said. "I'll be back to get you." With that, Hailey hurried out of the building.

The air was suffocating outside—hot, sticky, and thick. Hailey struggled for breath, making her crave the dry, cool air of the Rockies. She walked to the car and sat on the cushioned seat. Sinking the key into the ignition, she turned on the radio and boosted the volume, hoping some music would drown everything out as the warm air from the air conditioner blasted her face.

Obviously, Kevin still had some power over her, which she detested. She didn't want Kevin to have any influence over her or let him invade her thoughts, but, obviously, she was incapable of preventing it.

Hailey started driving. Memories from the night before flooded in. The moonlight, the ocean, the way she felt with Peter, the almost-kiss on the porch. Was it fair to see him again if she was having this reaction to Kevin's call?

All she wanted was to help Gramps recover and give some support to Gran. She did not want to have a relationship with anyone or, worse, get sucked back into something with Kevin. A grinding headache began to form. Before Hailey knew it, forty-five minutes had passed and it was time to get her grandparents.

Hailey trudged into the building and found them in the waiting room. She motioned for them to come over, because she didn't want to risk seeing Peter in the mental state she was in.

In the car, Hailey asked, "How was the session?"

"Good, I think," Gran said with enthusiasm. "Peter was very patient, and Harry even said a three-word sentence."

"That's awesome, Gramps." Hailey stroked him on the shoulder. "You'll be telling us your silly stories in no time."

Gramps gave her an indignant look as if his tall tales weren't outrageous.

"I have some words to practice with him," Gran said. "I made a list."

Hailey nodded. "We can add those to the previous ones we've been doing."

"Peter said to work on sentence structure, so Harry's brain can remember how to form sentences."

"Peter was happy with the progress?" Even saying his name made Hailey's stomach quiver.

"I think so."

Hailey wanted to know if Peter had mentioned her, but she didn't want to come out and ask about it. She hoped Gran would say something, but she didn't.

Hailey drove them back home.

"How about if I make some fruit salad?" Gran asked on their way into the house. "On a hot day like today, that's about all I want to eat."

"Sounds good to me." Hailey could almost taste the sweet fruit.

"I think I have all I need to make it," Gran said.

Gramps made himself comfortable in the living room and turned on the TV.

Gran bent down and kissed Gramps on the head. He looked up at her and touched her on the cheek. It made Hailey's insides feel warm and mushy to see the obvious love between her grandparents. Maybe someday she'd find that.

Gran walked into the kitchen and Hailey followed her.

"Aren't you curious if Mr. Stafford asked about you," Gran said casually as she pulled out a box of strawberries.

Trying to act as though it wasn't important, Hailey answered, "I guess."

Gran handed Hailey a cantaloupe and a small watermelon. "He didn't say anything."

"Oh." The disappointment stung.

"But I could tell he was unhappy that you weren't there." Gran pulled a bowl of blueberries out of the refrigerator.

Shrugging one shoulder, Hailey said softly, "I just couldn't."

"Why not?" Gran put her hand on her hip.

"Because hearing from Kevin made me feel all weird. Confused."

Gran peered at Hailey with a probing look. "Do you want to get back together with him?"

"No . . . I don't know." Hailey rubbed her forehead. "I mean, I loved him. At least I thought I did. But he hurt me."

Gran turned on the water at the sink and began washing the fruit. "Can you forgive him?"

That is an excellent question. "Maybe, but I don't know if I could ever trust him again." Hailey grabbed a knife from the drawer.

"And what about Peter?" Gran shut off the water.

Hailey's nerves reacted to thoughts of Peter. "He's sweet and fun and I had a really good time last night."

"Then it sounds like the choice is easy." Gran said it with so much confidence.

Hailey set the cantaloupe on the cutting board and sliced it open, releasing its sweet aroma. "But, realistically, it can't really go anywhere with Peter. And if hearing from Kevin makes me act so irrational, then maybe I'm not actually ready to date anyone."

Gran took a knife and started cutting up the strawberries. "Or maybe it *is* time for you to move on and you just have to decide to do so."

Hailey stopped slicing and gazed at Gran. "So what should I do?"

"I'm not going to tell you what to do, but Peter deserves an explanation why you didn't come to the session." Gran found a large bowl and set it on the counter.

"It's not like I'm required to attend the appointments, you know." Gran was making a big case out of nothing.

"But you've been coming, and now, after a date with him, you didn't come. He's probably thinking you're trying to avoid him," Gran said.

She has a point. "Maybe I am."

Gran wagged her finger at Hailey. "My lands, girl. Get it together."

"I want to." Hailey raked her hands through her hair in frustration. "I don't know what to do."

"We have another appointment next week, but I don't think you should wait that long." Gran motioned to Hailey to open the refrigerator. "I have some cream that we can whip up when it's time to eat."

"Here it is." Hailey pointed to it. "You think I should go see him? Wouldn't that be awkward?"

"What time does he get off?"

Hailey shrugged.

"It's up to you." Gran dumped a box of blueberries into the large bowl and then cut open the watermelon.

Hailey added some green grapes. "I don't know. Maybe I should leave it alone." That would be the easier option.

"Your call. But if it were me, I wouldn't want him to think I didn't like him. Unless that's true." Gran looked at her sideways. "But I don't think it is."

Hailey shut her eyes for a moment, then said, "Let's finish the salad."

Chapter 29

After they put the bowl of fruit in the refrigerator to keep it cool for dinner, Hailey spent some time inputting receipts that one of her clients had scanned and emailed her. She added numbers to a spreadsheet, then updated a few files, including one for a new client. She wished Mr. Michaels would stop sending her new accounts. The ones she had were more than enough right now.

"Hailey? Are you ready for supper? We're both hungry," Gran said down the hallway.

Hailey saved her work, then went into the kitchen.

"Would you please whip up the cream?" Gran asked, handing her a glass bowl.

"Sure." While Hailey whipped the cream, she thought back to her conversation earlier with Gran. She wasn't convinced that going to see Peter was a good idea. What would she say anyway? *Hey, Peter, I think you are amazing and I'd like to go out with you, even though I'm going back to Colorado, so it's kind of a waste of time. And, PS, my ex called me today and made me a little crazy and that's why I didn't come to the therapy session.* She shook her head. *Yeah, that makes me sound insane.*

Good thing Gran had interrupted them before they kissed last night or this would be even more complicated. Why did things have to be so confusing anyway? Best thing to do was to put it out of her mind.

"Door," Gramps said from the living room.

Hailey set the bowl of whipped cream on the table and went to the front door. She opened it to Peter standing on the porch, which sent her heart plunging into her stomach.

"Oh, hi," she said, trying to be calm and casual, but her racing pulse and moist palms wouldn't listen.

"June left this today." He handed her Gran's knitting bag.

"That's so nice of you, but you didn't have to bring it over here," Hailey said. *He's so thoughtful and kind to go out of his way.*

"I was worried she'd wonder where it was." He gave a slight smile.

"She probably was wondering." Except Hailey was certain her well-meaning, but quite devious, grandmother had planted that bag there in the hopes he'd bring it over. The image of the binder overflowing with photos and bios flashed through her mind. *Gran and her little band of matchmaking minions are such schemers.*

"Hello," Gran said innocently as she walked over to the door. "Won't you come in?"

"He brought your knitting." Hailey held up the bag, then gave Gran an I-can-see-right-through-you look, but Gran ignored it.

"Oh, *that's* where it was. I'd leave my head if it wasn't attached." She laughed. "Sorry to be such a scatterbrain."

Hailey didn't buy her act. Not. One. Bit.

"No problem," Peter said.

"Thank you for bringing it over. That was mighty kind of you." Gran slipped a quick glance at Hailey. "We're about to sit down and eat some fruit salad. Would you like to join us?"

Peter looked at Hailey. "I don't want to impose," he said.

"Don't be silly. You brought my knitting all the way over here. The least I can do is feed you." Gran guided Peter over to the table. "You can sit by Hailey," Gran said in her best bossy tone. "Harry, it's time for dinner."

"This looks delicious." Peter sat.

"It's been so hot and humid today it seemed like the best option," Gran said as she helped Gramps take his seat.

Gran dished some salad on Gramps's plate and then on her own. She handed the large orange bowl to Hailey, who spooned some onto her plate. She, in turn, passed the bowl to Peter.

After Peter filled his plate, he picked up his fork.

"We need to say grace," Gran said. "Everyone holds hands while we say it."

Gran is so transparent. Hailey noted the upturn of Gran's mouth, then reached out her hand. Peter slipped his hand in hers. The same warmth from the night before radiated up her arm, enveloping her in quiet contentment as if this were as natural as breathing.

Gran said grace, but Hailey was too distracted by the gentle strength of Peter's hand in hers to hear any of the words.

When Gran finished, Gramps said a loud and enthusiastic amen, which made Hailey giggle.

"Why don't you tell us about yourself, Peter?" Gran plopped a dollop of whipped cream on her plate.

"Not a lot to tell. I grew up in Orlando. My mom still lives there. I have a sister and a nephew that live here in Daytona Beach. I spend most of my time working, but I really enjoy my job."

"He also sings," Hailey said.

"Like an angel," Peter said under his breath, but Hailey caught it.

"Hailey mentioned you took her to one of those singing bars," Gran said. "What kind of songs do you like to sing?"

"Ballads mostly. But I enjoy country music, too."

"He also owns the entire collection of Beatles albums." Hailey bit into a grape and it exploded inside her mouth.

Gran sipped her lemonade. "I remember when they first appeared on TV on the *Ed Sullivan Show*. Harry has always been a big fan."

Gramps started to sing something that sort of resembled "Here Comes the Sun."

Peter joined in. Watching the two of them singing together made Hailey's heart feel happy and squishy. When the impromptu song was finished, she clapped.

"I told you he could sing," Hailey said to Gran.

They continued to chat as they finished eating.

After dinner, Gran said, "It's a little warm, but still a nice evening for a walk. Don't you think?"

"A walk would be nice. Thanks, Gran," Hailey said. Gran was completely entrenched in matchmaking mode.

Hailey followed Peter out the door. "Sorry," she said.

"About what?" He peered at her with his magnetic eyes.

"My grandma. She's so obvious."

Peter laughed. "I think she's funny."

They started down the street. The air was still hot and muggy, but, at this point, it was preferable to staying in the house with her grandparents. *Who knows what else Gran will say?* "I'm glad you came over," Hailey said, hoping it didn't sound too forward.

"You are?" Peter sounded relieved.

He was a good man. Hailey didn't want to play games or make him feel bad, so she decided it was time to be honest. "I didn't come to the appointment today because I had some thinking to do."

"Oh yeah?"

"My ex-boyfriend called earlier. Before the appointment." She paused while they continued to walk for a few moments. "It's a long story."

"I like long stories." The way he said it encouraged her to continue.

"Maybe I can give you the short version." She drew in a breath. "Kevin and I dated for a little over a year. I thought we were going to get married because we'd talked about it. We'd made plans. I expected a proposal, but instead I discovered he was cheating on me with at least two other women." The razor-sharp memory sliced through her. "He ripped my heart out with his betrayal. I felt so broken. So sad. I realized it was all a lie, and my world came crashing down around me."

"I'm sorry," he said in a compassionate tone.

"It was rough." She bit her lip, trying to keep the painful images from seeping into her mind. "When Gramps had his stroke, it seemed like a good opportunity to get away and heal. But then Kevin called, and it all came rushing back."

Peter nodded, but he didn't say anything.

They walked to a nearby park. Peter sat on one of the swings. "Would you like to swing with me?"

Hailey hadn't been on a swing in years. "I don't know."

"Come on," he encouraged. "Life's greatest problems have been solved while swinging."

She gave him a skeptical look. "Oh, really?"

"Absolutely." He pushed himself back and then lifted his feet and started to swing.

Hailey did the same, the thick air lifting the ends of her hair.

"I have to warn you," he said as he passed her in the air. "I'm the Lakeridge jumping champ."

"You don't say." She was never one for jumping out of anything, especially a moving swing.

"I could out swing and out jump anyone. We used to have contests every week at our neighborhood park. I always won."

"I hadn't pegged you as a swinging champ." She laughed.

"Kids came from other neighborhoods to try to beat me. But I won every time."

"Did you end up with some kind of trophy or something?" She imagined some bronzed swing as his prize.

"Nah. Just the recognition. I almost went into it professionally, but decided to go to college instead." He said it as if swinging were a real profession, and Hailey had to purse her lips to keep from grinning.

"That was probably a wise choice." She tried to sound authoritative.

"My mother agreed," he said as he swung past her. "Now I only swing for the enjoyment of it."

This conversation bordered on the ridiculous.

"I'm glad to learn this about you, Mr. Stafford. It engenders a whole new level of respect and admiration."

"Admiration?" He flashed her a smile.

Oh no. Did she say *admiration?* "I mean, acknowledgment of an amazing skill."

"I could be coaxed out of retirement for the right incentive." He leaned back in the swing.

"You mean a bet of sorts?" Hailey watched him. This man was competitive, but in an endearing way.

"Yes. If you're okay with losing again." He said it with so much confidence it could've been mistaken for conceit, but somehow it captivated her.

"I didn't lose," she reminded him. It was a little odd trying to have a conversation while swinging. She'd never done this before.

"Yeah, you did. And you owe me," he said as he whooshed past her.

"Wasn't it dinner?"

"I believe so," he said over his shoulder.

She was quick to say, "And you ate dinner tonight."

"Wait a minute . . . I guess, technically, that's true."

"Then the debt is paid." *Hailey one, Peter zero in this match of wits.*

He swung a few times, then said, "All right, let's bet again."

In her most innocent tone, she said, "I'm not sure about all this gambling, sir."

"Not gambling. It's more like a friendly wager. No money is involved."

She smiled. "That does sound better."

"Are you game?" He looked back at her.

"Sure." *I wonder where this will lead.*

"Winner owes the loser a dessert," he said.

Hailey scrunched her nose. "Don't you mean the loser owes the winner?"

"Nope." With that he jumped out of the swing. "See if you can beat that."

Hailey pumped her legs and then catapulted forward. She was at least a couple of feet short of where Peter landed.

"I win." He did a little dance that made Hailey start to laugh.

"Which means you owe me a dessert," Hailey said, pointing to herself.

"Yep."

She blinked a few times. "Somehow, this seems backwards."

"You got me." He held his hand up. "I want to take you out for dessert."

"That's coincidental. Because I love dessert."

He gazed at her with his inviting eyes. "I guess that makes us a good pair."

Suddenly, her heartbeat sped up—like four times. The air felt even heavier. Was he implying something? That they could be a pair, as in a couple? Was she ready for that? Feeling anxious, Hailey checked her watch. "I better get back to Gran and Gramps."

They began walking back toward the house, a sweet, flowery scent floating in the air. As they approached the front porch, Hailey's mind shot back to the night before. Would Peter try to kiss her goodnight again? Did she want him to? Even after Kevin's call? She hadn't kissed anyone since Kevin, and her feelings were still a little jumbled. Yet the thought of kissing Peter erupted into tiny sensations that congregated in a twisting motion in her stomach, and all she could think about was his lips on hers.

"I enjoyed spending this time with you, Hailey," Peter said with a frankness that left no doubt he meant it.

"Me too. Although," she paused, "I still think I could've beat you jumping out of the swing."

"And I still owe you dessert."

He stepped closer to her. The back of her neck warmed and her heart thudded with each movement he made as the anticipation grew.

Suddenly, her phone started to ring. *I thought I silenced that stupid thing.* She wanted to throw it across the yard and never see it again. But she couldn't. Because it wasn't just any ring—it belonged to her boss.

Peter stepped back. "Do you need to get that?"

Hailey wanted to scream. Her boss had the world's worst timing. "I probably should. It's my boss." She pulled it out of her pocket and tapped accept.

Peter gave her a wave, turned and left.

"Hello?" she said.

"Hailey, I need some figures right away for the Henderson account." Mr. Michaels seemed frazzled.

"I can get those to you," she said with assurance, trying to leave out the irritation she felt.

"When?"

"Now." She was grateful she'd updated the Henderson file earlier.

"I need everything from the last quarter." He sounded almost frantic.

"Yes, sir. I will send that to you." *You couldn't have called any other time for this?*

"Thank you." He ended the call. No time for pleasantries. Mr. Michaels was all business, especially when he was stressed. She glanced down the street at the lost opportunity with Peter, then hurried inside to retrieve the information for her boss.

After sending him what he requested, Hailey walked into the living room where Gran was knitting and Gramps was snoozing in his chair. Hailey flopped on the couch next to Gran.

"Tell me about your walk," Gran said with eagerness.

"You mean the one you set up?"

Gran put down her knitting. "I merely made a suggestion."

"It was fun." *Actually, it was awesome.* Hailey played with the fringe on one of the couch cushions.

"He's a nice young man."

"That he is," Hailey said, feeling wistful.

Amid the clicking of her needles, Gran stated, "And you are falling for him."

"I don't know." Hailey closed her eyes. "Maybe."

"You deserve to be happy."

"It's so easy to talk to Peter." Hailey leaned her head on Gran's shoulder. "And we have fun together."

"Sounds like there's a *but* in there."

"I'm not sure where it can even go." If she let her mind wander even the least little bit, it settled on all sorts of possibilities.

Gran stopped knitting and held Hailey's hand. "How will you know unless you give it a chance?"

"I'm afraid. My heart is still fragile. And Kevin's call has me all sorts of mixed up. I don't want to be hurt like that again." That kind of heartbreak didn't need to be repeated.

"Peter doesn't strike me as a man who would hurt you." Gran patted Hailey's hand.

"I don't know." She hadn't thought Kevin would hurt her, but he trounced all over her heart.

"Did he kiss you tonight?"

Hailey's head popped up. "Gran. Really?"

"Well?"

A smile edged across Hailey's lips. "I think he wanted to, but my boss called. Great timing, right?" She shrugged. "But I'm not even sure I wanted him to. I mean, I wanted him to, but I don't know if it's a good idea." Once she kissed Peter, she feared there would be no turning back.

That night Hailey lay in bed going over the second almost-kiss. This was starting to be a pattern. If Mr. Michaels hadn't called, she would've kissed Peter, but she didn't want to leave a piece of her heart here in Florida. Her career and her home were in Colorado. His home was here in Florida. This was doomed before it even started.

Hailey rolled to her side. She could enjoy some dates with him knowing it had no future, but that wasn't what she wanted. She moved to her back and stared at the revolutions of the ceiling fan. Could she do a long-distance relationship? If Peter was even interested in a relationship—maybe he wanted a fling. Wait, did he think she wanted a fling? No, he didn't seem like a fling kind of guy.

And what about Kevin? How did she feel about him? Did he deserve a second chance when she returned to Colorado Springs?

Her head hammered with questions, and Hailey didn't have any answers. She'd never had so many conflicting emotions ping-ponging inside her, making her whole body ache. Somehow, she needed to figure it all out.

Chapter 30

Peter sat on his leather couch and stared into the inky darkness. The moment had been right to kiss Hailey. Why did that phone have to ring and ruin it? He massaged his temples.

On the other hand, maybe it had done him a favor. What was he doing getting involved with Hailey? She'd go back to Colorado and leave him here. Missing her. That wasn't what he wanted. Or needed. Sara had already left one gaping hole in his heart; he wasn't anxious to have another one.

He laid his head back. Thoughts and images of Hailey swirled around his mind. Her contagious smile. Her dark hair, long and soft, falling past her shoulders. Her flawless face. The vulnerability in her voice when she shared her painful breakup. The way her mesmerizing eyes danced when she spoke about her grandparents. And to top it off, she was easy to talk to. To be with. It felt so relaxed.

It wasn't fair to compare her to Sara. Even in the short time he'd known Hailey, he could tell she was nothing like his ex-wife.

But his heart still struggled to believe it wouldn't be shredded. He'd thought his dream life was with Sara. He'd planned on it and dreamed about it, but it wasn't. His life was shattered when she left.

Now, in the dark, all his fears rose again, making him realize that he wasn't ready for this.

Early Monday afternoon Peter received a frantic text from Laura asking him to pick up Benji after school and take him to karate.

After they arrived at Seaside Martial Arts School, Peter sat on a chair inside the large, industrial-looking room and watched his nephew throw kicks and punches at a large punching bag. Benji then started sparring with a partner. Peter grimaced a few times and hoped no one would get injured. When the instruction concluded, the students bowed to the sensei. Benji came bounding over to Peter.

"Hey, buddy, good job out there." Peter held up his hand for a high-five.

"Thanks, Uncle Peter." He slapped Peter's hand and then glanced around the room. "Is my mom coming?"

"I think she's planning to meet us back at my place. We'll get some dinner to bring home."

Benji's eyes widened. "What are we having?"

"I don't know." Peter knew exactly what his nephew wanted because it was always the same thing.

"Oh, oh. Pizza? I love pizza." Benji licked his lips.

Peter laughed. "Then pizza it is my young padawan."

"Huh?" Benji wrinkled his nose.

"You know, Obi-Wan Kenobi and Anakin."

Benji stared at him blankly.

"You gotta be kidding me. *Star Wars?*" *Where has my sister been keeping this kid? Underground?*

"Oh, yeah. I've heard of that."

"You and I need some serious man time together. What's your mom got you watching? Chick flicks? Love stories?"

Benji shrugged.

Peter patted his deprived nephew on the back. "We shall remedy this immediately."

After they picked up a pepperoni and sausage pizza, Peter and Benji made themselves comfortable on the couch in Peter's condo and started watching *The Phantom Menace.*

"You are going to love these movies, I'm telling you." Peter bit into a piece of pizza.

"Maybe we should wait for my mom," Benji said.

"No way. This is *our* time. We are going to eat pizza, watch *Star Wars*, and bond."

Benji smiled.

About halfway through the movie, the doorbell rang.

"Probably your mom," Peter said. He went to the door and let his sister in.

"I'm so sorry. I didn't think I'd be this late. Thank you so much for getting Benji." She gave him a hug.

"No worries." Spending time with his nephew was more like a reward than anything.

Laura kicked off her shoes, then wound her hair up into a bun. "He went to his karate class?"

"Yep. And we got some pizza and now he's watching *Star Wars*."

"You're the best." Laura smiled. "Thank you. I don't know what I'd do without you. My boss is being so unreasonable lately."

"Do you want some pizza?" he asked.

They walked into the kitchen. Laura grabbed a piece and took a big bite. "I'm starving," she said with her mouth full of pizza.

Peter opened the refrigerator and pulled out a jug of chocolate milk. He poured a glass for Laura.

"You and your chocolate milk." She took a swig. "How was your weekend?"

"Good." He wasn't sure he wanted to get into specifics.

"Have you seen the woman from the restaurant?" She took another bite. "Heidi?"

"Hailey." Mentioning her name made him smile.

"So have you seen her?" Laura's eyes grew wide.

He nodded, knowing full well she would press for more information.

"Details, bro." Laura motioned with her fingers.

Peter leaned against the counter. "We went to the karaoke bar, and then I had dinner accidentally at her grandparents."

Laura quirked her eyebrow. "Accidentally?"

"Her grandmother left her knitting bag when they came for Harry's appointment. So I returned it and she invited me to dinner."

Laura gave him a suspicious look.

"What?" It was completely innocent. He was simply trying to do a nice thing for June.

"You *had* to return it personally?"

"I thought she'd want to have it." Why was Laura questioning his motives?

"You like her." Laura smiled and nodded at the same time. "A lot."

He shook his head. "I was only . . ." He let it trail off, because Laura was right. He did like Hailey—more than he wanted to admit—which was why his insides were like pretzels.

"When are you going to see her again?"

Peter put the milk back in the fridge.

"Well?" Laura asked expectantly.

"I don't know."

Laura sat atop the barstool. "What? Why don't you have plans?"

He had no answer. Except that he was afraid Hailey would work her way deep into his heart and then abandon it.

"You can't spend your life being scared that history will repeat itself," Laura said as if reading his mind. "You have to take a chance one of these days."

"I did. I took her out. Like you suggested." What else did she want?

"No. I mean a real chance." She took a swallow of milk. "At love. At commitment. At a future."

"But—"

"But nothing. Don't be stupid."

He crossed his arms in front of his chest. "She's going back to Colorado when her grandfather recovers." Laura would obviously see the futility of future dates.

"That's easy," Laura said.

"It is?" What did she mean?

Laura gave him a do-I-have-to-explain-everything kind of look. "Make her want to stay."

"I can't ask her to move here." Was his sister crazy?

Laura shrugged. "This is the first woman that's gotten your attention in years. Don't let her slip away."

Peter sat on the barstool next to Laura. "I'm not even sure she's interested in any kind of relationship."

"Why wouldn't she be?" Laura grabbed another piece of pizza.

"She just went through a bad breakup." Having gone through one himself, he remembered all too well how much it hurt.

"You can't keep one foot on the deck and one in the pool, you know. You have to jump in with both feet." Laura picked a piece of sausage off her pizza and popped it into her mouth. "If you don't, you'll never swim."

"Huh?"

"It means"—she poked his arm with her finger—"stop being an idiot."

He shook his head and then stood. "Let's watch the rest of the movie with Benji."

After Benji and Laura left, Peter sat on the couch and drummed his fingers against his leg. A tug-of-war raged in his mind. On the one hand, being alone was safe, secure. He didn't have to worry about being hurt and enduring all that pain again. On the other hand, he couldn't get enough of Hailey, and he wanted to spend as much time with her as he could.

Peter laid his head back and closed his eyes, delving into his psyche. He did want love, commitment, and a future. He still wanted the dream of a wife and kids living in a house in the suburbs. If he were being honest, Peter needed Laura to give him that proverbial kick. Left to his own devices, he'd probably become an eternal hermit to protect himself from heartache. But is that what he truly wanted—to guard his heart at the expense of missing out on something amazing with Hailey?

Peter opened his eyes and gazed out the window. He grabbed his laptop and surfed the Internet looking for ideas for another date. He'd lived in Daytona Beach for a few years but hadn't been part of the dating scene, so he wasn't sure where he could take Hailey. After almost thirty minutes, he found what he was looking for.

Chapter 31

Hailey sat on her bed, still in her well-loved pajama shirt, with her laptop open trying to get some work done before the office opened. Mr. Michaels needed some more files and she had reports she needed to send in. She'd collected the documents needed for Mr. Lanceton's audit and had sent those in. It had been harder than she'd thought it would be over the last month trying to work from Florida, but she was grateful Mr. Michaels had allowed her to. She didn't want to think about her time with her grandparents coming to an end soon, especially because she wasn't sure when she'd be able to return. And, if she were being completely honest, she didn't want to think about not seeing Peter anymore.

She stood and stretched. A glance in the direction of her laundry pile reminded her it was time to do a load or two of clothes. She began gathering her clothing when her phone rang. It was Peter.

Immediately, her hands started to tremble. "Hello?"

"Hi, Hailey. It's Peter."

"Oh, hi." She said it nonchalantly so he wouldn't suspect she'd already put all his contact information into her phone.

"Are you busy this evening?"

Normally she liked more notice for a date, but she was willing to forego that formality for Peter. "I think I'm free."

"Would you like to go out with me?"

"Yes, I would." Going out with him again was dangerous, but Hailey wasn't willing to say no.

"I'll come over after work. About five-thirty." His voice was light and upbeat.

She sat on the bed, excitement churning inside her. "Are you going to tell me where we're going?"

"No. But it involves the dessert I owe you."

"I'm not sure what that means, but it sounds fun." Anything with Peter sounded magnificent.

"I'll see you later." He ended the call.

She had no idea where they were going or what they were doing. How could she choose an appropriate outfit? Maybe she needed a new one.

After a shrimp salad for lunch, Gran said, "We have another bingo night tonight, would you like to come?" She began clearing the table.

Hailey didn't want to disappoint Gran, but she had no desire to give up a night with Peter to play bingo. "I can't." She handed Gran a plate.

Gran ran some water over the dishes. "More work?"

"No, not work."

Gran turned, stared at her, and then smiled. "A date? With Peter?"

Hailey nodded, trying to keep the smile from exploding on her face, but she failed.

"I'm glad to hear it," Gran said.

"But what about bingo?" She didn't want to make Gran miss out.

"I can always do that." Gran waved her hand. "Besides, I need to finish knitting the baby blanket for my new great grandson. And Harry and I can watch a movie."

"Are you sure?" Hailey didn't want to cancel the plans, but she could rearrange them to suit Gran.

"Yes, I'm sure." Gran wiped off the counter. "What are you going to wear?"

"I don't know." Hailey mentally rummaged through her clothing, but nothing stuck out that she wanted to wear for this date. "I was thinking about going to the mall to find a new outfit. Do you want to come with me?"

Gran seemed to consider the idea. "I'd really like to go with you, but some of my friends were going to come over today."

Hailey rolled her eyes. "More plotting for the love-challenged?"

"Now, dear, I know you don't approve of our services, but we do help people find each other." Gran gave a sharp nod. "And, goodness knows, the world can do with more love."

"I guess." Hailey still thought it weird that a group of old ladies sat around planning dates for unsuspecting victims, but it seemed to be relatively harmless, and it made Gran happy.

"I can reschedule our meeting, and I suppose I could ask Raymond across the street to come play cards with Harry."

"We wouldn't be gone long," Hailey said.

Hailey and Gran drove over to the mall and shopped in a couple stores. Hailey found a fitted red dress. She walked out of the dressing room and stood in front of a three-way mirror. The dress looked even better on her out there than in the small room. "That's adorable on you," Gran said.

"You think so?" Hailey twirled around.

"Really shows off your figure. Wish I had a tiny waist like yours." Gran patted her side.

Hailey stared at herself in the mirror. She loved how the dress made her feel—feminine and dainty. "Maybe it's too dressy."

Gran studied her. "He didn't tell you where you're going?"

"Nope. I think he wants it to be a surprise." Hailey wasn't too fond of surprises. She didn't care much for impulsiveness or spontaneity—she preferred to make plans and know exactly what was going on—but tonight she'd make an exception. Being with Peter made her want to branch out, even take a chance.

"He's a good one, Hailey."

"Let's not jump to any conclusions. This is a date, not a marriage proposal, Gran," Hailey said, reminding herself of the same thing.

Gran wagged her finger at Hailey in the mirror. "I still say he's a good young man and you shouldn't let him go."

"I don't *have* him. This is a friendly date. Nothing more." Even as the words left her mouth, she hoped they weren't true. She'd been moping around long enough after Kevin, and she was ready to move on. It was time for a new chapter. Actually, it was time for a whole new book.

Hailey purchased the dress and they drove back to the house.

Chapter 32

As the clock ticked ever closer to five-thirty, Hailey's stomach did cartwheels in anticipation. In the bathroom, she brushed her hair, dabbed on some perfume, and checked her makeup.

"Hailey?" Gran's voice echoed down the hallway.

"Coming." She checked herself one last time in the mirror, making sure she didn't have anything in her teeth.

Hailey strolled out into the living room keeping her nerves under control. Peter stood there in gray shorts and a black shirt that fit him snugly in all the right places. His eyes widened almost imperceptibly when he turned and saw her. "Hi. You look beautiful."

"Thank you." *This dress is a winner.*

"Are you ready?"

Hailey was more than ready. "Where are we going?" she asked.

A playful smile stretched across his mouth. "It's a secret."

"Sounds exciting," Gran said, clasping her hands together.

Gramps was sitting in his recliner. He adjusted his blue shirt and then said with some effort, "You t-t-wo, h-h-h-aaaaaaaavvvve fffff-uuun."

"Thank you. I think we'll do just that," Peter said brightly. "I'll take good care of her, Harry."

"You b-b-bettttterrrr." Gramps pointed at him and smiled.

Hailey bent over and gave Gramps a kiss on the forehead. "You and Gran going to bingo?"

Gramps rolled his eyes.

"Maybe you'll win." Hailey said.

"He doesn't enjoy bingo like I do. Thinks it's rigged," Gran said, her silver dangly earrings swaying as she spoke. "It'll do him good to get out for a bit. Dee will be here to pick us up soon."

Gramps shrugged.

Gran gave Hailey a kiss on the cheek. "I'll leave the porch light on."

Peter escorted Hailey to his car and they started driving.

"You really aren't going to tell me what we're doing tonight?" Hailey's curiosity kicked in.

"Nope." He smirked.

"I'm not a huge fan of surprises. Just so you know. I like to be prepared."

"This is a good surprise." He nodded with a grin. "You'll like it. Trust me."

That's *exactly* what she was doing—trusting him. She hoped it wouldn't come back to bite her.

They pulled into a parking lot. "Here we are," he said with enthusiasm.

Peter opened her door and they walked over to a landing pad. The sun was beginning its descent over the bay and a few birds flew overhead.

"I read some good reviews about this dinner cruise, but I haven't been on it," Peter said.

"Dinner cruise? I've never been on one. Sounds . . . fun." What she wanted to say was that it sounded romantic, but she thought better of it. Hailey didn't want to read anything into this date.

"I guess this is a first for both of us," Peter said as they walked across a bridge onto the deck.

The boat had a huge wooden paddle behind it, which reminded her of the Mark Twain Riverboat in Disneyland. When they entered the dining area inside, succulent smells of roasted meat, fresh-baked bread, and garlic floated in the air. White linen tablecloths adorned the tables, and a small bouquet of red silk roses sat in the middle of each one. A tall woman dressed in a white blouse and black pants directed them to a table for six next to a large window that overlooked the water.

"This is pretty out here." Hailey noticed all the vegetation along the banks.

Peter pulled out a chair for Hailey, then sat next to her.

Another couple was seated at their table.

"Hi, I'm Abbie," a platinum-blonde, petite woman said. "And this is my husband, Brad." She giggled.

"In case you can't tell, we just got married," the man with wavy brown hair and a goatee said.

Great. We're sitting at a table with newlyweds. This is going to be awkward. Hailey gave them her best smile.

"When did you get married?" Peter asked.

"Three weeks ago," Abbie cooed. "It was so romantic. Our ceremony was at the beach right at sunset."

Brad reached his arm around his bride and pulled her close. "And she was the most beautiful bride." He kissed her.

Two empty chairs were still available at the table, and Hailey worried another newlywed couple would sit with them.

Brad pointed at Hailey and Peter. "How long have you been married?"

"Us?" Hailey laughed nervously. "Oh, we aren't married."

"At least not yet," Abbie said with another giggle and then turned and snuggled into her husband.

What did she mean by that? Hailey was sure her face matched her red dress.

"This is our table," a middle-aged lady with short black hair said. She sat next to Hailey, then pulled out her phone.

A balding man with glasses sat across from the lady. "I guess we'll be eating dinner with you," he said. "My name is Rick and this is my wife, Samantha."

"Nice to meet you," Peter said, then introduced Hailey and himself.

Samantha kept scrolling on her phone while Rick leaned back in his chair and gazed around the dining area. Neither of them seemed interested in conversation with each other or with anyone else at the table.

Hailey turned to the newlyweds, but they were wound up in each other's arms. She gazed at Peter, who gave her a helpless look. It seemed that they had two people at the table who couldn't get enough of each other and another two who had more than their share. Where did that leave them?

"The prime rib is excellent according to what I read," Peter said, scooting closer to Hailey.

"I love prime rib. T-bones, sirloin, filet mignon. You name it, I love it." Hailey's mouth watered.

Peter gazed at her and raised his eyebrows. "You do?"

Hailey nodded. "Oh, yeah."

"Most women prefer chicken or no meat at all." Peter casually draped his arm across the back of her chair.

"Back in Colorado, we used to get a side of beef every year. Gramps insisted. He grew up on a cattle ranch." Happy memories of her childhood poured in, and suddenly she longed to share her hometown with Peter, but she quickly tied those feelings into a nice, neat package and tucked it away.

"Harry was a cowboy?" Peter's eyes widened.

"He sure was. And he used to ride broncs on the rodeo circuit."

"Really?" Surprise splayed on his face. "Never would've guessed that."

"Gran made him give rodeoing up after they got married. She wanted a family man who was home with the kids. They lived on the ranch, and Gramps took care of the animals and milked the cows."

Peter moved in closer. A whiff of his musky cologne floated past her nose, putting her nerves on alert. "How did he end up on the police force?"

"Hard to make ends meet on a ranch. His older brother took it over when my great-grandpa died, and Gramps thought that was a good time to make a change, but he still helped when he could."

"Fascinating."

Hailey twirled a lock of her hair. "Gramps used to take me hunting on the ranch."

"You hunt?" He blinked a couple of times.

"I'm a pretty good shot, if I do say so myself." She paused, then smiled. "And I do."

"You're blowing my mind." He blinked again. "I never would've imagined you were a hunter."

"Well, I was never a fan of gutting the deer or skinning it, but I love fresh venison." She could almost taste it.

"And you ride horses?" His full attention was on her and it radiated warmth like the midmorning summer sun.

"When I was a kid, I used to spend time during the summer there riding John."

"John?"

"He was a Quarter Horse. Big, deep brown, and full of muscles. Nothing better than riding him in the field and feeling the wind whip through my hair." The freedom and pure happiness she felt during those carefree days flashed through her memory.

"You are definitely a western girl." His fingers brushed her bare arm, sending prickles across her skin.

"I am." She leaned in. "What about you? I mean, besides being the Lakeridge Swing Jumping Champ, what else did you do?" Being this close to Peter made her heart flutter.

"After my many championship jumps, I retired and spent time at the beach."

"Beach bum, then?" It was easy to imagine him on the beach with his trim body and sun-bleached blond hair.

"Kinda." He smiled, his hypnotic eyes drawing her in. "I did a lot of scuba diving and fishing. My dad and I would drive over on a Saturday morning from Orlando and spend the day fishing at different spots. Spent a lot of time talking about life and waiting for the fish to bite."

"I used to fish with Gramps back in Colorado, and one time he took me on a big boat here when I was visiting. It was so much fun."

"Maybe we could all go fishing sometime. It'd be great fun with Harry and June." His gaze held hers, making her stomach twist and turn like she was on a rollercoaster while energy sparked between them.

"Excuse me," someone said, breaking the spell.

Hailey looked up to see a waitress with a salad in her hand. Hailey cleared her throat and settled back in her chair, noticing the temperature had increased several degrees. At least it felt that way.

After the salads had been handed out, Samantha wrinkled her nose and said, "This looks like that bagged salad you get at the grocery store."

"Maybe you could enjoy it, instead of complaining," Rick said without emotion.

"Maybe if we went to a place I wanted to go, I wouldn't have to complain," she said sourly.

"Are you kidding me? You said you wanted to go on a dinner cruise." Rick sat back, a look of disdain crossing his face.

"Not this weekend."

They began to bicker and Hailey made a mental note to never become someone like that. *What a miserable way to live.*

A few minutes later, the waitress placed the prime rib on the table. The newlyweds barely noticed. All they could do was gaze into each other's eyes with an occasional giggle from Abbie. Hailey envied that and hoped someday she'd have the same thing.

"This prime rib is excellent," Peter said.

"Practically melts in my mouth." Hailey took a bite of the asparagus drizzled with garlic butter. "I've never liked asparagus much, but this is so good."

"And the rolls taste like my mom's," Peter said. "But don't tell her that."

"I won't." Hailey patted her chest. "You can trust me."

Peter smiled.

Hailey took a few more bites of the tender meat. "This was a great idea. An awesome idea. A superb idea, in fact." She stopped herself from rambling on anymore and hoped she didn't sound too over-the-top enthusiastic.

"I agree." Peter bit into his asparagus, then licked his lips, drawing Hailey's attention to his mouth. All she could think about was feeling his soft, full lips on hers, tasting his kiss, and losing herself in his strong embrace. Her heart drummed a steady beat in her ears while delectable thoughts of kissing Peter circled round her head.

Peter looked up at her, making her realize she was staring and letting her mind go wild with all sorts of risky thoughts. She smoothed her hair and said, "Uh, yeah, I was just thinking that this dinner is so . . . good." It was the best she could do. *I'm so transparent. He totally knows I was thinking about him.*

"I'm glad you're enjoying it."

"I am. Aren't you? I mean, it's delicious, don't you think?" She sounded like a babbling teenager wrapped up in too many conflicting emotions.

Peter peered at her, making her feel dizzy. "I'm enjoying *everything*."

The way he said it didn't leave much doubt as to what he meant. "Me too," she said, steadying herself against the impulse to wrap her arms around his neck and kiss him. *Do not be impulsive.*

After they finished dinner, the waitress brought them each a slice of cheesecake with strawberry sauce.

"Your dessert," Peter said with a smile. "I've made good on the bet now."

Hailey took a bite of the creamy goodness. "You have."

"When we're done, there's dancing on the upper deck."

"Dancing?" *Could this night be any more magical?*

He nodded.

They finished the decadent dessert and then headed up the stairs. The music hadn't started so they strolled to the front of the boat. Hailey leaned against the railing. "What a beautiful evening." Twilight was settling in and a soft breeze blew from the south. The water across the bay rippled, then lapped at the side of the boat. Peter leaned against the railing, his upper arm slightly touching Hailey's arm. They stood there, gazing out on the water but not saying anything, while a peaceful, pleasant feeling encased them.

Some instrumental music began to play. Peter extended his hand and Hailey eagerly took it, loving again how his hand fit so comfortably around hers. They made their way back into the dance area.

A woman with long purple-streaked hair wearing a bright purple spaghetti-strap shirt lifted a microphone to her mouth and said, "Welcome to Moonlight Cruise on the Bay. We're happy you're here with us tonight. How about we get this party started?" The crowd clapped and a man in the back whistled. "First off, let's dance to one of my favorites, Tim McGraw," she said.

The guitar intro started to "I Like It, I Love It."

Peter said, "Would you like to dance?"

"Do you know the swing?" Hailey asked. "Not the jumping out of kind, but the dance steps?"

"Yes, I do. My mom insisted I take dance classes when I was twelve. I hated it, of course, but she wanted me to be a gentleman. At the end of the class, we all had a big dance." They stood at the edge of the dance floor holding hands and talking.

Hailey smiled at the thought of a twelve-year-old Peter at a dance. "Like a formal one?"

"Yeah. We dressed up in suits and had to ask girls to dance. It was quite the event."

"Especially at that age." She remembered being twelve and wasn't so sure she would've been game to take dance lessons.

"It's still seared into my memory." He tapped his forehead.

Certain he was exaggerating, Hailey said, "That sounds a little daunting."

Peter let out a whistle. "I think Carol Anne Stevens would agree."

"Oh yeah?" She *had* to hear this story.

He drew his brows together. "I did mention the girls wore long dresses?"

Hailey shook her head.

"And that I was clumsy?"

She shook her head again.

"And that when I stepped on Carol Anne's dress it kind of ripped."

Hailey covered her mouth. "A big rip?"

"The biggest." He pursed his lips and nodded.

"Oh no." She pictured a young girl standing on the dance floor with a gaping hole exposing her underside.

"So, yeah, *seared* into my memory."

"We can skip the dance. You know, if it brings back painful memories," she said with a grin and a playful nudge with her arm.

Peter placed his hand on the small of her back and guided her out to the dance floor. They began to swing. Hailey wasn't as graceful as she'd hoped and stepped right on Peter's foot, but he acted as though it didn't hurt. They scooted across the dance floor and did a two-step to the next song. Hailey was having so much fun and trying her best not to step on his foot again.

After some vigorous dancing, Peter said between breaths, "Let's go outside." He reached his hand out for Hailey and she readily took it.

The air wasn't much cooler outside, but it was a welcome relief to get away from the crowd on the dance floor. Dusk had turned to night.

"You are quite a dancer," Peter said.

"Better than your partner in dance class?"

Peter smiled. "Yes. And you aren't a foot taller than me, either. That's a bonus."

Hailey stood on her tiptoes. "Not into tall girls?"

"Not in middle school. Way too intimidating."

"You were intimidated by girls?"

He nodded emphatically. "Very much so."

"I find that hard to believe."

He turned around and leaned against the railing. "Let's see. I don't think I hit a hundred pounds until I was a sophomore, maybe even a junior, in high school. My nickname was Pee Wee Pete, thanks to a couple neighbor boys."

"I see." Hailey bit her lip so she wouldn't smile.

"I'd like to think I don't earn that name anymore."

Arching a brow, she said, "Fishing for a compliment, Mr. Stafford?"

He straightened. "No. I wasn't fishing. I didn't mean . . ."

Hailey let out a laugh. She found his humility charming.

"Can I get you a drink?" he asked.

"I'd love an ice-cold lemon water. All this dancing has made me thirsty."

"I'll be right back."

Hailey watched him walk away. He was the total package. Gorgeous. Funny. Fun. Kind. Compassionate. Their conversation was engaging, and she was having a wonderful time tonight. But how long could it last? She'd eventually go back to her life in Colorado and never see him again. Of course, they could enjoy some fun—except Peter wasn't the sort of man you simply had fun with. He was the sort of man you made a life with.

"As you ordered." Peter handed her a glass of water with a lemon floating at the top.

"Nothing quenches my thirst like water. And it's so hot here I think I must drink two gallons a day." She sipped the cool liquid, letting it slide down her dry throat.

"Florida heat and humidity are an acquired taste, I suppose, but I can't imagine living anywhere else."

When the music slowed and Taylor Swift's song, "Enchanted," started to play, Peter guided Hailey out to the dance floor. Peter pulled her close to him—close enough she feared he could feel her heart beating furiously inside her chest. His hand was strong and certain against her back, and in the other hand he clutched hers, slowly bringing it to him, making the nerves up and down her arm start to twitch. Swaying back and forth, Hailey lost herself in his capable arms—the music, the dancing, the romantic setting—and felt as though she could stay here and dance like this all night. Like the title of the song, she was finding herself enchanted by this man and hoping he felt the same. Despite Hailey's efforts to lock her heart, Peter had found the key.

When the song ended, Peter led her out to the deck. The warm breeze washed over her while the moon perched above them in the sky. Peter reached his arm around her as they gazed across the water. Neither of them said anything.

"This is a perfect night," she said, breaking the silence. Everything about this date was flawless. In the Great Book of Dating, this would absolutely be number one. The only thing that could make it better would be a kiss under the moonlight.

As if reading her mind, Peter turned her around so they were facing each other and peered deeply into her eyes.

Her gaze was drawn to his lips as he moved closer to her. A whiff of his cologne awakened all her senses. He ran his finger along her neckline, inciting a mass eruption of goosebumps from her neck to her toes. Her breathing became labored as his lips hovered over hers. She'd never wanted a kiss as much as she wanted this one. Right here. Right now. His warm lips brushed hers softly, delicately, leaving her breathless and yearning for more. Once again, his mouth covered hers, gently at first, but then more confidently. Her lips tingled and sent ripples of energy coursing through her body. He brought her even closer, their bodies melding together as one while his strong hands caressed her back. It was as if no one else existed on the boat, or on the planet for that matter. Every part of her was consumed with desire to kiss him long and hard and never stop.

He finally pulled away, drew in a deep breath, and then brushed a tendril of hair from her face. "I don't know what's happening, but I like it."

She nodded. *Definitely enchanted.*

"I don't want this night to end," he whispered.

Hailey loved his honesty. "Me either."

They spent the rest of the boat ride arm in arm. Hailey wasn't sure what all of this meant, but, at the moment, she didn't care. She only wanted to be here with Peter. Nothing else mattered.

When the boat docked, they walked leisurely with arms around each other to the parking lot. Inside the car, Peter grasped her hand and held it in his. He drew it to his mouth and lightly kissed each knuckle, sending such a strong current through her body that she was afraid it might paralyze her limbs.

On the drive back, Peter asked," What kind of music do you like?"

"I'm pretty eclectic. I like Twenty-One Pilots, Neck Deep, and Aerosmith. And I listen to Rascal Flatts, Boston, and I love a few of Taylor Swift's songs." *Especially* "Enchanted."

"You're right." He laughed. "That's quite a spectrum of music."

"What about you? Besides the Beatles, what other music do you like?"

He glanced at her. "I used to listen to heavy metal back in the day."

"Really?" That didn't seem to fit him.

"In high school, I played the electric guitar. I was even part of a band."

"Seriously?" She'd completely misjudged this man. What other surprises did he have? "What was the name of your band?"

"The Screaming Dolphins."

She didn't want to laugh out loud, but that was a ridiculous name.

Instead she said, "That's interesting."

"Yeah. We didn't make it too far down the road to fame and fortune." He paused. "Plus, most of our parents refused to let us practice in their garages. But, in our minds, we were legendary."

"You ever play the guitar now?"

He shook his head. "I gave it up when I went to college. I needed all the time I could find to study and learn as much as possible about language and speech."

Hailey gazed out the window. "Of all the things that could've been affected by his stroke, speech was the worst one for Gramps. He's had a hard time. I sure hope . . ."

"Harry is already beginning to regain his speech and have conversations." Peter squeezed her hand as if giving her encouragement. "With you helping him, he can't lose."

"Thanks." She appreciated Peter's positive attitude and his encouragement, and she hoped he was right. More than anything, she wanted Gramps to regain all his speech, and for things to go back to normal.

"I was thinking we could plan a picnic at Cocoa Beach," Peter said.

"That sounds awesome. We could—" Hailey's phone started playing "Hello." *Worst timing ever. I don't want anyone calling me right now. Why didn't I turn off the ringer?*

"You should answer it," Peter said.

Hailey reluctantly pulled her phone out and looked at the caller ID. "Gran?" she said.

"Oh, Hailey," Gran said through sobs.

"What is it?" Hailey's stomach clenched and her pulse beat erratically.

"It's Harry."

"Gramps?" *Please don't say he's had another stroke. Please!*

"Something's happened. I don't know." Gran wept. "I called 911. The paramedics are here."

"I'll be there as soon as possible." Hailey's eyes brimmed with tears and her throat swelled three times its size.

"Please hurry."

Hailey ended the call, blood rushing through her veins.

"What's wrong?" Peter asked with urgency.

"EMTs are at the house." Dread filled Hailey's lungs as she struggled to breathe.

"Another stroke?" His voice was thick.

Hailey wiped at her eyes, fear threatening to suffocate her. "Gran doesn't know."

"I'll get us there as fast as I can."

The drive over was a blur, a million thoughts pinging in Hailey's mind. A lump formed in her throat and grew exponentially the closer they got to the house. *Gramps has to be okay. He has to be.*

When they arrived at the house, Hailey flung open the door of the car and jumped out. With each step, she felt as though she were swimming against an unrelenting current. Finally, she made it to the front door and went inside. The thick, stale air weighed heavy on her chest. Two women wearing EMT uniforms stood next to the door.

"What's going on?" Hailey asked, her heart rapping against her ribs and adrenaline shooting through her veins.

The woman with black hair said, "When we arrived, we checked his vitals and couldn't find a heartbeat."

"You did CPR, right? He's okay." Hailey looked between the two women. "Gramps is okay, right?" A cold sweat began to envelop her.

"We've done all we can," the other woman with short red hair said. "I'm sorry."

"No, no, no. Do *not* say that. You keep trying." Tears spilled down her cheeks. "Do you hear me? You keep trying." Her voice felt rough and harsh, and her hands wouldn't stop shaking.

Gran came over and draped her arms around Hailey.

"He can't be gone. Tell them to keep trying." Hailey buried her face in Gran's neck. After several moments, she said, "This can't be happening. He was fine when we left. You were going to bingo." Hailey stepped back and wiped her eyes with the back of her hand. "What happened?"

Gran looked at her with red-rimmed eyes. "We went to bingo, and I even won a game." She took in several breaths. "Dee brought us home and I asked him if he wanted anything to eat or drink. He wanted to watch TV." Tears welled up in her eyes. "I was only in the bedroom for a short time. When I came back into the living room, he was slumped over in his chair. I couldn't get him to respond." Gran started sobbing, so Hailey hugged her close, refusing to look in the direction of his chair. "I had no idea he was . . ." Gran didn't finish her sentence.

Hailey and Gran stood there locked in a tight embrace. Hailey wanted to comfort Gran. She wanted to comfort herself. *He can't be gone. He can't be.*

"I don't know what I'll do without him." Gran seemed so tiny in Hailey's arms—so fragile, as if she'd break at any moment.

"What can I do to help?" Peter asked, reminding Hailey he was still there.

Hailey stepped away from Gran and shrugged. Her eyes were on fire. This couldn't be it for Gramps. Not yet. She wasn't ready.

Peter caressed her shoulder, then pulled her to him. Through her tears she said, "This isn't real. I don't believe he's gone." Hailey gulped for oxygen like she was drowning. How could he be gone so fast?

"I'm so sorry," Peter said softly.

Gran started sobbing, so Hailey went to her and held her.

"It could've been a heart attack or a stroke," a male EMT with glasses and wearing blue gloves said. "We've put in a call to the coroner." He gazed at Hailey with sympathy in his eyes. "I'm sorry."

"Thank you," was all Hailey could say to the paramedic.

The coroner, a dark-skinned man with gray hair, arrived a short time later, and spoke about arrangements for Gramps, but Hailey's mind was so muddled and her emotions so raw, she could barely function. *Pull yourself together so you can take care of Gran.*

Peter stepped up and said, "I'll make some calls."

"You will?" Hailey had never been so grateful.

"Yes. You need to focus on June. I can take care of this."

A flood of relief washed over Hailey. "Thank you."

"I'll be here as long as you need me." Peter gave her a hug, then pulled out his phone.

It was surreal—Hailey was there but not there at the same time. The air was dank and clingy, enveloping her in disbelief and sorrow. Her heart was shattered for Gran, but also for herself. How could this have happened? He'd been fine and she'd been enjoying a magical date with Peter. Then, in an instant, it all changed.

She and Gran sat on the couch in silence for what seemed like hours until a knock sounded at the door. Two men in dark clothing came in and loaded up Gramps to take his remains away. A piece of Hailey's heart left with them.

She turned her attention back to her grandmother, who was silently crying in Peter's arms.

"Let's get you a glass of water and then you can lie down," Hailey said.

"I don't know what I'm going to do. Harry was everything to me," Gran said. "I can't believe he's gone."

Hailey gave her some water, then guided her down the hall to her bedroom. "I don't want you to worry about anything. Please try to rest."

Gran sniffed. "I'll try."

Hailey made her way back to the living room feeling like she wore cement boots. Her whole body ached with sadness.

"Thank you for being here, Peter."

He pulled her into an embrace. "I'm so sorry."

Hailey let the tears flow as she hung onto him. "He was fine when we left. How did this happen?"

"This is the most difficult part of my job. It's hard losing people we love." He kissed her tenderly on the forehead.

"I wish I'd talked to him one more time. Told him I loved him one more time. I feel so . . . empty." She let out a long, mournful breath.

"He knew you loved him." Peter held her close. "No doubt about that."

"My heart hurts so much."

Peter guided her over to the couch and they sat. He put his arm around her, and Hailey snuggled into him, needing the comfort he offered. Hailey lost track of how long they sat there.

Finally, she said, "I thought he was going to get better. That he'd get back to his old self. I didn't think he'd die. I mean, I knew it was a possibility, but I didn't think it'd actually happen."

Peter stroked her hand, but didn't say anything.

"I thought I'd come here and help, then leave when things were back to normal. I thought it might take a month or so, but I figured he'd be better, and they'd both go on living for years." She shook her head. "I should've stayed here with them tonight. Maybe if I'd been here . . ."

"You can't do that to yourself." Peter said. "You can't second guess what you do."

"But maybe I could've saved him." If she'd been thinking about her grandparents instead of herself, Gramps might still be alive.

"I've learned in my career that I can't play the *What-If* game. I have to treat people the best I can and live the best I can and then trust God to take care of the rest."

"I feel so sad." *Sad* didn't seem to adequately convey the depth of her sorrow.

"Harry was a good man and he lived a good life."

Hailey sat up and wiped at her face. "What do we do now?"

"You'll need to make arrangements for the funeral."

A waterfall of tears splashed down her cheeks, and she slumped back against the couch. "I can't even think about this."

"I'm here to help in any way I can."

Peter was so kind and caring. He was a port in this unexpected storm, and she was grateful for his strength. "Thank you. I appreciate you being here. It makes me feel better."

Hailey leaned her head against his shoulder and closed her eyes. The next thing she knew, her eyelids flew open, and she was lying on the couch with a blanket tucked around her. Peter was on the floor, his head propped up on one of the couch pillows. Early morning light was streaming through the window and it all hit her again with the force of a speeding truck. *Gramps is gone.*

Warm tears slipped down her face and onto the pillow. Today was going to be hard, but she had to be strong for Gran, who needed her more than ever now.

Hailey glanced down at Peter. He looked so peaceful sleeping there. Her heart was touched that he'd spent his night trying to comfort her. He was a good man. The kind of man she could love for a long time to come. She shook that thought free. Gran needed all of Hailey's attention and focus right now.

Hailey went to the bathroom and splashed cool water on her face. Her bloodshot eyes stared back at her from the mirror. She had so much to do, including calling her mom and letting her know. And what about Regina? Hailey should find her and tell her, even though Regina was the last person she wanted to find. Under any other circumstances, Regina could stay gone forever, but Hailey knew the right thing to do was to find her aunt.

Hailey tiptoed down the hall and peeked in on Gran, who was still sleeping. What would Gran do? Would she keep living here? Go somewhere else? Maybe go to her sister's house? Or back to Colorado? Too many unanswered questions rolled around her throbbing head.

When Hailey returned to the living room, Peter was awake and sitting on the couch. He stood. "How are you?" he asked, his eyes full of empathy.

"Still trying to process everything." Hailey ran her fingers through her hair. "I'm sorry I fell asleep. I didn't mean for you to have to stay."

"I wanted to."

"But you probably have appointments today."

"I do." He nodded. "But I can cancel them."

"No." Hailey held out her hands. She couldn't ask him to give up work. Besides, she needed to focus on her grandmother. "You should go to work. It'll be fine."

He peered at her with compassion. "Are you sure?"

"Yes." She wasn't sure she could handle this at all, but somehow, she had to.

"Would it be all right if I came back after work to check on you?"

"I'd like that." *Actually, I'd love that.*

Peter smoothed his hair and adjusted the collar of his shirt. He made his way to the front door. "I'll see you later."

Chapter 33

Peter rolled down his window as he drove. The already too-hot morning air blew through the car. His heart was heavy—he'd miss Harry. True, Harry had been a bit cantankerous at times, but he always had a smile and a way about him that made Peter miss his own grandpa. He hated this part of his job and tried not to get too attached, but he'd failed with Harry. And not just failed, but failed miserably.

Then there was Hailey. He'd been attracted to her from the minute he met her. That attraction had grown as he'd gotten to know her and spent time with her. She made him laugh and feel something he hadn't in an exceedingly long time—something he'd worried he'd never feel again. It was a connection that went deeper than physical attraction.

He shook his head. "But her life is in Colorado." The words sounded hollow as they left his mouth. Peter didn't want to lose this chance with a woman that he could see a future with. Though he hadn't known her long, he'd spent enough time with her to know she was the kind of woman he wanted to build a life with. And share a home with. And a white picket fence with kids' toys strewn all over the lawn.

But maybe that was only a fantasy. Maybe reality was that women left. Sara left him and now Hailey would too—for different reasons, but the outcome was still the same. He'd be left alone. Again.

Perhaps it was better this way. He could get out before he was in too deep. Get back to focusing on his career and his plans to start his own practice. He had a good life. A great life, as a matter of fact. He didn't need a woman to complete it. He was happy.

Except he wasn't.

Chapter 34

Shortly after Peter left, Hailey heard Gran sobbing in her bedroom. She knocked on the door, "Gran?"

"Come in," came the shaky voice.

Hailey took two strides to Gran's bed and sat next to her.

"I keep thinking that if only I'd checked on him sooner. Or stayed there next to him. Maybe he'd still be here."

"You can't blame yourself." Hailey desperately wanted to take the anguish from Gran, but she knew she couldn't.

"I'm not ready to let him go. I'm not ready for it to be all over." Gran gazed past Hailey. "It seems like yesterday that I met him. He was such a handsome fella with his dark hair and big muscles. We fell in love deeply and passionately. Before I knew it, we were married and had your daddy and Regina. All-around American family—that was us. We were so happy." Gran smiled, lost in her memories. "Seems like I went to bed one night with my kids underfoot and woke up the next morning to an empty nest." She let out a long breath. "Of course, we had our ups and downs, but Harry, he was always there. My rock, that man." Her voice was filled with emotion. "When we lost your daddy," she paused, "that was a hard one. But your grandpa, he held me together, so we could be there for you girls and your Momma."

"I remember." Memories of the days and weeks after her father's death were inseparably connected to memories of her grandparents showering her and Brit with plenty of love and attention.

"He wasn't perfect—nobody is—but he was mine." Gran's lip quivered.

"And he loved you." Hailey took Gran's hand in hers, trying not to succumb to crying herself. "He loved all of us."

"Now he's gone and left me a widow. And your daddy's gone." She wiped at her puffy eyes. "I still have Regina, I suppose, but she doesn't want much to do with me." Gran cast her gaze downward.

"You have me." Hailey rubbed Gran's back.

"Gran patted her hand. "You're so sweet, but you have your own life. You've already done so much, and you need to get back to your career."

Gran was right, Hailey did need to return home for her job. She couldn't simply walk away from a career she'd worked so hard to procure, but how could she leave Gran like this? Her life, and her mom and sister, were in Colorado, yet Gran needed her more now than ever. An idea came to mind. "What if you came back to Colorado and lived with me? You'd be close to Mom and Brit. I'd love to have you live with me."

"That's a generous offer, but you don't need an old lady cramping your style."

Hailey had to laugh. "Cramp my style? I don't think I have a style for you to cramp."

"You know what I mean." Gran nodded. "You're young and vibrant and need to live your life without worrying about me."

"I can't leave you here," Hailey insisted.

"Let's not talk about this right now, it's too much." Gran rubbed her eyes. "I do need your help with something."

"Anything."

"Regina needs to know that he's passed, but I don't know how to find her." Gran lifted her hands in exasperation. "She leaves with no way to contact her."

"I'm sure she'd want to be here." At a time like this, family needed to bond together and support each other.

Gran let out a woeful breath.

"I'll see if I can find her somehow." Hailey had no idea how she might do that, but she wanted to offer Gran some hope.

Gran reached over and grasped Hailey's hand tightly. "If this had to happen, I'm so grateful it was when you were here. I don't know what I'd do without you. Thank you!"

"You need to get some more rest." She squeezed Gran's arm. "I'll take care of everything. Okay?"

Gran nodded.

Hailey left the bedroom and sank down on the couch in the living room. She didn't even know where to begin, but she had to figure it out, so Gran wouldn't have to deal with all the details.

In all the chaos of the night, and then the late hour, Hailey had neglected to call her mom. She probably should've called her right away, but she'd been so focused on Gran. Besides, she was a mess herself and needed Peter to just hold her. Pulling out her phone, Hailey tapped the screen to call her mom.

"Hi, honey." Her mom sounded sleepy.

"I'm sorry, did I wake you up?" *Two-hour time difference, remember?*

"It's fine. How are you?" Her mom yawned.

"Not good."

"Oh no." Her mom perked up. "Has something happened?"

Tears trickled down Hailey's cheeks. "Gramps passed away last night."

Her mom gasped. "Oh, dear. I'm so sorry to hear that."

"I wanted to call you," Hailey said, feeling guilty she hadn't. "But it was so late and—"

"Don't worry at all about that. How is June?" She could hear the concern in her mom's voice.

"Heartbroken. We didn't expect this at all." The shock still covered her like a lead blanket.

"I thought he was recovering."

"We did too." That was supposed to be what happened—Gramps recovered and Hailey went home.

"I'll book a flight as soon as I can."

"Mom, I have no idea what to do to get started." Turmoil set in. "I told Gran I'd take care of it, but I'm lost." She didn't want to adult today. *Adulting* was vastly overrated at times.

"First, call the mortuary. You'll need to make some decisions. June needs to decide where to have the funeral."

"I can't ask her that." Hailey bit her quivering lip. "She'll be too sad."

"It's difficult to make decisions right now, but someone needs to make them. Maybe you can give her some choices." For the first time, it struck Hailey with a jagged pain that her own mom had to go through all of this years ago, and her heart swelled with love and compassion for her mom.

"I just can't believe Gramps is gone." Hailey still couldn't wrap her mind around it.

"I'm thankful you were there for the last month."

"Me too. I am so, so glad I came when I did." *So glad.* What if she hadn't stood up to Mr. Michaels? What if she'd stayed in Colorado and missed out on this time with Gramps? Tears filled her eyes and fell down her cheeks as she realized how fragile life is and how easily she could've missed out on the last days of Gramps's life in favor of her career—a career she loved, but one that hasn't filled all the empty places. *Family is the most important and should come first.*

"Let me know what to do to help."

"I will. Thanks, Mom."

Hailey ended the call. She found Gran's address book and proceeded to make the difficult calls to Gran's sister, Mary, some cousins, and a few family friends to let them know.

She made an appointment at the mortuary and started thinking about what to do for the funeral. The grief and exhaustion overcame her so she lay down on the couch. The next thing she knew, two hours had passed. She heard some commotion in the kitchen.

"Gran?" Hailey walked in. Gran stood at the sink.

"I'm making something to eat. I'm thinking macaroni and cheese."

Hailey massaged the kink in her neck. "You don't need to cook anything."

"I can't lay in my bed and cry anymore. I need to do *something*." Gran opened and shut some cupboards as if searching for something.

"We could go out to eat," Hailey offered.

"I'm not sure I'm ready for that." Gran grabbed a tissue and blew her nose. "Besides, I'm not hungry."

"Why don't you come sit down?" Hailey motioned toward the sofa.

"I suppose we need to talk about the service, don't we?" Gran rubbed her eyes and then followed Hailey to the couch and sat down.

"I made an appointment at the mortuary. It's at four o'clock. Today."

Gran covered her mouth and rocked back and forth.

"I can go over and take care of everything. You don't need to worry about any of the details." Hailey didn't want Gran to feel any more pain than she already was.

Shaking her head, Gran said, "No, I'll go. I need to do this."

Hailey and Gran arrived at the large white building with pillars. Hailey parked the car and they took the long, agonizing walk to the entryway.

This is real. We are planning a funeral for Gramps. A tear edged down Hailey's cheek.

Inside, a short, bald man in a dark suit, said quietly, "Are you the Baker family?"

Hailey nodded. "This is my grandmother, June."

"My name is John Williamson. May I extend my deepest condolences? I'm so sorry to hear of his passing." He shook their hands.

"Thank you," Hailey said, noticing the cold, detached feeling inside the building.

"Please follow me." He led them into a small room with a desk and two large chairs. "Please sit down. We can get started when you're ready."

Gran drew in a deep breath. "Harry didn't like a big fuss. I think something simple at the church a few streets over from where we live would be nice. It's the Living Light Church."

"Do you have a preference for the time?" he said with a soft, respectful tone.

"Morning."

They continued to make plans and decisions, including picking out a casket. It left Hailey with a deep ache in her chest. She'd been too young to participate in much of this when her father passed away. She'd had no idea how emotionally draining and physically exhausting it was to make final arrangements for a loved one. Her mom had to do this for her dad, as did her grandparents. Now Gran was doing it again for Gramps. It was almost too much.

"I think I have everything." Mr. Williamson wrote a few more notes. "I'll see if we can get it all arranged for Friday morning."

Gran gave a quick nod, then stood. "Thank you for your help."

"You're welcome. Again, my sympathies for your loss," he said with kindness.

Hailey and Gran left the mortuary and made the drive back to the house without saying much.

When they got home, Hailey said, "Can I get you anything?"

"No. I think I need to rest." Gran trudged down the hall to her room.

Hailey began cleaning up in the kitchen. Her stomach growled, reminding her she hadn't eaten anything all day. She stared at the open cupboard, but nothing looked appetizing.

A knock sounded, so Hailey walked over to the front door and opened it. Peter stood on the front porch, his eyes full of compassion. Just seeing him gave her a sense of serenity. She wanted to throw her arms around his neck and lose herself in his embrace, but she resisted the urge. "Come in."

He had a couple of bags in his hands. "I brought some Chinese from a place down the road. I hope it helps."

"I was about to make something to eat, but this is much better. Thank you." Hailey took the bags from him. "Gran went back to her room, but I'm starving."

"Glad I could help."

"And you'll join me?" she said. The bags obviously held plenty of food, and she had no desire to eat by herself.

"If that's all right."

Hailey grabbed some dishes and utensils, and they sat at the small kitchen table. After she said grace, Hailey dished out some rice, sweet and sour pork, and an eggroll. She picked up her fork.

Peter gave her a distressed look.

"What?" Did she have something on her face or, worse, in her nose?

"Chopsticks." He handed her a package.

"Oh," she said with relief. She unwrapped them and tried to corner some rice. Using chopsticks made Hailey feel like she had three thumbs. How the Chinese could ever get any food into their mouths with these oversize toothpicks was beyond her.

Peter started laughing. "I have never seen anyone who was so bad at using chopsticks. Ever." He reached over and brushed some rice from her chin.

"I have no idea what the allure is to using these things." She set them down and picked up her fork. "This is how I eat Chinese food." She stabbed a chunk of pork and shoved it in her mouth, the sweet and tangy sauce perking up her taste buds.

Peter took a bite, then said, "How is June doing?"

"I think she's still in shock. We went to the mortuary and made plans for the service. We even picked out the casket." The bitter words tripped on her tongue.

Peter laid his warm hand on hers. "I'm sorry. Can I do anything to help?"

"Being here with me helps." Her gaze locked on his and suddenly her lungs squeezed tight, like they were unable to take in enough air.

After they finished eating, Hailey walked down to Gran's door. "Peter brought us some Chinese food. Would you like some?"

"No, thank you."

Hailey slowly opened the door. "You need to eat something."

"I'm not hungry." Gran looked at her with red-rimmed eyes. "I'll be fine. I need some time to adjust, that's all."

Hailey didn't want to leave Gran in her room to deal with all the sadness alone, but she didn't want to dictate how Gran mourned for Gramps either, so she simply said, "Let me know if you need anything."

"I will." Her voice sounded so small—almost childlike—that it made Hailey's throat thicken.

Hailey shut the door and went back into the living room where Peter was sitting on the couch.

"She doesn't want to eat anything," Hailey said, worrying that Gran needed nourishment.

"It's probably a good idea to let her rest." Peter said it with assurance.

Hailey sat on the couch next to him. When he put his arm around her, she snuggled close, breathing in his musky scent. They didn't say anything for several minutes. She reveled in the security that emanated from him and beckoned her to relax. She'd never experienced this with anyone.

Peter ran his fingers through her hair, sending tingles down her spine. Hailey didn't want to be anywhere but right where she was. Part of her knew it was going to end. It had to. But for this moment, she only wanted to feel his arms around her and drink in every drop of him.

The doorknob jiggled, and then the door flung open. Hailey jumped to her feet. "Regina?"

"Yeah. I'm back." She tossed her keychain on the small table by the door. "Things didn't pan out the way I'd hoped." She looked from Hailey to Peter and then back to Hailey. "Did I interrupt?" She laughed.

"I need to tell you—"

"Where's Momma? And Daddy? You run 'em out or somethin'?" Regina kicked off her boots.

Hailey resisted the impulse to choke her rude aunt. "Actually, something has happened."

Regina flopped on the couch and Hailey was sure it would've groaned if it could have. "Oh yeah? What?"

Hailey cleared her throat. "It's Gramps."

"Go on." Regina crossed her arms in front of her ample chest.

"He passed away." Hailey hated those prickly words.

"What?" Regina shrieked.

"They think it was a heart attack. Or maybe another stroke."

Regina thrust herself forward and perched on the edge of the couch. "Daddy's gone?"

Hailey nodded.

"But I . . . he was . . . how?"

"We're all in shock." Hailey wanted to give her aunt the benefit of a doubt. Maybe they'd all be able to help each other heal and possibly patch up previous wounds. Maybe.

"Why didn't you tell me?" Regina narrowed her eyes. "Were you gonna keep it from me?"

"Of course not." *How dare she accuse me of trying to keep this from her.*

Regina stuck her hands on her hips and with a defiant tone said, "Then why didn't I know?"

Hailey sucked in a deep breath of patience, reminding herself that Gran was down the hall and didn't need a big scene in her living room. As calmly as possible she said, "I didn't have any contact information for you. You left without telling anyone where you were going, and you don't have a cell phone."

"You're right I don't have one. They give you brain cancer."

Refusing to mock her aunt's tin-hat mentality, Hailey asked, "Then how would I have reached you?"

"I don't know, but somehow. Now I come home to find that my daddy's dead. Where's Momma?" Regina demanded.

"In her bedroom."

Regina stood. "I'm going to talk to her."

Hailey held out her hands, trying to appeal to her aunt. "She may be sleeping."

Completely ignoring Hailey, Regina ambled down the hallway.

Hailey looked at Peter. *He must think Regina is a total mental case.* "I'm so sorry. My aunt is . . ."

"Upset," Peter said.

"That's a nice way of putting it." *Leave it to Peter to think of a kind way to say Regina is a lunatic.*

"I should probably get going," he said with a hesitant tone.

As much as Hailey didn't want him to leave, she had to agree that with Hurricane Regina blowing through the house, it was the best idea. "Thank you so much for bringing dinner. You are very thoughtful." *And sweet. And kind. And wonderful.*

"It's the least I could do." He said it in such an endearing way, it made Hailey's heart melt.

She walked with him outside and stood by his car. The sun was descending in the west, coloring the wispy clouds with pinks and oranges.

"Please call me if you need anything," he said.

What I need is you. "I will. Thank you."

Peter lingered at his car, as if he wanted to say or do something. He turned to Hailey and in one swift movement, brought her close to him. Her heartbeat began pounding in her ears as his lips brushed hers. In an instant, their lips began a delicate dance—giving and taking in perfect rhythm and balance. This man knew how to kiss, so much so, it left Hailey feeling intoxicated.

Breathless, Peter pulled away. "I need to go. If I don't leave now, I might not leave at all."

Would that be so bad? Hailey took an unsteady step back. "I'll see you soon?"

Peter smiled and then got into his car.

Hailey walked back to Gran's house with a mixture of emotions churning inside her. She wasn't prepared for another heartbreak, which might be right where she was headed, but she was powerless to stop herself from falling for Peter. It was too late to protect her heart. Much too late.

As she neared the house, the intense anguish of losing Gramps hit her with full force. *I can't believe he's gone. No more card games. No more tall tales. No more hugs. And we still have the service to get through.* A lump the size of a boulder formed in her throat. *At least Mom will be here soon. It'll be better when she arrives.*

And then there was her aunt. Regina, Regina, Regina. What would Hailey do with her? Strangling her probably wasn't the best idea, but it brought a smile.

Hailey stepped inside the house. Gran and Regina were in the living room on the couch.

"I can live here with you, Momma." Regina's voice grated like the proverbial fingernails on the chalkboard.

"I don't know, Regina." Gran sounded so tired and overwrought.

Regina blinked several times as if surprised by Gran's reply. "Why not?"

Hailey wanted to give her an answer, but clamped her mouth shut instead.

"Would you like some lemonade, dear?" Gran asked Hailey. "There's some in the fridge."

"Sure. I'd love some." Gran made the best lemonade—not too sweet, not too tart. Hailey poured a glass, then sat next to Gran on the couch.

"My sister called. She isn't doing so well." Worry lines creased Gran's forehead.

"Oh, no. I'm sorry to hear that. Aunt Mary is so sweet," Hailey said, remembering visits through the years. "And she makes the most delicious chocolate cake."

"She won't be able to come for the service." Gran's mouth turned down.

Hailey slung her arm around Gran, hoping to buoy her up with love and support. "We need to go over some details."

"Yeah, I wanna know about the funeral," Regina said. "Can I say something?"

"You mean like the eulogy?" Hailey asked. She envisioned Regina standing up and tripping all over her words as she muttered nonsense about Gramps.

Regina jerked her chin. "I'm not sure what that is, but I wanna say something about Daddy."

Hailey looked at Gran, who shrugged one shoulder as if defeated.

"I'm sure we can work something out," Hailey said, trying to keep the peace.

"Who put you in charge anyway?" Regina demanded.

"Would you like to be in charge?" Hailey asked. She already knew the answer.

Regina sat back against the couch. "Oh. Uh. No."

Then keep your mouth shut. Hailey would sure like to tell her aunt where to go. "Then I'll work on the program."

"But it'll be simple," Gran said.

"Yes." Hailey turned to Gran. "Simple and no fuss, like Gramps."

That night, Hailey lay in bed. Her heart still ached, but if she kept busy it didn't seem to consume her as it had at first. The more she could help, the better. It'd keep her mind off the loss.

She turned to her side. What about Peter? *That* was the million-dollar question. Hailey rolled onto her back, too many thoughts colliding in her mind. *What am I going to do?*

One part of her wanted to tell him how much he meant to her, but the other part wondered what the point would be in doing that. An undeniable connection existed between them, but, in the end, did it matter? Next week, she was supposed to leave. At least that's what she'd promised her boss—to return before the next quarter. Hailey reminded herself to contact Mr. Michaels and beg for an extension to help Gran transition to life without Gramps. If her boss felt magnanimous he might grant her one, but that was a very big *if*. And it would still be only temporary—not indefinite—if she wanted to keep her job. So, where did that leave her and Peter? When she left, whatever there'd been with Peter would come to a screeching halt. Right?

Peter tossed and turned. He kicked his blanket off, then plumped up his pillow under his head. He let out a long, audible breath as he stared at the ceiling.

He'd finally met a woman he could possibly see a future with. A woman who made him feel alive again. A woman who made him forget how his heart had been shattered. A woman who . . . did it matter? Her life was almost two thousand miles away, and the reality was she'd be returning to that life.

It had been foolish to let himself become attached when he knew better. Seeing Hailey again would only make it harder to let her leave. He didn't need to become any more attached to her than he already was. He needed to cut his losses and put her out of his mind and heart. It was the only solution, and that's exactly what he intended to do.

He'd forget about her.

He'd forget her laugh. Her silky hair and soft skin. He'd forget the times he'd lost himself in the depths of her blue eyes. He'd forget the cadence of her voice and the way she blushed so easily. And he'd definitely forget holding her in his arms. Kissing her. Yearning to be with her all the time.

He'd erase everything from his memory and push the reset button. No problem. He could easily do that.

Peter laughed out loud at the lunacy. *Forget Hailey?* As if that were at all possible. His heartstrings were far too tangled with hers.

Chapter 35

The next day, Hailey accompanied Gran to the mortuary again to answer a few questions and finish the arrangements. Thinking about the whole thing made her body throb with pain, and all of this made memories of losing her dad resurface.

Gran put her arm around Hailey as they left. "We're quite a pair."

"Yes, we are."

"I think it's time for us to do something to lift our spirits." Gran squeezed Hailey's shoulder.

"What did you have in mind?" Nothing sounded appealing today.

"Let's get our nails done."

Hailey blinked, then studied Gran. "You *never* get your nails done."

"Maybe it's time I tried it." Gran shrugged.

Surprised, but willing to support Gran, Hailey drove them over to a nail salon, hoping it would make both of them feel a little lighter.

When they walked into of the salon, the strong scent of nail polish remover hit Hailey's nose and made it itchy.

Gran said to the desk attendant, "We want the works."

"A mani and a pedi?" the petite Asian woman with long hair asked in a thick accent.

"Yes. For me and my granddaughter."

Hailey picked out a pale peach color. She'd never had her nails done before. It felt almost decadent to have someone pamper her.

"This will make us both feel better," Gran said with assurance. "We need some spoiling."

Gran was right. After an hour at the small salon, Hailey didn't feel so heavy and sad.

"I'm not ready to go home," Gran said when they got into the car. "Let's go to the mall. I don't have a nice black dress."

Hailey wasn't anxious to go back home and deal with Regina either, but she didn't want Gran to feel obligated to buy a new dress. "I don't think you have to wear black."

"It's the proper thing to do." She patted Hailey's hand. "And I'll buy you one too."

"I have one, but I didn't bring it. I thought . . ." Hailey let her sentence trail off. She started up the car and they began driving.

"We didn't expect this to happen." Gran said. "But Harry wouldn't want us to be miserable. We need to celebrate his life instead of mourn his death. We should be grateful for the years we had with him instead of being sad because of the years we won't." Gran crossed her ankles. "I've given this a lot of thought since he passed. And I think I'm going to . . ."

"What?"

"Go to my sister's house for a while." Gran gave a strong nod indicating her mind was made up. "Mary needs me. I can stay busy helping her and we can get caught up."

"That's a good idea." Thinking of Gran with Aunt Mary made Hailey's heart happy.

"Nothing I can do will bring my Harry back. We had a good life. No," she held up her finger, "we had a great life together. I don't want to spend the rest of mine being sad. I'd rather remember the happy times we had together and be grateful for that. Not everyone spends their life happy. I'm one of the lucky ones."

"You are an amazing lady, Gran." Hailey was filled with a deep sense of gratitude that she'd been able to spend this time with Gramps and Gran. She was a fortunate woman to have such wonderful role models.

"I don't know how I would've gotten through this last month or so without you here. Thank you."

Hailey slipped a look at Gran, whose eyes glistened. With a thick voice, Hailey said, "I love you."

Gran smiled. "I know you do. You have always been good to us. Which is more than I can say about my daughter."

Hailey found a parking space and pulled the car in. "What are you going to do about Regina when you go to Aunt Mary's?"

"I'm going to tell her to get herself together. It's about time, isn't it?" Gran clucked her tongue.

Hailey wasn't sure she'd want to witness that conversation, but Gran would need moral support to take on Regina. "Yes. And I'll be there with you when you tell her."

Gran pointed at Hailey. "And then you'll need to get on with *your* life."

Hailey nodded, unsure of what that meant for her.

They both got out of the car and started walking arm-in-arm toward the mall.

"What will you do about Peter?" Gran asked.

"There's nothing to do. His life is here and mine is in Colorado." Hailey placed a lock of hair behind her ear. "It isn't meant to be."

Gran gazed ahead, seeming to be in thoughtful consideration. "Are you sure about that?"

"I have to be." What other choice did she have? She couldn't stay in Florida with no job and no reason to be here anymore. Her life was back west, even if that meant she'd leave a piece of her heart in the south.

After shopping for almost two hours, they both found dresses appropriate for Gramps's service. His death was sinking in and feeling more real.

When they returned to the house, Regina was lounging on the couch. "Where have you been all day?" She scowled at Hailey.

"Taking care of details." Gran set her bag on the table. "After the funeral, I'm going to Oregon." Gran said it so matter-of-factly that it even took Hailey by surprise.

"You are?" Regina said with a shocked expression.

"To be with Mary." Gran took off her shoes. "She needs me."

Regina swung her legs off the couch and with a pained expression said, "When will you be back?"

"I'm not sure." Gran walked into the kitchen.

"I can take care of the house," Regina called after her, then gave Hailey a smirk.

Less than a minute later, with a glass of water in her hand, Gran stood in the doorway and said firmly, "No."

Regina blinked a few times and shook her head like she hadn't heard Gran. "What?"

Gran squared her shoulders. "You need to get on your own two feet. For good this time."

"But, Momma," Regina whined.

Gran held her hand up. "You've been wandering aimlessly for years, Regina. I love you and always will, but it's time. You need to get it together."

Regina frowned. She stood and then stomped back to her room, slamming the door.

Gran looked at Hailey and shrugged. Hailey suppressed a smile. Regina was always doing the leaving, never letting Gran and Gramps know where she was or when she might be back. It was about time Gran stood up to her.

Chapter 36

Peter awoke after a fitful sleep. *Today is Harry's funeral.* He stared at the ceiling fan, listening to the whirring sound it made.

He wasn't planning to go. He soothed his conscience by reminding himself that he hadn't attended other funerals. It wasn't in his job description, and he shouldn't feel obligated. Harry was a patient. That was all.

Peter sat up in bed and massaged the knot in his shoulder. He couldn't go to the service because he had to get caught up on paperwork. He needed to do that. It was important to keep current on all the paperwork. Because there was a lot. A lot of paperwork.

He lay back down and kicked off his covers. Who was he kidding? He wanted to go to the funeral. He wanted to pay his respects to a man he'd come to care about. Even more, he wanted to see Hailey. He *needed* to see her. Even if it meant heartache when he had to tell her goodbye.

The day she'd been dreading arrived. Hailey picked herself out of bed, showered, and put on the new navy-blue dress Gran had bought her. She checked her phone. Her mother's late-night flight had been cancelled and she was on an early flight this morning. Hailey hoped her mom would make it to the funeral.

Hailey hadn't heard at all from Peter, which was odd, but she was too emotional today to try to figure out why. Besides, she needed to focus all her energy on supporting Gran through the service.

Hailey tried to apply some makeup, but her eyes were too tender. She brushed her hair and then walked out into the somber living room.

"I don't know what to do with these." Gran held Gramps's glasses.

Tears sprang to Hailey's eyes. She reached her arms around Gran and they both stood there, crying for a few minutes.

"I miss that old coot," Gran finally said.

"Me too."

Gran wiped at her face. "Are you ready?"

Hailey smoothed her hair. Was anyone ever ready for a funeral of a loved one?

Regina came down the hall wearing black pants and a cream-colored blouse. She'd brushed her hair and looked respectable. In fact, she looked good. "I'd like to go in the car with you." She paused. "If that's all right."

Hailey didn't want her unpleasant feelings toward Regina to interfere with paying tribute to Gramps. "Sure. We'd like it if you rode with us," Hailey said, trying to cut her aunt some slack.

"Thank you," Regina answered. She wasn't the nicest person, and she'd done plenty to hurt everyone, including Hailey, over the years, but Regina was still family. She was blood. And Gramps wouldn't want bickering today.

Hailey helped Gran into the car and they all drove over to the small, white church. No one said anything.

When Hailey parked the car, she turned to Gran. "Are you going to be okay?"

Gran nodded. "I survived your dad's service. I will survive this one, too."

Hailey marveled at her grandmother's strength. "I'm right here with you." She squeezed Gran's hand.

"Me too," Regina said from the back seat.

"Thank you," Gran said. "I'm glad we can be together today to honor a life well lived. No one could ever accuse my Harry of not living life to the fullest. I want to celebrate that."

They walked into the church. A sweet, potent, floral scent saturated the air while organ music floated in the background. Hailey spotted the smooth, black casket at the front of the chapel. A man with graying hair and gold-rimmed glasses approached them.

"Pastor Anderson, thank you so much for doing this service," Gran said.

He smiled, exposing a chipped front tooth. "This must be your granddaughter."

"Hi, I'm Hailey."

"And this is my daughter, Regina," Gran said.

"Nice to meet you," Pastor Anderson said softly.

"Same," Regina answered demurely, making Hailey do a double-take. *Is this my aunt?*

"I have a few details to go over with you, June. Can we go to my office?"

Gran left with the pastor, so Hailey and Regina sat together on the front pew. Hailey stared ahead, thoughts tumbling around her mind. *Gramps, I wasn't ready for you to leave. I still wanted to beat you at cards.* She wiped at her eyes. *Wherever you are, can you say hi to Dad?* Envisioning Gramps and her dad together brought her a sense of tranquility and peace.

Someone made a noise, and Hailey turned. She jumped to her feet. "Uh, hi, Peter," she said, her heart instantly reacting to his presence.

"How are you holding up?" His expression was a mixture of kindness and concern.

"All right, considering." She tried not to notice how handsome he looked in his charcoal-gray suit.

"I wanted to pay my respects and—"

"Hailey?" came a familiar voice from behind her.

She whirled around. "Mom?"

"My plane was delayed." She hugged Hailey and they stood there for several moments. "I came as soon as I could."

Hailey nestled into her mom's loving arms.

"I'm so glad I made it in time. I was so worried," her mom said, dabbing at her eyes.

"Me too. Gran will be so happy to see you. How is Brit?" Hailey snuck a look over her shoulder but Peter was gone.

"She's good. The baby is doing well, too, but Brit was sad she couldn't come. She loved Grandpa Harry." Her mom adjusted her black blazer.

"I'm so thankful I was here and got to spend some time with him before . . ."

"He loved you. Both he and June appreciated and enjoyed you being here."

Regina stood. Hailey's mom stepped over to her and gave her a hug. "I'm so sorry about your dad, Regina."

"Thanks," Regina said. "Daddy was a good one."

"Indeed, he was." Hailey's mom glanced around. "Where is June?"

"She's talking to the pastor." Hailey pointed toward the pastor's office.

"Look at all these beautiful flowers. It's like a garden in here." Her mom checked her watch and then wiped her forehead. "The service begins in forty minutes. I'm so glad I made it."

"I think everything is ready," Hailey said, slyly searching the room for Peter but having no success in spotting him.

"After the service, I'd like to go over to June's and spend some time with her." Hailey's mom smoothed her dark hair.

"I think she'd like that." Hailey wished the reunion were under different circumstances, but she knew Gran would appreciate time with her daughter-in-law.

With her brows drawn together her mom said, "You seem distracted, Hailey."

"Mom, I'm sad." It was true. She was sad. But she was also distracted by a tall blond man who seemed to have disappeared.

"All right. I'm going to find the restroom and freshen up a bit. My flight was long."

Her mom left and a few people wandered into the chapel and made their way over to her. They expressed their condolences. Another group of older people followed and soon the room filled up.

When Gran entered the chapel, everyone stood. Hailey sat next to her and grasped her hand. She resisted the urge to scan the room again for Peter.

The service was lovely, and Hailey found herself alternating between crying and laughing at some of the stories the pastor shared about Gramps.

When Regina stood and made her way to the pulpit, Hailey tensed. *I hope Regina doesn't say anything weird.*

"My daddy was a good, good man. Not a lot out there like him. I know." Regina sniffled, then continued to praise her father and share a few of her own stories. Hailey let out a breath of relief when Regina finished and even saw her aunt in a slightly different light, maybe even with some measure of sympathy. After all, she'd lost her father and the last interactions between Regina and Gramps hadn't been great. *Regina must be feeling pretty low.*

Afterward, Hailey stood next to Gran as people approached her and expressed their condolences. Regina stood off from the group, grief etched on her face. Hailey vowed to always let the people she loved know she loved them, because life was too unpredictable and too short.

Without warning, her thoughts turned to Peter. She cared about him a great deal, maybe even . . . *loved* him.

Shouldn't she take the risk and let him know how she felt? Wasn't it worth it?

She drew in a long, deep breath, trying to decide what to do.

After the internment at the cemetery, Hailey walked with her mom and Gran over to her mom's black rental sedan. Peter stood next to Gran's car. Seeing him made Hailey's stomach flip-flop. In her mind, she pictured him pulling her close, telling her he loved her, and begging her to stay here in Florida.

"Hailey," her mom said, "I'd like to take June home and spend some time with her."

"That would be nice," Gran said. "We have some catching up to do. I hope you brought some pictures of my great-grandson." Gran gave a slight smile. "The circle of life."

"I'll bring Regina back with me. Have you seen her?" Hailey glanced around.

"She was talking to the pastor," her mom said. "We'll see you back at the house."

Hailey watched her mom and Gran pull away. She turned toward Peter, trying to calm the ripples of nerves that coursed through her body.

"It was a nice service," Peter said. He plunged his hands into the pockets of his suit pants.

"Yes, it was." Hailey reflected on the music and words of the service. Gramps would've been pleased with it.

Peter kicked a pebble with his foot. "I'm glad I came."

"I'm glad you came too." Hailey wanted to say more. She wanted to tell him how she felt and how much he meant to her, but fear paralyzed her tongue.

Peter took his hands out of his pockets. "I'm sorry I haven't communicated with you."

He stepped closer to her, and her lungs felt as if they were collapsing, leaving her struggling to breathe.

Peter peered at her and all she wanted to do was to throw her arms around his neck, melt into his embrace, and let him smother her with kisses. "When do you leave for Colorado?" he asked.

A light bulb went off. He hadn't communicated with her because he figured she was going home. Whatever they'd had was great—even amazing—but now it was time to face the truth that it was over. He wasn't going to sweep her into his arms or confess his love. He was going to say goodbye. She stepped back, her heart squeezing so tight she feared it would stop working altogether. She cleared her throat. "In a few days. Gran is going to stay with her sister in Oregon for a while."

"And you have your life to get back to," he quickly added.

She nodded. *Unless you can convince me to stay.*

"I hope that everything goes well for you," he said.

"Thank you." She pointed at him. "Same."

He shifted his weight. "I've started looking at property for my own office."

"That's awesome. I know you'll be successful." She hoped all would go well for him. He deserved it, and she wanted him to be happy.

"Thanks."

"Thank you for showing me Daytona Beach. Even under the circumstances, I've enjoyed my visit." *I especially enjoyed spending time with you. I wish . . .*

Peter tapped his foot. "I guess I better get going. It was a nice service. I'm sure it would've made Harry happy."

She forced a smile, even though her lips were quivering. *This is it. This is goodbye.* Her body ached to hold him. Her lips ached to kiss him. But she resisted. Kissing him would only make it harder to leave, and he wasn't going to ask her to stay.

"Goodbye, Hailey."

She tried to swallow the shards of glass lodged in her throat. "Bye."

He walked away toward his car. Everything in her screamed to run after him and tell him how she yearned to have him part of her life, but it was no use. He'd made it clear that this was goodbye, so she hurried and let herself into Gran's car. Otherwise, she'd turn to putty and fall apart there on the spot.

Hailey rolled the windows down and let the moist air blow through her hair on her drive back to Gran's, convincing herself all along the way that Peter wasn't the man for her. He obviously didn't think so, either, or he would've said something. Disappointment welled up in her eyes.

When Hailey arrived at the house, her mom and Gran sat on the couch huddled together.

"Your mom is showing me photos on her phone. What a beautiful baby Thomas is." Gran's eyes glistened.

Hailey sat next to Gran and viewed the photos of her nephew with his head full of dark hair.

"How about I fix us some dinner?" Hailey's mom said.

"I think there are a few casseroles in the fridge from some of Gran's friends. And a chocolate cake," Hailey said, trying to ignore the deep sense of loss that gnawed at her heart.

"My lands, we'll never eat all of that," Gran said. "Where's Harry when I need him?"

Hailey cleared the emotion from her throat. "When will you go to Aunt Mary's?"

"Monday, I think. I spoke to my neighbor, Raymond, and he offered to come check on the house and take care of things while I'm gone, but I still need to figure out my bills."

"I can help you with that," Hailey said.

"Thank you. I'd appreciate it. I have a plane reservation for Monday afternoon."

"I'll schedule my flight at the same time," Hailey said. That would make it easier to not only go to the airport, but to leave Florida.

"So will I," her mom added.

"Hailey?" Gran looked at her with an odd expression. "Where's Regina?"

The blood rushed to Hailey's cheeks. She stood. "Uh, oh."

"Where is she?" her mom asked.

Hailey gave them a repentant smile. "I might have forgotten her at the cemetery."

Gran covered her mouth, but Hailey could tell she was stifling a laugh.

"I don't know how it happened. I guess I was . . . distracted." She shrugged. "I'll be back soon."

Hailey drove to the cemetery, preparing herself for the onslaught of angry words from her aunt. What could she do, except apologize? *I'm sorry Peter made me forget all about you.* No, that wouldn't work. She'd have to come up with a better apology.

As she entered Evergreen Cemetery, she spotted Regina over by Gramps's plot. Hailey parked the car and got out, steeling herself against Regina's tongue lashing.

Hailey approached and could see Regina's head bowed low. After a few minutes of silence, Hailey said, "I'm so sorry I left you here, I–"

"Stop," Regina said. She tilted her head back and looked up at the sky. "My daddy is gone."

Hailey didn't know what to say or do. She was afraid Regina might explode at her.

"I thought I had so much time. Time that I could use to make something of myself. Make up for my mistakes and make him proud." She whimpered. "Instead, he died ashamed of me."

"He wasn't ashamed," Hailey said softly.

"Why wouldn't he be? I've got nothing to show for my life." Regina looked at Hailey with bloodshot eyes. "I wasn't always like this, you know. I had so many plans when I was young."

"What happened?" Hailey was almost afraid to ask.

"I don't know. Guess I got all mixed up in the wrong things when I was younger. And when your daddy died, I was so angry. I drank the pain away and lost myself. Then next thing I know, it's all these years later and I'm still . . . lost." Regina's shoulders slumped.

Hailey wasn't sure what to do. She'd never in a million years expected her aunt's self-evaluation resulting in this confession.

"And I know I've been nasty to everyone. Momma, Daddy, and you." Regina wiped at her reddened nose. "I don't know what to do to make up for any of it. I don't even think I can." She sounded so broken. Hopeless.

"Why don't you start by coming back to Gran's with me?" It wouldn't be easy, or fast, but this could be the beginning of Regina's path.

Regina drew in a ragged breath.

"My mom is fixing dinner. And I know Gran wants to see you." Hailey's resentment from Regina's nastiness through the years began to melt away—a little—as Hailey witnessed her aunt's contrition and deep regret.

They started walking toward the car. Regina said, "I've made such a mess out of my life."

"Today is as good a day as any to make changes." Hailey wanted to offer her aunt some hope. Regina wasn't a monster. She'd made mistakes, and, truthfully, she'd been rather horrible at times, but she was still family. And family needed to stick together. To help each other. To love one another, warts and all. Gramps would want them together.

Inside the car, they didn't say anything, but Hailey's mind was moving a million miles a minute. She'd expected her aunt to be an angry, raving lunatic. Instead, she found a defeated, dejected woman searching for redemption. Maybe, with enough time, Regina and Gran could find their way back to each other.

After they parked the car, Hailey led the way to the house. "We're back," she said as she opened the door.

"Regina?" Gran said, looking up from the couch.

In a few strides, Regina was at her mother's side, tears streaming down her face. "I'm so sorry, Momma. For everything. I'm sorry for all the terrible things I've done. For the terrible daughter I've been."

Gran wore a shocked expression. She reached out her arms and enfolded her daughter within them.

"I know apologizing won't make up for what I've done, but I don't want to lose you," Regina said. "I'll do whatever it takes to make it up to you. Can you forgive me?"

Gran stroked her daughter's head.

Hailey's eyes misted. This is what Gran had been wishing would happen for years. Too bad it had taken Gramps's death to bring about Regina's turnaround, but at least there was hope they'd repair what had been damaged between them.

"Maybe we can both go to Mary's in Oregon and spend some family time together?" Gran said with an encouraging tone.

Regina nodded. "I'd like that."

"I'll make a reservation so we can fly together."

After dinner, they spent time visiting and sharing photos. Gran shared memories and Hailey listened intently, trying to soak up every moment with her grandmother. She wouldn't allow herself to think about leaving yet, because it was too painful.

Chapter 37

After making some phone calls and coordinating with Gran's bank to set up online billing so Gran could easily pay her bills from Oregon, Hailey finished packing her suitcase. She sent off a few emails, including one to Mr. Michaels, and then gazed around her room. Sadness washed over her. *It's time to move on.*

Hailey, her mom, Regina, and Gran took a cab to the airport. Their flights were all within an hour of each other.

After going through security, they all stopped to say goodbye.

"Thank you for being with me and for all of your help. Harry loved you so," Gran said as she embraced Hailey, her familiar floral scent enveloping them.

Trying to hold back her tears, but failing, Hailey said, "I'm so glad I came."

"But now it's time to go back to *your* life," Gran said while she caressed Hailey's arm. "I want you to promise me something."

"Anything."

"Don't worry about me. I'll be fine. Go out and live your life now." She peered at Hailey. "Don't be afraid to take risks and give yourself wholeheartedly to the one you love. It's always a risk, but true love is worth it. And that kind of deep, committed love doesn't come around very often. Take a chance, dear. Live the life *you* want."

Hailey knew exactly what Gran meant, but it didn't matter. Her chance with Peter was over. "Thanks, Gran."

"And, Shari, thank you for coming to the service. I know it was hard to leave your sweet grandbaby." Gran gave Hailey's mom a hug.

"I wish I could've made it here before Harry's passing. I love the two of you very much." She turned to Regina. "I hope things work out."

"Thank you, Shari," Regina said.

"I hope so too, Aunt Regina," Hailey said. Although she still wasn't her aunt's biggest fan, she hoped Regina would get herself together, and that she and Gran could begin to build a more solid relationship.

Regina managed a slight smile, and then Gran looped her arm through her daughter's.

"We'll talk soon," Gran said.

"Of course." Hailey would miss Gran deeply, but it was good to see her happy with Regina at her side.

Hailey's flight to Denver left before her mom's, so she flew back by herself. Leaning her head back against the seat gave Hailey ample time to think about the last month or so. Her heart was tender and raw, both from losing Gramps and from saying goodbye to Peter. She had hoped there might be a future with him, but that was only wishful thinking. After all, they had separate lives almost two thousand miles apart. It had never been realistic to think anything permanent would come out of meeting him, even if her heart desperately wanted to believe differently. She would cherish her time in Daytona Beach and tuck it into a special place in her memory.

Hailey caught another flight to Colorado Springs, then took a taxi to her apartment. After unpacking, she flopped on her couch and surfed absently through channels. It seemed like she'd been gone forever and yet it also felt as if she'd never left.

Someone knocked at the door. *Who can that be? I'm not expecting anyone.* For a moment, she let herself fantasize that Peter had come to whisk her off to a life of dancing and swinging with lots of cuddling and kissing. She let out a long sigh at the treasured memories.

The knock sounded again, jolting her from her reverie. Hailey opened the door to Kevin standing there. *I'd rather be stranded on a desert island with Jimmy Vaughn than see you right now.*

"Hi, Hailey," he said in a way that used to be charming.

"Kevin. What are you doing here?" Her shock was tempered with apathy.

He looked at her with the same deep blue eyes that used to make her heart skitter. "May I come in?"

Hailey didn't see the point, but opened the door wider. "I guess."

Kevin stepped inside. "You never called me back."

"No, I didn't." There had been nothing left to say.

He approached her, reached out, and grabbed her hand, but she felt nothing. Not even a flicker of anything. "Look, Hailey, I'm sorry for what happened."

"I'm sorry too, Kevin." She dropped his hand. "I wanted to have a life with you. Marry you. Have babies."

"And I messed it all up. I know." A pained expression crossed his once attractive face.

"Messed it up? No, Kevin, you destroyed it." She didn't want him to misunderstand her at all. "We had a great thing going, but it was all a lie."

"It wasn't a lie." He said emphatically. "I made a mistake. That's all."

Hailey pointed at him. "No, you chose to cheat. With more than one woman. I was the one who made a mistake to trust you in the first place."

Kevin stepped closer to her, his dark hair falling over his forehead. "I was so wrong to do that, and I've realized that you're the only one I love, not anyone else. Please, forgive me. I'll do anything."

Hailey held up her hands. "You've already done enough."

"But I love you, and I want you back," Kevin pleaded.

Hailey stared at the man who'd once held her heart. A man she thought she'd love forever. "Here's the thing." Hailey didn't want to purposely hurt Kevin, but he needed to hear the truth. "I don't love you anymore."

"We can make it work this time, baby. I've changed. I know you are the only one for me," he said. "And you still love me."

"But I don't." Hailey paused for a moment. "I love someone else." There she'd said it out loud. She loved Peter.

Kevin took a step back. "Who?"

"It doesn't matter." Sadly, that was true. It didn't matter that she loved Peter.

Kevin studied her for almost a minute. She assumed he was waiting to see if she'd change her mind and want to take him back, but she stood firm. After spending time with Peter, she could never waste her time on someone like Kevin again.

Hailey opened her front door and motioned for Kevin to leave. She was done and there wasn't any point to dragging this out.

"But—" he started.

"No buts. I've realized there's so much more out there, Kevin. And I deserve it. I'm not going to settle for anything less."

"Hailey—"

"I'm done, Kevin. Done with you and done with us."

"You don't mean that." He walked out the door. Over his shoulder he said, "You'll want me back."

Hailey shut the door not only on Kevin, but on that chapter of her life. Seeing him made her realize she was finally and completely free of him. Her time in Florida had cured her of ever wanting to be with Kevin, or a man like him, again. She deserved better—much better. Life was too short to be with a man that cheated. Period.

Chapter 38

Peter sat on the lumpy sofa in Laura's apartment, staring at the glass of lemonade in his hands when a pretzel stick hit him in the head. "Hey, who threw that?"

"I did," Benji said. "You aren't paying attention."

"I'm sitting here watching this movie with you."

"No. You're looking at your drink with a face like this." Benji made his lip pooch out and his eyes all droopy.

"That's ridiculous," he said. *What does a kid know anyway?*

"What's ridiculous?" Laura asked when she came into the living room with a laundry basket in her hand.

"How weird Uncle Peter is now," Benji said.

"That's not true. I am not weird." Peter pushed down his irritation.

"I gotta agree with Benji," Laura said with a tone that grated on Peter's nerves.

Peter took a gulp of his lemonade. "You're both weird."

Laura set the basket on the back of the couch. "And I'd say it started, what, about two weeks ago. Yeah, that's definitely when it started."

Peter knew exactly what she was driving at. He scratched at his neck. "Look, are we gonna watch this movie or not?"

"Evasive maneuvers, huh?" Laura gave him a you-aren't-going-to-avoid-the-subject stare.

"I told you, we parted on good terms. There's nothing else left to say. She's gone back to her life and I've gone back to mine." Why was this so hard for his sister to grasp?

"You mean the life where you go through all the motions, but you aren't really living? *That* life?"

He hated how pointed his sister was sometimes. "I don't know what you want from me." Peter sat up and placed his glass on the coffee table.

"It isn't what *I* want, Peter," she pointed at him, "you're miserable. You've been absolutely no fun since Hailey left."

"Yeah. What mom said," Benji interjected.

"Are you going to sit here and do nothing? Let love slip through your fingers?"

"Love? Who said anything about love?" Now the conversation was bordering on the absurd. He didn't *love* Hailey. Really. He didn't. They'd had some fun. That was all. And he didn't want his sister to stick her nose where it didn't belong.

Laura threw her head back. "Please. You're about as lovesick as they come."

Peter glanced at his watch. "You know, I need to get going. I have work tomorrow."

"What about the rest of the movie?" Benji asked.

"We'll finish it this weekend," Peter said. "Thanks for dinner."

He grabbed his phone and headed to the front door.

"Running away won't change the fact that I'm right," Laura called after him.

Peter jumped into his car and plunged it into gear. Even if Laura was partially right and the memories of Hailey and their time together still circled his mind, it didn't matter. He'd get over it. He'd move on. His plans to open his practice were on track, and his life was all falling into place.

Besides he wasn't in love with Hailey. He didn't miss the lilt in her laugh, or the way she watched him so pensively when he spoke, or the infusion of kindness in her voice as she interacted with her grandparents. He didn't recall night after night the time they spent together swinging, dancing, going on walks, and talking. And for sure he didn't think about her sleek hair, the warmth of her skin next to his, the curve of her lips, or the taste of peppermint in her kiss.

Nope, he was not in love with her.

Not a bit.

Chapter 39

Hailey spent almost two weeks staying late at work trying to catch up and get back on track with all her clients. Though she'd worked while she was in Florida, she was still behind.

On the way home from work, she stopped at the grocery store to pick up a few items. Back in the bakery department, she spotted Jimmy. *Oh, no. If he sees me, I'll have to talk to him and he'll try to come over to my apartment.* She ducked behind the cereal aisle to avoid him. If she never had to see him again, it'd be too soon.

She stealthily snuck around the corner, grateful she'd avoided the most annoying person on earth. Hailey bent down to grab a jar of spaghetti sauce, and when she stood, there he was. *Boom.*

"Hail, where you been?" Jimmy said in his nauseating drawl.

Her skin started to itch. "In Florida."

"Long vacation or what?" He slicked back his hair.

"Actually, I went back to help my grandpa after he had a stroke." *Not that it's any of your business.*

"Oh. So, how is he?"

"He passed," she said, her patience wearing thin.

"Oh, geez. I'm sorry. I didn't know. I was thinking . . . maybe . . .

we could get together tonight since you're home now."

"I'm really tired, Jimmy." *And will be for the rest of my life.*

"Uh, yeah." He bobbed his head a few times. "How 'bout I come over another day. We can get some pizza or something."

"I'm going to be very busy catching up with my job." *Very, very busy. Every day. For forever. Plus another ten years.*

He held out a hand. "You gotta eat."

"I'll let you know, Jimmy." *In 2045.*

He gave her his cheesy smile and then winked. "Catch ya later, babe."

Hailey hurried down the aisle. *Time to find a new grocery store.*

After loading her car with groceries, Hailey drove home, then rushed to her apartment and locked the door behind her. She put the groceries away while warming a can of soup. Sitting in front of her TV with her bowl, she surfed through channels trying to find something to watch. When nothing caught her eye, she absently stared through her window into the darkness.

Was this how she wanted to spend the rest of her life? Working, living in her average apartment, watching TV, and hiding in the grocery store to avoid Jimmy Vaughn? Even though she'd shed Kevin once and for all, she was exactly where she was before she went to Florida.

The promise she made to Gran at the airport shot into her mind—a promise she wasn't keeping. But what could she do about it?

Deflated and dejected, she got up, dumped her soup in the sink, and went to bed.

After spending most of her day preparing for Mr. Lanceton's audit, running quarterly reports for several other clients, and making a few phone calls, Hailey sat at her desk blankly staring at her computer screen. Working with numbers and making them all balance used to give her a thrill of accomplishment. Now it felt like drudgery. Her life was as bland and dreary as the numbers she worked with. *This isn't the life I want. It isn't what I promised Gran.*

"Don't forget about the meeting with Mrs. Winters. It's tomorrow afternoon," her boss said, jerking her back into reality.

Hailey nodded. "I have it down. Her reports are all ready."

"I'm sorry to hear about your grandfather." Mr. Michaels wore a kind expression.

"Thank you for allowing me to go and help him. It meant a lot." She'd relish the time she'd spent with her grandparents for the rest of her life, for more than one reason. And it was that one reason that had her so confounded. So conflicted.

"You're welcome. Now you can dive back into work full force?" He peered at her over the top of his glasses.

"Dive back into work full force?" She knew what he meant, but still repeated his words trying to convince herself to do just that.

"Yes. All of your focus and energy."

Hailey looked at him and blurted out, "No, sir."

"Huh?" He wore a confused expression.

"Huh?" Hailey said, equally confused. *Why did I say that?*

"What did you say?" He pinched his brows together.

Hailey blinked. She drew in a breath of courage. "I think I said no, sir. Because I'm not ready to dive into work."

Mr. Michaels cocked his head to the right. "Excuse me?"

Hailey stood, her heartbeat pulsing in her cheeks. "I made a promise to my grandmother that I need to keep."

He studied her with a probing gaze. "What does that mean?"

"I don't know exactly, but I need to go." She gathered up her bag. "This isn't where I belong anymore." *Was she really saying this?*

"What are you doing?" He narrowed his eyes and looked at her as if she'd totally lost her mind. Maybe she had.

"I'm taking a risk." It was suddenly so obvious. So clear. "I know what will make me happy. I've known it for weeks." She knew exactly what she needed to do.

"This doesn't make any sense," he said as he watched her.

"You're right." How could she explain this to Mr. Michaels? *I can't explain it.*

"Your job—"

"Has been great, but it isn't enough." As soon as it came out of her mouth, she knew. This was the right thing for her to do. She was done living her mediocre life. She wanted more. She'd had a taste of something better, and now she wanted it all.

"Where are you going?"

"To Florida." A flurry of tingles shot down her back.

"You're willing to give up your job?" Mr. Michaels said sternly, arms crossed in front of his chest.

Hailey drew in a deep breath. With complete confidence in her decision she said, "For a chance to be with Peter? Yes. I'm willing to risk it all."

Hailey packed her suitcase before she could think about her decision. She found a last-minute overnight plane ticket and purchased it. On the way over to the airport, she refused to let herself evaluate what she was doing. She knew it was impulsive and a little crazy—a lot crazy—but she had to go with her gut instinct and follow through. The greater the risk, the greater the happiness that could be hers. It was worth it.

During the plane ride, she tried to sleep, but all she could think about was Peter and what she would say to him. She blocked out thoughts of his possible reaction because that would make her turn around and return home. She wasn't naturally impulsive—she liked to consider and plan things and take time to think them through. This was the craziest thing she'd ever done. Ever. In her whole life.

The plane touched down in Orlando, and she freshened up as much as possible in the airport restroom. She rented a car and made the drive to Daytona Beach, all the while practicing what she would say, especially since he didn't expect her. She planned to drive over to his office and lay it all on the line. *I'm in love with you, Peter.* By her calculations, she'd be there before nine o'clock.

Deep breaths. I can do this.

When she pulled into the parking lot of the rehab facility where she'd spent time with Gramps, waves of emotions crashed over her. She couldn't afford to let the memories of Gramps affect her or she wouldn't go through with telling Peter how she felt.

She applied some lip gloss, fluffed her hair, and checked her teeth. *It's now or never.*

With each step, her heart threatened to leap right out of her chest. *How will he react when he sees me? Don't think about it, don't think about it, don't think about it.*

She entered the building and walked back to his office. Unfortunately, Joyce was at the front desk with her oversize gold hoop earrings and bright red lipstick.

"May I help you?" she asked with an edge to her voice.

"I'm here to see Peter Stafford." She said it as evenly as possible.

Joyce gave her the once-over and then asked, "Do you have an appointment?"

Hailey cleared her throat. "Uh, no. But I'd like to see him as soon as possible." She laced her shaking fingers together.

With a smirk, Joyce said, "He isn't in."

Hailey's shoulders fell. She hadn't considered that Peter might not be at the office. "When will he be in today?"

"He won't." Joyce seemed to be enjoying this interplay, but Hailey was becoming increasingly agitated.

Trying to remain cool, she asked, "Is it his day off?"

Joyce leaned forward and with an arch of her eyebrow said, "He's taken some personal time. I'm not sure when he'll be back."

"Oh." Personal time? Peter was gone? Hailey felt like she'd been kicked in the stomach. With stiletto heels.

"I can leave him a message if you'd like. I talk to him frequently." Joyce said it with an air of authority.

Tamping her disappointment down, Hailey said, "No message. Thanks."

Hailey walked out of the rehabilitation center. *Personal time?* What did that mean? And why now? Of course, the biggest question was where did that leave her? She'd put on her cloak of bravery and wasn't about to go back to Colorado without seeing him. Not when she'd come this far.

What should I do? How can I find him? She had to see him in person and tell him how she felt or she was sure she'd burst into a million pieces. After thinking on it for a few minutes and trying to figure out what to do, her only option seemed to be to call him.

Hailey pulled out her phone and rolled it between her hands, staring at it. *Should I call him?* If she wanted to see him, she'd have to, because there was no other way. Quickly, she tapped in his name, hit his contact info, and connected the call.

Her heart hammered and her stomach roiled in anticipation as she waited for him to answer. When the call went through, Hailey jumped right in because she didn't want to lose her nerve or momentum. "Hi. It's me, Hailey. Please don't say anything until I'm finished. I'm here. In Daytona Beach. Because I wanted to see you. I've been doing a lot of thinking. I need to tell you . . . I'm in love with you. I knew it before I left, but I was too afraid to tell you. Being back in Colorado made it crystal clear. I had to come back and tell you that I love you. That's all. I'm done now." She let out an anxious breath and waited for his reply.

She heard a cough, and then a strange voice said, "Uh, hi. This is Laura. Peter's sister. We met at a restaurant."

Hailey's face immediately caught fire. "His sister?" She'd just declared her love for Peter to . . . his sister. How humiliating was that? She wanted to crawl in a hole and die.

"Peter is here at my house," she whispered. "He left his phone on the counter while he went outside with my son. When I saw your name on the screen I had to answer. We don't have much time."

"Because?" Hailey had no idea what she meant.

"My stubborn brother finally figured things out." She chuckled softly. "He came by to say goodbye."

"Goodbye?" Was Peter leaving Florida? Why? Hailey was all sorts of confused.

"He's on his way to the airport. He has a ticket from Daytona Beach to Denver tonight."

Hailey's heart catapulted to her throat. She hoped she knew the answer, but she had to ask to be sure. "Why is he flying to Denver?"

"Seriously? To see you."

"What should I do?"

"You could come over here, but I'd have to stall him. Or you could meet him at the airport. He's leaving my house within the next fifteen minutes or so," Laura said with excitement.

"I can leave right now and meet him at the airport." Adrenaline pumped through her.

"He's flying Delta. Uh, oh, he's coming back inside. I'm going to delete this call so he won't see it. Good luck." With that she ended the call.

Hailey stared at her phone. Did his sister just give her seal of approval? It sure sounded that way.

On the drive over, Hailey replayed what she'd said to Peter's sister. *How embarrassing.* On the bright side, at least that had given her a practice run, even if the humiliation still stung. Maybe when she saw Peter she could express herself more eloquently. She gripped the steering wheel to steady her trembling fingers.

After she parked the rental car, she made her way to the entrance and paced back and forth. She was a jumble of nerves as she waited for Peter, hoping it would all play out as she'd fantasized.

Before she could wear a path in the dingy gray carpet of the airport lobby, she spotted Peter coming through the glass doors. He was dressed in khaki pants and a blue dress shirt and was pulling a small black suitcase behind him. When he looked up and their gazes locked, her heart did a nosedive into her stomach. He blinked, let go of his suitcase, and rushed over to her, picking her up in his arms and twirling her around. "What are you doing here?" he whispered in her ear as he set her down.

"Finding you." She peered at him, overflowing with love.

"But how?" His smile reached up into his pale blue eyes.

"I have my ways." She bit her lip and then led him by the hand to a more private area of the lobby.

"I'm so happy to see you." He embraced her again. "I was actually on my way to Colorado to see you."

"Oh yeah?" The idea that he was coming to see her made her heart want to sing out in joyous choruses.

"And here you are." He looked her up and down as if he couldn't believe she stood there before him.

"I am." Hailey wanted to tell him why she was there, but she found it difficult to think about anything except the way his eyes sparkled with intensity, the way his musky scent drew her in, and the way his strong and steady arms encircled her so perfectly. Finally, she said, "I was a fool."

"You were?" His eyebrows moved slightly and the corners of his mouth tugged up.

"I should have told you how I felt before I left."

"And I should have told you," he said, brushing a lock of hair from her cheek.

"Really?" Her legs were like overcooked noodles.

He cupped her chin in his hand. "I want to be with you, Hailey. Since you left, I haven't been able to think about anything else." He paused and then peered deeply into her eyes, making her feel like a thousand candles burned inside her. "I love you."

Her cheeks throbbed. "Oh, Peter, I love you too." This was even better than her fantasy.

"I don't want to spend another day without you," he whispered, his warm breath tickling her ear and making her eyelids flutter.

"Me either," she said, gulping for air.

He reached up and traced her lips with his finger, letting it trail down her neck until every cell was on full alert. He laid his warm lips on hers and each nerve in her body ignited, then exploded into a full-fledged forest fire. His lips explored hers tentatively as if he were asking permission for more. When she responded affirmatively, the kiss intensified. The deeper he kissed her, the more she craved it, as if she couldn't live without it. Passion pulsed through her body, making her limbs feel numb. She never wanted to stop kissing this man who had somehow captured her heart. She was all his.

Once he stopped kissing her and her brain reengaged, she asked, "But what about the fact that you live in Florida and I live in Colorado?"

He ran his fingers through her hair. "I'm not much for long distance."

"So, what will we do?"

"I'm ready to start my own practice, and Colorado is as good a place as any to start it. I've already researched what licensing I'd need."

"You'd do that?" He was willing to give up his life in Florida for her. Could he be any more amazing?

"You are all I want. I know that." He intertwined his fingers with hers. "My career will work itself out."

Hailey chewed her lip and then said, "Would you be offended if I said no?"

He wrinkled his forehead. "Why?"

"Because I'd rather stay here in Florida. Honestly, I love Daytona Beach and I want to be there for Gran when she gets back from Oregon. And your family needs you here."

"You'd move to Florida? Permanently?" Peter gazed at her in disbelief.

"Yes."

He pulled her in for a long embrace. "You are exactly who I've been looking for all of my life."

His words brought a sense of security and happiness she'd never experienced. He was exactly who she'd been looking for too. They'd both taken relationship detours, but now they'd found each other, and she wasn't about to let him go.

Chapter 40

Hailey stood in the modest foyer of the Living Light Church up the road from Gran's house. She smoothed the layers of tulle on her wedding gown and clenched the bouquet of red roses mixed in with golden rosebuds in her trembling hands.

A year ago, she'd said goodbye to Gramps in this chapel. But today, she was saying hello to a new life with Peter—the man she'd come to love even more deeply than the day she'd caught him at the airport. This last year had been filled with grand adventures and quiet moments, all shared with the man who had completely and wholly captured her heart.

"Look at my beautiful girl," her mom said, then kissed her on the cheek. "Your father would be so proud." She adjusted Hailey's veil. "You are a perfect bride."

"Thanks, Mom." Hailey still couldn't believe today was her wedding day. *Her wedding day.* She wanted to shout from the rooftops that she was marrying her best friend and the man of her dreams, but an internal "*squee*" would have to do.

"I'll take my seat with Brit and the kids at the front." She gave Hailey another kiss and then walked into the chapel.

"My lands, you are breathtaking," Gran said, her eyes moist.

Hailey hugged Gran and tried to keep her emotions from spilling out of her eyes. "Thank you."

"I wish Harry were here to see you and walk you down the aisle." Gran's eyes saddened.

"Me too." Hailey let out a breath of regret. She so wished Gramps could've been here on her wedding day. She could almost see him standing there and grinning at her.

"I better find my seat. Regina will wonder where I am." Gran disappeared inside.

The wedding march began on cue and Hailey couldn't stop the smile that enveloped her face. She stepped into the chapel. Flowers were draped on the pews and the cool air from the AC circulated around her. All eyes were on her, but the only ones she noticed belonged to Peter. He stood at the front in a black tuxedo with a deep red vest and tie and a grin that stretched across his handsome face. Hailey wanted to pinch herself to make sure she wasn't dreaming.

Today she and Peter would unite their lives and promise to love each other always—a promise she intended to keep every single day, just like Gran and Gramps. She drew in a deep breath that was sprinkled with a soft floral scent. Her heart skittered as she put one foot in front of the other and began the walk toward her one true love.

Keeping her gaze on Peter, she glided to the front of the church. As soon as he reached out his warm hand for hers, a gentle peace enfolded her. This is exactly where Hailey belonged.

The pastor began the ceremony and then turned the time over to Hailey and Peter to exchange their vows.

Peter cleared his throat. He caressed Hailey's hand and gazed deeply into her eyes, making her breath catch. "You asked me what your grandfather said to me before we went to the karaoke bar. He said, 'Be good to her.' And that's what I intend to do for the rest of my life. I pledge all of me to you, Hailey. I will spend every day loving you, honoring you, respecting you, and being true to you. I told your grandfather I'd be good to you and I intend to. In sickness and in health, in wealth and in poverty, during the good times and the stressful times, I will love you. I promise to build a life with you and to grow old with you. You are the piece of my heart I didn't know was missing, and from today until the rest of time, I promise to love and cherish you." His eyes misted.

She blew out some air. "My turn?"

He nodded.

Trying to keep her voice from quivering, she said, "I give myself to you, body and soul. I give my heart to you today, tomorrow, and always. In sickness, in health, in good times or bad, if we are rich or if we are poor, I promise to love and honor you from this day forward. And to walk with you wherever our life leads us. You are my everything, Peter Stafford." A tear edged out of her eye and Peter reached up to brush it away.

The pastor said a few words, then had them exchange rings. He said, "You may kiss your bride."

Peter took a step toward her and enclosed her in his strong, capable arms. "You've made my dreams come true, Hailey Stafford." He brushed her lips gently with his, sending a deluge of heat coursing through her. She melted into his arms, and their lips mingled together in a perfect rhythm of give and take while the world around them ceased to exist.

"Uh, excuse me?" the pastor said, interrupting them. "Remember, we're all here." He laughed.

Hailey pulled away from Peter, then leaned her forehead against his. She wiped at her mouth and said, "Sorry. We didn't mean to get carried away."

"Speak for yourself," Peter said with a wink.

The pastor clapped Peter on the shoulder. "Please welcome, Mr. and Mrs. Stafford."

Hailey had never heard such sublime words as those. *Mr. and Mrs. Stafford.* They danced on her tongue and sent a shiver of happiness down her back.

She looked out into the crowd, a sense of gratitude overwhelming her. A year ago, she'd come to Florida simply to help her grandparents, but instead found her destiny in the man who'd spoken to her heart.

Thank You

Dear Reader,

Thank you so much for reading *Speak to My Heart*. It was inspired by my own grandfather and his struggle to recover from a stroke. It was also inspired by my youngest son who has Down syndrome and struggles with his speech on a daily basis. In both cases, I had to learn about the building blocks of speech and learn how to help them communicate. I wanted to write a story that included a speech therapist and a romance. Life can be hard and throw us unexpected curveballs, but everyone deserves their happily-ever-after.

The best form of advertising for authors is word of mouth. You can help spread the word about my book by submitting a review. If you have an Amazon account, it's simple to submit a review on the product page. Reviews can help authors find new readers and help readers find new authors. Thank you!

Thank you to all of you who voted for this book in Kindle Scout.

I love to hear from readers and I respond as quickly as I can.

You can email me at rebecca@rebeccatalley.com. You can find me online at www.rebeccatalley.com, on my author page on Facebook, on Instagram at RebeccaTalleyAuthor, and on Twitter @rebeccatalley.

You can join my Reader News at www.rebeccatalley.com, and receive a free novella, find out about new releases, and gain insights into my crazy life with my big family. (Yes, I have 10 children and I'm still (almost) sane).

ABOUT THE AUTHOR

Rebecca Talley grew up next to the ocean in Santa Barbara, California. She spent her youth at the beach collecting sea shells and building sandcastles. She graduated from high school and left for college, where she met and married her sweetheart, Del.

Del and Rebecca are the sometimes frazzled, but always grateful, parents of ten wildly- creative and multi-talented children and the grandparents of the most adorable little girls and the most handsome little boy in the universe.

After spending nineteen years in rural Colorado with horses, cows, sheep, goats, rabbits, and donkeys, Rebecca and her family moved to a suburb of Houston, Texas, where she spends most of her time in the pool trying to avoid the heat and humidity.

When she isn't writing, Rebecca loves to date her husband, play with her kids, swim in the ocean, redecorate her house, and dance to disco music while she cleans the house.

Made in the USA
Middletown, DE
05 October 2018